DATE DUE			
JAN 2 8 '84			

Leila

J. P. DONLEAVY

Leila

Further in
the Destinies
of Darcy Dancer,
Gentleman

DELACORTE PRESS/SEYMOUR LAWRENCE

Published by
Delacorte Press/Seymour Lawrence
1 Dag Hammarskjold Plaza
New York, N.Y. 10017

Manufactured in the United States of America
First trade edition

Library of Congress Cataloging in Publication Data

Donleavy, J. P. (James Patrick), 1926–
Leila.

I. Title.
PS3507.O686L44   1983   813'.54   83–1970

ISBN 0-385-29260-0

A signed first edition of this book has
been privately printed by The
Franklin Library.

1

Taking the train, this empty lonely Dublin day of Sunday. Staring out the stained streaked window, westwards. With the sweet smell of turf puffed whitely by the engine out into a purple darkening sky of Ireland.

The snow deeper across the white frozen countryside. Streams and the canal iced over. Cattle standing dumb and still. A line of black figures on foot following a horse drawn hearse waiting at a barrier to cross the railway track. Ivy clad trees passing like multiarmed dark green monsters. Fluffs of snow blown off the shiny green leaves in the carriage's thundering windy wake. A farmer tossing forkfuls of hay from a cart to his hungry shivering bullocks.

Nearing the big midland town. Horizon glowing pink, the winter afternoon grown dark. Faint lights in the houses after the gnawing painful solitary stretches of empty fields and bereft bog lands. Compartment doors opening. The bangs as they slam shut. Flurries of snow blowing along the cold concrete of the station platform. A large ring and key handed to the driver. A shout. And off again. Rumbling along the lake's sparkling blackness and by the gentle whitened moonlit hills. Till the train wheels squeak and screech again against their brakes. Heft down my two bags from the luggage rack. Say goodbye to the pictures of watering places in the county of Kerry.

Unhook the leather strap and drop the window. Push open the door. And alight at last on this familiar station.

A priest, two nuns and a farmer with a box of pullets huddled out of the wind, emerging from the little waiting room, to board the train further west. The station master stopping to stare as if he were seeing some interloping stranger until recognition suddenly overcame his face.

"Ah it's yourself sir, Reginald Darcy Thormond Dancer Kildare. I didn't recognize you from the size of you."

Approaching in a battered dark trilby hat, the brim pulled down fore and aft, and a long black coat tied closed with a piece of twine. Sexton. Straw and cow dung frozen on his boots. The station light flashing across his face. A tear in his only eye and moisture seeping down from his eyepatch.

"At long last welcome home Master Darcy. And apologies for me appearance. I was out foddering the cattle when Crooks jumped at me with the message you were coming."

On the apron outside the station a cart collecting packages and mail off the train. Station master calling all aboard out of the darkness. A silent world so far away from the lights of a city. Sexton throwing up the bags behind the box seat of the victoria. And helping me by the elbow to sit up on the rugs.

"This weather with the snow and the wind biting the very skin off the face, would make you think you were living in Zhigansk Siberia."

Sexton's big horny hand so delicately guiding the reins, to the gentle beat of Petunia's hoofs muffled on the roadway. An automobile passing skidding and sliding along. Its lights blinking out and then on, and fading out again. Petunia shying and Sexton giving her a belt across the quarters. The sputtering choking automobile suddenly silenced behind us.

"Any fool out in a horseless carriage a night like this deserves a ditch in the darkness. Ah Master Darcy, the moral tone of the nation of this moment is very sadly low. There should be a requiem for the national anthem. And I see you're without a nosegay. Well out of the conservatory, I'll have a selection laid out for you in the morning. That'll knock your eye out. You'd be a foot taller. And it's a grand bit of smartly cut thorn proof tweed you're wearing."

"Kind of you to say, Sexton."

"And I'd also say now Master Darcy you've had an adventure or two. You'd learn lessons a little differently in the city than you would in the country. And I heard tell you became the owner of a great motor car up in Dublin that would give goose pimples of envy to them teetering on the very highest pinnacles of the aristocracy."

The cold moonshine casting black black shadows across the countryside. The straight road up and down these little hills and over the stone bridge of the canal. Another familiar mile. Another stone bridge over the river. Ivy clutched on the broken walls. Cottages, thatches white, faint yellow light in the windows. Through their turf smoke, the air sudden sweet. Ahead on the left, from this hill. That vast dark expanse of trees. Andromeda Park. In the magic silence. Strange drums thumping. Who doth it be. Awake. What stranger. Takes me by that grabbing hand. A music weeping. To lead me back. Under the purple bright stars. To those long lain now, faded in the grin of death. And to those still alive in the pain of living.

> Who ride
> Out of their troubles
> On a good horse

3

2

Beyond the snow capped walls, the moonlit towering shadows of the chestnut, oak and elm trees. Turning through the front gates, the lodge's broken door and windows, a sapling growing through the roof. Petunia shying, nearly overturning the carriage. A shadow at the side of the drive suddenly bolting behind the rhododendrons, swinging two rabbits by the ears.

"Ah by god, look at that now, no longer content are they to skulk around stealing and crawling out through a hole in the wall, they have the nerve now to try to come in and out the front gates. A blast of shot across the backside is what he'll get next."

The victoria's wheels crunching the gravel where the thick pine woods sheltered the drive from snow. Petunia's hoofs resounding, puffing like a train up the incline to the last turn between the plantation of rhododendrons. The looming great black silhouette on the landscape. Shutters closed on the windows. White curls of smoke from chimneys caught in the moonlight. Kern and Olav rushing out barking from around the house. Bigger, greyer, shaggier monsters. Their unbridled delight hooting yelping and howling. Jumping to put their massive snowy paws up on my shoulders.

"Only pups when you left, they'll be glad to see you now, Master Darcy."

4

Footsteps frozen on the snowy granite steps of the porch. Sexton reaching to turn the latch. The door already sweeping open. In the candlelit hall, Crooks. More aged and considerably more cross eyed and infirm. His unentitled old Etonian tie flagrantly hanging down his rather soiled detached shirt front, which breaking out from his lapels displayed beneath, a rugby jersey sporting his equally unentitled colours of Trinity College.

"Good evening and welcome home Master Reginald, trust you had a pleasurable journey."

Reginald Darcy Thormond Dancer Kildare, crossing the hall. A fire blazing in the hall grate. A tiny glow against the chill clammy damp. Crooks taking his hat and coat in hand. Heels clicking on the black and white tiles. Darcy Dancer's long hair pouring over his shirt collar. A yellow silk handkerchief struck in the greeny brown tweed pocket of his jacket. Stopping by the staircase hall under two mournful portraits of my mother's father's two wives. A whiff of whisky from Crooks' breath. Stains thicker on his coat. Larger swatches of grey in his hair, his cheeks hollower and his neck thinner. And here, all of them stand. Except Edna Annie. Perhaps finally indisposed by her ancient age. The familiar and fatter faces of Kitty and Norah. Catherine the cook, her hair coiffed in a mountain of grey, brushing her hand down her apron to shake mine. The others curtseying as I nodded to each. Crooks, displaying his best butlering, his ecclesiastical voice echoing.

"Edna Annie sends her best Master Reginald."

"Is she alright."

"Ah her fragile but willing bones are still washing and ironing. And this is Mollie. And this is Leila."

Hardly more than my own age, two unfamiliar faces. Mollie freckled skinned, her hair a frizzy red. Leila behind her. In the shadows seems raven black haired, and the darkest eyes staring from a smooth white skinned face.

The small contingent proceeding up the grand stairs. Candle aloft flickering in the breeze, a limping Crooks unable to lift the bags leading the way. Sexton following, kicking as he went, the brass carpet rods. Around the landing, past the great window, facing the grove of beeches silvery in the stilly snowy moonlight. Crooks mumbling back over his shoulder at Sexton.

5

"Boots in the house, boots in the house."

Halfway down the hall, just as a bat flew by overhead, Crooks turning to announce.

"Your bath is drawn Master Reginald. And supper will be at your convenience."

I could hear Sexton murmuring under his breath that last word should have the letters I and N in front of it. And by these sounds apparitions and sights, one did indeed know one was home.

Sexton lifting the luggage up on the oak baggage stand. The candles flickering. Darcy Dancer shivering in the damp room. Where under the long acquired dust nothing seemed touched or changed. Opening the shutters, the snow looking even colder out on the trees in the moonlight. The idea of a bath floating with icecubes fills one with dismay. At least Crooks need not worry about the debris and snow melting off Sexton's boots.

"The fire's out Master Darcy. I'll go fetch matches and light it."

"That's alright Sexton. Leave it till the morning. It will help me get out of bed."

"Now is there anything else. That would make your comfort kinder."

"No thank you Sexton."

"Master Darcy just let me say, it's good to have you back, you were sadly missed."

"I appreciate your saying that, Sexton."

"And by God, whose holy name we praise, we'll have the estate shipshape again in no time."

Sexton just as of old, always hating to take his departure, lingering, his eye sparkling and as always searching for any new topic of conversation. And I must confess, despite my famished cold condition, I had not the heart not to aid and abet him a little.

"Who are they Sexton."

"Who's who sir."

"Those two new girls."

"Well now the two of them arrived at the station. One is perhaps the dumbest creature God ever put on earth, and well she deserves the name Dingbats. Daughter of a blacksmith in Galway. Who I'm sure between belting the sparks out of horseshoes has been trying to get rid of her for years. The agent collared the two of them. Just the day be-

6

fore your father packed up his shotguns and was away to parts unknown."

"Is she addressed by the name Dingbats."

"It's cook who started calling her Dingbats. And as it's now universal, so you might too, being as she's familiar with the name now. Sure she'd smile back at you if you called her a tart, liar or layabout. And mind you, she's just enough brains to understand the two last at which she's best at."

"O dear me Sexton, do tell. Seems all so familiar."

"Dumb when it suits her. And the rest of the time she spends cowering around inside the house terrified of her own shadow seeing a host of ghosts. Swears there's a rat bigger than a cat in her room. Outside she's in dread of the dogs. And it's probably the only thing she's to be believed about."

"Well I can't think that that's going to do, Sexton."

"Ah but now the other young lady is a different kettle of fish altogether. Parents unknown. And was from out of the female orphanage. By god isn't she some looker though."

"I'm afraid I can't remark on that Sexton, she seemed to shrink somewhat back in the shadows."

"Shy she is. But her wits about her. With shopkeeping experience no less. And a set of teeth you wouldn't believe were her own. Sculpted they look by Galileo himself."

Sexton seemed to have revised his feelings about former departed members of the household. Speaking rather nostalgically of Mr Arland my tutor who would have surely corrected him on his reference to Galileo.

"She'd even be an improvement on the beauty of Baptista Consuelo, upon whom poor old Mr Arland wasted his love, and scourged himself with the evil pain of jealousy. But now there was a man Master Darcy, as who knew his Caesar and Cicero."

Departing off down the hall, as I closed the door Sexton went murmuring, et incarnatus est. Facit indignatio versum. One did wince at the papist bias in Sexton's Latin. And his latter phrase certainly, as I loosely translated it to mean righteous wrath creates poetry, did not materialize in my case as the dressing cupboard door, promptly as I opened it, fell off its hinges and my righteous wrath created a bloody blast and damn and a good kick to the shins of the wretched furnish-

7

ing. All my clothes too small. My dressing gown coming above my knees, the sleeves inches above my wrists. The faded mauve and the chocolate brown borders and facings which sported my mother's racing colours, now mottled with a dusty mould.

Going bathroomwards, a breeze blowing out the candle in the hall. And promptly tripping over the carpet to open a wrong door. To the scrabblings of a rat, and the fume of dead mice. A taste and sure smell of things to come. Dear god. Please. Give me fortitude to, by oneself, stomach such immense difficulties. I do not ask to lie on velvet. Or even to wine and dine well. Just merely to have some horses sound and be able to once more decently hunt, decently shoot and decently fish.

A relief to find the fragrance of bath oil in the ablution room. The towels dank, no longer aired as they once were in the kitchen oven. But Crooks had indeed drawn my brimming bath steaming hot. In which stretched immersed I immediately fell asleep. And with my head slipping under the water, nearly drowning. Dreaming momentarily of a rather recent night life moment in Dublin after the races. Of a waiter, wildly out of control, rushing from one of the better restaurant kitchens to dump a pail of freshly caught uncooked prawns on top of an American lady's head who'd incessantly complained she wanted really fresh seafood. I did on the real occasion witnessing it with my pal Rashers Ronald, who bent double at our table slapping both his thighs, also ungentlemanly laugh. But now waking not knowing where I was, I felt boiled like a lobster in a pot.

Darcy Dancer wrapped in a towel shivering back along the corridor. Seeing by the light now coming from the staircase. Avoid holes worn in this ancient carpet. My slippers too small. My dressing gown hopeless, split in half by my shoulders. Use its tattered girdle to hang myself when that time comes. Floorboards crackling underfoot ready to give way. Perhaps I shall move. Select a bigger, grander bedroom. More befitting my position. Better suited to taking my privacy. Decorate it in a manner of my recent preference for Regency. Somehow blackdog doldrums and despondency do not seem so soul scourging as when one can reach out and lightly caress a lavender scented rosewood furnishing in one's life. And damn it, it does not mean that one is in the least effeminate.

My door ajar. My hairbrush moved. My ties laid out on my dress-

8

ing table. Shoes neatly placed together. And a linen card propped against the mirror.

SIR: SHERRY WILL BE SERVED IN THE LIBRARY

A note written in the most elegant print, ever so slightly slanted to the left. And who now would know the use or meaning of a colon in this household. Perhaps of course Sexton, who would certainly pretend he knew. But he has never written such a fine hand. The pen's black ink strokes discreet yet bold enough. And curled as if engraved. Well, well. Dear me. Provided the sherry has the suitably fresh nutty tang of old, this could all be rather unexpectedly cheering. Requires a dig in my luggage for my silk shirt. And my gold best cufflinks.

Darcy Dancer in black tweed, a blue polka dot tie and silk hanky peeking above a pocket. A candelabrum placed on the window sill of the staircase landing. Making it all feel a little safer proceeding down these steps. Flame reflecting on the panes of the window. And right here where I stood once. A tiny innocent boy. When from the front hall foot of the stairs, my so called father, a sour cruel look on his face, called me a little bastard. And one does wonder. What now do all these portraits think. The long departed dead. Staring down from the mouldering walls. Grand aunt of my mother's. Painted as she regally sat on a dais in the ballroom. Her haughty beautiful face. A ringlet halo of hair. The indistinction close up of the thick mottled lumps of colour which come into miraculous focus as one stands away. The sumptuous finery of her black lace gown. Bejeweled straps across her pink shoulders. Sparkling necklace of pearls and diamonds upon her bosom. If artistic standards are to be considered, this is undoubtedly one of the finer pictures escaping theft by my father. Who upon being advised that certain paintings could indeed be genuinely by Giovanni Battista Tiepolo then assiduously denuded the walls of same.

Darcy Dancer passing by the open door of the library alight inside with another candelabrum. Stopping further down the hall. To push open these large hingesqueaking double doors. The massive cold darkness of the ballroom. Two bats aloft darting back and forth. Streak of moonlight across the dusty floor. Slanting in a window where the shutter hangs broken. I should so dearly like to hold some

9

very grand great party. Invite the better local ladies and gentlemen if any are still to be found. The ballroom chandeliers sparkling light once again. If an orchestra is out of the question make music on the old gramophone. Whoever wrote the note placed in my bedroom could manage the invitations. Do. O do come. Won't you. At home. For the champagne. Our buckets full of caviar. And your broken ankles. You most certainly will get my dears, dancing through the floor.

Darcy Dancer sipping his sherry in the chill fireless library. Poured from the decanter in all its nut fragrant pale brown gleaming glory. Warming the innards and the boulevards of one's memories as I glance by the spines of these leather worn ancient musty tomes that Mr Arland and I would crack open on the many rainy winter days, delighting over their fusty language of pompous travels and pretentious recall. Of socially distinguished gentlemen pulling their legs out of sharks' mouths and wrestling heroically with monstrous pythons. My how people did then take themselves so seriously. Of course there were accounts of intrepid Shackleton, especially admired by Mr Arland perhaps because of his Irish connections. And dear me before freezing to death here I had better soon be proceeding to supper in the dining room. Ah a creak of floorboards. A knock at last.

"Master Reginald, when you're ready, supper is served."

"Ah indeed. Thank you Crooks, I am in fact quite ready."

The shutters closed. A fire at least taking the chill off the dining room. Crooks equally at the ready with my chair. Something to be said for having dear old servants surrounding one who although frequently forgetting, do occasionally at least try to acquit themselves agreeably. Having been such a deliberately appallingly bad servant oneself, one of course knew of the endless opportunities a servant could find for making life utterly miserable for his employer.

Cabbage soup. Boiled potatoes. And stew with carrots and turnips. Not awfully exciting. But so starved am I one simply can't mind at the moment, having all I can do to not dive grabbing into the food like a pig famished.

"The likes of youse is no use at all when youse won't learn left from right when youse is tolt."

I was surprised to overhear Crooks mimicking in the gutteral overtones of a Dublin accent as he grumpily ordered Leila about in the pantry. One could not help feel that there was just a touch of jealousy at this new girl's albeit nervous efficiency. As she stood behind Crooks with Brussels sprouts one attempted to observe her but could only discreetly just catch sight of red swollen hands shaking gripped tight on the steaming heaped bowl, and the serving spoon banging. Crooks as he finished pouring wine at my right, snapping his fingers for her to come around to my left side. And just to casually lighten the atmosphere I pointed to the stained and soaked seat of one of the dining room chairs against the wall.

"Crooks what befell that chair."

"Ah more than a sup of rain has made a recent habit of coming through the ceiling. The chamber above is getting a spill from the chamber yet above again. Poor old Chippendale. When the snow melts Master Reginald you'd want to be dining here in a tent."

Unable to dance his attendance on his toes, Crooks holding his chin awfully high, and behaving with an autocratic attempt at efficiency one had never witnessed before. Announcing in sepulchral tones the year of vintage as he poured the decanted premier grand cru Margaux with its bouquet shrinking back in the glass from the cold. He was also very voluble indeed. Especially with his elaborate excuses over the more noticeable dilapidations of the house. And once such great bitter enemies, it was enthralling to now hear Crooks recall our previous housekeeper, Miss von B in glowing terms. Elevating her from that regrettable bitch to Princess, and tossing in her royal highness when invoking her name. And as he waved Leila to collect my plate he then stopped by the sideboard, placed his towel dramatically over his arm, and then took a Napoleonic stance to stare vacantly up at the ceiling.

"Ah isolated in these lonely hills. If only her Royal Highness, the Princess was here. Magnificent seamstress. Ah she could sew. Mends in the heels of socks like sparkling jewels. Linen folded with such perfection, would bring tears to the eyes."

And last night in Dublin I had a dream that Miss von B had come galloping on her horse, back to Andromeda Park. Coming up the front park lawn and jumping the fence to the drive. Dismounting and striding up the front steps to march into the front hall. Confronting me there in her rather severely styled foxhunting raiment, as a massive military band ceremoniously played outside. Trumpeteers sounding, drums beating. Her blond hair snugly netted gleaming, her velvety cheeks pinkly glowing. The front hall suddenly silent as a church. Then a soft music playing a lament. I trembled and trembled and shook and shook. Waking and staring about my hotel bedroom in the dark. A milkman passing, his horse faintly clip clopping up Dawson Street.

"Master Reginald, we've gone short of the d'Yquem that you and her Royal Highness so esteemed. There were great calls on it these past months. Decant a little port perhaps."

"Please don't bother Crooks."

"Not a bit of bother, not a bit. Port."

"That would be nice."

"Then port it shall be. Now I'd have the blue parlour fire going but for the jackdaws with a nest halfway down the chimney. I've had a chair put in front of the fire in the front hall."

I was quite surprised at my twinge of thoughtfulness concerning the staff's need to get off to bed. And pouring cream on top of the whipped cream of my second helping of trifle, I did not go on to have three helpings. Somehow too, the new girl's thinness gave one the uncomfortable feeling that it was inappropriate to gorge myself any further.

Darcy Dancer crossing the front hall towards the new girl mending the fire, which out of the shadows sent its dancing licking flame of colour up to the ceiling. And was doing it properly too, putting logs on from the sides and one across the back at the top, leaving the middle with embers to glow out. I pretended to examine the guest book on the hall table, my mind aflood with questions conjured up to ask her. All sounding so damn stupid and foolish. Like I understand young lady you are a lonely abandoned orphan who now works here. And how do you like it. But even as I thanked her she just cast me a nervous glance and hurried away. At least one was saved sounding like a patronising ass.

I did enjoy the jolly good port. Sipping as one stared into the crackling spitting flames beaming warmly against the feet, hands and face. And except for its being like sitting in Amiens Street Station back in Dublin one enjoyed the ear ringing silence. Which suddenly was rent by a shout.

"Jesus, Mary and Joseph, they're at me. They're at me."

The sound of pounding running feet somewhere upstairs. Now

other feet and doors slamming. And ten minutes later. Crooks with a candelabrum crossing to me.

"Forgive the upstairs intrusion Master Darcy. But that one Dingbats said a rat big as a fox jumped up on her in bed. Sure now if there was a rat it would be very surprising he didn't take a good bite out of her being as she's got a body on her like a boneless shoulder of pork."

One did at this moment find it physically painful to have one's quiet reverie and privacy so invaded. Perhaps a beam next would bounce down on my head. Or the assembled staff come lurching in, bottles to their lips, quaffing back, having been in the wine cellar. But this tonight is home. In all its hopeless insanity and crumbling dilapidation. Mine. Its land I do so love. Marked up and down and over hills with its mossy stone walls. Where I ran and rode. With sunshine joy, swinging in the lichen grey apple trees. My sisters chasing me. Peeking round the strong sinewed ancient trunks of beech, oak and chestnut. Streams and lakes streaking with trout. Emerald meadows of softest velvet. No footsteps heard. Lonely walks dreaming beyond these halls and rooms. Where I was born. And in such bygone pain. Saw my mother die. And what sadness now. Lies before my feet. Tongue of a vixen. Out there. Screeching. Across the white frosty night. An owl. Calls. Out of a sorrow cold and old. Who doth it be who hoots. And I must. Fight as I have never fought. Never give up. Someone must preserve the architecture. Someone must cherish the porcelain, paintings and silver. Someone must care about the trees, the flowers and butterflies. Someone must love again. The air, the waters and grasses.

> To keep
> Safe embraced
> A moment longer
> The jewels
> Of life

3

The moonlight gone. And a cock crowing waking me. A wind. My mind aswirl with the most indiscreet of dreams. Dressed as a bishop I was having it off with Lois attired as a nun back in her Dublin studio clacking her castanets. Reached into my side table for my piss pot. Kneel in bed to avoid freezing. And then freezing as one waited for one's fierce engorgement to subside. What bliss to take a long and most relieving pee. But good almighty grief, feel my knees growing wetly cold. Dear god in the very worst of worst horrors. One's warm piss is flooding out a crack in the bottom of this bloody pot to soak frigidly into one's mattress.

Of course frozen out of my wits, Crooks woke me just after dawn. From my nightmare of an arctic mid Atlantic ocean sinking. I had not the heart to tell him to bugger off and let me sleep. Until I was sorely tempted to do just that as the wet paper and sticks he attempted to light smoked up through the soggy turf in the fireplace. Crooks pumping the bellows, puffing out massive clouds of smoke, which joining the billows gusting back down the cold chimney, one could hardly breathe or see across the room.

"Breakfast's on the way and have this alight blazing now any second Master Reginald."

"O god Crooks, do please leave it. I'll go down to breakfast. And do please dispose of this cracked chamber pot."

"It would be that one Dingbats again."

"You must I think Crooks please see she is more careful."

"I've done everything in my power to train that one up. She'll swear on a stack of bibles that the pot wasn't cracked when she put it there. Set this fire as well so that the devil having a barbeque in hell wouldn't get it alight."

It was always hard to estimate the degree of madness any individual staff inmate had reached, being as they were all going mad together. The one true cooperation they genuinely shared. And the only sane consistent thing one could depend upon. But with the future prospects for Andromeda Park already so bleak the addition of the likes of Dingbats made it look dispiritingly quite uncomfortable indeed.

Darcy Dancer dressed. A thick herringbone tweed jacket and cavalry twill trousers. A thick cotton cricket shirt, two layers of woollen underwear. Tiptoe now out in the hall. Avoid alerting a new disaster. Only barely escaping this morning's asphyxiation. And the frostbite while the windows were wide open for my room to clear of smoke. Good god who's that. That voice. Crooks mumbling down the hall around the turning to my mother's apartments.

"Yes my dear Delia, your royalness, my true and only blessed virgin, I shall be back shortly, madam, with the hot towels, to dry your back."

My god Crooks is now taking the most diabolical risqué liberties in his ravings. As in the same way, having detested the sight and sound of Miss von B while she was here, raising her to beatified and saintly social heights while apparently demoting the memory of my mother to something regrettably verging on the lascivious.

My breakfast tray brought upstairs by Dingbats left abandoned on the landing. For a host of rats to eat, no doubt. The fire mercifully at my back in the dining room.

Sun glowing faint gold across the whitened landscape. A magpie, feathers shiny black and white, dancing up and down the branches of an orchard apple tree. Pigeons about. Await breakfast. Cold stiff fingered. Write out my purposes in my old blue clasp book. To inspect the horses, the farmyard, garden, old saw mill, the grove of beeches. As one hopes to see the mate of the magpie out in the orchard to avoid any ill luck of seeing only one. Some cheer to find Sexton's selection of nosegays laid out at my place. Choose the tiny braided bouquet of snowdrops. But it has already occurred to me even before the day has hardly begun that I shall have to find a very rich, preferably from brewing, heiress to marry. To pay for the repairs to floors, ceilings, halls, roof, never mind the plumbing, or replacement of the long disused electric wiring. Which latter at least, one is relieved to know, will still mercifully long remain unconnected to any supply. Otherwise instead of widespread light at one's fingertips there would be wholesale electrocution.

Darcy Dancer attempting to catch larger sight of Leila who held back nearly an arm's length as she served. The lace at the wrist of her uniform quite soiled. And upon her hand there seemed two words written with numerals in indelible pencil. When I said good morning upon entering she made no reply. Keeps constantly behind my back. And I must say Crooks snapping his fingers at her did irritate one. But then as she chose a moment as I was turned looking out the window to lift a platter from the sideboard, I found, as I suddenly turned back, that she was staring at me. Her face flushing crimson as she turned away and hurried pantrywards. It could have been that with copious cups of tea, I embarrassingly devoured four eggs, six slices of bacon, several slices of toast and marmalade, one jug of cream, all preceded by a quart of apple juice and large bowl of porridge. As any sensible person in his right mind would, in present conditions and circumstances. But she could think me unreasonably greedy. And now with Crooks growling out to her in the pantry.

"More toast, more toast, more toast."

In his own trembling inadequacy Crooks in pouring my tea put a good bit of it in my saucer and on the table. Which he ordered the poor new girl to mop up.

"Forgive me Master Reginald, it's been a bit of a night with hunting rats high and low, but tomorrow will have us right."

Leila returning with a rack of perfectly browned toast to my side, in murmuring my thank you I deliberately turned to look up at her. The brightness of the snow outside revealed her astonishing flashing eyes. The strange quiet beauty of their Oriental cast beneath her brows. The iris around the pupil instead of appearing black as it first seemed, was a glowing deep mossy green flecked with blue. And the longest black lashes I've ever seen. Her forehead and cheeks of the whitest smoothest skin. Her soft full but unsmiling lips. Her slenderness. And in her black uniform she did seem so hungry and cold and even god forbid, consumptive.

A malodorous sewer smell in the basement hall. Edna Annie tried to get up to bow as I entered her warm little room and I had to hold her and help her back into her chair but up again she stood, her white hair with a red ribbon coiffed and brushed up from her birdlike skull. Her gnarled fingers busy as ever knitting and grabbing me strongly by the arm. Making this supreme effort to leave her bedridden bed. Hugging me, the tears were welling and dropping from her old pale blue eyes.

"Ah Master Darcy you're hitting the ceiling with your head now. A gossoon no more, god love you. Sure I haven't been able to make soap now. My days are numbered. Out there soon under the sod."

"Nonsense, you look so marvellous."

"Ah flattery will get you somewhere."

Taking a peek in the kitchen a hot breeze blew at me out the door. The nervously collected snugly comfortable staff jumping to their feet at the snap of Crooks' fingers. Dingbats with her cheeks bulging out with cake. The rats had not upset her appetite. One could see the wooden backs and seats of the chairs shining with the months and months of polishing from so many human bottoms and shoulders. Table centre, large pots of tea, plates stacked with biscuits, cake, barmbrack. Mounds of golden butter. Pots of jams. Clearly no deprivation or starvation was going on below stairs. Kettles steaming on the stove. Blazing fire in the fireplace. Mouths chewing. Awful smell of cigarettes. Frankly it looked like a feast was going on.

Climbing back up the servants' stairs. Damp everywhere one looked. To push open this mahogany door to the old schoolroom. To step inside. My books as I opened them, their pages softened by moisture, nearly fell apart. The cobwebbed maps peeling down from the wall. Abandoned crayons and pencils. So many hours spent here. My dear Mr Arland. His sad yet noble life. The only man aside from Sexton and Uncle Willie upon whom I ever felt I could depend. Young as he must have been as my tutor, he so ably yet so gently led me into the old ways of the world.

As I departed in the front hall, I passed Leila, the only one not at the feast, on her knees cleaning ash out of the grate. One is now even more frightened of speaking than she must be of being spoken to. God one must get on. Sympathy for others in a household has a way of depriving one of convenience. My cap and scarf still miraculously where I last left them with my boots in the small vestibule inside the door. Shake off the dust and push my feet into my father's Wellingtons. Take a walking stick. Go out.

Darcy Dancer, blowing his clouds of breath out in the crisp cold air and kicking his feet through the snow. Stand looking out across the whitened park land. The river flowing darkly between its banks. The woods beyond up the hill. How can it continue. The massive roof to stay atop this house. One's spirit did crash down as one saw a new crack in the front hall and the plaster crumbling. Rain stains on the front hall tiles. The food pours down all these throats. The worst that can happen is I die. At least there is no shortage of graves. Lie next to my mother. But I did take heart again at the brief sight of Leila at the grate. Was tempted to summon her to the estate office. Mention the subject of a medical consultation with Dr Wellbeing in the town. And ask her. Would you please smile so that I can see your teeth.

Go now making a fresh path of footsteps towards the orchard. The snow dry and ice patches crackling underfoot. I would in Dublin be at this moment taking a mid morning coffee in the lounge of the Hibernian Hotel waiting for the likes of Rashers Ronald to come eagerly sauntering in. With some new plan for making a fortune or at least a fiver by lunchtime. And to dissect the previous night's partying. And hear his very English voice say bash on regardless. His face flushed with new further and better particulars of plans to marry a rich widow. And then his octaves dropping to his confidential whisper as he inevitably wanted the loan of a fiver till teatime. He would I'm sure tell me to pawn Andromeda Park, land, stock and chattels. And one supposes he would be right.

Push open this barred squealing iron gate. The apple tree branches weighted down. There ahead the potting shed. Smoke rising out of Sexton's tiny chimney jutting above the wall. The world I left here.

Cows gobbling up the juicy autumn apples. Chasing to catch fat frisky lambs as they would run for their tiny tail twitching lives. This old green door, brass handle worn so shiny. Well oiled hinges. The comfort inside of ancient smells. His Latin lists pinned upon the walls. This place in which Sexton offers up the toil of his life to beget beauty, bent at his bench whistling happily, gently lovingly packing his plant roots in turf mould.

"Ah good morning Master Darcy. I see you've come safely across the tundra. This weather's great for tracking the poachers. But now as soon as the frost's gone from the ground, I'm going to plant out in honour of your return, the greatest avenue over there of Acer Pseudoplatanus Brilliantissimum."

"Dear me Sexton, that is awfully thoughtful of you. But you must let me in on the secret, my Latin is awfully rusty this morning."

"Ah the noble sycamore, Master Darcy."

"I do wish that appellation Master might be dropped, Sexton. It leaves me looking rather too young in a task I feel requires one to seem a little older."

"Ah it's the habit of it. But certainly it's only right and proper, as gaffer you'd be now the viceroy, hospodar, pasha, tsar, and undisputed Squire Lord of Andromeda Park."

"Well we needn't be quite so extravagant about it, the mere word sir will do."

"At your command sir."

"And saluting Sexton is certainly not necessary."

"Ah now this morning you'd not be I see in the happiest of moods."

"Well I have just cause. The sewers."

"I know sir. Conduits burst, pipes blocked up all over kingdom come. Not a drain working. A blessing it's all frozen by the cold. Everything on the blink. But for us born here in Ireland, where God has long looked down on us smiling, and kept us safe from the world's scourges and disasters, its floods, earthquakes, poisonous spiders and snakes, and from the foul diseases of impurity, we should remain truly thankful."

"One is quite aware of our gifts from God but somehow it's still all quite bad enough. And I should be glad if it does not ever get worse. God did however send us famine."

"Only to remind us of our favoured position."

"I see."

"Well it's not the half of it now, I was only getting you ready to hear the finale. Two old cows who should have known better frozen stiff as statues as they lay down by the lake to sleep. We'll have to wait till they thaw to move them."

"I'll have the agent buy in new stock."

"Let me buy the stock Master Darcy, ah sorry that slip. Sir it is. And never mind that agent. Up there in the estate office like it was his own private preserve, Napoleon calling for that Leila to fetch cups of tea all morning when he wasn't at the whisky in the wine cellar."

"Where exactly did the agent find her Sexton."

"Now you've got me there. I'd only know he's very sweet on her. Comes stealing my indoor flowers no less to present her with. He found that other one of the frizzy hair in the scullery of a pub, breaking so many glasses and dishes the poor old publican was ready to pay to have her taken away at any price. The agent he'll lie low now you're back. But sine dubio the espirit de corps of the household is very low. You might say, it's made no one any saner and that's a fact. I wouldn't let them cut or remove a thorn tree, there beyond, in case it would bring any more ill luck."

"Perhaps one should raise wages Sexton."

"Ah god abandon that good intention straight off."

"Well at the moment there are no wages, so why not raise them."

"Ah I like your existentialism."

"I'm afraid Sexton, I don't know what on earth that is."

"It's what at this very moment they're thinking and practising in Paris, the very latest that's what it is."

"Good god, Paris. I'd be better advised at this moment to know what they're thinking and practising here in Andromeda Park."

"Now meaning no disrespect to Ireland, I'd say what you need now to add to your intellectual might is a trip to the cafés of that city."

"I see."

"Ah the social, cerebral, not to mention noological activity of that capital would give you a style that would make them Dublin intellectuals cringe in shame of their backward concepts."

"Sexton I did not know you have been to Paris."

1

"Ah don't mention the Champs Elysées to me. The soaring spires of Notre Dame. Mere commonplace. The Prado."

Proceeding at last to the stables it having taken till nearly lunchtime to extricate oneself out of the intellectual ferment of Sexton's potting shed. One does feel however that just as sure as the Prado is not in Paris, one was as certain that Sexton had a loyal heart. And he noticed with pleasure my selection of his nosegay of snowdrops.

Darcy Dancer walking down this familiar road. Just steep enough for a sledge to glide. But no time for pleasure. Not here even a day. Two cattle already dead. How dare the agent assume a romantic prerogative with one of my staff. An old trick to take advantage of an innocent menial. Awfully damn insolent. Play pop with him. Filthy minded type for whom the blessing of marriage is not enough. But he who is without sin fling the first stone. And I have on too numerous an occasion been so sordidly and disgracefully indulgent that my arm I fear, must remain stilled at my side. Carnal mindedness must be in everyone's blood. Two defrockings in the family history, both of archbishops who had a difficulty to curb a taste in young boys. Plus my mother's father and grandfather, old reprobates who had similar tastes for young girls. Especially those serving in the household.

Darcy Dancer at the bottom of the little incline. Crossing the bump of cobble stones beneath the snow. Hungry pigeons sheltering up under the eaves. Make a nice pie had one a shotgun to hand. Hay rake and ploughs rusting in a corner of the yard. Whoever it is alerts to my coming. Hear the noise of activity. Step through the mended, tottering and remended stable door. Puddles on the stable floor. Horse piss fumes. Cobwebs like lace ball gowns hanging from the ceiling. Faint smell of oats and strong stench of stable dung. A stall full of musty hay. Rusty leaking buckets. Standards here. Appalling.

"Good morning, Master Reginald, and welcome home."

"Good morning, Slattery."

"I am getting it tidied up a bit here. It be a hardy old winter. Will you be hunting when the weather improves."

"Yes I shall."

Slattery's ear looking blue, chewed and flapped over and whitened at the edges. Where his son Foxy had nearly bitten and torn it off. The two reddened indented marks still on his skull where Foxy had struck him with a hammer. Intrepid Foxy Slattery. His fighting spirit never vanquished. Fought so at every authority. Indulged in every desecration. Introduced me to my early weaknesses of the flesh. Would ride any mount or steal the pennies off an old dead woman's eyes. Under what part of the bleak blue sky does he rascally now go.

"You'd be back staying a bit with us Master Reginald."

"Yes."

"Be a blessing when this hardship of a winter is over. Not been one like it in living memory."

Head groom Slattery's careful preamble to letting one know of the dead cows. Leading me to the news gently. Count the horses in their boxes. Petunia. Nutmeg. Molly. And my god, what's that. Eighteen hands of giant black beast. Weaving back and forth. Hot red fierce burning eyes. Massive head and neck like a colossal snake looming in some dark jungle ready to strike.

"Be careful there, Master Reginald that's Midnight Shadow, I meant to warn you."

The huge black stallion shooting out its head to snap its teeth at the bars. Nostrils flaring. Darcy Dancer jumping back. As its forelegs rear and smash against the teak door. Trembling the entire stable. The latch nearly breaking open.

"You'd be best away out of here now, Master Reginald. Before he has a go at the door. That savage has killed one old farmer already. And maimed a dozen. Kick you to death as soon as look at you. Daft. His mother was daft. His father half daft. And he is completely."

The stallion turning in his stall. In the billows of rising straw, dung and dust. His immense quarters letting fly his hind legs north, south, east and west. Hoofs sending sparks off the walls. And finally crashing open the door of the stall.

"Begorra he's loose, get away out. Out now."

The animal backing out of its stall kicking and bucking. The groom Luke grabbing a hay fork and shoving Darcy Dancer out the door in front of him, slamming the outside stable door shut. The roars and hoofs slashing inside. Luke turning the knob to close the latch as hoofs crash at the other side. Stone chips hitting windows and then the panes of glass flying out into the snow.

"This better hold the blackguard. Or we'll be taking our next piss in purgatory."

The stable door splintering in two as Luke jumps back. Another and another hoof comes crashing through. Screws flying out of the hinges in the rotted wood. The stallion, filling the doorway. Its chest heaving, blasts of breath out into the chill air. The black giant neck craning forward, its head lowered, teeth bared, as it charged.

"Run for your life Master Reginald."

The snow flying, the stallion pounding across the yard after Luke. The beast's ears flat back. Hulking great head, jaws agape, bearing down as Luke turns jabbing with the hay fork. The animal's head dodging the prongs and forelegs rearing to knock the fork flying out of Luke's hands. Slattery shouting.

"Call the dogs, call the dogs."

Darcy Dancer letting a piercing whistle out into the air. Luke by the stable wall arms raised, jumping backwards seeking safety by the side of the rain barrel. The gutter pipe coming asunder, banging Luke's head, as he slides stunned arse first into a deep snow drift covering the drain. Kern and Olav bounding round the house at the top of the road. Tails like rudders in the wind, steering them down into the yard. Henry and Thomas, who should have been out foddering the cattle, emerging from somewhere comfortable into the fray. And just as quickly seeing what it was about turning their backs inside again. A voice heard as the door slammed.

"Begob I'm not sending my soul to heaven yet."

Luke, one arm clutched over the edge of the frozen rain barrel, pulling himself up again against the wall. Kern leaping to bite the beast's giant hind quarter. Olav sent flying with a hoof catching him on the shoulder. The stallion's yellowed curving teeth tearing the shoulder out of Luke's jacket. The graveyard is going to be put into use again sooner than one imagined.

"He'll have us all kilt Master Reginald."

The black monster slipping on the stable cobbles. Kern's fangs bared at its neck. Goes down on its haunches. Darcy Dancer tearing off his jacket. Rushing flinging it over the massive horse's head. Luke squeezing and crouching further behind the rain barrel. The vast animal getting to its feet again. Turning blindly rearing round in a circle bucking in the air. The earth trembling, dogs barking.

"Quick Master Reginald back inside now out of sight."

The two figures running for the door of the turf shed. Luke tugging, kicking and pounding on the door frozen shut. Oaths turning the sky pink. A final thump of Darcy Dancer's shoulder smashing it open. Banging it closed behind them. Peering out a cobwebbed window.

"Jesus, Mary and Joseph, I'm telling you Master Reginald, only a shotgun blasting a couple of times in each ear would put some manners on that black terror and then he'd eat you napkin and all."

Darcy Dancer's jacket hanging over the mighty beast's one eye. That bucks its head left and right. And one's best tweed coat goes fluttering down into the snow. Kern dodging and snapping around the stallion's hoofs as it stands vertical on hind legs, bellowing, pawing at the sky. And lands again, feet asprawl on the snowy cobbles to turn looking around the yard. Just to see if there's anything left to kill. A snort out its nostrils. A shake of its head at Kern, as it charges again. Another lash of its hoof at a limping Olav. Till its hind legs sending a lump of snow flying, the monster beast turns to gallop pounding away up the stable yard road. In a soaring leap clearing a five foot wall by two feet. Glistening black against the pearly park land. Its legs reaching racing out into its snowy white miles of freedom.

> Midnight Shadow
> Would be
> Better named
> Morning Earthquake

4

A mild moist westerly wind fading the snow and ice away. Dripping from the trees. And the dining room ceiling. The moisture blackened roof slates drying a lighter blue. The drains and gutters gurgling. The front park land glowing emerald green again in an afternoon sun. The unfrozen cows hauled with chains to the side of the field and buried.

Before the beams crack and walls finally crumble I thought that I would move into my mother's apartments. Calculating to recline there of a morning on the soft satins of her chaise longue. My langorous limbs enveloped in my silk dressing gown. Where one could await the news of any new disaster in some comfort. Dear me, and how pathetically did one dream of such serenity. In the cock crowing silence, my head against a pillow, not a bother on my mind. And there deep in eiderdown ensconced, having breakfasted peacefully abed and one's ablution hour over, to then, in the delicious pain pleasure throes of ennui, peruse the pages of some light and preferably silly novel. Populated with insufferably haughty top layer la de da people living in similar country houses but with unsimilar tiresome pursuits and debacles to mine own. Such as, while savouring biting into an unburned piece of toast slathered with a particularly tasty and unmouldy

25

gooseberry jam, Dingbats went running through the halls screaming she'd been scalded with soup thrown at her by cook in the kitchen.

"I am this minute scalded. I am this minute scalded to death."

Then there appeared in what seemed nearly the next minute, an envelope clearly penned by Leila and delivered to me by an arm bandaged Dingbats with breakfast. She of course also wearing her expression of the most depressed of the apostles at the last supper. As well she might having forgotten napkin, the salt, the butter, cream and a cup to drink from. But did remember to make sure that nearly everything one touched was either tacky with honey or slippery with grease. I must confess I was so damn tempted to upend my tray and shout something quite rigourously untoward and blasphemous. But one could so plainly see the poor creature despite her big tits and fear of rats and dogs, had not more than five brain cells in her head.

"Ah Mollie, I do think we are minus salt butter cream, a cup and saucer and napkin."

"Are they not there on the tray sir."

"No in fact apparently they are not there."

"O. I put them on I did."

Clearly a ghost with wings had stolen them on the way from the kitchen and now one was going to spend enough time while my cold breakfast was getting ice cold, discussing it. And in one's impatience one does do dastardly things. I pointed silently downwards to the kitchen. Suggesting Dingbats to go there. Before I much noisily rose from my bloody bed and booted her well larded arse stairwards. Damn insolent creature by the tone of her voice I knew was suggesting I could do without the salt, the butter, the cream and a cup to drink from. And one overheard her mumbling just as she was closing the door.

"I haven't had me own breakfast yet."

Good lord, not back here long enough to catch my breath, with hardly a single moment of peace and with such brazen ungratefulness, one wonders why on earth I bother to stay. Debts mounting hourly. A most recent insalubrious communication from the local bank manager with clearly an increasingly careless regard for his social betters, demanding to see me. At least one will dig out a spoonful of this still

26

lukewarm congealed porridge while I opened this envelope addressed unmistakably under Crooks' instruction.

Master Reginald,
c/o The Apartments of
Delia, Her Late Ladyship.

And well you might know he would choose to have such message written on one of the last few sheets of engraved notepaper left in the house. And that put into one of the last few engraved envelopes. And that sealed with my mother's grandfather's wax seal. With a coat of arms that one hates to admit this tender hour of the morning, may be quite bogus.

I beg to inform you kind sir that your obedient and humble servant is due to the recent apparition presently indefinitely indisposed.

CROOKS.

Just as one needed, in the soothing interests of one's spirit, some very top butlering these mornings, you might be damn sure that nothing of the sort could be expected. Having as I had just elaborately enumerated and posted new unbreakable rules for the household and estate. Instructing that only one pound of butter and one quart of cream be allotted per meal at servants' meals. Of course including tea this still means four bloody pounds of butter, and one ruddy gallon of cream down the hatch, plus endless grumbling from the men in from the yard. That nothing of the kind could happen in my mother's day. Further to which Sexton, of course enlightened me.

"Ah there would be complaint no matter what but sure harmless enough are the passing remarks that you're a Protestant alright, and next you'll be counting out the raisins baked in the bread."

One does shrink in horror at the bias of such bigoted words, but not much milk comes out of the udders of two dead cows, even Catholic ones. And unless I galvanize this mob into some semblance of corporate efficiency they'll all be lucky to be eating potato and cabbage

27

soup. Of course one is one's own worst enemy. To feel abed of a morning that one's blankets and counterpane somehow shielded one from the rigours of facing another day. Of turd congealed sewers. Of hungry coughing sick and dying animals. Of fences broken. The muddy deep ruts of carts where timber had been stolen. Every tool if not broken, twisted out of shape. Or worse, lost. Game poached. Beasts strayed. Or a neighbouring farmer's cunningly trespassing cattle. And before one even arises to get out into the fields, so much internally is already amiss. A knock right now on the door. Dingbats with the missing items of my breakfast.

"You've still forgotten the cream and butter Mollie."

"Ah sir it is the new kitchen rules to stop the wastage."

"Did you have cream and butter for your breakfast."

"I haven't had me breakfast."

"Will you have cream and butter for your breakfast."

"I might."

"Well I might too, if you please."

If nothing else, Dingbats' four brain cells recently five, clearly could energise enough to provide an instant countenance of insubordination. Flouncing about in her tracks, big tits shaking and closing the door behind her with far more than enough force to shut it. God knows what they were all doing in this house all the time I wasn't here. Rereading Crooks' message, one takes a damn poor view of his word indefinite. Find him in urgent hysterics blinded over another vision of my virginal mother draped in her array of pearls arisen from the dead. Better I suppose than finding him having abruptly terminated his employ by committing hara kiri in our butler's suicide room. Where from whence Crooks now claims, the previous butler who had hung himself from the ceiling, came making a nightly ghostly appearance with ampoules of whisky. And as Sexton said to me in the garden.

"Sure it's nothing more than proof incarnate with the residue of bottles and glasses and stains staring anybody in the face that your man Crooks is a raving alcoholic."

Three days of continuous rain later. Fields flooded. Buckets all over the house under leaks. And waking from a dream. Of having discovered my mother's jewels. From their years secreted. A glowing glittering ransom. Of diamonds, necklaces, her tiara, strings and strings of

28

pearls, ruby and emerald bracelets, all stacked in their steel chest. And at last found. To release me. From all future want and impoverishment. Naturally I reared up in bed shouting something like hooray and Crooks jumped back, trembling and rattling the breakfast tray. A white bandage, as if a truce had been declared, tied conspicuously over his striped trouser at the knee. Doing me the honour of personally attending to my morning nutriment.

"Master Reginald are you alright."

"Sorry Crooks. I was in a dream."

"You reared up at me. For a second there I thought I was to get the belt of a clout."

"Yes well I think I was momentarily excited."

"No harm done. Breakfast now, here hot and ready when you are. And I shall be back presently to take instruction concerning our Tuesday impending lawn meet here at Andromeda Park."

A hobbling Crooks in a regalia hardly suitable for top drawer butlering. But at least everything in place on my tray and carefully spreading my napkin for me. As he leaned over the bed his boiled detachable shirt front bent straining like a bow to perhaps catapult off and reveal his rugby jersey beneath. Even as one eye looked east as the other peered due north west one could see how quite red eyed he was. And grunting disapproval at the displacement of my mother's things. Kept most irritatingly screwing up his nose each time he reached to replace a small artifact to its former position.

"Permit me Master Reginald if you will, to preserve the arrangements your mother her late Ladyship Antoinette Delia Darcy Darcy Thormond would have desired to be kept."

Dear me, such equally pretentious palaver can pour from Crooks sober as well as drunk. Flinging titles about left, right and centre. And together with his attempting to preserve every furnishing in my mother's rooms as it had been, plus his hindering interference in removing my mother's collection of bath salts I'd become fond of using, did make me think it merciful for us all if he were soon found swinging from a rope in the butler's suicide room.

"Where are the bath salts Crooks."

"Ah the bath salts, the bath salts, the bath salts."

"Yes the bath salts."

"They are from Paris."

"I know they are from Paris, Crooks."

"Created by André the greatest of great perfume makers, fragrances fit only for a queen."

Of course it's an indelible characteristic of servants to first please themselves before pleasing oneself. And although utterly infuriating, I let Crooks hold on to his precious bath salts. Expressions such as fit only for a queen, had nothing to do with my decision. But one could sense Crooks on the verge of making a remark in that risqué direction. But of course taking my acquiescence as encouragement he also promptly rearranged the bedroom to its original and inconvenient manner. One even finding he would shove my brush and comb and studs out of sight somewhere in the bureau drawer, making my dressing for dinner unnecessarily maddening. Avoided only when I decided to dine taking supper on a tray upstairs with a fire. And already prepared for bed in gown and slippers, ready to disappear buried in blankets and counterpane with my digestion undisturbed.

"Crooks I shall take supper here tonight."

"Very good sir. It will be lamb this evening."

"Then do you think we could have a suitable claret."

"We're in a bad way in the cellars."

"O dear, please, do find what you can."

"I've been scraping and scrimping every way imaginable to keep this household in one piece."

"I did only say Crooks find what you can."

"After long service such as mine, Master Reginald, you take to heart the tone of words as much as you would their mere meaning."

"Well I apologise for my tone then. And I do think you're due some improvement in your clothes Crooks. We must look smart for the lawn meet."

One regretted instantly having ever opened one's mouth. Crooks putting on his most painful expression of deeply injured pride. As if one had accused him of rape murder and sacrilege.

"I beg your pardon Master Reginald, but these garments are fit for the likes of any of them turning up here on their high horses I assure you."

One deliberately decided not to take lunch. As the beetle browed agent was the next on the list of sons of bitches one was to play pop

30

with. Close off to him the comfortable mecca of the rent office where he has been holding court. Dispensing petty cash which when totalled over last week amounted to more than his wages. But by god with a thousand more trees gone missing, it will be more than injured pride he will get. Needless to say since my return he was little to be found in evidence except to report via Luke that Midnight Shadow had left a trail of destruction across the countryside. Running amok in sheep, cattle and cows, and driving the whole parish shivering in fear behind their doors.

And one caught him brazenly in the rent room opening the safe with his own set of keys. A fire blazing cozily in the stove. A tray on the desk with a bottle of best claret, slab of roast beef, vegetables and pudding. So much for Crooks' scraping and scrimping. No bloody wonder things are in a bloody bad way in the cellars. And would you believe it, a cigar singularly resting on one's best Meissen.

"Ah, it's you is it sir. Back once more from Dublin's fair city is it. I was just getting down to a bit of business thinking you would be at your own lunch and not wanting to be disturbed."

"I understand there are legal threats over the runaway horse."

"More than threats they be sir. And it's only facts of the matter, only the facts now as I'm telling you to your face sir. Writs for damages ready to be served by every solicitor able to read and write in the town."

"I suppose there will be further shenanigans from the owners of every mare that Midnight Shadow had committed rape on the sloping quarters of their luckless nags."

"They'd be cheering instead of complaining of that now. Only there isn't a mare in miles that could take the shaft of that monster."

"Well hooray that at least is a blessing."

"But I'm only suggesting now that a mere fistful of fivers slipped at the right time into the right hands would soothe many a ruffled feather before things get legally antagonised as you might say. And I was at the safe here for that purpose."

"I'll attend to the safe in future if you don't mind. And there won't be any fistful of fivers given into the right hands. And I would appreciate your leaving that set of keys. I also want all account books available for inspection. From your scribblings posted there on the wall,

31

the list of stock, feedstuffs, timber and machinery is not only incomplete, it is, from my having counted the cattle and checked the barns and woods, also entirely fictitious."

"I will not be spoken to in that manner, I won't. With years trying to get blood out of a stone in this place. I won't be spoken to with the likes of them remarks. Not from you nor nobody like you. You'll have my notice of resignation."

"And I'll accept your notice."

"Who are you suddenly. Tell me. Thinking you can run this place and you still just out of short pants. And the likes of you who wouldn't know a bullock from a heifer."

"I think it is more required I know a rascal from a yeoman."

"I'm due thirty acres by the old school house on the main road for my services over the years. And I'll have that from you."

"You'll more likely get the end of my boot to put you out of this room if you're not singularly careful."

"I'll not forfeit my rights. Call yourself a gentleman do you. Threatening me with violence are you. I'll get the Guards to you. And a writ. I'll give you a writ for your trouble. Accuse me of embezzlement will you. Fraud is it. When I've been patching this place together so the buckeen likes of you and yours can twiddle their toes in the bathwater to go lie on your backsides in silk under the crystal chandeliers. Recruiting hardworking young ladies to sweat for you."

The agent wisely sidling round to the other side of the rent table. As one must confess I was just then aiming a fist straight at his beetled brows to knock his bowler hat flying. Which of course he had the insolence to persist wearing in my presence. Tugging it now jammed down over his ears. Throwing keys on the table and pulling open a drawer taking what appears to be a parcel wrapped in mouldering brown paper. Delicious to see his eyes glancing at his lunch tray. Cork pulled and the full bottle lying in such magnificent comfort in its wicker basket. Whose label upside down I could at last read. Chateau Clos d'Estournel. And which I must say, did give me an immediate ruddy roaring appetite.

"I'll have freehold my thirty acres out of you and more before I'm finished."

"You get out that door this second, or by god I will throw you through it."

"I've been slandered. Threatened with violence. I'll put a writ on you."

"Get out. Or you'll be murdered long before you get to a solicitor."

"A writ. Gentleman you call yourself."

A series of distant doors heard slamming. Darcy Dancer ensconced at the rent table. Elbows sawing back and forth cutting nice chunks from the thick slab of beef. Napkin tucked over his gold pinned polka dot pink and blue cravat. A spot of sun beaming in the barred window. Bringing to light three ancient bullet holes in the portrait of my grandfather which were meant for and missed his then very alive head. My lips at the edge of this, his armorially engraved glass. Sipping the musky smooth velvety brick red nobility of this wine. And hugely bursting into laughter between nearly every mouthful. A quarter pound of butter in a dish. Half a loaf of Catherine's soda bread like the most delicious cake. Swirling the claret to perfume the air and further tempt one's mouth. The roast beef a little overcooked but refreshingly tasty nonetheless. Just as one found most unrefreshing the bitter hatred suddenly erupting from the agent which had obviously lurked smouldering in him over all these years hidden beneath his smarmy smiles and obsequious genuflections. However he did rather conjure up a very nice image indeed. Twiddling toes on one's backside swaddled in silk. Awfully nice. And perhaps even popping grapes down one's gullet while watching up into the celestial bliss of one's crystal chandeliers. Quite delightsome. Before of course such ceiling glassware unhinges out of its rotted anchorage and plummets straight down onto one's previously idyllic countenance.

"Jesus, Mary and Joseph."

"Do come in Mollie."

Dingbats transfixed in the doorway with another tray. Containing a bottle of port, Cointreau and brandy. Saw me with cigar alight and nearly dropped the lot as she looked around the room, glancing even under the rent table and beyond the old oak filing cabinets. Now looking suspiciously side to side for more ghosts as she puts the liquors down and quite quickly moves again backwards to the door. Blessing herself in the usual manner.

"Was it you it was wasn't it I brought the lunch to."

"I think so Mollie."

"I could have swore. I'd swear. And you'd think I was a liar that it was himself the agent, so help me god was here in the flesh ordered lunch. If my mind is not playing me tricks."

"Your mind Mollie is playing you tricks."

The men having spent the previous day with ropes wandering the countryside hoping to somehow entangle the wild stallion and blindfolded get him back to the stable were all now, even including old Pete and Willie both retired and pushing ninety, sitting around in the tack room, plotting useless strategies, the premier one being that of merrily wasting time. One realised one would have to head out oneself. And after such a good lunch, claret, brandy and cigar why not join them in the fun. One did attempt to put the task to them in the most indirect way possible.

"Well I think perhaps we might give that old stallion a try again, keep him on his toes."

Needless to say we were the first time coming upon that old stallion again running for our lives in all directions. Those at least who couldn't climb a tree. Out of which I nearly fell laughing watching Luke go splashing face first into the bog. And luckily for him totally submerging long enough that Midnight Shadow seeing him disappear chose another victim in sight. One suspected of course that the four footed monster was completely enjoying himself. Routing us all, taking a sleeve here, a lock of hair there, the bottom out of someone's trousers or landing a kick as he did in Mick's belly which deposited its luncheon contents over the meadow. And then the beast rearing and with a triumphant victory roar taking off gale force cross country, black mane and tail flying.

"Are you alright Mick."

"Not a bother on me, just a bit of this ould blood leaking up me throat that spit out now here all over the grass will grow great clover. Sure all I need is a kick in the backside now to put me stomach back out where it was."

Although one could level a litany of criticisms, it had to be said that no matter what physical evil or maim seemed to befall the man that one never did hear even the most minor complaint. But after crashing through hedgerows, trampling forest meadows and bog lands mile after mile, one was oneself not only too exhausted to complain but hardly able to speak. And one was damned if one was going to do another inch of search this night or suffer such efforts to worry further of what murder and mayhem the savage animal might still do. But one thing one was sure of. Just as the stallion could not be trapped or caught, that if ever the damn creature could with its monster tool, put a decent civilized kind mare in foal, you could end up lucky with a sane two year old such as would be just wild enough to have a stride and jump in him that would leave every other nag gasping furlongs behind in the Grand National.

An owl hooting. Darcy Dancer returning up the front steps of Andromeda Park. The great door scraping open to internal darkness. Boots kicked off in the hall. The sweet scent of turf smoke from the fire. Go wearily feeling my way climbing the stairs in stockinged feet. Hair congealed with salty sweat. Mud spattered up and down one's brow. Blood dried down cheeks. The stiffened strains in one's guts. Dublin life has softened the muscles, weakened tendons, shortened the breath and nearly civilized my mind into finding life out in this wild wilderness grossly uncomfortable. And a sorry beaten mess one feels.

"I am Master Reginald having the towels as of old aired for you in the oven."

"That is much appreciated Crooks."

"Sir now you shouldn't take a mad horse to heart. Sure with miles to gallop he'd be dead tired like yourself and bring harm to no one this night. And you'd find him tamed and exhausted enough to bring in in the morning."

Darcy Dancer stretched in a hot bath. The window and mirrors steamed. The candle guttering. In safe at last. But Crooks doesn't know his ear from his elbow about horses. Or about that death on four legs marauding out there in the bleak black dark. Close one's eyes for a sacred moment of warm peace. Except for a rat or hopefully a giant mouse gnawing at a timber somewhere. Time for toe twiddling prior to reclining a backside in the silks. Creaking floorboard in the hall. The bathroom door is opening.

"Glory be to god."

A gasp from Dingbats coming some few unnecessarily prolonged seconds after dropping the oven hot towels on the floor. Blessing herself and mumbling some indecipherable expression in Irish before running out the door. Dingbats has seen another ghost. Lying here quite rude to be sure. With my pole up like a periscope. Which warm soothing waters always seem to do to me. Teach her a saucy lesson not

35

to barge in doors without knocking. But one does hope that after reciting the act of contrition and saying a rosary or two she might again reappear with my dinner. Which of course she did.

"Dinner is served sir. Shall the tray go on the table there."

"Half an hour late Mollie."

"Sir there's been terrors of stories told down the kitchen about the mad horse. Sure he could come back and get at us up the stairs of the house."

"I shouldn't worry Mollie. But you might come back yourself and up the stairs with the condiments, wine glass and fork."

"There are too many shocks for me in this house to remember me name, never mind the condermints or whatever they're called."

Her frizzy red hair previously well camouflaging her brow and eyes now brushed in a new off the face style. Maybe so she can see more nudity. I did think sight of me in the bath did do something improving to Dingbats' behaviour although not to her overpowering musky smell. One knows of course of the chastening effect the nakedness of the master or mistress of a house seems to have on staff. Putting them into good humour for days on end. And now rather than a stupid frown overcoming Dingbats' face, as usually happened when racking her brain for some asinine excuse, one found her mischievously smiling. Rendering of course her asinine excuse.

"Ah sir them condermints must have jumped off the tray in the kitchen as they were all there just this minute ago."

One would swear too that her chest was sticking out somewhat further. And still on her freckled face was what one could only describe as a Mona Lisa smile. Which I fear gave her countenance a rather sickly appearance, especially as she was now conspicuously licking her tongue around her lips. And engaging me in what for her was unusually familiar conversation.

"It's a better sort of evening sir, this evening now with the stars out."

O my god, how does one now get a moment of privacy. Previously she seemed to be quivering in fear and couldn't wait to get out of one's presence and now one is informed the stars are out.

"Ah you don't say Mollie. Pity the shutters are closed."

"I'll open them sir."

"No. Please don't bother. I'll look at the stars I think later. Thank you very much Mollie."

Mollie departing and after feasting I was woefully suffering randy pangs conjuring up previous Dublin nights. Of a naked svelte castanet clacking Lois in her studio. One regretting all her portraits of me were in the nude. Otherwise one could hang one right here. Hammer it in with nails safe from Crooks' removal. So soothing now to have in my hand a glass of Trockenbeerenauslese. Poured from the very last bottle of this nectar left in the cellar. And to be for chaste distraction, perusing my mother's scrapbooks and about to dig into my first spoonful of rice pudding in which I fully intended to count the raisins. So pretty too to contemplate the strange evening beauty the candlelight gives to the wild bog flowers there in their vase so delicate and rare. As if one had never really seen that porcelain before.

Darcy Dancer, legs folded gently in his slippers. Thick white Aran Island stockings warmly on his feet. In air that must be growing chilled in the starry night. Turning to this page of my mother's memories. O god damn it, a knock on the door, what is it now. It's altogether too soon to collect my tray. One does lose all one's savoir faire. And makes one shout in my loudest voice. O god damn it. It will be Dingbats out in the hall squeaking that she is in a hurry to get to bed and has come for my tray. But there seems utter prolonged silence. Yet someone still remains outside lurking. Forcing me, wouldn't you know it, angrily to get up and see. I'll drag old smelly Mona Lisa Dingbats in by her latest styled frizzy red hair. Which is perhaps exactly what she wants me to do. My god. My heart stopped in my chest. Leila, here in the hall darkness. Her eyes averting shyly.

"I've come to collect your tray sir."

"Please I am sorry, I rather shouted, please do come in."

Leila reaching to close the door to the chill draught blowing in from the hall. Unlike Dingbats who would let the wind blow me out the window. Leila glancing about at the changes Crooks had this very evening wrought. My mother's fire screen back against and shielding her chaise longue.

"I'm sorry sir, I didn't mean to intrude."

"O no, please, by no means, you didn't."

"But you're not finished."

"O but I am nearly."

"I'll come back."

The dignified presence of her straight slim shy form standing in the shadows just inside the door. So comforting at a very moment when one was feeling immensely sad. Having transported oneself into the past. Solemn with the sweet strange pain of another's memories. Pressed tiny flowers of primrose, violet and snowdrops. Between vellum pages affixed with faded photographs. Conjuring up my mother's face and voice. Her kisses I knew as a child. Upon my face abed in the dark as she returned from hunting. And in these years of her life long before I was ever born. Her parasols. Her beribboned straw hats. Her gentle gaiety and laughter in this house. These pictures of her so gaily posed. On front lawns of great houses. Sporting and carefree at Aix les Bains in sun and demurely risqué in bathing costume. Her cold mouldering coffin there beyond amid the yew trees. When once there were these chaps in polo tournaments changing horses between chukkas. Be now such old men. Chewing cigars in their clubs. Gout in their joints. When once they swirled and danced attendance upon my mother. Their autographs she collected at parties and hunt balls. Her standing next to a stalwart mounted on a motor bike. Then animated at race meetings. Her smile. Gone from her flesh. Covered purple in the snows that night of my return. And long lain now. Faded in the grin of death. In dust lie quietly. Where all vanity vanishes. Where too my own life will go. Out hunting. As hers did. Flung down from her horse. And placed peacefully. Back into the land she loved.

"I have intruded, sir."

"No. Honestly you haven't."

A gust of wind rattling the shutters. A whiff of turf smoke down the chimney. The mirrors of the candle lamp throwing shadows on the walls. How does one make one's voice sound casual. To ask. Out of one's deepest loneliness. Join me in a glass of wine. As she steps across the room. Bending to the low table. Pausing. Her dark head turning. To the scrapbook open at a large picture of top hatted gentlemen and frilly frocked ladies at Goodwood week. Another picture beneath of my mother in her long white flouncing skirts ready to play tennis. And on the page opposite her signed dance card at a grand ball in England. Among her friends. In her flowing gown. Her

38

pearls, her tiara, and jewels glittering. And a poem drawn in a rust faded ink in my mother's large neat hand.

> Before wedding bells chime
> How I do love this time
> Would it could never change
> This sweetness of my dream
> Of being sweet seventeen.

"I think the poem and she are so beautiful."

Still with my glass of wine raised in my hand. And I nearly dropped it. Finding her words spoken as if she were standing inside my soul. Caught so unaware. And speechless. As I was just three previous days ago. When from the main staircase landing where always I pause to look out at the so stately silver boughed grove of beeches. I had just turned from the window to step down the remaining stairs. To see Leila standing on the black and white tiles of the front hall. She seemed suddenly taller. Her well turned slender black stockinged legs. Black hair swept back from her face, her chin raised. And I hardly know any other word one can choose but aristocratic, to describe her at that moment. As she looked up at the painting of my mother's grand aunt. I froze frightened to move. The seconds dragging on. And still she stood there looking. Desperately not wanting to disturb her, I tried to retreat back up around the landing. Promptly of course kicking and clattering loose a carpet rod with my heel. And startled, she saw me. I felt so mortified to have intruded upon her in her quiet communion. I wanted to say. Please. Do. Go on watching. It's my favourite painting. But even as she rushed away, I knew, that though we had yet to speak, it was as if we had already spoken. A spiritual language that only ancient friends can speak. And go as silent companions touching in each other's lives. And there she stands now staring me straight in the eye. The chilblained redness it caused me pain to see in her trembling hands. And nervous as she clearly is, I am even more so. My dressing gown sticking out in an inexplicable randiness so that I must move behind the back of the chair. A cow moaning somewhere in the distance. The thump thump of a chimney cowl spinning. Her face flushed pink in the fire and mirrored candlelight. The white skin of her neck a bright red.

"I should not have taken such a liberty. To say that. But I could not help seeing, open as it was the other day to the page on your dresser. And some might think such a poem trivial but it so clearly came from the heart."

The precise, confident sound of her voice. Yet so soft and sweet. Her words. Intrude. The word trivial. Coming from her soft moist lips. Leaving me awed that she should have the solemnity of spirit to think them in her mind. Under her thick black hair. Behind the alabaster beauty of her face. Surprising me so much I find my mouth opening and not a word of my own coming out. Clearly now she thinks she has overstepped her position. Before one could reply suitably. Moving her shaking hands behind her back in embarrassment. Watch her fingers move plates to balance the tray and lift it deftly. Her black stockings on her slender but strong legs. How does one deal with disaster that steals so stealthily into one's life. So at a loss. What does one say. Stay. Put back that tray. Don't please go towards the door. Speak your beautiful voice again. Don't avert your eyes. As past me you go. Berry bright luscious lips pressed together as if any moment tears will pour from your eyes. Head bent. Door closing. Your feet. Gone. Leaving me more crushed and dismal now than ever. Offending you. Cruelly bruised your spirit. Nothing seems to go right in this place. Everything becoming like a dirge forever playing in one's heart. Her words. Said again. Intrude. Trivial. How can I ever find other words to say to you back. And what I could not ever admit. Those previous three days ago. That after watching you in the hall. That later that day. At a water trough. And closing an old iron gate into a low rushy field. My hand on the wall. An evening sun coming over the rising western hills, warming one's back. And suddenly I felt as if shot. That every energy left in me would burst forth in tears. Your name on my lips. Leila. And again. Leila. And good god it cannot. It must not. It will not. Happen. That I stand here. Tonight. As I did that afternoon. Trying to make you know. I want to touch. Place my fingers against you. Press lips to your hair. Leave them there.

> Like the snow lies
> On the tree branches bent
> To breaking

5

Since the night she spoke of the poem in my mother's album, nothing could drive the thought of her out of one's mind. I knew the touch of her hand everywhere. My breeches, stock, jersey, laundered by Edna Annie, now carefully neatly folded and placed on my mother's dressing room chair. My socks in a symmetrical pyramid on top of my underwear. I stood staring not wanting to move them. To leave them just as her hands had. Wondering where her fingers had rested. Seeing where she creased to make the folds. And then finally lifting the clothes in a sacred bundle, making space and placing them away in a bottom drawer of my mother's dresser. Where they stay untouched.

I had thought life had so hardened me to have made me free of such wretchedly painful sentimentality. To atone for such lapse these last days before the lawn meet, one brandished out at dawn saddling up to exercise horses before breakfast and again every afternoon before teatime. Still searching for the stallion. But only finding the furrow marks of his hoofs and where he had removed great patches of bark from trees and chewed saplings to the ground.

One abysmally attempted to have the servants' bell to my mother's apartments reactivated, the wires and pulleys clearly having been rusted into total disuse. And for one's trouble one got a twisted ankle, falling in the dark into where the floorboards had been removed. And on that exhausted evening, I ordered an early supper and went to bed. Hoping desperately that Leila would come with my tray. But Dingbats did instead. And wouldn't you know she would with one bloodcurdling crash, not only fall over the upended floorboards but with her leg plunging through the ceiling below, send my meal over the hall rug for the rats to have a feast.

One did hope for a cheering day to dawn soon. Heading out after breakfast to find as always, Sexton safe in the warmth of his potting shed. One of the few places one could take refuge. And pass the time of day.

"Ah how are things in Katmandu this morning Master Darcy."

Things were certainly not good in Katmandu, especially in the afternoon. With an irate farmer coming thumping a walking stick on the front door. And a family of tinkers found milking half our cows. Dingbats poured a bucket of hot grease down the sink and as it congealed the kitchen was flooded. Crooks attempting to get the dumb waiter to the pantry working once more, had his knuckles crushed for his efforts and Catherine wondering what all the screams were about looked up the shaft to have the dumb waiter come crashing down on her head. I must say, one did just pop out of the maelstrom for a Madeira behind the locked door of the library. No wonder the country houses for miles around were full of their drunken inmates.

One felt quite tipsy saddling up Petunia to ride out. To view land a rather rat faced farmer had bought surrounding a distant choice field to which he said I no longer had a right of way. Suffice to say I rode straight through his feeble fence. And found myself where banks were washed down along the big river and a flood was pushing out across the fields. I was planning to have a gallop across the long meadow joining Andromeda Park to the land of the great castle. And maybe catch a glimpse of the exotic goings on one felt must be in evidence there. Low dark clouds and heavy mist were lowering from the sky. Suddenly the great castle was out of sight as one got lost descending through an ancient oak wood. Too far from roads even for the agent to be bothered stealing. Surrounded by a plantation of gone wild rhododendrons, merging into another wood. Dripping spooky fern. Mushrooms sprouting out of the boggy tangled roots. Nearly dark now. Along the river the bridge is half down. Remains of an old farm road. Rotted trees. Foundation mounds of abandoned cottages. Centuries ago, feet trod and lives were lived here. And something is ahead there. On the little stone bridge. Rein up. There is something. Petunia shaking. So am I. In the white wisps of mist. Like a christening dress. In long flowing veils. Someone is standing on the ruin of the bridge. A figure. Swathed in white. Long dark flowing hair. Her garments move as she stands so still.

Petunia shying, rearing, falling sideways and throwing Darcy Dancer to the ground. His skull crashing back banging the bulging roots of a beech tree. Petunia struggling up shaking her head and with reins slapping loose, galloping away. Darcy Dancer getting to his feet. Stumbling forward on the wet boggy ground. Turning to see Petunia pounding and crashing up through furze, bracken and briars. Abandoning me. If anything a horse hates it's a ghost. Almost feel cracking my head open is a relief. Sticky on the back of one's neck. Blood. Not a sign of anyone or anything on the bridge. Amazing how one's troubles finally drive one into having visions. Just like everyone else mentally unhinged at Andromeda Park.

Darcy Dancer once more catching Petunia's reins as she stood finally grazing the other side of the hill and halfway across the bog. With the brown chill water filling and spilling out over the tops of one's boots. Nearly dark and nearly lost. Just shadows on the horizon. Without a sign of any light or life. Except snipe, wings beating as they chirp speeding left and right, away into the sky. Can't even see the top turret of the great castle. Walk Petunia quietened out on the edge of these wild uncharted lands. Without disappearing forever into a bog hole. Dump the moisture out of one's boots. Bless oneself like Dingbats does when she sees a ghost. Or my highly exaggerated penis engorged.

Darcy Dancer returning over another two miles. By the forest and around the lake. To at last find one's way to the park land meadow. Without a horse between one's thighs one's legs would be frozen. Cross the stream. Head up the hill. The house looms darkly with all its shuttered windows. Except one. The whim room. Behind the shiny black panes. A figure standing watching. O god what new strange haunting is afoot.

Following a hot bath I lay shovelling more sherry than was good for me down my throat. And wrapped in blankets on the chaise longue reclined waiting for supper. Imagining that Dingbats had gossiped below stairs about seeing me with a raging erection in the bath.

43

And Leila would think one a shameless debauchee. Returned from wallowing in the fleshpots of Dublin. With ill met dissolute friends. And at the knock on my door. Hoping with all my present indisposition that she would come. I was utterly disconsolate when Norah did instead. Saying it was everyone else's night off. And a dance in the town. With a brandy I went to bed. And lay practising dying. Somehow muchly preferable to being killed. By the bloody worries here. Even the men taking my mood from the nosegay of a morning. Made one choose to wear a dried purple cornflower. No point in letting them think I'm happy and that the time was ripe to ask for a bit of hay, straw, firewood or extra milk. As one was often asked for anyway. And one did not exactly scowl but I tell you my demeanour was considerably less than ebullient.

Needless to say in finally tossing and turning to sleep one had a nightmare of a dream. Of being attired in pyjamas in the front lobby of the Royal Hibernian Hotel unable to pay my hotel bill. With Rashers Ronald behind me with his very best British military accent blasting out pretending to be my adjutant and me his general. Rashers demanding to see the manager and rather loudly and pretentiously declaring that I was a man of enormous land holdings. Plus being the Marquis of Delgany and Prince of Kilquade. Who was not about to be insulted by a hotel clerk's insolence asking for settlement of an account. But somehow in the dream one was insulted. And I think referred to as a chancer. And Rashers Ronald, as he once did when so called by a clerk on a similar occasion, loosed his fly, unreeled his prick, and peed all over the lobby. Of course Rashers was peeing too over one's heels and it wasn't till Crooks himself woke me from my thrashings about the bed that I realised it was all a dream. Crooks with his arm in a sling. A limping Dingbats putting a tray by my bedside. Reassuringly set with Meissen. A plate of six sausages, two rashers, and three fried eggs. But somehow even a stack of toasted soda bread and slabs of butter only minus a knife, pepper and salt did not lighten a blackdog depression crushing down upon one. To put a shotgun barrel to one's head in this loveless life. Condemned. By convention and birth. To the great granite shell of this mansion. To all these prying eyes and ears listening. And who would care if I were found mortally wounded. A few screeches out of Dingbats perhaps at the blood and gore. A message to the victualler in the village. To prepare the body. And in one of our own sycamore coffins I'd be lowered in the ground. Sexton would mind. He would I think be quite sorry to miss our talks. But none other would much give two or more hoots.

"And how are things in Shangri La this morning Master Darcy."

"They are Sexton I suppose, as per usual."

"Well let me tell you. Right straight from the contentment here in the intimacy of all these growing things. And having recently travelled up to Dublin and visited the Botanic Gardens of Trinity College, that what we need now is a new heated plant house in which choice and tender exotics can be grown. The professor himself from the college will come down to consult."

"Well in my opinion Sexton, I do, I really do think instead of a new plant house that this entire island of ours should with suitably strong tug boats, be shifted many latitudes further south. Especially now that upended floorboards have been added to cracked ceilings and walls held together only by the debris choking them."

"Well take consolation sir now that if the dust and debris filled chinks and crevices were ever cleaned, dusted or scrubbed away out of the big house, the winter winds would penetrate all that more arctic into your bones and likely freeze you and the rest of the occupants to death."

"While I take no consolation I do quite see your point, Sexton. Clearly a dirty house is a warm one."

"Fronti nulla fides. And that Latin translated, means, There is no trusting to appearances."

Between Sexton's botanical dreams and Latin references one did want to broach the matter of the figure on the bridge as casually as possible. If anyone was left sane enough in this place who might give one a reasonable explanation of the previous evening's events it was Sexton.

"And by the way, Sexton. I was out exercising yesterday evening. Went beyond Thormondstown to Thomastown. Got quite lost. Petunia has put on rather too much condition and is not as fit as one would like. Thought a good long run would do her good. Just happened on the way by the old ruined bridge."

"Ah the old stone bridge that's tumbled down by the oak forest over the big river."

"Yes, and I wonder is anyone ever to fix it to be crossed again."

"True vaulting in the arches that was built with. There isn't a stone mason about if you searched a dozen parishes around here that could do a job the like of that. And if there were he wouldn't go near it."

"Why not."

"Begob. Why not. I'll tell you why not. Been a couple of heads gone white overnight with fright. That's why not. The ghost of the lame girl haunts it she does. Nineteen summers old she was. Her horse threw her upon the stones that once built the bridge over the river. Her back and neck broken. Lay a whole night before she was found in the morning. Begob I was there wasn't I. Helped lift her. Her black long hair spread on the grass. A face like your mother's. Her beautiful blue eyes staring up at you. O god it would crush your heart. Her hat found a mile away afloat on the river. But her horse nor saddle have never been seen since. I'd say ended up in the clutches of some villain."

A chill struck one's spine. The hair rose to stand on the back of my neck. Felt the blood draining from my face. And greeted with my silence, Sexton turned his one eye up from the plant he was packing in a pot.

"Sure now you look as if you'd seen a ghost."

"Who was she, Sexton."

"A visitor to Thomastown Castle. Had the merest limp, one leg slightly shorter than the other. But by god for beauty she had no shortage. About to be married she was. To one of the richest peers in England. Trousseau packed. Sure the lass could quote the poets, as she would of a morning constitutional when I was a groundsman over at the castle with my starvation wages. I put many a flower on her grave, would coax and cuddle them. But not one would grow. A sure sign her body was elsewhere. But I'm not pretending there's a word of truth to the ghost of her on the bridge."

"You don't yourself believe in ghosts do you Sexton."

"Ah now it's this way with me. After the Holy Ghost, one ghost is the same as another. If you've seen one you've seen them all. I take them as they come. But then the diehard members left one late evening of the hunt ran a fox to ground a stone's throw from the very spot. And having roused him once more off into the mists swirling, followed by the huntsman, the whipper in, the Master, the Mad Major and the Mental Marquis and one of the sisters, they all saw her the other side of the river. Standing in white on the end of the little stone bridge. Made the Marquis, mental enough already, even more mental. Sent him drunk for a week."

I accompanied Sexton to a new layout of vegetable garden already dug over he planned for Indian corn, sunflowers, artichokes and asparagus. One always took heart from his horticultural enthusiasms.

"Be eighteen feet tall they will. Sunflowers that will set the whole garden alight with their glory. They will surmount the wall. But now coming over that bit of broken wall there didn't I catch redhanded the other evening, a trespasser and you'd never guess what he was after."

"I don't think I would Sexton."

"Ah they're all bleating and moaning lovesick since the dance. Sure this one told me it was none of my business what he was doing here. Skulking around. I said I'll do for you. With a boot sailing up your backside. Ran him off I did. O but such beauty as that Master Darcy is trouble I'm telling you."

"Sexton, what on earth are you talking about."

"Sure didn't you hear about the dance the other night. That Leila went to with Kitty and Dingbats. Mademoiselle created a sensation. For every lass furious at the sight of her there were two lads with their tongues hanging out in awe."

One did all too soon find oneself out of the garden and back in the library. With one's teeth clenched in pique and one's heart pained with jealousy. I too was bleating and moaning. Albeit inwardly. But outwardly, at the thought of her, my trousers were sticking out a mile. Just hoping she would come in the door. That we would confront as we had a previous time upon my entering. And she had suddenly grabbed up her jar of wax and polishing cloth, nodded her head and before I could on some pretext engage her in conversation, she vanished out the door. And I wondered why she would rush so out of my presence. Until the reason became apparent from Crooks, to whom I tried striking a cheerful note as I sensed he was about to present me with a highly unwanted difficulty.

"Crooks, the library does seem so awfully neat, dusted and frightfully well polished these days."

"Master Reginald, sir, that may be but not without some shocking liberties being taken. And I refer to that girl Leila. She must be taught her place. Completely out of order she was. In here reading books."

"O dear. Pray tell what books."

"The porcelain and pottery if you don't mind, laid open on the tablature over there. And surveying with your magnifying glass if you please."

"O dear. O dear."

"Well she's been placed back down below stairs until she has some better manners put on her."

"But surely Crooks is it so sacrilegious. The young lady may have been merely trying to improve her mind."

"Sir with the greatest respect I submit that is not what she is serving in this household for."

What a terrible prig Crooks is. Sounding like an awful pompous barrister at times when his accent wasn't assuming its unpleasant Dublin undertones. One nearly feels like blowing him up with some strong language. But as he stood about to deliver an envelope the sight of which spelled immediate danger and embarrassment, one decided to take unpleasantries one at a time. And deal with the documented ones first. Crooks placing the salver in front of one as one imagined some high court judge might, handing down a sentence of death. I slit the letter open.

"That Johnny Gearoid, sir, brought it this few minutes ago. Face red as an old beet and puffing like he would explode, and, forgive me sir, stinking of stables. I gave him a shilling and sent him down around to the kitchen."

One knew Johnny Gearoid well. A gentleman short of stature and long on thirst, who for the price of a few pints of stout, held horses while hunt members either peed, cohabited in the bushes or drank to inebriation in the pub. And this letter he carried comes from that unpleasantly familiar old firm of solicitors in the town whose rambling dusty offices are full of gossipy spinster women and ancient creaking mahogany desks. One felt it should not have the dignity of being opened in the library or of having its bearer stuffed with refreshment.

48

Containing as it does such arrant nonsense and the ridiculous assumption I give two hoots about proceedings.

Dear Sir,

We are instructed by our client J. Quinn, Esq., to protect his interests in this primary matter, among others, concerning his position at Andromeda Park.

Our client not only was disparaged, slandered, and with menace, was put in fear not only of his good and respected reputation, but of his very life and as a result has since been under the care of his physician.

Clearly you are of the assumption you are a law unto yourself, which is inconsistent to say the least to the standing your forebears have enjoyed in this community. And in this context we advise you that our client is owed five years of uncollected bonuses promised our client by your father. Further he is entitled to have conveyed and registered to him thirty acres, four roods, three perches or thereabouts, of that land in the Parish of Thormondstown adjoining the old school house and extending south west to the bank of the river from the main road.

We would be glad if you would forthwith take the necessary steps to convey such land due to our client failing which we are instructed to take proceedings on this matter and the previous matters aforementioned.

Yours faithfully,
Fibbs, Orgle, and Justin, Case, Fluthered

Imagine elevating a low fellow like Quinn to the dignity of esquire. One remembers this firm when their name was somewhat different, tussling with us over something previously disagreeable. And now they again think they can put the wind up me. How abysmal the world suddenly is just before lunch this morning. With a sudden predominance of Protestant names in the obituary column of the newspaper. To which the religious clue was given by a scientifically motivated gentleman donating his body to the College of Surgeons. While a list

49

of much loved and deeply regretted Catholics were complacently content to proclaim their joyful reunion in heavenly places. Clearly certain their papist corpses will luxuriate in eternal happiness. And one suspects there are more than a few Catholics in the company of Fibbs and Orgle. By god I shall out of the library's legal tomes hurl such torts, rebuttals, grievances and summonses in reply, they will be sitting around their rickety old offices wondering what counter claim to use to wipe their arses with.

"Will there be anything else Master Reginald, sir."

"Please Crooks throw this letter in the fire."

Lunch was a singularly solemn affair. The ceiling nearly ready to collapse from the unsolved chronic leak somewhere higher in the house. And Dingbats dropping the sauceboat breaking on the table. Its oily contents flooding across the mahogany. Then using a priceless lace doily heirloom to wipe it up. And refusing to come out of the pantry again because one had quite under one's breath expostulated, O god, at her. Seeing the mess Crooks pretended a heart attack. As soon as a moment of escape presented itself, I donned boots and sou'wester to oversee the men build a stockade to drive the stallion into. And that collapsed like a pack of cards as soon as someone leaned against it. The rest of the afternoon one retreated indoors taking tea in the north east parlour with rain splashing the windows and the wind howling. Viewing the ceramic tomes Crooks had found Leila reading. Waking then after falling asleep, a rug drawn up over me. So carefully folded and tucked, I tortured myself thinking it Leila who had come collecting my tray. I bathed. Dressed for dinner. Sat in the salon and pecked at the piano. And then in some melancholy took supper. With one of Dingbats' long frizzy hairs wrapped around one of my sausages, and another stuck in the mashed potato. You'd imagine presenting oneself as I did in black tie that some semblance of civilization would arise from my effort.

"Port, please, Crooks, in the library."

One sat watching the glowing turf flames, sipping strength from this dark noble silky wine. Thinking of words Sexton had said and one always imagined applied to someone else.

"Far from being land poor, the poor devil was impoverished by his staff, a consistent bunch of no do gooders and layabouts who ever feathered their own nests."

Sexton talking about the years ago occupant of the great castle. And only this morning I took to task Slattery and Luke sheltering idly under the stable eaves and then minutes later I chanced to overhear Luke grumbling the other side of the orchard wall.

"Sure himself up there in the bedroom has spent himself enraged over the breakfast he's been served and is out here next in the stables later biting our heads off. And sure he never thinks a second that between the time he's had his breakfast in his dayroom that in the three hours the poor likes of us have been out here being soaked in the inclemency."

To prevent the final crumbling of one's spirit, I called for still more port. And quaffed far too much. I was in fact talking to myself standing in front of the library mirror as if in parliamentary debate, the fate of the nation at stake, shaking my fist, showing my teeth. And altogether reminding myself that I was an imperialist, a squire, pasha of Andromeda Park, and would never, never be dragged down to being a common sort. I do like the sound of my own voice. But just slip over to the door now between tirades in case anyone is lurking in the vicinity listening. Not a soul. Empty halls in all directions. Must confess one is just that little bit piqued no one is crouched overhearing. Will push aside this brass keyhole cover so the interested may peek through. I did I thought strike one or two impressive posturings. While one was expressing some rather eloquent turns of phrase. The sort of thing one would never hear in the Dail Eireann but one might encounter in the House of Lords.

Darcy Dancer tugging the servants' bell. Turning to the library shelves. Pulling out volumes. Opening them and shouting out the title and author. Slamming them shut. Flinging the volume flying, pages fluttering across the room. Knocking over the tripod of the telescope at the window. More and more books pulled out. Tossed over his shoulder. Chucked up into the air.

"If someone wants to bloody read, let them by god read. Ah. My dear Mr Arland's favourite reference to health. *A Domestic Homoeopathy*. Let us gentlemen deal with. Ah constipation. A condition widespread in this household. Brought on by the continued unrelenting wolfing down of buckets of butter and cream. Yes, on page two twenty three. Confined bowels. And the great torpor thereto. With the sensation as if they were paralysed. If opium does not afford speedy relief. Then by god an enema. Otherwise the whole staff is full of shit."

Darcy Dancer shouting. The door coming ajar. Crooks' head peeking in. His crossed eyes momentarily uncrossed. Night cap on his head. One of my father's wool dressing gowns wrapped around him. And a pair of Wellington boots on his feet. Thinking I suppose there was a fire.

"I beg your pardon sir, did you ring."

"Crooks I'm drunk. Of course I rang. Do please observe that the port there is about running out. More port."

"I shall decant another bottle immediately sir, but."

"No buts. No ands. Nothing but port."

"Very good sir."

"And to hell with this place."

"I beg your pardon sir."

"I said to hell with this place."

"Very good sir."

Door closing. Darcy Dancer reeling. Tripping forward over volumes on the floor, stumbling into the fire grate. Catching a hand on the mantel, and leaning down to pick up a fire iron. Slowly pulling himself up to stand again. Raising the fire iron above his head.

"I say Hilderson, your day and night alarum clock is about to no longer sound alarums day or night."

"Please sir, you mustn't."

"Who doth it be. Who goes there. Who doth it be who tells me. What I can. Or what I can't."

Darcy Dancer swaying, turning himself towards the door. Slowly lowering down the fire iron from behind his head. Jacket open, the bow of his tie hanging loose. Leila standing. Her eyes moistly sparkling in the yellow candlelight. A swatch of her black hair slanted across the corner of her brow. Her dark uniform. Her two feet placed together.

"It is I who tells you."

Darcy Dancer, the poker hanging at his side. Staring across the books stacked on the library table. These golden letters of the alphabet written up higher under each shelf. The peeling leather bindings. The gramophone in the corner. The wind. Still whines. The shutters still shake. Rain drops splatter the window panes. Above the sill where a pair of grey doves came once on a grey August morning, with their dark tails and light grey breasts and whiter heads and they flew to sit in the deep dark green of the pine trees. Just like the pair of silver two pronged strawberry forks under glass on their blue velvet in that case. Tolerate ridicule now. As you would tolerate praise. In this room of sorrow. Room of even sadder days. Who doth it be. Who goes there. Who doth it be who tells me.

> The tears I weep
> Are tears of sleep
> Of death
> And others dying

6

Standing confronting Leila in the fading light of the guttering wall sconces, neither one of us moving or speaking as we stared at each other. The tears drying on my eyes. I silently said words that I had not the nerve to even whisper. Crush my heart against yours. Kiss your soul with mine. Die with me. Paltry trivial sentiments of course. But the sort of thing one is apt to proffer when pissed out of one's proprieties.

"Good god. Ouch."

With the stink of scorched cloth, Darcy Dancer jumping out of the hearth and stumbling into the library table. Leila hastening forward across the room.

"Sir you're on fire."

Leila grabbing a pillow, and swinging it at Darcy Dancer's hind-quarters.

"Good god I am actually on fire. Ouch."

"Hold still sir, hold still."

"Bloody hell this is a clear indication of an inferior fabric perpetrated by an inferior tailor."

"Hold still sir."

"I am. At least attempting to. In the heat of the moment."

Leila battering the pillow up and down the back of Darcy Dancer's legs as he slaps with his hands and dances forward about the room. The pillow seam giving way. A cloud of swan's down exploding out, billowing up and wafted by draughts all over the library. White floating tiny boats on the air. Is all that's left of one of my mother's Paris made, escutcheon adorned pillows. Just as I was somewhat embarrassingly enjoying being softly buffeted.

"I beg your pardon Master Reginald."

Crooks at the door. Nearly tottering to the floor in a faint with his tray of port. Leila, one hand holding the emptied sack of the former pillow and her other bent to feeling at Darcy Dancer's backside as he lurched losing his balance.

"Come in Crooks. Been a slight misadventure. I do believe in the midst of a slight daydream I have scorched the back of my trousers in the fire."

One could have sworn that Leila laughed audibly not only when the pillow broke but also at the sight of Crooks looking as he did like a clown out of the circus, in the voluminous crimson plaid bathrobe, Wellington boots and a flower embroidered sky blue nightcap. I had all I could do to suppress my own threatening explosion of mirth. At least Crooks' ample dressing gown provided a little chance had he keeled over, that the wearer's privates could, by an unexpected parting of the folds, confront one.

"I would respectfully ask Master Reginald, if the fire brigade from the town should be summoned."

"The flames are, I think Crooks, thanks to Leila here, now under control."

Leila, sidling away backwards replacing the deflated cushion, gave as she passed, a half curtsey to Crooks. Whose face contorted in a variety of grim directions as he sputtered a bit like a fish out of water. Just as the Hilderson alarum clock on the chimney piece appropriately struck midnight. And a little parade of woodlice migrating over the floorboards to what one imagined was a safer refuge of rotting wood away from the blazing fire. Amazing how one's drunken attention can be distracted. Even with Crooks growling his Dublin accent under his breath.

"Youse is a disgrace, youse is."

"That will be enough of that Crooks please. It was entirely my fault."

55

Leila brushing away the feathers stuck to her dress. Her usually pale cheeks unusually bright pink. One did want to take another pillow to bust over Crooks' head as he glares at Leila. Her voice so soft and reasonable.

"I will leave you now sir."

Crooks, one hand trembling gripping the tray, the other sweeping the folds of his dressing gown tighter around him. One sensed his world had suffered a severe setback from the curt way in which he rounds upon Leila.

"You certainly will not leave, you will tidy up in here."

With a distinct flavour of insubordination, Leila performing a sweeping curtsey to Crooks from the door. Certainly Crooks himself seemed rather embarrassed by his outburst. My god the little lady not only can fight fires but is a bit of an actress. And one did notice too, her glancing at the chess board by the window where I had been playing a half finished game with myself, taking a turn either side of the table. And now to just listen to her well chosen elegant words.

"As you wish Mr Crooks but if I may please withdraw to get the sweeper."

"And ah would you mind awfully Leila also fetching me up a spot of cheese from the kitchen."

Leila's merest faintest smile and tiniest genuflection of the knee. Gently closing the door. Leaving Crooks frowning disapproval. Blowing away the swan's down from the side table and loudly lowering the tray. Placing the port bottle and cork on a napkin and the decanter next to my glass. Clearing his throat with each manoeuvre, to remind one of his presence. He is quite fond of imagining himself a much grander butler in a much grander house. Where the occupants would merely murmur the word cheese. And white silk stockinged and emerald liveried footmen would glide wheeling in an entire stage set with Brie, Camembert, Wensleydale, Cheddar, and Stilton. Not to mention the silver capped glass bowls housing myriad water biscuits decorated with coronets. One does under all these circumstances try to pull oneself together. Put a bit of starch back into the conduct of the evening. Distinctly made slack by events. With Crooks clearly aggrieved.

"Sir I am behooved and it is incumbent upon me to inform you that my resignation is in order. I am no longer able to endure the erosion of my authority by newcomers in this household."

"O damn it Crooks do stop saying those damnably big words to say so damn little."

"Sir you have my resignation."

"Crooks go to bed will you. There's a good fellow. Make sure the hall candles are snuffed. And don't for heaven's sake, fall through the floorboards."

Crooks rather archly sidestepping the books strewn on the floor. Grumbling inaudibly and then hardly without a limp imperiously withdrawing. In the frame of the doorway, the dim candle glow from the hall making his silhouette look like some broomstick riding witch. Must say, a few direct words here and there seem to have a salutary effect upon me if no one else. What a bunch of bloody children they all are. Lurking about with their grudges, resignations and resentments. Complaining of their years sacrificed in dutiful service. I would adore to accept all your bloody resignations. As bloody hell I don't think I can last much longer before one sinks under the waves. Any day one's name featured in *Stubbs' Gazette*. The rate collector yesterday insistent to collect the rates. Which alone nudge one to the edge of bankruptcy. Each tumbled stone, brick and slate one places back, another two more seem to fall. No wonder one flings books about. Or wants to smash a clock. No wonder one calls for port. And lifts this fortified spirit to one's lips. For the encouragement it gives. While the dried brown fabric of my trousers disintegrates. The white of one's recently donned woollies showing through, but at least saving my legs from combusting. And one so feels that in the youth of one's life, there should be at least some idle years. Poised in the perfumery of flowery phrases echoing above the tea, hot buttered scones, clotted cream and raspberry jam. Of being invited to ensconce on other satin damask sofas in the silk walled drawing rooms of various stately country houses. Where one's ears are lulled in contentment by pretty ladies rustling their silks. Or as my mother so ably did. In her salon. With her two admiring clerics. Who wore their handkerchiefs up their sleeves. While distilling their verbal admiring reflections on her porcelains. So many of which have been purloined by my father. And no one has invited me anywhere to cast my own comments abroad upon an agreeable teatime air. To coax further and similar comments from other cultured lips. Isn't the Meissen utterly divine. Words reassuring. To cast a spell of comfort. To glow at least a moment in the emptiness of these boggy miles about. To remind one's mind that we are the very best people. We call each other my dearest, my darling, my oldest and nearest friend. Of whom I have none of course. But if I did, our knees and elbows would be cocked in the deportment of anciently inherited privilege. Our arses couched comfortably in the bosom of large fortunes. Our lands fenced away by their stone built walls. Enfolding the miles surrounding our mansions towering upon their hills. Where admiring guests are drawn between great piers of great gates. The park arrangements pleasing their eyes along a winding pebbled drive. In short not this bloody desecrated place. Where a rat has more comfort than a squire. Sour milk served in my coffee this morning. Torn linen on my bed nearly strangling me in the night. In a dream of Miss von B. So meticulous as a housekeeper. So warmly limbed to lay in the soft ease of her flesh. To then awake alive here in a pair of baked trousers. When I could be back in Dublin. Racing, feasting and squirting one's sperm somewhere appreciated. Instead of suffering a lonely pain in the groin. With about one's only pleasure left, to sink softly in the depths of drunken self pity. Pat oneself reassuringly on the back. Say again and swear one will never sell. Rid oneself of all this estate, lock and stock. But first drink the barrels. Or maybe better, burn this mansion to the ground. Yet in the very next regretting breath I always know that even in the worst of worst miseries I cannot leave. And lower the flag of one's honour that waves above this crumbling pile of stones. That would let them think that my land might be had by their greedy grabbing claws. By god instead. Make them even greater resent the lustre, brilliance and splendour of one's style. Show them implacable eminence. That will make them bloody well cringe even lower in their inferiority. Anyone who hasn't touched the heady brew of being so much better than one's insufferable common man will never know what the joy of imperialism is all about. Even in this land whose pathetic only claim to fame is, as my dear old tutor Mr Arland used to say, its floating location way out west of Europe sodden under its watery skies unloading yet another day of head chilling back bending rain.

"Excuse me sir."

"O my god, I'm talking aloud. I'm sorry. I didn't realize someone was there."

"May I come in with the cheese."

58

"The cheese. Yes. Do."

"Catherine being asleep, I'm sorry this is all that could be found."

"Ah well, it's enough for a rat or two. Or indeed even three. Of our larger rats of course."

"I'm sorry for breaking the pillow."

"That is so nice to hear. You are the first one I have ever heard in this place apologise for breaking anything. And I should, shouldn't I, really apologise for appearing ready to demolish the clock. No don't go."

"I have the sweeper just outside the door. To tidy up. I'll pick up these few books, sir."

"O do leave it all. I rather like the effect. Of the feathers. Makes everything rather more lighthearted, ha ha, in this gloomy room. Open books on floor giving an air of erudition. Ah. I suppose that isn't at all funny is it."

The leather chair creaking. Darcy Dancer sitting back with a half drained glass of port. Leila standing, a book held open in her hands. A moan of wind and the screech of a fox out in the night.

"What is on the page of that book."

"A map of the battle of Rathmines, sir."

"Ah wouldn't you know hardly a volume on Ireland can be opened without a war of some sort occurring. But I've been meaning to ask you a question. May I. I hope you won't think it silly or impertinent. But dear me. Perhaps it is not silly but indeed it is impertinent."

"If you wish to, ask me."

"Well. If I may. And perhaps I am the worse for port having loosened my tongue. But do tell me. Just who are you. O god. To ask you any question at all. You must think me a crass fellow."

"You are enquiring concerning my parentage."

"O no, nothing as impertinent as that. I already know you are an orphan. I'm half a one but I've always wanted to be a whole orphan. Somehow it must be so relieving not to have any parents at all who haunt one's life. You have such fine handwriting. And your elegant handling of linens. One nearly imagines you a product of a ladies' finishing school. O dear. How patronising of me. To have said that. Now I know you must think me a crass fellow."

"No."

"You don't."

"No."

"What do you think of me."

"I think it is time that I withdraw. And leave you further to your port and cheese. Sir."

"Damn the port and cheese. I asked only for the cheese so that I might have you back here to talk to."

"Yes I know that you did."

"You are uncommonly honest aren't you."

"Yes. My honesty however, is not for everyone."

"Is it for me."

"Yes."

"Then, just who are you."

"I am as you find me, sir."

"That of course tells me nothing."

"Perhaps it is as well."

"You are being uncommonly evasive."

"What reason is there for you to know anything about me other than just as I am."

"Because whenever you enter the room I feel I should stand. I am indeed sitting. But I feel as if I should not be. Why."

"I'm afraid sir you will have to answer that for yourself."

"It was you wasn't it watching the other day out of the whim room window as I rode up the front lawn."

"Yes."

"I knew it was you. But sometimes one's eyes imagine things. The figure standing there seemed to be the mistress of this house."

"Is that censure. Or a compliment."

"I think you have, haven't you. Just dumped me between two stools. Where of course, my remark quite deserves to put me."

"I think one of us is taking unreasonable advantage of the other, sir."

"O damn, isn't that what life is all about. And damn calling me sir in that accusing way. You are of a calibre so far above that of a servant that I am suspicious. Which is not to of course insinuate in any way a denigration to the station of being a good servant."

"You're full of snobberies, aren't you."

"Yes. Indeed I am riddled with them. And of course when all is said and done, one must also have servants who are utter snobs and who will put on the dog at the drop of a chapeau. But you are an outspoken lass. And therefore I beg your pudding. Plus your pardon. Madam."

"I don't mean that you are not very nice too."

"Thank you. Here, I think we shall get you a glass and you have a bit of port."

"No thank you."

"You're refusing to drink with me. You don't perhaps really like me. Not that I give a damn."

"I like you. I think you a very lonely person. And you do give a damn. But you do imagine things."

"I imagine all sorts of things. And I imagine you are curious about the life I live in this house. Observing me."

"Now you are impertinent."

"Should I apologise. For drowning my sorrows. Sad as a king, drunk as a lord. Damn it. I won't apologise for being drunk. For if I were not drunk I would not have the courage to converse with you. How is it that you do, for a humble serving girl, have the voice and manners of a lady."

"Are such things forbidden me."

"No. But I think they are deserving of an explanation."

"I acquired them out of practice from books I have read. Sir."

"Indeed. I dare say you are mistaken. Such things are not available from books and manuals. They come by following the intimate good example set by those of rank. And don't continue to use that awful word, sir."

"It's my way of assuming in a de bon genre manner an advantage of you, too, n'est ce pas."

"Ah oo la la, I see, you even speak some French. And with a most impressive accent. You are clearly of the haut monde in some kind of incognito. You must not attempt to fool me. You see. I was a lowly servant once. You are amused. You don't of course believe me."

"No."

"Nevertheless it is entirely true. Started as a common stable lad and was promoted indoors where in fact I was then caught enjoying my employer's drawing room sofa and reading with my boots propped

61

up, much as Crooks came upon you perusing that tome on porcelain there. Of course for my presumption I was chucked out."

"Perhaps you should, for my presumption, have me chucked out."

"No. I think not. I would find your absence from this household an abysmal matter. For you do by your merest glances erase the loneliness and neglect in one's life."

Darcy Dancer, and his fingertips slowly moving his glass of port closer on the side table. A piece of glowing turf dropping through the grate into the pile of coral coloured ash. Leila's head bowing. The small purple ribbon in her hair. Her eyes averting. Their deep mossy green, tiny spheres of black in the dim light. Her neck and face will blush pink as I know they must. At my words. More than hinting. Much more than just affection. My own pangs. The pain. Like a sour seed in the sweetest fruit. Of love flowering. In its joy of yellow blossom. And in its green leaves of jealousy.

"I should not have said that."

"I am very happy that you said it."

"Why."

"So that I can tell you. That if you were ever alone and needing my care. I would come. From wherever I was."

"And you say that."

"Yes I say that."

"O lord, what am I to say."

"Please don't say anything. Please. Let my words stay as they are. And just say what they mean. Please."

"I am further now than ever knowing about you."

"You will know. One day perhaps."

"Would you come to my bed."

"Please don't ask me that."

"Would you."

"Please don't."

"Why."

"Because I don't want to say no. And because we have something between us now. That should not be changed."

"You are an uncommonly strange girl."

"And I think I will have a bit of port. No please do not get up. If I may I shall sip from your glass."

"Ah mademoiselle, how wonderful, how marvellous, how splendid. Port. Of course. Yes. Note how this purple fine liquid rises for you in the glass."

"Thank you. It is the first time I have ever tasted port."

"Ah from a grape trampled by the naked foot, this is a vintage. Lain waiting twenty years. You are in for a treat."

"It's very nice."

"And too there is Malmsey. That you must try. Served after dinner. Equally dark in colour, rich in bouquet, luscious to the lips. Like yours are. O please. Please. Let me ask you again. Come to my bed. Come. Please."

"I must now stand away from you. You must not make me leave."

"I would command you to come back. As you know I do not tolerate disobedience in this household. I tolerate flooding, breakages, malingering. But not insubordination."

"I shall start calling you sir again if you are not careful."

"That would be too sad. It has taken so long for me to say what I have said to you. You indeed had to break a pillow over my arse. And you do know that it was my feverish thinking of you that set me on fire. Ah when you laugh you have the most beautifully perfect teeth I have ever seen."

"Yes I think of all the things that could happen to me, that I would be saddest if something happened to my teeth. Before I came here things were very bad for me for the last many months. And my teeth were what I most worried about. But I will not bore you with my trivial life."

"Honestly I would not be bored."

"Ah you would. Similar tales have so often been told. And I will not add to them telling mine."

"Are you a country girl."

"Yes but I have lived in the city too."

"You're fond of fine things. And I frightened you away when I came upon you viewing my great aunt's picture."

"It's a beautiful picture."

"You go dancing."

"Yes I love dancing."

"To the local dance."

63

"Yes."

"And gentlemen have been trespassing to pursue you. Ah you do not know what to say."

"What should I say."

"Is that what gave you such fine legs. Dancing."

"I did not know my legs were fine."

"Thoroughbred. As one would use the term if one were not applying it to horses."

"Well I have gone many miles on my legs."

"What miles."

"I have often walked seven miles to a dance and danced half the night and walked seven miles back."

"Please. Let me see your legs. If you would. By standing, just a little over there."

"You've made me shy. By your many questions."

"Ah but you must know so much about me. And I know so little about you."

"I will tell you about me. But only a little at a time."

"Tell me a little right now."

"No. I prefer to ask you something. You forget that when this night is done. That you might not in the morning feel as you do now."

"I shall."

"You might indeed confine me below stairs. As Mr Crooks has already done."

"You shall be so confined, no longer, mademoiselle. I give you my word."

"Can I ask you if I might play chess with you."

"Ah so you play chess as well."

"I have watched your game, you play with yourself. And I would with your permission take white's next move. I shall play my move dusting in the morning and you might make yours in the evening."

"By jove you are a kettle of strange fish. You ride of course."

"No."

"Ah a yawning gap in your accomplishments."

"I have been on a horse."

"Ah. That answer is redolent of possibilities. Your topper. Your veil. You would of course stun the field. Your legs too, aptly placed upon the side of the saddle. I can see it all."

64

"Are you making fun of me."

"No no. Upon my word not."

"If you are I must warn you I can become very angry."

"I should hate more than anything to make you angry with me. But you must not go on standing. You must go and sit in that chair there. Of course there are about five eyes and seven ears at the keyhole. You mustn't alarm. That is of course a joke. But as you must well know, to eavesdrop is a great staff hobby in country houses. Where there is so little else to entertain. But never mind. Ah, you see, how properly ladylike you sit. Knees so perfectly together. Legs slanted, ankles crossed. I adore your deportment."

"Mr Crooks would have a fit."

"Never mind Crooks. He's an old grouchy souse. Who'll just sprout weeds out of his ears and fade, as all faithful butlers do, into the wainscoting. Or indeed he may choose to hang himself at an appropriate time in the appropriate place chosen by previous butlers."

"You appear to have a low opinion of servants."

"Nonsense. I shall of course give him a marvellous funeral. The wake shall be held in the middle of the hall. A few fiddlers and a piper. And a chap playing the spoons. Ah god we'll have a grand old time I'm telling you with a barrel of good Guinness stout. We'll have him up out of his coffin and dancing with us."

"He's not dead yet."

"O no. Quite. But when he is he'll be a lively corpse. And meanwhile we must plan the obsequies. The farm cart suitably draped. Hauled by two black plumed horses. A throbbing drum. Best elm coffin. By god. I think a choir. On the front steps. Why do you smile."

"I would never have thought such thoughts would go on in your mind."

"I am much interested in the style in which life is conducted. What other defence have we to the long winter gloom but to raise our raiment against the sodden skies."

"That is beautiful what you have said."

"O my god, who are you. That your mind listens so. I would not have known that what I had said was worthy of being admired. I daresay most have regarded my thoughts as being quite otherwise. It is wonderful to sit and speak as we are doing. I have not spoken so since the sad departure from my life of the worthy sensitive soul of Mr Arland my tutor."

"I like your intelligence. And you too, I think, have a nice soul."

"Hardly anyone has ever thought that about me. I am quite cheered, I must say, by you. You are a jolly encouraging lass. Deserving of more port."

"O no. No more thank you. It was lovely."

"Ah now I catch you. That word lovely. It is lovely. Indeed it is lovely to hear you say lovely. But a lady would never say lovely like that. O god. Now I have offended you. O you must bloody well forgive me. You do, don't you, think of yourself as a lady. Has the cat got your tongue."

"No but the wisdom of my better manners is holding on to my hand. Which would slap your face were I closer. And I think you are both rude and cruel. If you will excuse me now."

"Please. Don't please go."

Leila getting up from her chair and turning towards the door. Tripping over a book in the dim light. Darcy Dancer rising to his feet. Without a backward glance she goes. The door firmly closing and she's gone. The brass knob on the shiny mahogany. That I had reached up to turn as a child. And see my so called father sitting in the chair I sit in. Similar glasses held in his hand. Of whisky then. Its wheaty fragrance floating over the room. His rude and cruel voice. Shouted and growled. Go to blazes. All of you. Go to hell and be damned.

Darcy Dancer falling back down in his chair. Reaching for his glass of port draining it and pouring another. Abandoned to all the nightmare of what wrong will happen next. A whole world of beauty crushed. Luscious lovely lips closed. Over her lovely teeth. Her lovely eyes. Her lovely legs. Hair and skin. She came she sat and she conquered. As have now all my edifices of rhapsody spiralling up into the joys of my future, crumbled. Left lonely. And unlovely. Gale still blowing outside the shutters. Rain drops down the chimney sizzling on the hot grate. Left cast here. Aseat like a Byzantine emperor behind one's thick curtains. Impotent in all one's power. Inured against the slights of the world. Yet have one's heart pierced by an arrow. The night yet to live. Drowned in all one's despair. Her sound gone. Ascend to her lovely bed. Who doth it be. Who is her god. To whom she

offers prayer. To whom I can pray. Not to take away. Her lovely
silken step that goes upon that dark stair.

> Your lovely
> Purple ribbon
> Worn
> On your lovely
> Black hair

7

In the blackness of the library one woke near dawn. Knocking over the tray of cheese. Kicking the lumps in all directions. Leave a feast behind for our resident rodents. Already scrabbling somewhere. Slits of faint grey moonlight through the shutters. The fire dead. The chamber stony cold. Feeling to find candles and matches, and creaky limbed stumbling over the disarray. To make one's blind dreary dazed way to bed.

The flame of the candle wick extinguished halfway up the stairs with the damp. Out the landing window the skies broken and the clouds racing under the moonlight. The shining silver bark on the grove of beeches. Carry apologies to her. On a salver as silver as those haunting trees. Find her in her bed up somewhere high in this house. Genuflect in all the courtesies known to mankind to gain her forgiveness. Put my arms around her. And surely be told to go away. Instead push open my mother's bedroom door. Back into one's own lonely life. To awake another morning to fight anew. Lie mine own head on the pillow. On the cold linen.

In the tossing turning ferment of my sleep, one dreamt of Mr Arland my tutor. I went searching in Dublin to find him. Where he lived in desperate digs down a dreary commercial street, having taken some humble schoolmasterish employment. He said as I came up his rather dingy stairs, ah Kildare you find me rather without kit, yet I do still have the utensils for tea. Come join me in keeping body and soul together and both our hopes warm on my gas ring.

"Good morning sir."

Dingbats with breakfast, banging the tray noisily and kicking open the door. Her arm bandaged. Her eyes glancing around the room at my clothes flung everywhere.

"There's a great mess this morning in the library sir. A cat and chickens got in. Tore out the books. They had a right old fair for themselves."

"Dear me. Is that a fact."

"With Kitty and Norah sick, and Leila not allowed by Crooks in there I will have to clean it up myself."

"And on your way there Mollie to do that please tell Luke to groom Petunia for hunting."

"It's fierce windy still this morning sir to walk out in the mud after all the rain to the stables and catch me death of the new monia. When I'm doing all the work and the rest on their backs."

One wanted so much to shout to big tits frizzy head that she'd better tell him or be sacked, never mind the new old or any of her monia. Obviously the household overnight had turned into the usual hospital as it instantly does when anyone chooses to sniffle and cough, and they all follow suit to take a leisurely holiday one after the other. Indolence and bickering. The only bloody thing they have in common. And while they would not do a stroke of extra work, they'd crawl a mile backwards to rub one another the wrong way.

"Ah you're quite right Mollie, make sure then to pop on a pair of boots and sou'wester."

Following extending her chest out at me as she did these days, and exhaling deep sighs as she opened the shutters, one did rather long for the fumes of summer, its mossy bliss and sweet perfumes. A whiff of which strongly comes off Dingbats. Who seems to linger longer each time bringing breakfast. Giving me sidelong glances. And one did at the moment under the covers have a rock hard obelisk poking up centre bed into the counterpane. And still inebriated just enough to want to plunge it somewhere soft and cozy for safe keeping. Ye gads. Dingbats. Amazing how one's standards can plummet. And dear me if I did. Try to put it in her I'd have, instead of a mental institution, a holiday camp on my hands. As surely she'd never do another stroke of work.

"Would there be anything else now to your liking and satisfaction sir."

"No thank you very much, Mollie."

"Ah then you'd want me to be going. If there's nothing else you might want."

Now there, if ever there was, is a stream of suggestive remarks. Tell her to strip down. To her freckled skin. View her marvellously strapping legs gaiting about. Then she could say her act of contrition first in the middle of the floor. Before jumping with big tits bouncing on top of me in bed. Even though cohabitation with one's household does lead to insubordination, it at least provides a chance of some good blood getting about the peasantry. Help instil in them some spark of nobility and serenity of spirit. Instead of the malcontent surly impertinent insolence one hears from Dingbats departing in the hall.

"Sent out into the wet. Before I even have me breakfast sticking to me ribs."

My fingertips pressing into a thick smear of butter on the bottom of my tray as I reached to lift it. The cream sour that I poured on my porridge. Yolks fried solid on my eggs. And although congealed in their fat, at least my sausages weren't wrapped in hairs. But on lifting the cover to the pot, a dead summer mummified fly was on top of my raspberry jam. In one's awful blackdog doldrums. I thought damn it eat the damn thing. Serve a penance. For my snobberies. Perhaps one has as pasha indeed put on the dog in a somewhat exaggerated fashion. But damn it all why must anyone take something so triflingly innocuous so seriously. Just like the overly sensitive papist she must be. How otherwise could one take offence at my most well meant remark. Even to think that she had the makings of a lady but was not yet quite a lady in absolutely all respects should be taken as a compliment. And with standards so low as they are it is so easy to improve oneself above one's station in Ireland. Certainly her wrists, hands and fingernails could be better groomed. A jewel or two on her fingers. Her lapses into brogue eliminated. And in proper dress she could pass off as a lady in any but the most discerning of drawing rooms.

Darcy Dancer attired in ratcatcher, heading down the grand stairs. Squinting his eyes at the light. A crow tapping at the window and flying away into the beeches. Hand on the bannister. A boot squeaking. Taking a whip from the console table beneath the painting of one's grand aunt. I had not intended till one's own lawn meet to go hunting. But by god to wake in such sour gloom one has to clear the mind of cobwebs and despair. Plus it always encourages an air of excitement in the household. That perhaps I shall come back with a broken neck and Crooks can unlock the wine cellar and the household have a one great last grand hooley over my corpse in the hall. And be stretched dead as a ruddy door nail under the watchful eye of this painting, its austere dignity and bright colours so admired by Leila. And O my god, there. At the front hall grate, a bucket of ash by her side, only these few paces away. Crouched, sweeping up. She ignores the footfall of my boots going by. Cuffs of her uniform rolled back. The muscle flexed in her arm. Her cold looking hand shovels out a heap of powdery ash. The draught of air from the door blows it about. And up in her face. Serves her bloody well right. Getting on her high horse with me. Yet O god. So near her. To pass. Within a touch. And be our worlds apart. Crooks at the open front door with my cap. Out there awaits the cold grey day. How do I tell her. There on her knees. Forgive me.

Mounting in front of the house, one was at least slightly improved in spirit. Petunia's hoofs had a high shine and one's leathers were supple and gleaming. Stirrups the proper length. The air blowing cold on the face down the drive did buck me up. And at the end of the grove of rhododendrons I jumped Petunia over the fence. Trotting out cross country under the low cloud. A drying wind blowing. Thump of Petunia's hoofs on the ground did stir one for my first appearance in so many years. Let's go old girl. Hear the hounds. Find him. Chase him. Heat up the blood. And charge across the green.

Darcy Dancer emerging from a rocky boreen. Turning left. See down this hill. The hunt collecting at the crossroads. A few familiar faces raising whip hands in greeting. Clattering now down the asphalt to the pub. Where half the hunt are in there stoking up their courage. Muddy booted locals, their backs leaning propping up the walls. Sniggering remarks to one another under their shadowy caps. Johnny Gearoid struggling to hold the reins of several horses, while attempting to pull his forelock at me, and getting knocked for his trouble this way and that, his friendly fat red greasy face under his greasy hat.

71

"How are you boss. How is it going."

"How is it going with you Gearoid."

"Fine. Fine. No complaint. None. But could you spare a tanner or two now for a pint of stout."

Rather a lot of lipstick on the mouths of the ladies. Two of whom had American accents. And a distinctly spiv looking type from England in a large motor car, snapping pictures of a few rather overly smart, and distinctly of an upstart aspect, interlopers, clearly down for the day from Dublin. And my gracious they were preening and posing on their mounts. Thinking much of themselves. One supposes from now on infiltrators will be much in abundance. As they clearly regard me and my ancient mended tweeds, down their noses between their horses' ears. One was reassured by the other motley array composing the field.

"Ah hello Darcy Dancer, you're indeed a much taller sight for sore eyes."

One of the flaming red haired Slasher sisters. Who at least seems to approve of my appearance. And is eager to be off. Backing her horse right into the Mental Marquis of Farranistic, who with the Mad Major emerging from the pub, were busily clapping each other heartily on the back. Amnesia Murphy the farmer of course, since his head was bounced off a rock years ago, did not know me from Adam and gave me a muddy look. But Father Damian, my mother's most admiring cleric looking rather splendid himself in top hat and ecclesiastic garb under his hunting coat, remarked on my transformation as he called it, from prince to king of my principality. Clearly one invites that sort to tea very soon. But of course the most ebullient of welcoming words came from the hunt secretary knowing my sensibilities should be kept soothed to contribute a large subscription and to clearly encourage one to provide port sumptuously at the Andromeda Park's lawn meet. As he normally always consumed at least a bottle.

"I say there Kildare, damn jolly good to see you out. Long time no see."

One did object to this silly American Indian affectation of the hunt secretary. Long time no see. Like in the constipation affecting many of Andromeda Park household staff. One tends to assume the rather wretched thought. Long time no shit. But one does know that to pass these long winter evenings, tomes were laid open all over these remote

72

parts of Ireland, with landowners nightly reading into the dawn about America's civil war and the cowboys and Indians. Ah but all was British to the nth degree it would appear, upon my introduction to the recently imported Master from England, barrelled up as he was with surnames.

"And meet our new Master, Kildare. Wing Commander Buster Lawrelton Ryecrisp Brillianton."

"Jolly good to meet you Kildare. Look forward to your lawn meet next Tuesday. Be a wizard prang I'm sure. Hear there's a lot of fine hunting over your estate."

I did think his reference to my estate rather too pointed. And my word, imagine, wizard prang. Where on earth does he think he is. One is tempted to disclose that one has a personal mad house he might take off and land in as well as a mad stallion at large to bite off his display of sandwich and brandy pouches. But one could see the man would not listen an instant, so overly concerned is he with the impression he is making on the ladies with his far too overly thoroughbred horse, pink coat, white leather breeches, ivory handled whip and other Londonish appurtenances. And dear me with two grooms in attendance. One driving a strangely shaped motor vehicle of a renowned make, containing as the hunt secretary put it, a veritable Bodleian library of cocktails. This latter remark of course being the most erudite thing heard in the county for a century.

"Jolly good day for a scent."

I say, gracious me, that's a rather nice bit of alright. A very superior attractive golden tressed lady just trotted by on that rather even more attractive skittish bay mare. I must catch her up and take her up smartly on her remark.

"Yes indeed, jolly good day for a scent."

One had only a moment to see her strangely familiar face as we moved off single line down a track and were then but a moment at the first draw when a fox was found and we were off and running like antelopes. On a line towards the big hill above the great bog. Seventeen in the field. Pounding across a great meadow. Swept by the fresh winds. Blowing the gloomy cobwebs out of the mind. Wafting the clinging doldrums away into the sky behind. Mists wet the face. Soft turf under the hoofs flying up backwards in the sky. The whipper in, first casualty. His mount catching a front leg in a deep rabbit hole.

73

Shooting like an arrow head first and astonishingly perpendicular, clearly a foot into the ground. His two legs thrusting like a frog's into the air. His poor hobbling horse barely able to stand on three remaining legs, awaiting a belt of a sledge hammer on the brain to be put by some local farmer out of its misery.

"Gung bloody ruddy ho."

The secretary shouting out at the height of his apogee, as he was catapulted up into the sky. His horse having somersaulted caught on an old bedstead hidden at the top of the first wall. It was quite remarkable his head over heels trajectory landing him quite embarrassingly but mercifully arse splatteringly centre of an enormous not too long deposited cow pat. He did at least have the sporting sense of spirit to express his euphoria at the safe but distinctly brown landing. And to later bravely groan out to the golden tressed lady offering the only assistance.

"Carry on my dear. Landed on a spot of brown I did. Soiled me but jolly well broke my fall."

Of course even I from a distance could see the vanquished secretary might have a broken leg and from his one arm hanging limp, also an arm. But attended to by a sensible chap who was closing gates the secretary was now being helped to his feet. While his horse, still running and stumbling in its reins, did a complete somersault over the next wall as if to demonstrate a victory roll to the new Master. And gracious me those American ladies, heading for the same gap, both trying to stay on the Master's tail, crashing together, their mounts both thumping to the ground and throwing them flying. So marvellously entertaining. Both ladies of course in search of titled husbands. Perhaps if one could rid them of their awful whining accents, one would be tempted to marry one of them for her money.

The Huntsman and pack had put the fox to ground on a rise of furze bushes. And I was pleased to see approaching the blond tressed lady who had offered the secretary assistance, and who had mentioned the jolly good scent.

"Hello."

"Hello."

Somehow I could not, racking my brains, put a name to this attractive face. And so stunningly pretty. Large eyes, and long lashes. And one was quite taken aback when she smiled and without the merest of introductions called to me from a couple of lengths away. And O my god I know now. Dear me who it is. Those blue eyes. None other than Baptista Consuelo. Of course I'm sure she doesn't recall after these few years seeing me as she lay on her back with the hairy arsed Mental Marquis pumping between her legs when one unavoidably had to jump the pair of them prostrate upon each other aisle centre down an overgrown avenue of lime trees.

"And how are you, Darcy Dancer."

"I am fine thank you. And how are you."

"I am bored thank you. And I'm beginning to think you don't know who I am. You don't, you don't, do you."

"Well as a matter of fact, I do. And it was sporting of you to offer assistance to our downed secretary."

"People are so bloody selfish aren't they. I simply could not put my pleasure before coming to the aid of another who might need it. Of course I know you're only pretending to remember me. I am Baptista Consuelo. You had a tutor, such an amusing man I thought. A Mr Ireland or something."

"Mr Arland."

"Yes that's it. Arland. Couldn't ride, could he."

What could one say as she smiled again, the steam of her horse rising round her. Amazing how one could have been such ardent enemies once. And now out hunting to adopt a friendliness forced upon one by one's impossible randiness. Further inflamed of course by that scene. Of the Mental Marquis' perspiring skull. His very hairy cheeks of his arse. And pounding away between her flailing legs. Clearly she has lost some of her aloof stuck up nature with which she had tortured my dear Mr Arland. Who never in his desperate unrequited love for her, had a single cheerful moment to be amusing. She does have indeed a pair of good strong thighs.

"I hope you're coming to the lawn meet."

"Wild horses couldn't keep me away Darcy Dancer."

O my god. I am rather sucking up to her. But what is one going to do for a lady. Someone to whom one could make naughties without suffering the gnawing pangs of love. Perhaps knock her off her horse down some ravine after this fox is dug out of its earth. And the two of us could sensibly on my coat do some things together. But to now want to reach to place my squeezing hand on one of her thighs, is a total shock to my sensibilities. When one thinks of all the revenges one should take for her treatment of Mr Arland. Of course the Mental Marquis of Farranistic does have vast estates. Does rather make ladies open their legs. And my poor Mr Arland had not a pot to piss in. And she must be back from England, by the sound of her. One could get the gossip from Sexton. One is sure she has across the water been madly attempting to meet someone of social stature. In her desperation to get married. But clearly the sort who would finally succeed in doing so will be a less socially acceptable type but considerably rich. A merchant perhaps considerably much older than herself. Showering her with gifts of jewels, houses and racehorses. Her quarters if anything are enlarged somewhat. But what an awful shockingly ambitious urge they give one in their pneumatic moundiness peeking out under her flapping coat, to plunge in there between them. Deeply. Just as our fox has gone to ground, dug in as the field waits for him to be dug out.

"Of course I am now Mrs O'Shawrassy McFlynn O'Toole. My husband is in textiles."

"I see."

"He's back in Manchester. I absolutely hate Manchester."

"O dear."

"One can't see one's hand held in front of one's face for the smoke."

"I see."

"In fact you can't see. Ha, ha. Ah but let us ride together. Darcy Dancer. You are aren't you I believe the namesake of that racehorse."

Dear me. She seems to have no timidity. And seems to know considerable personal about me. I wonder does she know that I have actually seen her bare arsed in a Royal Hibernian Hotel bedroom whipping the besaddled Marquis crawling before her across the floor. Ye gads. Tally ho. We're off. I shall burst my fly open with the present obelisk one sports. O god what a mercurial lot ladies are. Never bloody well know what they want. Wanting everything. And getting something. Always wanting something else. How shall one ever find a suitable wife with a decent dowry. One to whom one might read aloud of an evening in the library. Whose sensibilities are refined enough that she would know an ode from an octave, and an octave from an orangoutang. Yet possessed of nerve on the hunting field.

And who did not neigh like a horse as some do. A lady interested in madrigals. The finer things. Paintings and porcelains. Opera and ballet. One to take up the responsibilities of being mistress of an estate. Seeing that one's housekeeper sees to the linens. Commanding the servants suitably. Putting a stop to the malingering and indolence down every hallway. And to do so in such a fashion that it did not induce the cook to pop deadly nightshade in the cabbage soup. And not to go nuts. As Miss von B used to say. I did I suppose fall madly but not perhaps too fatally in love with her. And my god what tits she had. Her waist I could nearly join my hands around. And slender yet well fleshed strong limbs. She could nearly best me when we upon occasion wrestled together. Indeed she did once pin me to the carpet. Of course I was distracted by her utter nudity at the time. Tussling with naked ladies especially one's housekeeper, being entirely new to me. Her skin so smooth, and always so freshly clean. Marvellous to witness her sedately squatting to perform her gracefully executed ablutions upon her more intimate bifurcations. And then she would rub cream into her glowing limbs and torso. One does feel that women of this island are so gauche in their intimate matters. And those such as Miss von B from the better families on the Continent are so elegant. Of course in that part of the world, they are much cleaner and neater than we are. Miss von B was, or at least her collection of photographs professed her to be, raised in the better and larger castles. She did rather let her superiority be known. More than once addressing me as you dirty filthy Irish little bastard. She was, I hope, merely trying to be charming. As she would go wiping about with her white gloves. The household keys jangling. Vas ist das. Das ist dust. Der dirt. Dee grime. Der stink. One was indeed at times awfully smelly of course. But I don't think deserving of some of her less flattering references. Dear me when the blood gets up having a gallop, the thoughts one thinks out hunting. One would plunge it up anything at all. Like blind Mick McGinty does up the back of his heifer instead of his wife. But one must never allow oneself to suffer the misery of falling in love again. Shove it in. Bang. Bang. Take that you lovely darling. Bang bang. But leave my ruddy soul alone. When one thinks of it. I have indeed been up many ladies. At least four or so. Maybe five. But who's counting. As each was nearly more unsuitable than the other. And too many of them by half old enough to be my mother.

The married lady I went to bed with on Howth Head had such enormous nipples. Which I tweezed lightly between my fingers on her grand staircase. Not that I hold age or large nipples against her or any other mother who had them. But as one is quickly approaching one's own prime one does definitely choose a mare whose breasts are pinkly budding and whose loins and legs are at their galloping best. So many lying down cows getting up step on their own teats. My dear you're awfully long in the udder. No. I must put it up a female whose body is stately enough to adore. I shall never stoop so low as to consider a servant. Leila's luscious lips or even fine legs would be entirely wrong. Her beauties simply wouldn't be right. Perhaps if she had a decent conformation, pasterns, hocks, loins, quarters, neck and shoulder in the right manner, I would do well to choose someone plain of face but dependable. A parson's daughter. Found somewhere in England. Raised in a modest manor house on the edge of a village. In short a decent sort. Fond of hymn singing. Who would, when the verger was ill, light candles for her father before services. And whose blemishes might in themselves be attractive. A type who would not be spoiled by the seeming grandeur of a large house. A wholesome steady sort, interested in bee keeping, jam making and gardening. Beautiful ladies do appear in the end to be such a nuisance. They do I suppose give one a cachet while parading in public. While giving one a pain in the arse in private. And damn all they do is to attract the envious attention of other men. And what good does that do the pleasures of one's own prick. Which after all should have priority in one's passions.

"You must, Darcy Dancer, come over and see me sometime. I'm only an hour away by motor car."

Dear me that is an invitation. If one only had one's motor car I was foolish enough to sell in Dublin. I must knock her in the ditch before the day is finished. She has my tongue hanging out. After all married ladies are best in avoiding the worst. And meanwhile if only one could persuade oneself to be satisfied with some not altogether homely type and not a Leila taking insult at the drop of a hat or floating of a feather. And perform her duties good naturedly. And my coat is flying open. One's buttons are hanging off by a thread. If one dismounted at the moment I should be most embarrassed by my obelisk. I must say one does get unaccountably enraged if things happen at one's inconvenience. I simply must put it up some lady soon.

And not be driven to fantasizing about one's female servants. Jumping up from bed and grabbing Dingbats. Taking her uniform off. Monstrous boobies bursting forth into one's hands. As she demurely murmurs what are you doing to me sir. Shoving her down on the chaise longue. Get your arse spread across that you. And shut up. I'm going to give you jolly what for. In the form of galloping jollies. Up the joyful bifurcation. Very good sir. Damn right very good sir. O god. I'm out of my mind with lust. A deadly serious situation. Which must be controlled. One wants so much to be a carnal tour de force without being a complete arse hole as well. Last night's port is giving me this day's randiness. There on the horizon. The great castle has come into view. And the earl's flag flying. By the sound of the hunt hollering ahead we shall be in the bog by the woods on the edge of Thormondstown. A lasso would be the thing. Hurled to settle gently around Baptista's shoulders and then yank her down off her horse. Then bang, bang. O god. Petunia. Whoops there you go. Nicely over this dreadful wire. O my god. They're coming down like ninepins behind one. On their bunch of damn foolish horses that can't see what they're looking at. Such amateurishness doesn't bear thinking about. I must hold out. For an elegant wife. One with the common touch. Who could as my mother did go amongst the peasantry, and would, invited into their cottages, not wince at their primitive ways and their seemingly endless inexplicable stupidities. Who would be tolerant of their pagan ancient ignorances. Cheer them in their doldrums. Commiserate when the lower orders, as they do, laugh and point at each other when seeing someone suffering pain. As one witnessed visiting the ancient old lady O'Grady down a mile from one's own front gate. Her five pet chickens picking up crumbs from her earthen floor. Named saint this and that. And as she sat on the hob as one took tea with her, she pointed and roared as her spinster fifty year old daughter agonizingly contorted over a toothache. I must say I did myself chuckle inwardly a bit. It is in fact bloody rather enjoyably funny when another is groaning away in torment. And unable to contain myself, I too started roaring. As old lady O'Grady started slapping her thigh with such force she fell off the hob. O dear. I suppose these days, to find such a tolerant mate, as who could find such a scene perfectly acceptable, is a little too much to ask for. With evidence already so blatant in the land, of ordinary people putting on airs. Keeping up

79

with the Kellys. Even to raising their voices in the lobby of the Royal Hibernian Hotel. About crates of champagne being delivered to their front suburban doorsteps. Blast them all to hell. I simply must get Baptista in the furze somewhere beyond there, now that we are on firm land again out of this awful bog we've been mucking through. Wouldn't take all that long. To smash a bull's eye on that easy target. Bang bang.

Darcy Dancer following at a gallop the upraised white rear of Baptista Consuelo bouncing in front. Streaking up the hillside. A blood curdling scream ahead. And another. To scream in lust, rage or high spirits is acceptable but to scream in utter fear on the hunt is simply not done. Must be one of these ruddy interlopers whose nerve is being severely tested. But dear me riders are scattering in all directions. The hounds even fleeing. Huntsman will soon split the copper of his horn with his blowing. The whipper in trotting on foot lashing out around him. As if he were whipping enslaved souls in hell. O my god. That's awful. One of the American ladies, her mare being mounted from the rear by another entirely naked monstrous horse. O no. It's him. My god Midnight Shadow. On the attack.

"Help. I'm being ravished."

"Begorra madam you must own a canyon if you can fit the like of that up you."

Midnight Shadow, teeth out, hind hoofs gouging emerald clumps skywards from the land, locking its forelegs around the quarters of the Virginian lady's mare. Her yellow gloved hands outstretched as she pitched forward once more to the ground as this stallion killer humped away with his vast shaft. The yelp of hounds being stepped on. Riders scattered in all directions. Those at least who were still aloft on their mounts. And the unstuck escaping like scurrying crabs over the grass.

"Get off my land you fucking Protestants."

A crouched farmer with the barrel of a gun stuck over the wall discharging shot. The Master's horse rearing up at a salvo and tumbling him backwards arse first on top of Amnesia Murphy previously a mile back deposited wedged in the fork of a tree. A sound of the distinct crunch of bones and a long low groan. And it would appear Amnesia Murphy, who had long forgotten to pay tradesmen's bills for miles around, could still remember he was a Catholic.

"Begorra I want the last rites. I'm kilt."

The Huntsman, fist to his face, attempting to stifle his guffaws. The whipper in doubled over convulsed. Even the irate farmer standing up grinning behind his stone rampart, to promptly get a muddy sod smack in the face. The Mental Marquis falling off the side of his horse trying to empty the contents of his flask of brandy. And even prostrate on the ground was still drinking without dropping a drop. Mr Fox should he glance backwards from the bog whither he has so wisely flown taking the hounds in his wake, would surely too have a rare droll old time.

"Help."

Baptista, her reins flying loose disappearing in a hollow on the landscape, clinging to her mare's mane. Darcy Dancer that gentleman galloping after her. Petunia blasting farts from her quarters down the hillside. The other side of a ploughed field Baptista's mare breaking through a briar hedge. Head for that hole. Shield one's face. The thorns ripping past. One does wish chivalry didn't accost one at such times. But of course appearances must be kept up even in the worst melee. Otherwise the whole hunt could quickly give the impression of a collection of abject cowards.

Baptista hanging half off flying down a long slope, boots out of her stirrups, arms now wrapped around her mount's neck. At a turf ripping speed up and over a wall and pounding in a cloud of steam across a gorsey field. O my god if I recall correctly from previous hunts over this terrain behind that next wall lies the deepest of ditches. Clearly a lady is about to be in further deep distress. And what a bunch of namby pambies back there. Of course one was as clearly scared as anyone. Knowing Midnight Shadow of old. And relieved to be heading in a direction which happens to be homewards. Leaving far behind silhouetted on the gentle meadow mound a complete ruddy circus of terrified hunt members to whom one does not want to admit ownership of the lethal monster in their midst.

Darcy Dancer nearly catching up Baptista as her mount struggled belly deep thrashing across the ditch and scrambles up the other side, her bun hanging loose from her hairnet. Dear me, Petunia is getting stuck. I'll say that for the dear girl, she's not easy to shift out of the saddle. And holy ruddy hell while I'm being nearly bucked off with Petunia peering down into this abyss, she's reaching some sure footing on high ground.

Darcy Dancer back tracking to take a running jump across the ditch. Petunia refusing at the edge. Darcy Dancer catapulted forward over Petunia's head. In a somersault plunging completely submerged. Picking himself up chills, splattered and battered, soaked to the skin. A gallon of bog water down the throat. Lost my cap. My whip. H two O as Sexton calls it is pouring out the top of one's boots. Blobs of mud caked dripping from face to feet. And crawl and claw up the sides of the ditch to finally stand at the top. With Petunia galloping loose and Baptista utterly out of sight. A brace of ducks overhead. Minding their own business. As I should have minded mine. And left chivalry to the devil.

Darcy Dancer chasing Petunia across two Irish miles of moorland until she finally stood up to her belly quietly grazing the edge of a bog. And in one long swallow downing the sweet winey contents of one's port pouch still intact. To lead Petunia back across drier land to the shelter of a quiet glade in some pines. Shield from the chilling breeze. Empty my boots and squeeze the buckets of water out of one's clothes, numbness creeping into one's bones. Both of us nearly exhausted.

Darcy Dancer redonning his underwear. Waist coat, jacket and breeches hanging over the branches of a tree. The matches in one's pocket too wet to start a fire. Lean against Petunia for warmth. O my god Midnight Shadow may have already killed people only a mile or two away. And all he was trying to do was have a daylight orgasm up the what for of some American lady's in season mare. Which was exactly what one was thinking of doing to Baptista. Which would be as calming for me in my nervous state of celibacy just as it would be calming for Midnight Shadow.

The crack of a twig and a nearly blood curdling laugh behind him. Darcy Dancer quickly turning around. There mounted calmly as you please, framed by the pine's boughs, her head back roaring, Baptista. Hairnet in place and just a flake or two of mud splattered upon her immaculate person.

"O you are aren't you such a mirthful sight I can't help laughing. I'm sorry."

"I don't, if you don't mind, think it's at all funny."

"You must forgive me. But you do look so completely ridiculous."

Baptista popping down to the ground. Standing snapping her whip against her thigh. And there we were. Nice as you please. Together. Alone. In the glade. Me in utter muddy half naked ignominy. My obelisk about as rigid as any obelisk can get without its exploding altogether and conspicuously propping out my rather tattered underwear. Our mounts side by side gobbling up the grass. The foam at the sides of their mouths turning green.

Darcy Dancer struggling on one leg trying to get back into his breeches, hobbling to Baptista's giggling as he stuck a frozen foot through the wet fabric. Baptista coming forward to lend a hand. And one turns one's obelisk pointing in her direction and reaches arms around her in playful affection before one falls flat upon one's face.

"And what on earth do you think you're doing Darcy Dancer."

"Might we not rest on the grass while our mounts graze a little. They must be exhausted."

"Of course I'm appreciative of your efforts to rescue me but I don't mind saying. You have your nerve. To think I would get down in the mud with you. While people by those distant screams are indicating that their very lives are still in danger."

Darcy Dancer eyeing her highly undeserved hunt buttons and staring at these lips and large eyes. So full of their past deceits. What utter pish and pother. Who the bloody hell wants to lay hand to you anyway. O god I've trod again in the nettles. Always so prevalently sprouting in the garden of one's carnal desire. Stinging my poor bare feet with the hottest pain. Which they just barely feel being so god damn presently frozen.

"You are in your primitive way an amusing young lad."

"I beg your pardon."

"You would wouldn't you like to seduce me. Married as I am. That's shut you up hasn't it. You are rather handsome you know. But far far too young for me, not physically of course. But intellectually, and actually, if the truth were to be known, I rather prefer men who are brainier than myself and you are but a callow youth. A country bumpkin. While I have been a habitué of sophisticates. You do understand don't you. Well why don't you say something."

"Because madam I am totally speechless at your pathetically incredible presumptions, but one does allow for them, being as you so regrettably are, of the common mediocrity."

Darcy Dancer pulling on boots and jacket and striding off to the grazing Petunia. Taking up her reins and prodding her in the ribs and on the run jumping into the saddle. Galloping off and passing Baptista's mare, leaning out to land an almighty swat on the quarters as the two horses pounded out of the glade breaking branches and trampling the shrubs of gorse and blackthorn.

"How dare you, come back, come back."

Hanging from the western clouds a grey veil of rain approaching. And south, a streak of golden sun slicing across the distant meadows and hilltops. With three rainbows blazing one on top of another across the eastern sky. And a faint sound. Huntsman calling the hounds. While she's back there abandoned. A nice wet trek of a mile or two through uncharted countryside will quick cure her of her sophistications acquired in Manchester. One of course should have flung her down and pricked her arse goodo in the gorse. Her bloody over ample quarters need trimming down anyway. To begin with she arrived late to hunt and then promptly headed the fox into the bog without so much as an apology to the Master or huntsman. And can you imagine anyone getting so full of themselves in the English industrial midlands. I mean one can understand if she said she had spent a few weeks in London rounding off her rougher small town Irish edges and then if she had to go north she could at least have gone to Harrowgate which according to my dear Mr Arland does have an adequate preponderance of the better sorts. But for her to now think she was on stage with the top crust in the county well, she would be entirely better off boasting she was a scouse from Liverpool. And at least then be able to be taken as being the genuine article. Too many of those solicitors and shopkeepers on the edge of town whose front gardens have completely gone to their heads, thinking they are as oneself, an actual member of the landed gentry. When hardly yet distinct from tradesfolk. And for the matter of that.

Even from
Lesser educated
Apes
In the animal
Kingdom

8

Although one does not mind being a cad, one simply did not have it in one to be an unmitigated cad. And before sheepishly returning to Andromeda Park one circled back cross country to where one had abandoned the poor creature Baptista. Leading her mare who appeared from its hang dog look to be pretty well knackered and as shiveringly cold as I was.

"I'll have the big house likes of ye off me land, I'm telling you now."

Another farmer gone hysterically ape with his pitch fork dancing a jig up and down on his pathetic acres to which Petunia's dung, plopping out of her quarters, must have been the first beneficial thing that had happened to them in years. And having trudged through bog and clambered over stone walls again and come across stray hounds, one had of course expected to find Baptista up to her ample arse in muck throwing her arms about one in grateful tears. But she was nowhere in sight.

The sky clearing, a still night descending. The sight of the first twinkling cold star on the south west horizon as Darcy Dancer, Baptista's mare in tow, cut across through the ancient oak wood and rhododendrons on the overgrown old farm road. Frost on the grass. Fog hovering over the low lands across the countryside. The sound of the river through the mist. By the mossy mounds and ivied broken walls of these abandoned cottages. The ruin of the old stone bridge ahead. The sound of a voice. Singing. Petunia shying to an abrupt stop. Baptista's mare rearing up, pawing the air and nearly braining me. Horses backing away. And god. There is something there again. Something moved. My heart is pounding and Petunia's thumping. And bloody Baptista's mare bolting, tearing the reins out of my hand. And now it will surely break every leg crashing away through the thick undergrowth. Enough has happened today without my hair not only standing up on the back of one's head but I'm sure it will shortly be turning snowy white.

Darcy Dancer giving chase. Baptista's mare disappearing in the dusk. In the distance, a fox barking. Just to let me know. With every shivering stride home. What an awful arse one has been today. Hands and feet blue numbed with cold. Only sensible thing left is to sink in the safety of one's hot bath. Except for my privates, thorns nearly in every other part of one's anatomy. What one wouldn't give to be back amid Dublin debauchery. Lois her tits wagging and her castanets clacking. Instead of crossing through these beech woods. Mouldy death and gloom. Shutters closed on the back windows of Andromeda Park. Lower one's head in the darkness of the tunnel to the stables. A relief to hear one's horse's hoofs on the cobbles. Soon a long recline in a steaming tub. Expunge the offending splinters and thorns out of one's epidermis. And my god, out of one's soul.

Darcy Dancer passing the stable window. Luke, Henry and Thomas toasting themselves in front of the roaring tack room fire puffing on cigarettes. The three of them jumping up. From where their arses were planted on soft seats of hay stuffed in buckets. Nearly as fast as Henry did in his last discontent when Thomas left a bottle on a shelf labelled apple juice and filled with piss. Be the first effort they'll have made since lunch. Be dredging up their best blandishments to improve one's sour appraisal of their idleness.

"Sir was it a good hunt you had. Sure Petunia will be glad to be in her box. Looks like she had a few miles under her belly at the gallop."

Darcy Dancer walking up the incline and turning to enter the house by the side door. The heavy ancient latch. Polished by so many hands. See how many others are lolling about.

"Ah sir you're back."

"That would appear to be the case Crooks."

Crooks coming out of the kitchen with two decanters of port, in bandaged hands. Soupstained no doubt. And you'd think his hand crushed in the dumb waiter would have long since healed. He does so like to remind one of his injuries.

"Well excuse me sire for incommoding you at this moment of the evening Master Reginald. There's an urgent gathering upstairs. In the front hall in their muddy boots. Hunt members wanting to have a serious word with you. Barged right in the door past me they did. And I thought it best to have refreshments served to assist in calming them."

"Not with my bloody port I hope. Tell them to please fuck off."

"I couldn't do that sir now. Not in that language. By the bloodthirsty looking condition of them they'd set upon me."

"Well then tell them in the rudest way you can. To bugger off. And draw my bath please."

The faint candlelight. On the great slabs of stone. The smell of damp. Crooks trembling. O god, he's going to collapse. Just as one is hoping to run into Leila. Contemplating in one's mind her small swelling bicep. And the blue vein in her arm with its white tiny knot of an artery. When once she went by me carrying a water filled vase. The only member of this household I've ever known to roll up her sleeves. And now the whole entire world seems to intervene between us.

"And sir as for the matter of this port. This is for the dining room and library, seeing as you have been calling for it recently. And the two extra for dinner. Lady Christabel and Lavinia should be at this very moment arrived at the station and Sexton has gone to fetch them."

"Good god."

"A cable came while you were out hunting. Shall supper be at your convenience."

"Yes. I think most certainly yes. After a day like today."

Crooks ushered first up the servants' stairs. Darcy Dancer following. In case with an attack of sudden staggers he should collapse. Sound of voices down the main hall. Shouldn't be surprised if Crooks doesn't drink half a decanter and spill the other as he did one night on the carpet outside my bedroom door. One distinctly felt the thwack of a large spoon upon the top of one's head at the mention of one's sisters. Eye gouging. Secateurs clipping one's ear lobes. Hair pulling. Bath splashing. Attempted drownings and hangings. Shoves, pushes and punches. Toys and teddy bears ripped from one's hands. And upon their being shipped away to better things of England, not lost upon me are all the intervening years of peace.

Darcy Dancer soaking back in the hot waters of the bath. Window panes steamed over. The fire at last beginning to glow in the grate. At the finish of a day's hunting, agreeably tired, one should be purring with the joy of still being alive. Instead of haunted with singing ghosts and a killer stallion at large. And that uncomfortable feeling that while one has been away the day that nothing at all has been done by anybody. With the exception of course of Sexton, Leila and old Edna Annie. When one sees a member of the household or estate not with their hands actively on some tool, and wielding it in the motion and manner for which it is meant, one must suspect the worst malingering. And my god added to it all now could be the two more mouths of my sisters not to mention the mouths of any horses they may fancy to hunt. Where and how in this world does one make a monstrous amount of money. Or get to own something like a brewery. O god it's ruddy shocking how the terrors of impoverishment and ruin do gnaw at one's vitals.

Darcy Dancer in dressing gown, standing on the landing listening to the din in the front hall. Proceeding further downwards and stopping. Sound of distant feet pounding up and down the back stairs to the kitchen. The clatter of boots on the tiles. Sounds like a ruddy bash in progress. Candles blazing. The utter incredible nerve. With the whole ruddy household running hither and thither ferrying cakes, barmbracks. And my god big tits Dingbats, lugging by the neck two utterly heirloom precious bottles of brandy rolling her eyes demented with the delight of it all.

"And where Mollie are you taking those bottles."

"They be brandy sir."

"I know they're brandy. Which happens to be pale and extremely old."

"It's for inside there."

"Take them back to the cellar."

"Sir there's a thirst on them visitors in there that would make you think their bellies were screaming their throats were cut."

"Well their bellies can go on screaming."

Dingbats turning on her heel. Heavily pounding off back down the hall. Feel the floor joists tremble. Lots of ruddy power could be harnessed from her haunches. Tie her up to one of those machines they use pumping water in China. Burn off some of the butter she gorges. And by the smell of her she has worked up one of her more highly musty pongy sweats. Surprisingly quite stimulating to the gonads. But this is no time for an erection in one's front hall.

Darcy Dancer with an imperious sweep proceeding out amidst all these unheeding elbows so busily bent upending glasses to their mouths. Hunt servants in a decidedly sheepish little huddle by the fire. Not one of them noticing me in the pale blue brown and white racing colours of my dressing gown. Nor my black, white polka dotted silk scarf at my throat. Astonishing how one can suddenly feel a complete interloper in one's own house as a gang of invaders make jolly familiar. People making themselves entirely at home as if they were bloody well invited, most of whom I have never spoken to and some I've not even seen before. And wouldn't you know, like a gang of starved rats partaking from a table laid centre hall. Stuffing their empty bellies. Slurping up my tea, slathering on my butter and munching up my breads and already quaffing my wines and liquors. Behaving as favoured guests with one another at one's own conspicuous expense. But O my god, my port. There. The hunt secretary's hand already reaching for a decanter to take a refill. So much for damn Crooks' reassurances. Bloody servants love to be generous with one's viands and most precious tipple. Especially pouring the latter down the throats of perfect strangers. One does not mind being bled white by the consumption of bread and butter but it is a little bit bloody much to reach that anemic condition when it's one's most anciently preserved and cherished wines being gulped.

Darcy Dancer fetching the two decanters away to a sideboard around the hall corner. Followed rapidly by the bow legged hunt secretary Major Bottom clomping across the tiles in his boots, a cream bun and a glass of port clutched in his hands.

"Ah there you are Kildare my good chap. Damn good port. Quite right to get it out of the way of the uninitiated. Sorry to have to come at you like this but in a man to man fashion I'd like to have a word with you. That loose stallion of yours and all that. And I have it on some authority that a lady's horse was stampeded and she was left abandoned. I'm sure it's all a misunderstanding. Jolly fine vintage this port. And you know it's not been since your mother was hunting that I've been in this house."

Coming up behind Major Bottom, another face one vaguely remembers from a race track somewhere. By the look a horse trainer down from County Dublin. His blond slathered back hair conspicuously parted in the middle. And objectionably long sideburns. Type who's made a few bob being in the know on a few races and now thinks he's god's gift to county hunting society. And who's this type pushing in front of him.

"I contradict what the hunt secretary has just said sir. And I say we have a definite bone to pick with you. Letting a stallion run wild. And then the damn shabby treatment of a lady."

And my word this objectionable sort does think the world of himself and has the obtuse nerve to be pompously attempting to sound like an administrator of justice interjecting in front of the secretary, with the horse trainer at his elbow and with more hangers on collecting behind them. To all stand listening to the present utter silence. And the lot of them to a man with glasses of whisky and cream cake in thick gobs stuck to their faces.

"Well sir, you heard what I said, shameful shocking treatment of a lady."

O my god this is coming from one of those ruddy bloody asses who's got up on top of a horse to hunt and with accent improved thinks he need never again make his living selling lavatory articles door to door in the hinterlands of Dun Laoghaire or Dalymount.

"Why don't you bugger off and go about your usual business which is I am sure supplying purgatives to those who like yourself need them."

"I say look here sir we are not going to mince words. I'm in fact a major supplier in the sanitary fitting line. And you stampeded a lady's mount is what we have heard."

"Well hear this then. Clear out the lot of you."

"I say sir that's simply not good enough. We want an apology."

"What you'll get from me is your head stuffed in one of your crappers and a good swift boot of my foot in your goolies if you don't get out."

"I say you are a rude bounder sir."

"You heard me, out. Before I bodily throw you out."

The hunt secretary Major Bottom frowning his thick bushy brows and loudly clearing his throat while licking away the whipped cream impeding the vowels attempting to get out of his mouth.

"We must remain civil about this matter Kildare."

The sanitary supplier placing his feet well apart. Striking a stance. His eyes flicking left and right to see if his seconders were still behind him. The horse trainer nodding encouragement. The sanitary supplier taking another step forward.

"And I say I should not be so tricky if I were you Kildare sir."

"Tricky. I'll show you who's being tricky you twit."

Darcy Dancer grabbing the sanitary supplier by the lapels, shoving him backwards. The group parting behind him as his arse thumps on the tiles. Major Bottom stepping around the back of Darcy Dancer to grab an unguarded decanter to pour port.

"I say Kildare that's highly uncalled for."

Darcy Dancer striding away out into the front hall. Where hands were still reaching sweeping trays clean.

"Everyone out. The party's over."

Crooks coming momentarily out of the shadows to take up the cry.

"You heard the Master now. You've had it. The bash is over."

The horse trainer and sanitary supplier, followed by their group of hangers on, creeping up behind Darcy Dancer. The horse trainer leaping on his back. Closing a head lock across Darcy's throat. Darcy Dancer bringing an elbow back into the horse trainer's belly. The head lock loosening and Darcy Dancer sending the horse trainer flying forward over his shoulder. The horse trainer crashing on the tea table, skidding across it and off the other side. Taking in his wake the cloth, the tea, jam, scones, cakes. Together with the butters and bottles. The sanitary supplier, his mouth gaping.

"I say good god, the man's a demon. Clearly the lady's correct in her accusation."

Darcy Dancer pointing towards the door. As the horse trainer congealed in jams, glass and honey, stumbles up on his hands and knees. Wide eyed Dingbats's hands to her fully jammed mouth which might have been aghast but was still busily chewing. Crooks carefully retreating out of harm's way into the back hallway. Major Bottom strolling up, his port glass refilled.

"That's a poor show Kildare. Not what one would expect from the Thormonds. We should settle this like gentlemen."

The horse trainer getting to his feet, slowly wiping his honey congealed hands together, and murmuring a stream of oaths as he attempted to dislodge an entire pound of butter adhering to his breeches.

"By god I do rather resent this. From a stripling only out of short pants. I'll fight you Kildare. Sure you'll not get away with another lucky shove like that I'm telling you."

"I'll give you more than a shove, I'll bloody well give you a thrashing."

Major Bottom coming forward, his port well to the side out of harm's way as his free arm is held across Darcy Dancer's chest to hold him back. The Major raising his voice.

"Sir I think that challenge is highly inadvisable, remember we're guests in this man's house."

A band of accomplices gathering behind the horse trainer as he adopted a hand to hand combat pose of an Asian flavour, making lunges as he emitted loud grunts, one of which got awfully loud as one foot squeezed deeply into the butter only recently dislodged from his breeches. Darcy Dancer pressing away the hunt secretary's arm.

"You take one more buttered foot forward you simpleton and I'll break your back across my knee."

"Simpleton is it. I'll show you who's a simpleton. You'll not break my back, you'll not."

Most of the indoor staff of Andromeda Park retreating behind Crooks who was edging his way back behind them making the whole contingent resemble a big many legged bug crawling backwards. Along with a cold blast, more figures arriving in the front door. Voices on the sidelines taking up viewing positions.

"Ah your man is an expert in the Oriental art of self defence and he'll soon put paid to that Kildare."

"Ah I wouldn't be too sure about that now. By the way that Kildare flipped your man flying, I'd say he'd be getting a lesson from a gentleman well versed in the Gaelic art of pure mayhem and murder."

Hunt members closing closer about the protagonists some with whips raised, others clutching crockery to let fly. One swinging his fist prematurely and landing it on the face of another hunt member as Darcy Dancer landed him back a punch to send him sailing on his arse, blood exploding out of his nose. Town idlers among the hunt followers, making haste to descend upon the strewn sandwiches and cakes. A cry clearly from Crooks.

"Hit him in the haggis Master Reginald."

And a louder cry going up in the shadows. The black beetle browed agent with three others emerging from the door of the long unused west parlour. The timber merchant from the town taking up the rear at whom one had to discharge shot when he was generously helping himself to oak trees not that many years back.

"Come on lads. Together. At the buckeen. We'll take him."

Gearoid with a bottle in one hand and a candelabrum held aloft in the other.

"Ah it's the charge of the Light Brigade all over again. I'm telling you."

The middle of the hall, teacups breaking on the tiles. Candles knocked over. Hunt members rushing to pile on top of Darcy Dancer. The scrum of bodies teetering. Grunts and thumps. Boots skidding on the tiles. Green and blue collars of red coats torn in the grabbings. Kitty and Norah arriving around the hall corner ferrying trays heaped with more sandwiches up from the kitchen. Dumping them on the floor. Amid the screams and shouts, slabs of bread, beef and ham flying.

"Jesus, Mary and Joseph there's murther and slaughter."

The indoor staff of Andromeda Park retreating back. Kitty and Norah halfway up the grand staircase. Dingbats crouched shivering next to Crooks. Both peeking out over a heavy marble topped console table pushed out from the wall. Proving Crooks had plenty strength enough when needed. His Dublin accent slipping as he announced.

"Ah now don't lay a hand to me I'm an invalid I am."

More hunt members and followers, agent and accomplices climbing the heap burying Darcy Dancer. Bringing him kicking, tearing, punching to the floor. Bottles on the sidelines emptied down throats and wielded as weapons. Ear twisting, eye gouging. Hair uprooted. Knees pummelled into crotches. Boots socked into ribs front, back and sides. Whips snapping. A door knob stuffed in a mouth. A hard leather toe sinking into the spine of the horse trainer. Huntsman blowing the horn. An English lady hunt visitor retreating backwards eyebrows raised behind a glass of cherry brandy.

"Dear me, the noise and the people."

"Bejesus you're killing me when it's him we're after."

"I say the bugger's strong. Get him."

"Constrict his oesophagus."

"God save the king."

"Bugger the king. Up Ireland."

"Put the boot into him."

"Bloody hell I've just busted my toes."

"You cowards."

A dull lethal thud landing on someone's pink coated back. The victim spilling out his breath, slumping forward on his face. Another hunt member turning round to raise his arms to ward off a blow aimed at his head. The further upraised iron poker which had just flattened his associate, descending on an upraised wrist. A howl of pain as an ulna, radius and metacarpus fractured in twenty places. A voice of reason.

"For Jesus' sake almighty tear that fucking thing out of that woman's hands."

"You cowards."

Leila sleeves rolled up two handed belting the thrashing mound of backs. Aiming her poker swipes at another rolling to escape across the tiles. The attackers covering Darcy Dancer unpeeling and turning, to protect their heads. Darcy Dancer left on the floor with one head squeezed in a scissor grip between his legs and another with his arm locked across its throat gasping, tongue hanging out and a face turning deeper and deeper blue.

"Your man's choked for the love of Jesus will you let go before he needs the last rites."

A mud splattered Mental Marquis striding in the door, turning momentarily to fill a tall glass with brandy, and putting it to his lips, draining it to a drop and reaching for a refill as he surveys the battle.

94

"Ah this is developing into a nice bit of damn evil amusement. And who, may I ask of somebody who knows, is that utterly beautiful creature wielding that warhammer so brilliantly."

Leila swinging her poker back and forth, advancing upon the retreating phalanx of hunt members and interlopers. The hunting priest followed by his elegantly ecclesiastic parson friend coming in the door. Both accoutred half in clerical garb and half in their hunting kits tailored in Paris.

"Stop this violence. O glory be to god what infamy is this afoot. That you should break this man's priceless china and delft."

"Get out of the way parson. And you too father. Or you'll have Meissen in the eyeball."

Urgent pounding. The front door slamming open into someone's face and shut again with a scream over someone's foot. The parson pushed forward to his knees. The hunting priest, his collar popped up across his eyes blinding him. Farmer Amnesia Murphy's coat pulled over his head, raging around in circles like a fighting bull. The Mad Major waving his red coat as a cape taking Murphy through a faena. Someone present familiar with Spanish.

"Olé."

The Slasher sisters parked near the fire quietly munching sandwiches. The fat faces of Kitty and Norah back again peering around the corner of the back hall. And a shout from the front door.

"Step back. Back I'm telling you."

Sexton, his hob nailed boots skating on the tiles, a bill hook raised in his massive hands, its curved blade glinting.

"Move another muscle any of you or touch another hair of the head of the master of this house and you'll not only get a hit of this across the humerus that will send your infraspinous fossa flying but your noggins when I'm done splitting them won't know which side they're buttered on. I'm telling you."

The silvery shiny sharpness of Sexton's hook cocked back over his shoulder hovering in the smoky air. The assembly coming to a rigid standstill. Major Bottom wiping a splotch of cream from his face. Kern and Olav roaring and barking out front. Leila, veins standing out on her neck, her lungs pumping up and down in her chest, her whitened knuckles still holding the poker aloft. Sexton turning his one eye around the hall.

"Ah god this is a time when arma pacis fulcra. Dominus vobiscum."

"Stuff that bloody popery."

"Who said that. Come on and bejesus I'll swipe this right through you in bellum lethale."

In the raging silence, Darcy Dancer loosening his grip on his two unconscious adversaries. Both lying stretched and still. Any moment now Sexton's going to decline a series of Latin very irregular verbs. As far away as could be from amo amas amat. At least in the sea of staff betrayal two have remained loyal. And dear god what a wonderful blissful ensoothement it is to feel that one has for a change not only some brave brawn but also beatific beauty on one's side in this world.

"Take your hands from interfering under me skirt."

A shout and a slap from beyond the console table. Dingbats standing up in high dudgeon. Crooks cringing in low. Eyes turning. Dingbats brushing down her uniform. Crooks rising, chest out shoulders back.

"Lay hand to me girl, how dare you. I have never never before been accused of such a heinous thing in my entire career of service you insolent wench. And you go this instant and get the brooms."

"I was. I was interfered with."

Dingbats flouncing off down the hall. Crooks loudly clearing his throat adjusting his tie and doing up his waist coat buttons. Sexton herding the remaining assembly out before him. Past those allowed to stay. Gently nodding to the Slasher sisters, the Mad Major, ecclesiastics and Mental Marquis.

"Now the lot of the rest of you be off before you're all minus your ears."

"Lapdog of the gentry, that's what you are. Arselicker of the gentry."

Sexton prodding the agent in the spine with the handle of his hook. The agent sneeringly raising his fist and scurrying out of the way of Sexton's lunge.

"And the crooked likes of you were conceived, born and bred from the bowels of the devil and him an evil damn devil at that. Fuck off out of here now. And pardon the language ladies."

Candles relit, Crooks stepping forward over the remaining incommoded bodies removing the still held glasses and clutched bottles. As the two asphyxiated on the floor suddenly revive, sitting up, the hunting priest in a priestly manner making the sign of the cross and blessing with mumbled prayers over these remaining highly irate currently prostrate Protestants. Wondering what foul popery was afoot. Sexton shouting to those still able to walk down the front steps.

"And don't set foot this way again or you'll get the same. I'm telling you."

Chill blasts of breeze in the door. Fire blazing bright. Darcy Dancer dressing gown retied. Standing one foot in a sock the other in a slipper. Sleeves and lapels ripped. Crooks dabbing a napkin on the buttery finger marks.

"Imagine, me a rapist. The utter cheek of the trollop."

"You mustn't mind Crooks."

"Locked away in the pig curing room a night or two she should be, Master Reginald, with her imagination getting plenty of exercise with the ghosts raping her."

The parson carefully picking up pieces of a shattered plate. And into a piece of sideboard crystal pouring himself a glass of port. Holding it aloft crossing the tiles. His beige silk handkerchief hanging from his sleeve.

"Well well Kildare. You're in residence. Well well. Not the best surely. Not the best. But really. One would think in this modern day and age one could expect better manners to be about. But is there not something inherently unseemly emerging from the behaviour of the Dublin middle classes. Too many of whom I believe were down hunting today. Your mother would have been quite beyond herself with indignation. Thank heavens she's safely resting in peace from such."

Dingbats sweeping up. Raising dust, delft clanking and her broom knocking the furniture. The remaining household, all except Edna Annie, peeking around corners into the front hall. Raised voices out in the dark. Horses being mounted. Fast trotting hoof falls heard in the still cold night far off along down the drive. And more coming close of new arrivals.

"I do so thank you Sexton. Quite honestly they nearly had me done for. Had it not been for you and Leila."

"Ah that is a one who's a great brave lass. Just look at her now. Not a bother on her. There busily engaged in conversation with the Mental Marquis. And Master Darcy lucky for you I was in me cot-

tage sitting semper fidelis in front of the fire studying me seed catalogue and heard the rapid commotion of hoofs going by on the road.
Like the Boer War. I knew by the rush there was something afoot.
Could hear the din miles away. And I went like the wind on me
bishop's bike."

Darcy Dancer turning. Towards the corner of the hall. Leila, her
poker lowered. Soft silken skin flushed. Her arm brushing back her
curls of dark gleaming hair. O my god. She's smiling. Standing beneath the painting she so admires. And one's heart is stopped. So
painfully to see. To helplessly watch. Her paying attention to his silly
loftiness. The Marquis. One leg cocked forward. And would you believe it, a bloody hand on his hip. I'll break his bloody titled arse if he
thinks for one second that I'll tolerate his familiarity with a member
of my staff.

> And my loyal
> Lady
> From whom
> Every unblessed day
> Keeps
> My love

9

Darcy Dancer, a glass of port to his lips. The front hall door opening wide. A roar of draught up the chimney. Two ladies standing, their gloved hands politely up, smiles vanishing on their faces as Gearoid's quickly widened on his greasy one.

"Ah jasus wasn't it a good hooley gone great they had in here."

"Well, isn't anyone going to say hello to us."

Darcy Dancer turning round to the sound of this familiar voice. My god. My sisters.

"How do you do."

"O dear, how formal. We are your sisters you know."

"Yes of course, indeed how are you. Forgive me. We've had an entirely unpremeditated small disagreement here this evening."

"Well you must forgive us for not giving you more warning. But we thought as we're now back in Dublin we'd pop down and see the old place."

"Delighted to have you both I'm sure."

"Well we are glad to be home, especially for the hunting as a matter of fact."

"And so nice to have you both."

"I'm afraid this person here has presumed to help us with our luggage. And I'm afraid we're rather short of change."

How of course are they to know that Gearoid with the face like a toad, is a now and again unofficial footman at Andromeda Park, and officially permitted as a one time farmer to wear his cap and muddy boots in the house and to stink to high heaven of horse piss, stables and farmyards, while making familiar with guests and as an equal helping himself to copious of his host's wines and beers in order to keep himself happily half out of his senses. And how are they to know this goggly eyed, shabbily attired crew before them are the same lot who in our mother's day ministered in such impeccable splendour. I suppose if they ever dreamt of this place over all these years it must be one ruddy rude awakening. As good grief tennis racquets in their luggage. What on earth are they expecting. Of course in one's sunnier moments one did think of restoring the tennis court to playing condition. And needless to say soon find oneself lobbing balls up into the rain sodden clouds as one splashed muddily underfoot splattering one's white playing garments and sending gobbets of muck unhelpfully into one's partner's eyes. Perhaps from childhood, one is overly alarmed by their sense of presumed ownership being as the pair of them purloined my toys and constantly plotted to frighten me out of my wits. Even to threatening to snip my penis off with a scissors. And now, by the sound of their first few words, they return such utter Sassenachs. And I am as Sexton says. Undisputed Pasha of Andromeda Park. At least one is relieved to find them quite mature looking ladies of attractive facial appearance. Hope to god their high flown vowels, gay laughter and light jokes, will distract the Mental Marquis' rabid gaze and attention from Leila. Which is so utterly enlarging the hole at the bottom of my sinking soul. And of course, as would embarrassingly happen, my sisters' names, on the tip of my tongue, have gone both flying straight out of my head. Quite maddening as one does at least want to make a decent impression. But bloody hell the Marquis has cocked his other leg forward, changed his drink from one hand to the other and is now smilingly pointing out Leila's most admired painting to her. As my blood drains away into a groaning yawning abyss of jealousy. And O god. I am completely ignoring my sisters. But that bloody man is there brazen and blatant, clicking his heels on the tiles and clearly adoring to hear himself talk while his engorged prick is absolutely forcing his breeches out a mile. Leaving me in deep spiritual snooker. Yes, that's where you are my dear chap. Blue bloody bananas, how incredibly stupid it was to have invited him to dinner tonight. But then he did kick one or two interlopers in the arse and one was flattered by his back slapping camaraderie and jollity in nearly regarding me as a long lost friend. Of course it will relieve oneself of one's sisters' prying questions. For instance, where are our dear mother's jewels. To which I would adore to lay hand to, myself. Of course the Marquis does occasionally display a sensitivity of spirit that comes of deep melancholia. And his words did rather cheer me up.

"I say there Kildare. Can you imagine the bloody insolence coming into a man's house causing a disturbance like this. Demands a boot up a few holes. But damn it. I do seem to accost you at the most delicate of times. How are you my dear chap. Not seen each other I do believe since last we met at the barber's. Following your delicately relieving me of a fiver in the Royal Hibernian Hotel. Caught me incognito you did. As I was reflecting on St Paul's Epistle to the Ephesians. But you're the first man who's ever touched me for a fiver and repaid it by god. But apropos of this season's hunting don't you think it nice that we have a Master of Foxhounds with the signal advantage of having particularly strong piss to release in our various badger and fox holes. And by god cause any fox getting a sniff to definitely avoid seeking shelter therein and to go on merrily chased running for his life. Don't you think that a damn good thing Kildare. Except that the thirsty chap has to damn near quaff all one's whisky to do his required peeing."

Of course I did fervently think that an absolutely marvellous benefit. And indeed did watch close up the Master unravel his astonishingly long penis and take several of his pisses, till he lurchingly missed a hole and stank up my boot. One can't suppose the Marquis is all bad. In fact his taste in women appears to be too damn good. He's awfully hairy arsed of course. And I'm sure he knows it was me galloping along the old avenue of lime trees, and thundering down upon him to jump flying over on the Master's stolen horse as he rogered Baptista on the mossy ground. The vision of him pumping away between Baptista's unbooted flailing legs, totally unconcerned for my mount's hoofs scraping the top of his balding head, will go with me to the grave. Provided the Royal Hibernian Hotel keyhole sight of him with his chastisement equipages and his besaddled hind quarters being whipped as she giggled and gasped around the room doesn't blot it out. And I cannot bear to contemplate him even standing near Leila never mind being nudely on top of her. Especially as the bastard is used to riding such big enormous horses. Perhaps one's sisters changing décolleté for dinner out of their rather less than fashionable clothes may attract him. My god it wouldn't be the worst thing to end up with a brother in law with sixteen thousand walled in acres, possessed of a damn good trout lake, salmon river and a castle where your voice echoes in the front hall.

"Now there you be your ladyships. Weep not. And both of you sine dubio let me tell you are a sight for my one sore eye, dominus vobiscum."

Sexton. Saviour of his master, and utterly in his element. Having all those years ago danced so much previous attendance on my sisters. His little goddesses he called them. For whom he now runs twice back and forth, both arms loaded with the rest of their luggage which Gearoid, spotting a nearby whisky bottle, suddenly found too heavy to carry. And the amount of which my god does ruddy indicate much more than a short stay. Two vast steamer trunks. Five suitcases. And at least eleven hat boxes clearly means as many as a half dozen race meetings. Sexton, obviously intending to continue severe social elevation of my sisters' entitlements. And thank god, reminds one of their names.

"Ah Lady Christabel. Ah Lady Lavinia. Sine dubio too long has this great house been denied the great beauty you took from it upon your departure and now bring back to it upon your return."

"O how nice of you to say, Sexton."

One must confess. It was pretty damn nice and just in the ruddy nick of time. And Crooks thank god, blessedly minus soiled bandages and not looking like some down and out alcoholic person, has emerged too. Into the desperation of one's inadequacy. And bowing to each of them.

"Lady Christabel. Lady Lavinia. Welcome home. I trust your journey did you no discomfort that your ready and waiting hot baths will not completely dispel."

My god. Listen to him. Why don't I get some of this ruddy elegant attention occasionally. He really is on his best behaviour. Of course the Marquis does rather tone up the atmosphere. And damn him, is pretentiously conducting Leila around to further paintings, spouting out what god awful guff one can not imagine. As I'm damn sure the only culture he's ever been acquainted with is the curvature of his prick. Which bloody hell is now even more pointed in his breeches. Somehow one wishes one had Crooks' crossed eyes. When no one can even remotely guess where you're looking. Can be such a help sometimes. Since I can see so straight. At this painful sight resulting in one's most painful sour demeanour. And then the next awful embarrassment. Triggered off by Crooks.

"Shall I show their ladyships to their rooms."

With Christabel stretching her neck out of an emerald green satin scarf and pointing her nose upwards, taking it upon herself to suggest.

"Thank you Crooks, Mummy's old rooms will do for me."

"I'm afraid your ladyship, I venture to regret that her late ladyship's apartments are already occupied."

Even then one should have quite clearly known it was already obvious how the wind was blowing. And to get a further blast of it as one was an hour later descending dressed, for drinks to be served in the library. Overhearing one's sisters just at the bottom of the stairs.

"I think I shall any moment scream aloud."

"Why Christabel."

"Because Lavinia, it is so damn cold in this house and so wretchedly dirty and dusty."

Of course no dirt or dust on them as they did appear, teeth flashing at the Marquis, well washed and brushed up. Although mountainously goose pimpled and blue on their much exposed anatomies. The Marquis immediately taking to announcing over his full whisky glass a rather boastful account of his most recent hunting mishap. While Christabel and Lavinia, fanning their arses feverishly at the fire, tittered and titillated over their sherries. The Marquis obviously just waiting to roll his vowels concerning his horse rolling on him as each time Leila came in the library from whence she was removing two candelabra for the dining room. His eyes flicking up at her. Ignoring my sisters' adoration. And my distinct irritation. I must say even as rich as he is rumoured to be one does even vaguely, and very vaguely think one should hint of a substantial dowry available with the better built of one's sisters. Who by present cleavages would appear to be Lavinia. Perhaps a little plumpish on the upper arm. No matter. She's slightly taller than Christabel. And broader in the beam. That helps in breeding. But I do think she has, on further real scrutiny, smaller tits. Yes she does. Of course who's ever to notice when for the rest of their Irish sojourn I'm sure both will be bundled up in long flowing armour plated thick tweed suits. And boots of one sort or another. But O god one just knows, that those self same mounds on the chest of Leila would be revealed as such rare delicate gems. Nor are my sisters' good legs apparent in these most awful ankle boots edged with sheep fur they're still bloody wearing, thinking they can't be seen under their gowns. Obviously not taking any bloody chances with the temperatures in the dining room. Of course their best points are their accents. British in the extreme. Damn Marquis ought to appreciate that. But of course doesn't. Arse is the only thing on his ruddy mind. They must have both said jolly good show twenty times in the last five minutes. And would no doubt have said it fifty times if they weren't so busy smiling their heads off at him. And then had the nerve to look about at me at what one irritatingly suspects are one's occasionally more than slightly broguish vowels. And that's now the second bloody full glass of whisky he's downed. Just as one turns around. First he's there toying and touching a brimming drink you think he's never going to put to his lips. And then presto. The glass is empty. Perhaps one ought to bolster one's own spirit, and quaff an equal amount. Then in the luxury of loose tongues remind his lordship of his station in life. Not ruddy done to prance about with one's prick pointing at someone else's servant. Divert his attention back to one's sisters. In the shabby hope that mauling about in a drunken coupling somewhere discreet upstairs he might get one of them pregnant. Ah, at long last, Crooks. And look at this. White gloves. We are on parade tonight.

"Sir, Master Reginald, dinner is whenever you are."

The dining room lit like a ballroom. And the fire blazing so hot in the grate Lavinia said her back was getting sunburned. Serves her right. Crooks barking out orders. As if he were really on some ruddy parade ground. Or even on the bridge of a ship. The latter distinctly in a hurricane. Leila, Kitty and Norah, and even Dingbats. Bumping into each other. Cutlery continually clattering on the floor. But only two plates breaking. Which Dingbats accomplished taking away his lordship's too soon, to which she clung as he tried to grab it back. A nice exhibition of impeccable appetite if not manners.

"Hey where the hell again my dear do you think you're going with that when a chap is as famished as I am from hunting all day."

"I am sorry your majesty."

"I'm not a bloody king."

"Pardon me sir."

"I'm a potato digging bog trotter like the rest of you. Just have a few more acres than most to do it in."

Of course my sisters loved every word out of his mouth. Even laughed as he ladled a little gravy on his pate. And rubbed it in to make as he said, his hair sprout. Of course he was not known as the Mental Marquis for nothing. And I must confess myself finding him occasionally damn funny. But one's amusement wore damn thin each time he actually stopped talking waiting for Leila to come back into the room.

"Ah wait, we must wait, till all our beautiful ears are listening."

Shovelled in along with his Brussels sprouts, eight slabs of lamb he consumed. Pucks of potatoes. Quaffed two bottles of my best claret. Interrupted three of my best jokes. Of which I only know four. And he of course would take ages helping himself to anything Leila was serving. Remarking on how marvellously steady she was holding the dish. When anyone could see she was shaking like a leaf. And finally one found it a solace when my sisters withdrew. And I found it increasingly difficult to remain civil and execute one's duties as a host. Crooks with the cigars and Leila placing the port on the table.

"Ah there now Kildare is a combination. Exquisite decanter held by an exquisite hand."

One simply could not look at Leila's face. In case she was pleased by this quite pedestrian observation. Plus she did have chilblains. Crooks did however close proceedings with one of his sepulchral announcements concerning the decanter's contents.

"Laid down the day upon which you were born sir."

"Ah Crooks are you referring to me or his lordship."

"To you of course sir."

"Ah I do apologise Crooks but you will forgive me for saying so, I did think you were looking at his lordship."

105

Needless to say we were all getting crosseyed. Crooks happily not taking my comment amiss. Clapping his hands going back in through the pantry door and whispering to those assembled there.

"Get your ears back away from here listening at the door, the lot of you. Be quick about it."

The Marquis knowing of his eager audience, beaming in a broad smile pouring himself a port and pushing the decanter at me. The wind bellowing and rumbling up the chimney just as one imagined one heard a slate crash off the roof somewhere. Or was it a member of the staff crying rape. All sounds were getting to sound the same.

"Kildare, dear chap. Jolly good dinner. Jolly damn good port. Jolly damn good as my own. But let's get down to brass tacks here, as hunting men. She is, quite without doubt Kildare, the most exquisitely alluring elegantly beautiful creature I have ever seen. And what's more with a surname quite out of the context of being a servant. Surely you're not keeping her here like this are you. I mean forgive me my dear chap I have no intention to meddle in your domestic affairs, none whatever. But come come. Out with it now. The lady, for that's clearly what she is, knows about art."

"She does quite."

"Does quite. Does more than does quite, damn it. Telling me about the Florentine, she was. Giotto, Donatello, bloody Michelangelo. This o and that o. Of course I was mostly tight as a newt when I was in Florence. And the dear creature has hardly even been to Tralee yet. Got a mind as impressive as her beauty. Damn good port this. I mean to say dear boy, one does get one's fill of empty chatterboxes occasionally. So nice to talk a moment of the finer things. But the middle ages are over. Can't keep a girl locked away. I mean to say a man is now and again caught with his kilt up, like any man who likes a gallop."

"I can't see what exactly you're driving at sir."

"Damn it Kildare I'm not your grandfather, call me Horatio, that's my Christian name. I know behind my back I'm called something else. But there's a lass for which one lays down one's future. Of course I've got my past plethora of indiscretions. Of course I have. Skeletons clacking in the rear vestibule pantry closet, and that sort of thing. One does get in an occasional spot of bother as a fledgling flying officer. Then as you rise up in rank you tend to try to stop your junior officers making the same sort of high flying fools of themselves. I could do with going up for a spin in a Spitfire tonight. What about that Kildare. I'll come over in an aircraft one of these days. You've got enough level meadow for a landing field. Have a few wizard bloody prangs. Take you upstairs. Buzzing the bloody peasants hereabout downstairs. But now admit it. What's a young devil like you doing with a girl here as a skivvy whose sidelong glances could one day change the course of nations."

"I'm afraid I rather do regard your remarks as being transparent."

"What. Bloody hell, Kildare. I don't like the sound of that word one bit. But since I'm drinking your damn fine port let's not quarrel about that, especially when the subject of brains is at stake. Now don't you agree that a woman's mind is of some importance. I mean let's face it man to man. You put your old what for up their well meant for and you do your best done for and then you want to be immediately a mile away shooting snipe. Wouldn't it be better to be able to have a civilized word with a woman one has just pranged. What the deuce is the matter with you Kildare. Don't you see what I'm talking about here. It's a matter of principle."

Of course both of us calling for still more port were finally quite tight. And totally forgetting my sisters. Till Crooks appropriately clearing his throat at the door reminded one. As much as one found the Marquis' designs on Leila a bitter thought one does admit it could brighten her future. And also rid me of one of my very best reasons for remaining alive. Which does make one considerably angry especially as he keeps dropping more than a little of his cigar ash on the carpet. But one does still find him amusing. As well as suddenly sad. Sitting there. Staring into space. Looking terribly lonely.

"You see Kildare. Fraud, artifice, overreaching and deception are fundamental to democracy. Therefore I believe in socialism. You know what that is do you. Fair shares for all you know. We've been kicking the damn peasants around for too long. Now they're trying to kick us. I don't mind them poaching a few of my bloody salmon but some damn rogue has killed about two hundred of my trees. Hammered a copper nail into each wretched one. Our way of life is going you know. We want to be ready. When socialism comes. Yes siree as they say in Amerikay. You know power to the ruddy people and all that kind of cod's bloody wallop. It's a pity, but brains are not going to matter in the future you know. Fault of too much damn thinking getting nobody anywhere in the past. The war you know. Made too many people realize you had to kick someone in the goolies if you wanted him to do something. Man to man Kildare, what does a brainy chap like you think of socialism."

"I have not as a matter of fact recently thought about it."

"Well you think about it Kildare. But by god when you've a female item like that gaoled out in this neck of the god forsaken bog."

"I'll thank you not to refer to her as an item."

"What. What. Good god. You're not, are you. Smitten too. By jove you are. You well and truly are. Your face may be affected by the wine dear chap but a bloodier blush than that I've never seen. Now look here Kildare. Just shut up and listen won't you for a moment. Girl like that. Should be in London and Paris. I've got a proposition to make you. Now here it is in a nutshell. You agree to my taking her, quite properly chaperoned of course, over to my place where she can be trained up, and if a spade's to be called a spade, also groomed damn it, and polished. Made fit for society. And not bloody high society am I talking about here. I mean good bloody sound society. And if you'd only shut up and listen Kildare. The girl already knows some French. And we'd teach her some Italian too. Chi nasce bella nasce marita. If you get my meaning. I mean someone's going to steal her Kildare. And it may as well be a damn decent kindly chap like me."

Who the hell does he bloody well think he is. Expecting me to hand her over like a sack of oats, just because his damn decent kindly prick's been recently rigid over their lofty cultural conversation. All he is, is just a bloody Marquis. And all she is, is just a bloody servant. O god. How the hell do I tell him to fuck off to mid Sahara. And there having erected the appropriate scaffolding go and cohabit with a camel. I even see her face when I stare at the wall across this room. Every damn place I look. Outside on the stones. Her eyes, lips, teeth. Gems in the moss. While I think of her. And am so desperate to know. If she thinks of me.

"Sir, you rang."

"Yes. Bring a bottle of champagne. His Lordship and I also require a sabre."

Of course Crooks, returning cobwebbed from the gunroom was half an hour finding the latter and nearly jumped through the ceiling as

108

the Marquis sent the blade whistling through the air knocking off the champagne bottle's top and cork with a single cut.

"Forgive me your grace for me jump."

"That's alright Crooks. I'm not a duke yet but I'm a bloody good swordsman, what."

"You are indeed and no mistake sir."

"Bring some to the ladies Crooks, please. Tell them we'll be joining them."

"Very good sir."

"No on second thoughts, wait. They may drink it all."

"This is a fairly big damn room you know, Kildare. What you need down that end either side of the window are a couple of Regency carved giltwood girandoles. Just happen to have a pair collecting dust. Commemorating Nelson's victory at the battle of the Nile. As you scoop up your pudding, you contemplate his sterling triumph knocking any of those wogs for a loop. Don't want to be a spiv about it, but I could let you have them at a decent price if you've a mind. Damn decent price in fact. Bit of decorative ornate gold leaf would cheer this place up. And you ought to have a Kingwood parquetry commode right there. Also happen to have one which would suit. Or is that damn presumptuous of me."

"O no. Not at all. I like people to come into my house and cast their eyes around and comment freely upon one's shortcomings. Especially when they appear to have a warehouse full of exactly the items necessary to correct one's poor taste. Gives one, how shall I say it, a certain confidence that one day in the future, provided I avail of the splendid bargains being offered, that my house will be properly furnished. Nice to have something like that to aspire to."

"You know Kildare. I like you. Think we could be damn good friends as a matter of fact. Ah, and I deserve that. Damn it. Quite right. You Thormonds always did know how to grasp the nettle. As if it were some pulchritudinous lady's limb. And, as I understand from quite a few voices, you were indeed trying to do out hunting today. That Baptista dear boy. Bit of a trollop. Don't look at me in all innocence. As if your eyes are going to fall out. And don't turn your nose up at my girandoles. Sixteen hundred quid, the pair. Seven fifty for the commode. No. Let's make that thirteen for the girandoles, five for the commode. Both cheap at the price."

"I haven't seen them yet."

"See. Are you doubting their middle eighteenth century authenticity."

"Well they could be falling to bits."

"Well as a matter of fact they are but it's a damn bloody reasonable price I'm asking. Good carpenter put them right."

And finally on the way to join the ladies in the east parlour. Heading along the hall to the slow military clomp of his Lordship's riding boots.

"By the way Kildare how are you off for shotguns, have a pair of side lock ejector Purdeys."

"I'm fine for shotguns at the moment, but there wouldn't be a bend in the barrels."

"You're cheeky Kildare. Very cheeky. Offer you a bargain and you riposte with a bloody slander on Purdeys."

Crooks following his tray held much higher than he usually manages bearing the champagne and glasses. And patiently waiting for his Lordship to sell me a few more console tables for bare spots along the hall wall. I'm not sure that the damn man is not trying to unload all his castle junk and take more than a few quid from me at the same time. This house must give him the impression I have more money than my ancestors had taste. And if that's his conclusion, instead of in his trees, the Marquis must have had put in the baldest part of his head a bloody copper nail which is killing off his excess spivvy brain cells. Dear me, who knows, but just like me, he may not, for all his land presently have a jade pot to piss in. Although his ruddy father the Duke owns enough to start a couple of small nations. But one does have the impression seeing him standing there that he is utterly happy and utterly contented puffing on his cigar. Just as must be his horse utterly uncomplaining presently out in the stables munching up my hot bran, beetroot, hay and oats. Of course Dingbats did rather heap whipped cream in place of mayonnaise on his salmon. And then of course in one's bonhomie inebriation of winey bliss to make up for it, as one does, and to make matters even worse for oneself, one did do the unbelievably stupid thing. And offer the Marquis a bed.

"Kind of you Kildare but my hunter Rapscallion will take me home. Can fall asleep on that old fellow, and wake up on my front steps. But hold on why not, now that you mention it. I think I would damn welcome a bed. Just as my poor old tired horse would welcome not to have to hack miles in the dark."

And now Crooks is going to any second collapse with his lordship going off on another tack.

"But by god, what's this Kildare, a Tiepolo. Surely not. But by jove, it is, is it. No. Not. Maybe from the school at best. Want to sell. Good price."

Poor Crooks his arms beginning to waver under the weight of the tray. When one thinks of it, Crooks is sometimes a real dedicated servant. When he is not goosing another member of the staff. My god when one does think of it, poor sod is up there in his celibate cell for years on end. Of course one would mercifully hope that he was past it at his age. And not poking plaster out of the walls in search of self satisfaction. As one is nearly doing oneself except that any fervent attempt would certainly crash this whole place to the ground. Crooks does seem to take pleasure from the Marquis remarking on furnishings and paintings. And is shaking his head up and down in assent at even his bloody wheeling and dealing, as if he knew the girandoles were the answer to our prayers.

Darcy Dancer and his lordship followed by Crooks entering the north east parlour. Lavinia and Christabel purple with cold huddling forward over the fire. And would you believe it, both now wearing what to my eye looks like my mother's evening slippers. Indeed they are. Bloody, bloody nerve. Must have gone into my apartments and bloody rummaged around in my mother's closets. And as his lordship and I nearly fall in the door cigar first, Lavinia plumping down on the settee swinging up her dress with her pasterns showing. Two of them holding open copies of *Tatler and Sketch*. Clearly they must have been straining their eyes reading in the light of two candles.

"Good gracious me. I did think we had been abandoned."

"Ah my lovely ladies. It is I who have I fear been transgressing good manners with a too long prolonged talk on politics and furniture and pictures of your more than tolerant brother."

"O dear, you were both being brainy."

"Well, attempts. Attempts. At best."

Of course one does take one's dinner and always awakes next morning not remembering a single topic or word of conversation one had the entire previous and agreeable evening. Proof that the exercise of one's intellect is not needed to aid one's pleasant digestion. But dear me, what ladies won't hysterically do when sniffing even the vaguest hopes of becoming a Marchioness, not to mention ultimately a Duchess. If of course the Mental Marquis' equally dotty father, the present Duke, demises. Astonishing how women size men up. Not quite like they would the best cut of beef in a butcher's. But by memorizing every ruddy line of lineage in Debrett. Don't care if your hair is falling out of your head and growing in profusion on your arse. Or if you're wobbling along like a frog on two flat feet providing you're doing it on your own endlessly extensive acreage. Or even if your toes are webbed. Which of course is awfully nice if you're intending to beget children who shall wish to go fast as swimmers.

Christabel demurely lowering *Tatler and Sketch* as if it were some article of strip tease, which indeed she thinks it is the way she is batting her eyes.

"O how wonderful champagne. But whatever happened to the bottle, Crooks."

"It was madam, sabred by his Lordship."

Lavinia looking at Christabel as if this were some custom they were soon to have to come to terms with in this loony bin and the less enquiry the better. God. There the two of them are. Possessed of breasts and quite hysterically pukka vowels. And not that many years ago they were trying to stuff me into their toy pram. Calling me their own little baby. Nearly suffocating me with covers over my face as I struggled to get out. And then when our mother died would call me their own little orphan. Exhibiting me to guests and saying, now watch, watch how we can make him cry. Then putting a comforting hand on my shoulder, they'd say, your mummy is dead isn't she, your mummy is dead little brother and she will never, never come back again, will she. And of course I would cry. But the pain of this was never as searing as it had been when my mother still lived and they'd say your mother has gone away and left you little brother, little boy. And then I would get down on my knees and join my hands and sobbingly pray aloud, O please dear God, I beg you please bring my mummy back. And then they'd say, she's out in the hall, we just heard her come back from hunting. As many times as they had previously played this trick on me I would still arise and rush out into the dark hall desperate with hope. And where, as I stood there sobbing, they'd say, O dear she's not here she really has gone. So racked and wretched was I that I would press my face and body against the wall. Listening to the sound of winds shuddering up the chimney. All else in the empty hall a howling silence. And when it did finally happen that my mother came through the door to die I imagined for the longest time it was a dream, even to watching her coffin placed away. Down slowly in the ground. And so strange then that I shed not a single tear.

"O this is nice champagne. Dear brother. If you don't mind my calling you that, and also asking, whatever has got you so lost in reverie. Brainy matters I'm sure."

"No, not particularly. In this rather dumb part of the midlands it does not do to think too much."

"O dear we are cynical. Dear brother."

One did attempt all the usual avenues of polite conversation, that not discussing horses and hunting allowed. Which meant, one is ashamed to admit, of hardly being able to say a word. But the words said did soon present the Mental Marquis, his head sunk back on the sofa cushion, his eyes slowly closing and faded out of consciousness, uproariously snoring. One did feel a little sorry for one's sisters although they would understand that even drinking cauldrons of coffee, no one can keep his eyes open after hunting all day. Happily instead of taking umbrage, they laughed.

"Dead to the world. And I think we ought to achieve the same dear brother and retire. It has been a long day. I've ordered breakfast for eight and a horse at ten. And if any of the motor cars are working again, and the petrol is to spare, we might motor to visit about. Who is there now who's chauffeuring."

"I'm afraid the cars are laid up."

"O what a nuisance."

Dreadful feeling. Only once have they voiced during the evening that it was nice to be home. Christabel clearly thinks this place is utterly at her beck and call. And ah, that was a grimace of distinct distaste. As my god I do believe the Marquis not only snored, but at the very apogee of his nasal wind also shuddered in all his limbs and exploded in a sonorous manner a regettably long and what is to my aware nostrils a lethal fart. Producing on one's sisters' faces a look of having just been slapped. Indicating that they might like his ruddy title considerably a whole lot, but certainly do like much less than a little, his impending fume. I knew that something terrible was going to happen tonight. And this is a sound and smell of more to come.

"Well upon that note, sisters."

"Yes indeed upon that note we bid you adieu."

"I do with all apologies say goodnight on behalf of his Lordship."

"Yes quite. Goodnight."

"And goodnight, Dancer."

The parlour door closing. The hounds loosing long mournful wails out in the night. Lavinia's voice so much less strident and softer than Christabel's. And I suspect perhaps even comes of a kinder heart which still holds some affection towards me. And she and I at the other end of the wood were always seeing a leprechaun sitting on the end of a long log and as we got close and he ran we would find a great old spider's web and an old shoe. And then when I could at a very early age finally outdistance her either on my own legs or that of a horse, she chose of all my names to call me Dancer, after that great steeplechaser, for whom I was christened.

"Kildare. My god Kildare. I must have dozed off. Did I fart. I did. Hope the ladies weren't offended. One thing to remember about the fart it does no one any permanent physical damage. Unless to the perpetrator himself who attempts to hold it in. Have another glass of that damn good champagne. Wake me up."

One was tempted to tell the Marquis attired out hunting in black coat and bowler, he could be mistaken for a groom. He is of course entitled to wear pink as a former MFH. Adopts these little tricks to trip people up. Who want to talk to him because of his entitlement but who otherwise would ignore him. His hunter Rapscallion reputed to be eighteen hands one. Nearly as big as Midnight Shadow. Who if anyone could ever get near enough to the beast to make a measurement official, might find him eighteen hands two.

"You're staring at me Kildare. I know one does look a bit of a scruff. Keeps the arse lickers up from Dublin at bay. And a man's mind on his hunting instead of damn whores. You know, not a bad little place you have here. Came as a child a few times with my dear old mother. Time flies. Damn it you know if one discounts the happiness of foxhunting, the world when you look at it is pretty damn sad isn't it. I drink too much. I'll be dead in five years or less. Damn sad when you think of it. Damn bloody sad. Bones shovelled in an old coffin. Piper playing a lament. But let's bloody well hear some of the damn Count."

"Count what or Count who."

"The Count of course. You've got a gramophone. Damn Count is called for."

"Well I fear you do have me foxed."

"I mean the bloody tenor of course. What's wrong with you Kildare. McCormack. The great John. Garden where the fucking praties grow. Walk me by the fucking Grecian Bend. You mean you don't have his records. Don't tell me that."

The clock tower bell striking two a.m. when it was not yet midnight. The Marquis deprived of the Count sang in an astonishingly good voice some very common Irish songs which to my mind had their origins in Tin Pan Alley. But quite entertaining nonetheless. Tears welling in his eyes as the words the sun or moon or something sank on Galway Bay. He sabred another bottle of champagne, nearly taking off my head and exploding and splashing the wine around the room. Broke the face of the clock on the chimney piece with flying glass.

"Damn sorry about that Kildare. Fucking up your chattels in this way. Can't always make a clean cut. But let's drink."

Turf embers glowing in the grate. The room growing chill. The Mental Marquis, mud spattered on his stock, his boots off, stretched back deep in the swan's down.

"Beware of the women Kildare. I speak as a man already had by three wives. During which time it took five damn expensive mistresses to give me some kind of damn comfort. No children, that's the pity. O I've got a bastard here and there alright. Of course the mistresses would have me marry them too. To be bloody twelfth marchioness or is that thirteenth. Even if it's a title in courtesy only, that's a hell of a lot of damn marchionesses, what. One damn well ends up like a factory manufacturing marchionesses till they'll bloody be tuppence a dozen. What. And all running off with the family jewels. Bloody last one got off with four necklaces, three bracelets, two rings, never mind a mass of earrings and an emerald and diamond stomacher brooch. That alone could have when I'm finally skint, kept me in comfort in some nice little boarding house in Folkestone till I get cremated. One's not a piker of course. Just want the dear girls to leave a little something for the next marchioness, that's all. Instead of buggering off on my emolument to Monte Carlo, Spain and a lot of other woggish places. One hates to be feeding, housing, clothing another man's piece of ass, as the Americans refer quite aptly to such slices. Bloody hell, Kildare I support the bloody lot, lock, stock and bloody barrel. I'm being impoverished is the sum of it. And if one of them ever bloody well remarries I'll gladly eat my hat. In fact I'll eat all my bloody hats, including my coronet and flying helmet and goggles without salt. Lock's stock and bloody barrel if you get the pun of the first. And as one has been sparse on top that means more damn headwear than my old abused guts could digest in a hurry. Makes a man realize that pranging a down to earth prostitute is man's cheapest way to satisfaction. And you know, you are an agreeable chap to listen like this. To my rantings. But I suppose any man who takes a fiver off me the way you did knows the ways of the world. And damn if you're not a dozen years my junior. Always feel a con man chancer is deserving of the deepest respect."

"I think I must beg your pardon."

"Now don't bloody well be offended Kildare. You have the makings of a great con man chancer. Without people like you the whole world would be in revolution. Thieving is the escape valve of the lower orders."

"I beg your pardon."

"You're a commoner Kildare. A bogman. Pure and simple. But since you use a bog to shoot snipe in, it makes all the difference."

Having been a past below stairs servant and groom one did not easily tolerate his lordship's remarks. But amazing the presumption a title gives. He went on rambling as we proceeded out to the stables to see Rapscallion. One thing to be said, he really adored his horse.

"Look at that kind eye, Kildare. That noble head."

His nag however was back at the knee, upright in the pasterns, dipping in the back and sloping in the quarters. Never mind, fondness makes up for all that. And outside owls hooting, we had a look up at the stars utterly splendid cold and daunting to one's tiny presence taking a long piss on the lawn. And at last to bed. His lordship an arm around my shoulder and leading him lurching up the stairs. In candle smoke smell, snuffing them out behind us with a long handled church snuffer. Down the hall to my old bedroom. The Marquis pausing, muddy boots grasped to his breast as he leaned towards the last candle.

"Kildare you're a brick you know. Con man chancer but a brick. But you don't ruddy know how to snuff out candles. Squeeze the flame. Wet your fingers."

His lordship's quizzical eyes. The dried spots of mud on his lapels. A frown furrowing on his brow. Putting a hand up to the side of his head.

"My ruddy ears ring all the time, Kildare. Too much aircraft engine noise during the war. Makes you sometimes want to blow your head off."

A candle already alight in my old bedroom. And Crooks of course, wouldn't you know, has placed with a glass and decanter of water, a bottle of my very best pure Scotch whisky on the bedside cupboard. Not that one begrudges it. But bloody hell yes, one does begrudge it.

"Kildare, that's a damn decent highland malt there. This is very hospitable of you. I must put you up for my club in London. Only a handful of very very select members. Took over an old battle scarred house. Popped a couple of hunchback brothers down the cellars, one cooks the other does the portering and waiting. As we are not heavily endowed as a club, fees are a bit steep. But the ruddy wine and privacy is unexampled. Except for the hunchback brothers fighting in the basement. Bit of occasional early morning screaming, shouting and slamming doors over which one is to put out the garbage. Give you a bed in London. Into which, provided you don't fuss up the other handful of members you can comfort yourself with a bit of crumpet of an evening. But don't get the bloody idea I'm a ponce or it's a whore house. Hope I'm not giving you that impression Kildare."

"Well no not quite yet as a matter of fact. But of course I'm still listening."

"Ha I like you, Kildare. I damn well like you. Consider yourself a member. Phonecall by four p.m. will get you a supper. But roll in any time for pot luck. Along with suitable bare breasted ladies on the game, we invite a guest of honour quarterly and amusingly insult the ruddy shit out of him at the end of the table. Of course the food and wine are so good the ruddy fellow is too busy eating and drinking to give a damn. It's how of course one is accepted to membership. Nice old commodious house too. Donated it to the common cause. The old boy the Duke doesn't know it yet, but I've named it the Putney Club, after him. Man must have a reliable place to bring his occasional fly by night bird. And if you don't intend her to be permanent in your coop, other members who are momentarily short of the avian species, why they go aerial with her if you get my meaning. But it's no ruddy whorehouse remember. Nice young chap like you, the world lies before you Kildare. The world. Never forget that. Don't get skint like me."

"I am already skint."

"O. Sorry to hear that. Damn nuisance for you. Damn sorry. O that is a pity, isn't it. Well we have reduced memberships at the club. I'll bring it up with the secretary. No need Kildare to worry. Goodnight."

"Goodnight."

Pop of cork out of the whisky bottle. The Mental Marquis pouring himself a drink. Darcy Dancer, hand on the door knob.

"And O, by the way Kildare, Bangkok that's the place where you might plan to go and have a damn good fucking. Marvellous place for the ladies, both for the ones already there and the ones you bring with you. Cool season is November to February. Young man like you wants to be properly schooled in these things. Only damn sensible thing my father did was to recommend it to me. It's a great art you know. And one never gets done finished learning. I mean you know about fucking. Never get finished. I mean learning about damn good fucking. Goodnight Kildare."

"Goodnight."

One proceeded feeling one's way by the wall, back down the hall. Bangkok, good lord. Damn good fucking. I mean to say, chap obviously thinks me a rank amateur. Certainly there is no question as to what Leila's paltry fate would be at his hands. Shoved half naked into his London club. Members sitting around dinner with harlots' knickers over their heads. Jumped upon and pranged by the other members who had gone inebriatingly aerial. The hunchbacks no doubt rushing about with wind socks and suitable flags giving the signal and direction for take off.

Darcy Dancer removing his clothes in the damp chill. Peeking out the window shutters. A clear cold sky. The moon shining. My mother's wardrobe door open. Two of her gowns draped over the back of a chair. One's sisters do take signal liberties. What a day. What a night. Nearly asleep on my feet. O god. If only I could press my lips to Leila's. Instead of crawling alone down between these icy sheets. Ah, thank god. A hot water bottle. If it's not leaking one can anticipate a modicum of sensual voluptuous comfort. I suppose everyone is looking for a beautiful but decent minded woman. That she should be entirely thoroughbred in her figure, cultured in her mind and gay in her demeanour. Who would when one required it, put her hand on top of one's own and say soothingly to calm one's worries, there you are, you mustn't trouble my dear, we will, both of us manage somehow. O god, to know that such a creature does exist. To know that she lives and breathes under one's own roof. Where one wakes each day. And now sleeps. Sleeps. In a dream. Of the most delicious sensation. Enveloped in the soft arms and legs of one's past housekeeper. Ensnaking warm cozy comforting limbs of Miss von B. Her soft if somewhat commodious aperture. Into which one could dip so delicately. Holding her smooth silken miles of skin. Her voice in my ear. Vas ist diss Bangkok. You little naughty creature. Vy you need go Bangkok. Your bang bang cock so nice right here. You baby. Ah. Yes I scream. In your ear. You hear. My dear. Mein Bauernlümmel.

"Shush you fucking noisy heifer."

A voice out in the hall. Darcy Dancer squeezing a pillow, sitting bolt upright in bed. My god I think I heard most god awful screams and screechings. And naked feet pounding. Stopping just outside my door. Huffing and puffing breathing.

"Will you come back now you bloody wench."

"Jesus, Mary and Joseph, you've already been after interfering a finger in me sacred tabernacle."

"Begorra I'll interfere more than a finger with me stone rigid credential bulging up your essential."

Feet proceeding again. And speeding elsewhere. Going around the turning in the hall. And upstairs in what is commonly referred to as a damn quick hurry. Leila. Her feet would never make such heavy pounding. O god. Dingbats. No. Norah. Or Kitty. But one thing is bloody certain. It's his lordship whose vowels are pretending to be a bogman under that stage Irish brogue. Clearly thinks he's in his London club. Taking off in his Spitfire. With his hunchbacks clattering dustbins, signalling him down the ruddy runway. Shove my overtaxed senses back under pillow and eiderdown. Stay here. Until I smell floorboards or joists burning. Or the authentic screams of my sisters. Crying rape. Or O my god. Must have dozed asleep again. Hoofs thumping the gravel.

Darcy Dancer going to the window. Pulling back the shutter. Has there ever been a colder night. And down there in the moonlight. Has there ever been a madder one. The Mental Marquis. Galloping. Tally fucking ho. His hair flying. Atop his horse. Lashing his whip back across Rapscallion's quarters. And up, up and over the fence. There he goes. Down the front lawn. Fading in the shadows. Pounding the frosty ground.

Darcy Dancer padding back to bed. Stretching down deep beneath the covers. When is this night ever going to end. Pull up the blankets over my head. Cover ears. Ah dat's better. Peace and quiet reigns again. And leaves me so tortured. Prick pained without love. Close eyes. Stare away the dark. The Mental Marquis said. Although expensive for her own soul, how cheap a whore's price is. Cynicism hurts and stings. The closest thing to truth. And will I ever hold her. Touch my fingertips across her pale soft cheek. Kiss her brow. Will I ever put my hand deep clutching in her black hair.

Before I
Shut away
This brain
The last thing
That dies
In this body
The last thing
That lives

10

The day of the lawn meet. Dawning. On a bad bad old day. A night storm bringing a thaw with its gales and buckets of rain and flooded pastures. Slates off the cow house. Chimney toppled, ancient oaks out in the park uprooted, and utter utter misery festering in my heart. As one makes fervent plans to abandon this crumbling pile of stone and devote the rest of my life to whoring and reckless extravagance in the better fleshpots somewhere miles from the gossiping tongues of this rain sodden parish. Yesterday, a hint of disapproval in Sexton's voice as he stole up behind my shoulder in the corner of the orchard as I watched the rooster cohabiting with a hen just as it was growing dark and you'd think the rooster would be thinking instead of a night's sleep.

"Sure you'll be carrying on like the Duke of Portland in Welbeck Abbey, with shutters closed and no one seeing you for days on end."

"Many things Sexton to look after in the office, keeps me in."

"And now wasn't that something. Our little beauty Leila, our St Joan of Arc. Masterly, masterly. Now twisting that eejit Marquis around her tiny finger. Did you hear about that."

"I heard, Sexton."

"Writing to her he is. She'll soon move in the highest circles in the

land. She'll rule nations that one. Gone from here in a trice. Saw the
envelope meself. The coat of arms there emblazoned in the red wax."

"And it does seem to me, Sexton all quite improper."

"What, to write to a beautiful woman. When was that ever improper."

"I am merely suggesting Sexton that she merely works here in a not
particularly esteemed position."

"And didn't she acquit herself in that that evening after the hunt.
Let me tell you it wasn't, was it, as if Apollo was playing his lyre to the
muses. Ha ha. Cromwell at Drogheda was more like it. Except now
the boot is on the other foot. Struck in defence of you. Fought by your
side. Saved you by her loyalty. Ah now Master Darcy, with all due respect to your Protestant forebears, an Irish lass can rise to the heights.
Sure who hasn't in low moments prayed dear God, teach me how to
accept the awful scourge of being Irish and that so many other lucky
nations and lucky men are not. I've thought it I have. Plenty. When
they'd shoot you down in England upon the sound of your voice."

That darkening evening I found myself walking away from Sexton,
passing his Stations of the Cross. Veronica wiping the face of Jesus.
Jesus falls for the second time. Yes. Leila. Loyal. If you were ever
needing my care I would come she said. And she did. And now. Like
the gay sound of some summer laughter on the air. She may be gone.
Leaving me bereft as I wake yet another morn. So hard to disturb my
bones from a bed. That at least keeps the frost off my knees. But not
out of my heart. Silent in the household. Always a sign that everyone
is warmly collected in the kitchen shining the seats of the chairs. Bent
over tea, bread and butter, fried eggs, rashers, sausages. One even has
given up making loud noises of my approach. To scare them back
outside to work again. At least getting them as far as the underground
tunnel. With all its blessings and grievous drawbacks. Built to avoid
the aromas of manures or the sight of servants. But certainly more
used as an idlers' paradise, with a smell of contented tobacco smoke
coming out the high end.

"Sir. Sir. It's your breakfast out here I'm waiting with."

A thump on the door. Darcy Dancer turning to face the slit of light
creeping on the carpet. Yanking up blankets close around the throat.
This pre dawn moment one does lie muscles stiff in bed utterly shattered and beaten. And back a week ago, one thought it was another

dream. Or nightmare. But the cheeky ruddy nerve. The Marquis galloping off in the night. Having run amok among one's female servants. The whole ruddy lot could end up pregnant beyond belief. The place a maternity hospital. Full of his illegitimate heirs.

"Come in."

Dingbats, tripping into the room and clattering the crockery on the tray. The faint hall candlelight behind her. Her hair uncombed, looking like it'd been struck by lightning. My shutters rattling. Closed hopefully against new ill winds. Barred against the hysterical bank manager's letters. And a dream I had last night of the agent and the timber merchant cutting down a giant old beech, and his men swarming over it like a nest of ants, taking it away. Then seeing just beyond the ridge that the whole park land was denuded. Stumps of oaks, elms, sycamores, chestnuts, the meadows scarred and rutted.

"It be dark. It would be drowning rats, such a fierce wild night sir. Wait now while I feel for the box of matches and light the candle."

On the chimney piece three candles alight. Discomforting my eyes. The rest of the night awake with a ton slate coming adrift on the roof. The rumbling slide. The crash on the front steps below. Pity it didn't wait to hit the agent's lawyer or even better the bailiff who's soon to be banging on the door. Instead of leaving a gaping hole up there somewhere for the rain.

"Would I put the tray here now, sir."

"Is it clean Mollie on the bottom."

"Sure it's the one I fell down with and wiped later I did."

One has to take every precaution. This day after my sisters announced they were having a ball. Can you imagine. To meet amusing people they said. Bloody hell the house is full of amusing people. A ruddy vaudeville. Dingbats herself two mornings ago on the servants' stairs carrying a tray, fell tumbling down head over heels covered in butter, coffee, sugar and cream. Claiming she was goosed on the top step by Crooks who laughing so hard himself, fell after her. Both promptly spending the day in bed. And after the night of the Mental Marquis, rape was the talk of all the staff. And Kitty and Norah locking doors. Giggling. Hoping no doubt someone would break in and jump on them. Crooks rumoured seen past midnight without the merest trace of a hobble or limp, flitting and pirouetting down the hallway in a flowing gown and lady's Ascot hat. Isn't that bloody amusing enough. Transvestites anonymous. Without having a ball. Of course outside, there's a circus. Luke tossed by the bull into manure slops, and getting up running like a blind pickaninny. Straight into a loose pig he clung to and was then dragged into the stable where he ended up covered in barley seed. Crooks then flouncing about the house with a walking stick, and imitating Miss von B's most officious manner.

"I won't have outdoor staff using the indoor comforts of this house, not while I'm butler here, I won't."

And Luke in the hospital. Because washing the muck and barley off himself and never having been in a bathtub before in his life, slipped and broke his arse bone. Crooks loftily announcing.

"Serves him right taking the presumption of cleansing himself in the manner to which he is clearly not accustomed."

And the ferocious bull was all the talk of the house till Foxy Slattery's younger brother to whom Foxy must have taught every trick thought he'd have a go with him. And got flung up into the branches of a tree. Then the little eejit caused a fire in the tack room chimney while heaping up logs and toasting himself asleep. The tiresome little scoundrel then pouring lamp oil on it to put it out. The only thing he seems to know how to do is to every five minutes sneak into the house to get biscuits from the kitchen. Or if Catherine is resting after her lunch, to fry up a cauldron of eggs, bacon and sausages, enough for an army. And then into the jams and preserves, and after scooping out half their contents the little fucker tightens the caps on everything in the larder so that cook can't open them. Till Dingbats tried breaking them open with a poker and serves me broken glass in my breakfast honey and jam. Meet amusing bloody people. My god. Someone too, of course, was also being amusing supposing to entertain me by placing a rubber mouse in my bed, not realising that such creatures were already scampering across my face very much alive and waking me from sleep in the middle of the night. Meet bloody amusing people. My dears. They're right here under your noses. Of course they're no doubt wanting their potential suitors at whom they invariably were turning up their noses, to all be arrayed at their disposal along the ballroom walls. That is if Lavinia wasn't already hiding behind various pieces of drawing room furniture, as she did when Crooks came to announce a caller who was it appeared, enamoured of her, and of whom it would also appear, she was not enamoured, while Christabel at the same time was throwing herself with a screech prostrate in a faint on the soaked garden lawn to attract his attention.

"Now there's plenty of light sir."

Darcy Dancer pulling himself up from under the covers. Dingbats lighting the bedside candles. And would you believe. Performing a curtsey. Her concern over my upper nudity would not appear to be as great as it is over Crooks' alleged prodding finger.

"And now while the door is open behind me, should I be back to you sir momentarily. With the more of anything you may want."

"There's yesterday's newspaper in the library, if you'd bring it please Mollie."

"Very good sir, I'll be back, momentarily."

Dingbats withdrawing. Tiptoeing towards the door. She closes with a new silence I've certainly not heard before. And of course one will wait momentarily. And wonder momentarily whyever she is increasing her vocabulary so formidably. Especially with a word unheard of in this household since I'm sure it was built. There was of course momentarily a risqué moment with one's chest exposed in the dim light. O god and why does not my loyal lady ever bring me breakfast. Ever come in that door to my lonely dark. And she. She is what I want. Your lovely purple ribbon. On your lovely black hair. To take up its satin in my fingers. To undo. O god. As I might. Your body. To lie it stretched soft sinewy beneath mine. Souls clutched in warmth. Side of a slender neck to kiss. A brow to touch and tender. And have nothing. Except all these days to try to shut out all the thoughts of her. The jealousy. Like a great massive void. Cloaks my brain. Not once, not even once to speak to her all these days. Not even thank her. Except to see her come and go in the dining room. The inane conversation of my sisters. I'm sure appalling her ears. Of the dances and balls in London. The horses and hunting in Leicestershire. Racing at Newmarket. And the most grim and terrible embarrassment of all. Lavinia suggesting that she smelled. One knew Leila heard by the cold implacable fury rigid on her face, followed by her sudden departure, with a crash of crockery in the pantry, and resounding slam of a door. Dingbats leapt backwards into the dining room with a blob of whipped cream between the eyes as Crooks, his shoes and lower trousers splattered with trifle, reappeared, his one eye staring directly east and the

125

other at the north west corner of the ceiling which at that unfavourable moment started to leak.

"Forgive me sir, and your Ladyships, but the pudding lately prepared for this evening is regrettably indisposed."

O god one did wish one's sisters would soon go elsewhere. With their now written commands following breakfast in bed. Making suggestions as to decor, mealtimes, servants' rosterings and issuing orders all over the place. Each wanting their own private apartments and the silver on their dressing tables daily polished. And my best horses to hunt. Complaining about the lack of hot water, and the overabundance of cold sheets, their bedroom fires untended and draughty rooms. That tea was late to the parlour. And that it was Indian and not the China with lemon they preferred. Dingbats at least this morning seems all intent upon dancing better attendance upon one. Having in the middle of the night one of her more normal occurrences. With Kitty banging at my door in her nightdress. Come quickly sir with the shotgun, a vampire bat is flying round Mollie's head and a rat has her cornered in her room. Of course we were all minus our ear drums as a result. With the explosion sending the bat to kingdom come along with two panes out of the window. And the whole household peeking out their doors thinking the world had just ended. The only constructive thing being, that it was obvious to anyone watching Dingbats jump and leap up and down on her mattress that she did have such a great pair of tits, of which any poor understocked farmer would be immensely proud to find on his best cow. And here she is now. In my bedroom door. Actually breathing heavily. Back sooner than one expected. And believe it or not with the newspaper.

"Sir here you are now and did you ever hear tell of what happened to that man Hitler. They say he's living. In secret seclusion. Not ten miles from here."

"I'm sure he is Mollie."

"And is there anything else now I can do sir."

"No thank you, Mollie."

"Draw your bath."

"Ah yes, you might indeed."

Awfully difficult to know what prompts a servant's sudden diligence. There's no doubt one's previous nudity helped her to take one more seriously. Although god, this is bloody last month's paper. They are such an utterly stupid lot. Certainly one's sisters would agree. Yesterday, while I took tea in the estate office, they had theirs in the blue parlour. And which on this particularly mournful occasion, Leila brought. And concerning which, joining them later for drinks before dinner, Lavinia bitterly complained.

"She's insolent. She should be let go. She's talking back. Not only refusing to do what she's told. Do you know what she did. Threw the tea strainer at me from the door. Nearly struck me. Then she lifted up her uniform at me. Above her thighs. After bringing us Indian tea again. And having been told China."

I must say I was tempted to say it was a pity the whole thing wasn't dumped on them. To get them up off their grand arses which only shifted out of their beds to either recline in feather upholstery or sit on a horse. And then I did say it.

"It's a pity she didn't dump it on you to get you up off your continually leisurely arses."

"Well damn you brother, for your privileged information, she did dump it on us."

Then monopolizing the gramophone in the library. And playing their ruddy rhumba over and over again. Bloody Brazil. Which record if I hear it just once more, I shall break. Then switching the wireless on and off when they see fit. And more often than not absenting themselves and running down the battery requiring its recharging in town. Their imperious descent of the grand staircase. And as they did so, invariably issuing in their lofty grand manner some inane request to any servant seen in the vicinity. Especially Crooks.

"I wonder Crooks could you see if the library fire is bright as I shall be there presently sitting."

Crooks of course on one occasion did take the opportunity to pretend he was in a ducal house exercising his lofty command in delegating the precise division of duties. And he did split his infinitives calling and clapping and finally pulling the bell to summon one of his charges to pump the bellows at the library fire. But with Kitty, Norah and Dingbats repaired to an attic bedroom where Foxy Slattery's brother had brought them up biscuits, tea, scones and jams and where they sat around a fire smoking those Woodbine cigarettes, and I believe telling quite salacious stories, the servants' bells clinked and clanged unheeded down in the kitchen hall. Serving only to annoy

Catherine, who of course much mumbled to herself these days having her own small farm to worry about. Dear old soul did do me many a kindness. Dear me I think that one could easily get bitter. End up forever pursuing the things of enjoyment in life without much enjoyment. Must not lose sight of the fact that menials have their own worries. And at least less a nuisance is Christabel once off her arse. She did succeed in putting a new born calf sucking to its mother. Always remember her kinder to animals than she was to humans. But of course my sisters as a pair did as soon as our nanny's back was turned try to poke out my eyes. Explaining, we want a blind little baby brother so we can lead him around by the hand. Or if I were to crawl on the front lawn or hall, they would drive their prams over on top of me. We want a dead little baby brother so that we can hold a funeral. And while I screamed, and if Nanny weren't on her instant way, they would kick me. We want a wounded little baby brother so that we can play hospital. And not a toy could I pick up that they wouldn't rip it away out of my hands. Leaving me screaming. We want an unhappy little baby brother so that we can make him happy again. And dear me one nearly feels one is still facing these previous inclemencies of body and soul. Only my poor dear man, Mr Arland ever succeeded in making me feel that someone cared some little bit for my welfare. There we were all those many hours in a chill dusty schoolroom lodged in under the servants' stair. Even he grew moderately impatient trying to pound some Latin into my so obtuse brain. The lonely sadness in the man, so much like the sadness I felt myself. Being able to do or say something to cheer him cushioned and encouraged my own spirits. And then how cruel life was to him. Mocking all his kindly ways. Baptista Consuelo spurning his so shyly proffered attentions. Then death tearing his dearest love from his life. No god could ever make another Clarissa for him to cherish. Or such a Clarissa who had loved him. Whither now has he gone. His homeopathy book to cure his bodily ills. But no book to cure his grief. Where e'er he walk. That solemn man. Under what tiny piece of sky. Does he wander in his own abyss of sorrow. How find him. Hear him speak. Make me in my own sad dilemma. Not so sad.

Darcy Dancer in hunting coat, breeches, boots, coming down the main stairs. Rain stopped. The wind still howling. Pause here on the landing. The bark on the grove of beech, wet and dark to the west and silvery to the east. High in the tip top branches crows squawking. So often one stands here to look out. And see visions. Something I saw in a dream during the night. That I was an older man. Looking back into the past. Seeing a life that one had so long ago lived. Yet a life older than one's childhood. Before I had gone away to other lands in search of my fortune. And now returned a rich man. To an Andromeda Park standing empty. Roof caved in. All its inmates gone. Ivy growing through the walls. And I walked past the kitchen. The blackened hearth and stove cold, that years ago glowed warm. Stepping slowly on the wet stone. Between the mildewed and crumbling corridor walls which once kept the chill damps at bay. The brass servants' bells hanging from their coiled springs, corroded green and grey. And I stopped at Edna Annie's basement room, where her whole life was spent going about her lonely ancient chores. A fuchsia hedge growing through her broken window. The bedstead rusting. The rain dripping through the ceiling and falling on possessions one cherished once. A sailor doll of blue long lashed eyes, so many times warmly hugged and kissed and cuddled closely abed. And which lay unsheltered, broken armed and cracked on the rat holed mattress. Its little head upturned. A rain drop for a tear in one of its eyes. And I stood there. Tears in my own eyes. Till a sound behind me made me turn. A mist. Sound of water. And the hunting lame girl killed by the old stone bridge over the river was standing there. And instead of white she wore top hat and flowing dark hunting garments. Her face smiling. With the splendid white teeth. And lips of Leila. Slowly lifting her skirts above her slender legs. Slowly over her knees, higher on her thighs. And there in the ruins. She spoke. Her soft voice coming from her dark haired beauty. I am the mistress of Andromeda Park. She said. Then I woke. Shivering and cold.

Darcy Dancer stopping further down near the bottom of the stairs. The arriving voices. Distant bark of hounds. A breeze blowing through the house. Hunt members pouring in the door. The front hall with tables laden. Sausages, hardboiled eggs, smoked salmon, soda breads, barmbracks, butters, beers, creams, port, sherry, brandy. How far now the day that will dawn on the last drop of wine and the last morsel left.

Major Bottom already with a brimming glass of port to hand, striding up to Darcy Dancer. His grey brows going up and down as his ruddy face contorted in his attempt to smile.

"One would have thought Kildare, with the condition of the land, the hunting would be cancelled. Instead of making mires of small farmers' pastures. But it's damn jolly good of you to lay on such warm hospitality. But with the wind drying, clearing the sky and the fields brightening in a bit of sun during the morning, perhaps not too much damage will be done."

Of course the truth of the matter is the hunt secretary couldn't give a damn about making mires of small farmers' pastures and in fact delighted in parading his big bloody hoofed horse straight across their winter sown wheat. But not before he's drunk all my best port and turned the whole ruddy hunt breakfast into a luncheon party. Good heavens. Motor car horns sounding outside on the drive, and pulling up in front of the house. Horses rearing and bucking at the beeping. Who on earth could be arriving. Doors opening. Unloading folk. And who clearly climb up the steps. And wade into the hall. O my lord. A voice. O my god. No ruddy mistaking it. That one has heard uttering so many a time previously. Bellowing above the rising din in Dublin. My goodness, what on earth do I owe all this to. Being visited. One does so miserably dupe oneself with the false notion that people are fond of one for oneself and not for something which will be to their exclusive benefit, as indeed one finds dismayingly is always the case. People are, on the whole, aren't they, such a ruddy reprehensible lot.

"By jove, as bloody sure as most bloody houses in suburban Ireland are called Sorrento, damn chilly journey has given me a roaring appetite. Enough to eat a cold pail of muddy unpeeled potatoes."

Rashers Ronald. In the most outlandish of outlandish tweeds. His ever ready smiling face, front teeth protruding even further and the gap wider between them. Through which he occasionally resoundingly whistles. Cheeks and nose brightened. No doubt by clearly alcoholic refreshments, numerously taken at many stops on his journey here. A signally orange wool tie. With a totally contradictory stiff white collar attached to his light blue shirt. A sprig of bog heather as a nosegay. And although one does slightly quake at his unexpected appearance, a smile does erupt in one's heart at seeing him. Crossing

130

these black and white tiles. Grinning ever so mischievously and ever so slightly shy, proffering his hand outstretched to shake. Which I do believe I have never previously shaken before. His English vowels superseding those Irish where it mattered most.

"My dear chap Kildare. My dear chap. How good it is to see you again."

"Well this is a surprise, how nice to see you."

"Surprise. Nonsense. It's shocking. Being as I am the fox. And spiritually naked as I usually am. And indulging in the foolish temerity to appear in the midst of foxhunters. But when confronting such foxhunting fixture prominently tacked to the lobby wall of the Shelbourne Hotel, and a knowledgeable chap at my shoulder informing me with an insistent jab of his index finger that it was no other than you who was residing at this most impressive country seat. I'll be quite frank. I rushed here to presume upon our previous acquaintanceship. But also to return to you two fivers you were gracious enough to temporarily entrust to me. You see I stoop to grovel where others might merely pretend to fawn."

"Well thank you very much."

"I'm not entirely sure but I think I detest foxhunting and those who pursue it. But then, who am I my dear chap, to cramp anyone's bloodthirsty style, especially as one's own mouth is so wide open for drinking and chewing. To think I had been promoting you as an outrageous chancer just like oneself. And I believe introducing you, in the interests of making one's company at hand more agreeable of course, as the authentic Marquis of Delgany and Kilquade. As nice as such titles are you clearly are already a squire needing no such embellishment. And by god, commodious and substantial are the words for this very nice mansion you occupy. Fair takes my poor debtor's breath away. How are you my dear chap. How are you really. I sweep up in one little heap the debris of my fondest wishes left from so much disappointment in my life and humbly offer them to you from the labyrinths of my undeserving soul. And I do apologise for my flowery speech. And for not at least having brought you one of the better quality boxes of chocolates. You know with the chewy nougat and deliciously crumbling truffle centres and so forth."

"Crooks, please. Some champagne. For Mr Ronald."

"Of course sir."

Crooks giving, as he withdraws a single pace backwards, the proper and merest nodding inclination of the head. People who rather cut a figure always seem to inspire Crooks to his very best butlering. Albeit Rashers does more vaguely resemble a race course tout. However Crooks did, being a past Dubliner, listen to Rashers with rapt attention, a twisted smile tugging at the corner of his mouth. Which with his crossed eyes, made him look a trifle daft. But suddenly endearing. Between of course his more obtuse irritating moments. Especially his continued attempts at putting his finger in places where the rest of the female staff find it most unwanted. Not to mention what he may do with his fingers during some of his more bizarre recent night time fetishes.

"Of course my dear fellow I'm in utter awe. Clearly there is no need for you, as I have found the need in my line of adventuring mountebankism, to use the old nom de guerre instead of the old nom de famille and thereby keep the old incognito intact, if you follow me. But damn it, here you are, with ruddy eggs, barley, wheat, oats, milk and butter at a hand's grasp. And yum yum yummy filet mignon within the tap of a sledge hammer, and a few slashes of a carving knife. Of course I expect to find a few damp patches on the wall and also a headless chicken or two rotting behind the drawing room drapes which are customarily found in the better Anglo Irish house."

And as one stared out over Rashers Ronald's shoulder, listening amused and calmed as one might be by a bird singing, there she was. Out of a blast of sunlight in the doorway. White gloved hand holding her bowler and whip. Blond hair coiffed back on her head. So soigné. Striding in her slightly military manner across the hall. Straight for me. My heart thumping uncontrollably in my chest. My private enlarging in my breeches. Even as one of my ears still listens to Rashers Ronald rambling on.

"I would so adore to be a bookmaker. One of course with a couple or so shop fronts in say Duke or Anne Street. Even in spite of your enormous win my dear fellow. My betrothed keeps insisting she will back me. To the hilt. Which with her accountants shouting in unison that she shouldn't, could mean the business end of the sword up one's arse. I take a damn poor view of that short sighted attitude. But you must meet her. Before the dear gallant girl gets too much further the wrongish side of sixty. Two face lifts have kept her damn presentable.

Leaves her expression a little sphinx like as a result. But who minds. Perhaps a little blet in the quarters and thighs. And knobbly hocks. A regrettable consequence of her grazing too much on her boxes of chocolates. The dear dear creature's only failing, however. And added to her two previous tobacconist's shops she now has three more. O but I bore you."

"No not at all."

"Well then I damn well bore myself. Except for the fact that my dear betrothed has now instead of three hundred, four hundred and fifteen acres, three roods and two perches. Of the very nicest possible well watered and fenced acres in County Dublin. Stabling for sixty. Fifteen horses in training. Five footmen, eight gardeners. Of course I exaggerate for the sake of accuracy. Knowing that anyone listening to what I'm saying will take it with a grain of salt. You know I'm convinced, there is something to this country life. But dear girl wants to know if my intentions are sincere. That I'm not after the easy way of Jammet's restaurant life so to speak. That's where we are dear boy, every evening in my utter struggle to impress her that my intentions are hallmarked sterling. I mean what more can I do but sit there paying the bill and holding back tears that would otherwise be pouring down my cheeks parting with the fiver it's costing me. And all the while saying, I love you, darling. I love you. But the dear lady is taking such a long time to accept my proposal. I had to ruddy purloin this shirt and my present pair of socks from her butler. And can you imagine, damn chap had the sauce to request them back. I mean there I was on my way to take a pee having bid two spades during bridge. Damn uncomfortable feeling you know. Bad enough the collar's ruddy too tight. Ah but you do listen to me don't you. And you are wondering what I did, aren't you. Well I took off my coat and handed him back his shirt and took off my shoes and handed him back his socks. And went back to the bridge table and bid three no trump. Taught the ruddy chap a lesson. Didn't it. He then, gave them to me as a present neatly parcelled up in green tissue. But I mean my dear chap, I'm only the merest maybe thirty or forty or so years her junior. Why should my youth be such a hindrance. What matters is our common interest in horses, our companionship at the races. And what should be significant is we hold hands on our way there. Of course we couldn't do that if it weren't for her chauffeured car."

Miss von B stepping close to Rashers' elbow. Nodding to him as he stops in his speech, and she turns to smile at Darcy Dancer.

"Reginald Darcy Thormond Dancer, the genuine aristocrat. I presume."

"You do so presume correctly Madam. But I would rather present myself as your faithful potato digging bog trotter at your service."

My god, if I had not got those words out my mouth it would have stayed opened long and wide enough to become a swallow's nest. If anything she is even more beautiful than I remember. Her teeth whitely shining between salmon pink soft lips. Glowing mahogany of her boot tops and their lower leather so black gleaming. Glimpse of yellow vest under her white silk stock pinned with a gold and emerald pin. Her long and sinewy legs without her breeches. Not a hair or thread out of place. And a god awful crash had just happened down the hall somewhere, no doubt of the usual irreplaceable crockery breaking.

"Ha, by zee sound of zat the old place it has not changed so much."

Rashers recoiling at this rude interruption and turning away, just as oneself did turn at the expensive sound. And catch sight of Leila disappearing down the hall towards the ballroom. And see deposited upon the hall tiles, in her wake, a large vase in some many considerable pieces. While here in front of me within the smell of her sweet breath, Miss von B. Stands almost as one had dreamt. That she had come back into this house. And of course as luck would have it, she is surveying me from head to foot.

"Ah but that is just as we would expect, kaboom, something precious becomes no more. And so let me look at my trotter bogger."

Who was instantly noticed in his effort to shield my most embarrassingly largest tumescence I am sure I have ever had the arousal to have. Puts me in the extreme weakest position possible to show her any indifference. And so obvious to anyone even remotely acquainted with the breeding of horses. One even feeling that the thinness of one's riding crop, although being as ludicrously inadequate as it is would at least distract and give the appearance of a rival stiffness. Good lord what a hopeless image one conjures in the present desperation. To ask her to stay. Do sleep here tonight. My dear. And I shall, using my celibacy as a parachute, descend quietly upon your quarters and ruddy well prod them good and proper. And erase in one throbbing evening of love all the yearning hurt. Of your ignoring me back in Dublin. Ah but maybe one should not be so easy on her. As this now is my supreme moment to be utterly cool. As she has been in her so oft practised manner. And yet here I am, one's equilibrium already betrayed by one's inadvertent primal instinct. O god never mind tonight. What kind of an awful day might this be ahead.

"Ah the Rashers Rashers Ronald. You know."

"Indeed I do, madam."

"He is of course a fortune hunter. You do not seem to keep such worthwhile company."

Crooks with glasses of champagne poured. Delivering on his tray a glass to the elbow of Rashers upon whose face one catches a glimpse of utter stricken sadness. As if as a once celebrated actor he'd been suddenly swept aside in the middle of his final curtain speech to be told that it was his last. And dear me, the front hall of Andromeda Park is thronged. Voices of the thirsty hungry horde raised. Mouths stuffed and throats gurgling like drains. One hates to think so ungenerously but I'm paying for it all.

"Madam please do, take this glass. Crooks, didn't you, you knew her Royal Highness was coming and had her champagne ready."

"Yes Master Reginald and it is felicitous to see you again your Highness and looking so well."

"Well thank you so much Mr Crooks."

"Always entirely delighted to be at your service your Highness."

Crooks withdrawing back into the fray. And bumping into Gearoid, who with a glass of Guinness in each hand, drinking from both spilled their contents down the front of his greasy rain coat. And at his elbow watching in smiling admiration, the Dublin Poet known in the vicinity of Harry Street as The Bard Wandered Over From Duke Street and in the vicinity of Duke Street, as The Bard Wandered Over From Harry Street. And often called Grafton, for short, this being the street connecting the two. His mouth now, instead of spouting verse, gaping open to pour back his tall glass of whisky. Dear god, the denizens of Dublin. These inhuman beings. Erupting out of the past. All come to have a bash. The few incorrigibles of the permanently dispossessed who closely cling to the flotsam and jetsam, still afloat on their recent fast dwindling legacies. The temporarily rich and momentarily praised heroes of ignominy. Who sail the storm tossed waves of the Dublin night. Could there be even more of them off the morning train. Or another load out of another motor car.

"Ah but your eyes are lost in thinking, my too kind host, my boggy trotter."

"Yes I am Madam. And although that term is occasionally funny I sometimes wish you might find some other droll expression to use."

"Ah still so sensitive you are. But why. Why are you not proud to be from zee bog."

"Simply because Madam I am not from zee bog. The bog is more than two miles from this house."

"Ah, if you go round by the wood, but if you go as zee crow flies zee bog is right over there."

A minor commotion of pushing and shouldering at the jammed up front door. And entering in their thick to the floor tweeds, the bunch of flowers. One after the other. The spinster sisters, Rose, Camellia, Marigold, Pansy, and Iris. Holders of the world record for sisterly celibacy totalling more than three hundred years. Obviously come to sample my standard of home made bread, butter and jam. As they always do. And flying out of their camouflaged midst, my goodness, my dancing master. The Count Brutus Blandus MacBuzuranti O'Biottus. Waltzing right this way.

"Ah, so. So. And my dear you are wearing lavender water. Such fragrance. I smell you. I smell you. A mile away. You have done it. Reached maturity my dear. Quite captivating of you. You have managed such a mix. Of people my dear. Both the wickedly moral and respectably immoral. Clearly as we do no longer see you in the very naughty city of Dublin, we have had to come see you. Among these awful people with the blood thirst. Of course what you forget is how we miss your such young beautiful good looks. You must you know come to the Cats. Lois, who as you know is such a great artist could not tear herself off the canvas to come but she asks so much after you."

The Count tossing his head and blond curls as he glanced in his fifty directions for every three words out of his mouth. Smiling and nudging Miss von B who glowered at the mention of Lois's name. And the Count himself smelling to high heaven of lilac. One did put a drop of one's mother's lavender water under the tunic which one instantly regretted as the sweet scent fumed up one's nostrils. Of course the smell of some members of this gathering would send one into a coma if one sniffed too much. And one does avoid attempting introductions of these nearby faces of these catacombers, out on a spree, knowing of course everyone is already numbed to death having met again for the fifth hundredth time. Not counting the numerous unremembered occasions with their brains afloat intoxicated out of their skulls. Or when confronting each other in the blackness of some closet, alleyway, larder or wine cellar, groping at orifices and protuberances which if they didn't yield the satisfaction sought, were then punched, twisted, pulled or scratched.

Darcy Dancer excusing himself. With a shudder. Finally observing the pieces of vase on the floor. Which Mollie is busy chipping further with her furious sweeping. And O my lord. I suppose it is indeed bloody valuable. My mother's treasured glass vase. With its intercalaire overlay and marqueterie de verre. Cracked forever. One does not know whether to save one's tears for something worse. My sisters. Descending the stairs. Faces plastered with smiles as they enter down into the din. And smiles fade. Clearly regarding these Dublin interlopers as distinctly not amusing people but as heinous inhumans to be avoided. Especially Rashers Ronald from whose vicinity they have already decided to rush. But who it appears is not to be easily shaken off. Following right by their elbows as they take up new smiling poses at the sideboard. And by their hysterically animated voices, they are being presently utterly captivated by Count O'Biottus. Who has rushed to them. And every time I look at my sisters now, reminds yet of another string of awful perpetrations they wrought upon one. During a picnic, having shown me how to carefully do a pooh pooh in Nanny's best summer bonnet as she went to fill a bottle at the lake. And in the course of waiting for Nanny to put it back on her head, she instead sat on it. And the water Nanny had gone to get was for a stew they had asked could they cook over the fire for little baby brother. That they had brought their own little special bag of chopped up sprigs of yew and laburnum. Which they heaped into their brew. It was the only time she ever slapped their faces. When Nanny sniffed the spoonful being lifted towards my lips. And I must say I do remember being extremely pleased. My sisters clutching each other screaming to high heaven, and saying in unison, we hate you Nanny, we hate you. Only the day previously they had taught me

137

words to use to ask for another piece of cake at Mummy's tea which would assure they said its being given me. And I strolled in. Delighted with my frills and patent leather shoes and relishing this rarity of being invited to the sacred sanctum of the blue parlour. My sisters pushing me in the back to exercise the words they'd rehearsed with me. Nice polite words they'd picked up from the stable yard. May I please Mummy have another piece of that fucking shit, please. But Mummy took the wind out of their sails. Of course you may my dearest, have another piece of this fucking shit, but next time you must ask for simply cake. But dear me, there now my sisters. Craning their necks to look Miss von B up and down. Staring at her white leather snugly encased thighs. And swell of her buttock. And resenting clearly the attention she is getting from both the ladies and the gentlemen.

"How are you boss, it's good to see you again."

Darcy Dancer turning. To confront this shyly smiling face and mischievously sparkling eyes. Last seen so many years ago, hungry, cold, bedraggled and shunned by the world. And now in a smart, perhaps too checked jacket, his hair slicked back, cavalry twill jodhpur trousers. A rather overly colourful and overly shiny tie that one suspects might be American. And his shirt and collar not exactly pure white or ironed to perfection. But it is none the less, Foxy Slattery himself.

"Foxy what a surprise."

"I was to seeing the father over in the hospital. Only for the sake of the mother. And if you don't mind me saying, he's still the same old mean cruel bastard he always was. And I was just now down there for a look in the stables. A right old mess they are. In the care of me little brother. Worse than when I was looking after them. Dirty bad old hay. Dung everywhere but on the manure heap. Hear he's a bit of a devil like meself. I'm training the odd horse now. Over at the Curragh. And I sell a motor car or two on the side. SAI three eight nine, eight seven nought six ZC, five two four two LI."

"Ah I don't think I quite understand what you're saying Foxy."

"Ah that's the registration numbers on the cars parked outside. Now I'd be able to tell you the history of each one of them."

"Well Foxy, not really knowing of course but I suppose that is useful to know. And you do look as if you have little to complain about."

"Had a few tough times. But for the moment, there's not a bother on me. Made a bob or two. I wasn't exactly a saint, but sure when the world with everyone in it was against me, you always treated me right. I'll not forget you bringing me a sup of food out there beyond. When no one in this place cared whether I starved or died. I'll remember that. Didn't think you'd mind me stopping in a moment. I wouldn't but for you treating me well, come into the big house like this otherwise. And I had to laugh. Crooks over there still got an eye on me and nearly fainted at the sight of me when I walked in. But the Kraut Miss von B, you'd think never clapped eyes on me before. But we did clap eyes on plenty of her in our time. But if there's anything I can do for you now, legal or illegal, I'd want you to let me know."

"Thank you Foxy."

"Not much has changed in the old place. But there's an odd face here now I'd know from Dublin. But I won't outstay my welcome."

"Foxy you're entirely welcome. Please, do have a drink."

"Ah I'm on me way now. And you'd already have your hands full with the lot of them here. And I'm keeping people away from talking to you. I'll maybe grab a nip of something and say goodbye now and good luck. And any time you want to do business in the way of a motor car you know who to come to. And I'd have plenty of petrol for your tank and rubber for your wheels."

Darcy Dancer watching Foxy Slattery stride away. Heels clicking on the tiles. And we did indeed the pair of us clap eyes on the beauteous Miss von B, lying stretched bosoms floating in the steaming bathwater. And over there. Rashers Ronald. Wearing a more contented enthusiasm on his face. Sizing up the paintings and objets d'art with the practised eye of the pawn shop habitué. Dear me. He sees me. Of course he would know what one is thinking. He and the Mental Marquis would make a great pair. And here he comes smiling.

"You are kitted out, my dear boy. Quite kitted out. Totally possessing all the nice appurtenances which allow for an unrivalled, nay an utterly unassailable role in life. At the very top. I mean I haven't had a chance to fully count your servants yet. But I mean all, everything is very nicely splendid, thank you. If it were not utterly ignoble of me to do so, I would ask for my two fivers back. But the gentlemanly thing requires me to instead borrow them back from you. May I."

Darcy Dancer taking the two crinkled white five pound notes from his side jacket pocket. Where they had been so contentedly crumpled. Placing them in this apologetic but none the less deliberate hand.

"Damn decently sporting of you, Kildare. It really is. It's a damn denomination so prized by serious race goers. And I mean do you think, I might also presume a little further on your splendid hospitality. You must say no of course, if it is of the slightest even of the teeniest weeniest slightest inconvenience to you. But as a matter of damn fact I've been chucked out of my wretched basement. And into another worse basement. In the catacombs. And frankly dear chap. In that place. The rodents, mayhem, murder and perversions are the very least of it. I just simply can't take the irreverence. To the principles of behaviour one upholds. I don't mind the physical insult, constantly assaulting one, it's the social maim and injury one can't stand. Having to rub more than one's elbows with gurriers and newsboys. Who wouldn't know an ode from an ox. Imagine one of them greeting me as an intimate on Grafton Street. And then with other collected awful tramps in abundance, having to spend the night in their filthy disgusting proximity. Foul personal habits appall me. Is it too much to ask. Just to be away a sojourn from all that. I will sleep on the floor. Just show me some hearth rug in some little out of the way corner. And my dear chap I only speak as fast as I do, not wanting to let you say no, until I've made, I hope clear, how desperate my absolute desperation actually is. Need just a few moments to simply my dear boy gain my confidence back to face my dear betrothed. While her accountants are persuaded in my favour to fund my efforts in taking up my professional duties as a bookmaker. Or rather, turf accountant, as those residing in Foxrock would better have it."

My mouth when it opened first, simply did not speak. The stricken look again so overtaking poor Rashers' face. How to tell him. That this oasis he perceives is a mirage. On the most disappointing of deserts. And just as Sexton would say. Ah it's a great morning for delusions of grandeur. Plus I did nearly die handing him back his ten pounds. After the utter pleasured relief of putting in instead of taking money out of one's pocket. A symbol of what was happening in my life. Wages for three for a week. And now. To add the thirst of one more throat to slake. The hunger of one more mouth to feed. How does one make that rare display of perfect manners which shields the truth behind it. Yet I know his discerning wits would find me out. Simply must gather up all my resources of firmness and even cruelty. But search all over one's brain for the most uncruel words. To say the most cruel thing.

"I'm terribly sorry Rashers, but I think that that would be a rather difficult idea at the moment. You see."

One stopped. So utterly in one's tracks. And in the din of other voices all around one's ears. To see the vast tears aflood in his eyes. Their shiny tiny spheres breaking over the lids. Streaking down on his red ruddy cheeks.

"I understand. And why I may not be wanted. I know I'm a chancer. A fraud, hoaxer, fortune hunter. And that our past acquaintanceship is trivial. I am sorry that I have asked you. What clearly I should not have asked."

Rashers' shoulders folding forward. His head slumping on his chest. His voice breaking into racking sobs. Tears spilling blotting their dark spots on his bright orange tie. My own heart welling up. With the only words. That could come to my mouth. And there remain mute. For only my mind to hear.

> In the solemnity
> Of pain
> In the bright
> Key
> Of E major
> Let music
> Reign

11

I led Rashers into the front west parlour. Dead flies falling out as I opened the shutters of that dusty unused museum of a room. Smelling of musky damp. Full of its glass cases of porcelain and bric a brac. I'm sure one was mistaken but I thought the tears did dry rather quickly as Rashers' eye swept round the statuettes and bowls, the trinkets and cups. Nonetheless I did give him an Andromeda Park best linen napkin to mop up any remaining grief.

"Kildare. I do apologise for my unspeakable behaviour. Such a thing has never happened to me before. You must think me a weak kneed, spineless fellow. I suppose these past cold months of winter have rather knocked the stuffing out of me. I don't want to continue boozing and whoring. But sometimes it's only way to keep warm. I want some respectability in my life."

"Rashers. You may. Indeed please. Do stay. Crooks is already seeing to it."

"No. I must go. This is too much. To impose upon you. Damn it I'm nearly a stranger to you."

"Well you are."

"Well I thank you Kildare for being damn honest about it."

"I'm sorry. I don't know how that quite slipped out. But of course you're not. A stranger. You know you are absolutely welcome."

"Well since you put it with such insistence. Alright. I'll stay. Only because you absolutely entreat me to."

Hunting may not sweep all sadness from the mind but does indeed quite quickly erase misery from the soul. And one did feel relief at the Master's signal to move off. With the usual shouts and hoots from the gung ho contingent. But not ten yards from the front door of Andromeda Park, two members of the hunt already nosedived on their heads, having in their efforts to mount, got up on one side of their horses only to tip over to plunge down the other. And Gearoid holding the reins of both, while still clinging to a glass of Guinness and trying to swallow its spilling contents, was dragged off bodily. One did look back at the house and the fuss. And there up in the whim room window, catch sight of Leila. Staring it seemed down. At the top of the heads of hunt followers and of the assembled staff arrayed watching on the front steps. And waving goodbye. Sexton rushing up to me with a nosegay.

"Ah now you'd not want to be without a bit of colour taking you with its beauty flying through the wind safely."

One presumed the front hall had been left to scavengers. Cousins, aunts, uncles, nephews of one's staff. Who make themselves known from the lower reaches of the house when the grand folk have gone. Sexton of course directing traffic and hoofs to keep us off his sacred preserves of flower bulbs and grass. Down the drive someone dismounting. Secreting themselves behind a piece of broken statuary and heaving out their guts into the rose bushes, sounding as if in their death throes. You'd think that that terrified, they might rather retire safely quiet in front of the fire, and read about the more active moments of the hunt in *Horse and Hound*. Which periodical as it happens has sent a lady associate just arrived to report today's outing. Although I don't suppose she'll be reporting that in the thick of the rhododendron plantation there, white breeches can be spied of similar folk crazed with terror, depositing their hunt breakfasts. Which, who knows, will quite possibly be gladly gobbled up by one of the very devilishly clever foxes we shall chase.

It would seem that the advent of the use of the motor car again has brought a plethora of the nervous of heart to hunt. For not even a quarter way to the first covert, an extremely pinched faced lady down from Dublin, her face a mask of make up, which nonetheless underneath could be seen turned entirely green, keeled with a sighing gasp from her lips, in a dead faint straight out of the saddle and stuck like a pole into the ground. The hunting priest did stretch her out and do his well meant mumbo jumbo over her unconscious face, till the lady awoke and it would seem was distinctly and irately Protestant. Of course one does feel a shiver or two oneself. But at this casualty rate we will soon be minus the field before finding a fox.

Approaching the second covert, the first finding no fox, and just beyond and at the edge of the wood. The breeze not so cold in the snatches of sun. But the cloud brought a shuddering chill as we waited. And one did think. That not that long ago one sat in solitary enjoyment of one's privacy. The sole lonely occupant of one's house and served by its staff. Whose exact number one always has trouble to calculate. And now bloody hell. The place is overflowing. But if I were merely to count up the mouths. It would amount to more than a dozen more than I can afford.

"Tally ho."

A fox found. And off straight into the woods. To make sure we're all scratched to pieces if not knocked senseless.

"Watch out."

A shout just behind one. And a silly chap, absolutely belted backwards off his horse by that branch of a tree under which Petunia and I have just ducked. Blood exploding from his nose before he hits the ground. Miss von B following him, to whom he was obviously turning to display his charms. And who at the same time, shouted to him to watch where he was cantering. Poor damn sod. Immediately pretending to Miss von B as she offered to help, that he was tough as nails and completely alright. And then as she rode on, whammo, the Mad Vet, lately arrived at a gallop out of the trees, flattened your man once more. Poor wretched sod, just as he was sitting up to hold together his various parts of his loosened skull.

The field veering suddenly. Hounds barking hell bent on yet another fox. And foolish doggies. Down a hillside. Over a stream. Dear me, the injured gentleman's riderless horse has just scampered by. Which being on our way once more, everyone pretends not to see. And those who can't avoid being seen seeing, pretending to grab and tussle about with the reins, and of course as I see is happening, letting them go at the first opportune unobserved moment while shouting loose horse. They really are, just like oneself, such a bunch of damn self centred pleasure seeking hypocrites caring only for indulging their own sport and enjoyment. Rather like the Mental Marquis of Farranistic for whom one does keep an eye open to come thundering out of some copse, like the last charge of the Light Brigade. Which of course exactly happened the next second as his lathered horse came up beside mine. And god, he does look at times awfully insane. By his own admission having been rapped constantly on his head by a perverse nanny who maintained it was a good way of knocking sense into him. Only on one occasion she used the leg of a table.

"Damn sorry Kildare to have missed my stirrup cup. Damn car blew up other side of the village. Damn silly fellow can you imagine came lighting a cigarette to examine why my petrol tank was leaking. Set the horsebox on fire. Burning bloody inferno. I say, see a few nice pieces of crumpet out today."

One heard while waiting at the next covert that instead of anyone coming to the flattened chap's assistance, poor damn man ended up crawling to the nearest cottage where he was nearly shot. The farmer not only loosing a load of pellets over the poor bugger but nearly garotting him pulling his head gear off and trampling his top hat with his muddy Wellington boot. It's not stylish to wear a cord attached to your top hat. But I suppose the poor polite foreign fellow will have learned a thing or two before this day's out. Among which is, that he does not quite present the pleasure one gets fetching a beautiful lady in her muddy soaked finery out of a bog hole. And that an injured gentleman is quite likely to be left for dead. Perhaps a reason why more gentlemen of the inclination to prefer gentlemen, should be encouraged to hunt.

"Go get him."

The Huntsman with a terrier released into a foxhole. The whipper in nearby furiously digging with his spade to fill in an escape route. The stragglers slowly arriving. Gossip being savoured on various lips. Miss von B off to the side with a bevy of bug eyed still slathering at the mouth gents in eager attendance. And directly behind one. Sounds like a waterfall. Must turn to see. My god. Baptista Consuelo. Who obviously has avoided my hunt breakfast. Now suddenly here. Reined up and tightening her girth. Probably ready to accuse me of further and better particulars of my previous heinousness various. Her horse taking one incredibly noisy pee. Which one can't help marvel at. The stream coming out of what one must certainly term an inordinately large equine penis. Exactly what one would expect her horse to have of course.

"I would prefer, if you do not mind, and in particularly you, not watching while my horse is peeing."

Of course one turned away. Who bloody well wants to watch her damn horse peeing. While she is preening and making all her usual efforts to look captivatingly splendid while at the same moment also haughtily attempting to ignore the collection of chop licking gentlemen surrounding Miss von B. And it is amusingly clear that she and the Marquis currently utterly detest each other. I suppose some brands of fucking can breed later abhorrence. And dear me, over where the fox has gone to ground, an altercation already. The Master raising his voice to the Mad Vet.

"Sir I order you to leave the field."

"I certainly will not. Not for the pansy likes of you me boyo."

"Sir, that insult I shall deal with in due course and I repeat, I order you to leave the field. You left a man injured, having jumped over him."

"Bugger off. Wasn't he minding the beauty behind him instead of the danger in front. Daft fool's better off left. He was already half dead in the head before ever he came off his horse."

As the loud shouting match continued, other hunt members distancing themselves from the scene of disciplining. The hunting field is always the perfect place to hurl an insult if you've got one reposing in your bonnet. You damn silly fucker. You stupid ass. You absolutely ox witted obtuse unthinking noodle noddled nincompoop. You jerk. Very American that last. But quite effective. But then when one finally turns for home at the end of the day, one is supposed to forget all that was said and done. And as one invariably does, to sit fireside over one's whisky in smouldering fuming utter indignation and wrath. I'm sure rage must release into the blood a lot of unpleasant chemicals. But I suppose one must take it as refreshing that foxhunting gives rein to the basic instincts. And to quote the Mental Marquis. Especially the tendency incited by the blood spattered hounds at a kill for a gentleman to fish out his pole to put same plunging up some likely lady.

"Tally ho."

146

The fox. Dug, shouted at and disturbed out of its hole. We're off. Pounding. Just as I was bloody well hoping to see a really good fight for a change. One in which I might be the observer instead of the observed. No one giving a tinker's damn now, about the poor maimed and perhaps dead left in the wake of these present aerial sods flying behind down this hillside. And up on high ground again. See the red of the Huntsman on the far hillside. And one can make a very neat detour here.

"O do please get out of my way, won't you."

Copycat Baptista, of course, knowing I was taking a short cut, cutting in front of me. As if she were the one who knew this country well. Thinks she's such a fine horsewoman. Ruddy cheek. And listen to her pedantic English hunting references.

"I say, the hounds are feathering on the fox."

Instead of saying the damn silly mutts have decided to go off in a dozen different directions. And that ruddy howl just emitted is her ruddy horse incompetently stepping on a straggling hound. I'll soon bloody well show that overly endowed rump of hers a clean pair of heels. Come on. Petunia.

Darcy Dancer slamming his whip across Petunia's quarters. The mare in three vast strides overtaking Baptista. As the two mounts nose to nose head for the same low spot in a vastly high wall of boulders. With so much mud flying it was rather difficult to perceive how dirty the dirty look Baptista gave one was as I cruised past her on this brief stretch of flat meadow. Baptista bending her neck to growl.

"Keep out of my way. You wretched boy. Damn you."

"And you get out of my way. You wretched girl."

The pair of horses thundering abreast across the pasture. A stone's throw to go. To the wall ahead. The ground gently rising. Sun's rays flashing across the fields. A massive double rainbow arched on the horizon. Hoofs still stretching over the grey lichen encrusted outcroppings of granite, peeking up out of the emerald green. Baptista hissing out words she must have picked up hunting with the Quorn or Beaufort. Or some equally esteemed hunt in Leicestershire. Or elegant one in Gloucestershire.

"You fucker Kildare, fuck off."

Darcy Dancer swerving his horse away. Petunia's hoofs, carving a thick wave of turf up out of the ground. Foam flying from her mouth

147

and landing in little lumps of froth in the grass. Baptista's nag rising up into the sky. And disappearing. With a scream. Down the other side. Which was down and down. Deep into a ditch halfway to hell. It does help so to know the countryside well at such times. And to be able to smile deeply inside one's soul. Instead of plummeting into a chasm of bog water.

Darcy Dancer dismounting. Stepping to take a peek over the wall. And down into what is the very deepest gulch in this parish. Good lord. Her wretched animal is flapping on its side like a fish out of water. Gasping for breath. Legs atremble in its death throes. And she with her tresses strewn from under her disturbed hairnet and hat, is spreadeagled drowning next to him. Of course there was nothing for it but to be chivalrous. And slide down the bank into the abyss. I do damn myself sometimes for being such a gentleman. Drag her ashore under the armpits. Pour the water out of her boots. Slap her face back into consciousness. Mumble the last rites over her rapidly dying horse. And wonder how soon others would catch us up if I had the temerity to revive her further with an attempt upon her easy virtue to end my long excruciating bout of celibacy.

Of course Petunia ran off to graze in some longer grass she spied in the corner of the field. And Baptista's half submerged horse now dead. Its lips hanging loose away from its teeth. A fore leg snapped in two and the bone poking whitely from the brown bog water. I fell dragging Baptista out of the deeper mud and then attempting to further drag her up the impossibly steep bank, came crunching down my two knees landing on each of her shoulders. Which did not make her make an awfully nice sound.

"O god I can't move my legs and you're trying to kill me."

We both of us slipped back down three times before I got a foothold and lugged, dragged and tugged her heavy carcass to safe grass again at the top. Where it appeared her legs could again miraculously move and where instead of thanking me for saving her life.

"You did that deliberately, letting me jump that wall."

Luckily three stragglers with the previously creamed foreign gentleman's horse in tow, arrived. And I took the opportunity to be immediately gone. Until two parishes away, horse foamy mouthed, steaming in sweat, one finally caught up. But damn silly ineffectual hounds lost the scent. But my god what a wondrous melee was in progress.

Whips snapping and the air smelling of hot leather. The Mad Vet and Master entangled on the ground. Gouging at each other's ears and eyes. Rolling over in some splendidly deliciously fresh cow flop. O god, my stomach so bloody well paining me with laughter that I fell off Petunia as she reared away from the two embroiled figures. Their fists beating on each other's backs rather ineffectually as they clutched. Gloves blackened with dung. Who would believe that some of these same human beings might actually know who Tiepolo is or that Meissen is preferable to some other crockery. Even though they might not know a Neapolitan table top on a Chippendale frame. The lady reporter, who proves to be a good rider, is of course stunned out of her senses to witness the unbelievable physical rudeness in progress. And eyebrows raised, she's putting quietly back in her pocket her notebook. Clearly not needed when events are seared on the mind.

"Stop stop gentlemen. Disgraceful behaviour. In front of the ladies. Disgraceful."

The secretary wagging his riding crop over both the protagonists and pushing back some of the local grinning populace. Who must have materialised acrawl out of the thicker hedgerows or from behind the larger mounds of moss and granite. And were now most contentedly pulling forelocks and nodding to hunt members as they took up discreet ringside positions watching the gentry punch each other to pieces. As more hunt stragglers arrived up the hill. Followed by a loud bellowing voice.

"Ah much jolly nice. Not even a fox roused and yet mucho beaucoup frappé, I see."

The Mental Marquis taking a swig from his brandy pouch. Not even offering one a drop. And his nerve. To assume such a nonchalant indifference having written members of my staff letters. I'm simply never going to let him land his airplane in one of my fields. But one must suppose that together with his aerial acquaintanceship with the downed Master, the Royal Air Force is here in strength. And dear me, we are taking sides aren't we.

"Kick him. Come on. You've got him now. Squeeze."

And now the top hatted and today red coated Mental Marquis with reins dropped over his hunter's neck is putting his hands to his mouth and shouting.

"Hit him in the haggis. Twist his fucking halo out of orbit for him

149

Jonathan dear chap. Can't damn well tell who's winning this fight. Seems we should simply let them get on with it Kildare, don't you think."

His lordship still grinningly watching the battle. Wiping his crimson sleeve across his dripping nose. Taking up reins again. His massive horse, its eyes rolling in its head, snorting out its nostrils. Till suddenly overcoming the Mad Marquis' face, a look of alarmed consternation. His brow creasing and his eyes looking concernedly askance. As he shifts his weight around in the saddle and slaps his whip against his thigh.

"Good god Kildare, I just remembered. Left my bloody groom in the blazing horsebox. Shut it up after I got the horse out. To stop the damn draught burning the ruddy thing to a pile of ashes more quickly than it might otherwise. Do you think the poor fellow might be a cinder by now."

"Wouldn't he have yelled."

"No he wouldn't. Hasn't murmured a word for donkey's years. That's what I liked about the chap. Kept his mouth shut. So that you don't even know he's there. O well too late to worry about that now. But damn nuisance losing a good groom like that. Poor fight here don't you think."

And then just as one was turning one's attention away from the melee there was Johnny Gearoid holding one's mare. And how on earth did he two footed miraculously get here a dozen or so fields in from any road. No point in taxing one's brain over that one. But obviously he'll be looking for five shillings for his services. Knows just when to be around. Just like many of one's staff. One always finds them so clever in the wrong way. Perhaps their saving grace is they're too dumb to know what stupidity is and I suppose if they ever found out they'd be twice as dumb. But what are these words at one's shoulder.

"That's the kind of thrashing the likes of you should get trying to rape a lady."

Would you believe it. The words are addressed to me. Of course this ruddy smarmy pipsqueak has a moustache which twitches on his unpleasantly sneering face that one vaguely remembers from the battle of Andromeda Park front hall in the last melee. Son of a bitch sitting high up on his horse does not think he is in any danger with another imbroglio in progress, and is totally convinced he is nicely out of harm's way. As one grabs hold of the silly man's martingale. And goodness, imagine, bloody man is trying to lash me with his riding crop.

"Let go of my horse or I'll give you a bit of Swaine and Adeney across your uncouth bog face you Irish savage."

Darcy Dancer, whip blows raining down in his head, arms and shoulders, sinking his ten fingers agrip in the top of the man's boot. And in one downward wrench dragging him plummeting to the ground. Man's horse swerving round and kicking out its hind legs. Two hoofs catching the back of the secretary square on each rump and lifting him skywards to descend on top of the still battling Master and Mad Vet, now grunting and wheezing with exhaustion. Just as a shower of rain unleashes and two more peaceful rainbows blaze glowing purple orange gold and green in the eastern sky, one intersecting the other.

Darcy Dancer wrestling the moustachioed man to the ground. Dear me, by the facing on his collar, a Master of Foxhounds of a Leicestershire hunt. Must admit the son of a bitch is unexpectedly strong. With a good pair of lungs which he puts to good loud use as I wrench the cartilage within and nicely break two of his smaller fingers. Knee him for good measure in the kidneys. Elbow him for additional measure across the adam's apple. I'm a prince. You cunt. A prince at least in moral fibre. And now it's just about time to render you unconscious with a fist between your eyes. And wham. Am I actually seeing stars. I am. In an astonishing looking solar system. Good heavens. One is actually floating. Around in one's life. Yes there goes Sexton. Dressed as a cardinal. And O yes. There's Mollie. Her tits being milked by Luke. Into a pail held by Crooks. O good, Catherine's going to churn it into butter. Or am I waking. Staring up into her face.

"Hello my little bog trotter, ah your eyes, they at last open. Are you alright. Can you move."

"Yes I can move."

Her Highness covered in mud and debris. Her face scratched. The awful churned up muddy battlefield nearby empty. Just the darkening sky and cold breeze sweeping the hillside. And the faintest distant sound of the horn of the hunt.

"What happened Madam."

151

"Ah what happened. Of course, you. You are what happened. And I. I am what happened. Coming to rescue you."

"My god, I've a lump the size of a hoof on the back of my head."

"She kicked you. Sent your hat flying."

"Who."

"That one. Consuelo. While you were on the ground. In the fight."

"My god."

"And I must say. There was another battle. Between this Consuelo and me. This time not with whips. But sock sock."

"O my god. Are you hurt."

"Of course not. I knock her silly."

"That was kind of you Miss von B."

"Kind. Never. It was stupid. I have lost my pin. I have torn my jacket, two precious buttons gone."

"O we'll look. We'll find it."

"Find. Never. My horse I hire. It had no go. Till now. And is gone. With your Petunia. Dragging away that little man."

"But we are at least here alone together."

"Ah that kick in the head has not lost you your presumptions. And there is some blood on your lip."

"Madam, you are using big English words. It is rather nice however to wake up out of one's unconsciousness and find oneself in the kindly care of a beautiful woman."

"You little foolish arse. That cloud coming. It is going to rain again."

"I don't mind Madam, a little rain."

"You don't mind. I mind. I am already wet enough."

"Don't you have any romance left in you, Madam."

"And what is left in you. I can tell what, looking into your eyes. And I think I am seeing the lust."

"Ah Madam you have a very cunning mind, but would you mind telling me, are you being honest and sincere."

"What a crazy question. The rain is pouring. I do not think I have to answer."

"But you must."

"But why must. Get up please."

"Because you have been unfaithful to me."

152

"What, Mein Gott. Unfaithful. To you. What right you got I be faithful to you. You impossible little pup."

"I'll have you know, I am now a country squire, Pasha and lord of a thousand acres."

"And still the little snob you are. I see you with the Marquis. O so friendly. Do you still, how does one say, break your arse to kiss the arse of titles."

"How unforgivable of you Madam, how unforgivable to say such a thing."

"Ah now you are an actor playing on the stage."

"Damn soakingly wet one if I may say so, Madam."

"But you are at least funny sometimes. You know, don't you, my dear little darling. That I could see your breeches out a mile and your eyes so popping out of your head when I come into zee hall. And you know. I should not tell you. But I will. I was myself feeling such thoughts that you were thinking."

"O god."

"Yes. But I am sad I did not say something to you in Dublin. But how. I did not see you. What could I do."

"O Madam I do think you did, you must have at least felt my presence, and thereby you ignored me. I was crushed. You were so clearly with another man."

"And why not."

"We did have a deep abiding relationship. Of kindred souls. Our love had been consummated. That's why not. That's why it was unfaithful."

"What to have dinner. What nonsense."

"I knew by the look you gave him."

"What look. I don't know who you even talk about."

"It was a look of love. I saw it on your face. I know that look. In the expression of your eyes. And the way you leaned towards him. And there was wine. And during horse show week as well. I know it was your lover."

"You know. You know nothing. Except you have a piece of grass coming out of your ear. And listen. The horn. You hear. And a cow. Go moo moo."

"And there, a rooster Madam. Go cockadiddledo."

"Yes my little bog trotter. And my arse is frozen leaning over to talk to you. And the rain. Go drip drop. On top of us."

"Where do you live now in Dublin."

"Such conversation. You think we are having an aperitif on the boulevard. In Paris perhaps."

"Yes. In Paris. Now where do you live in Dublin."

"Ha you would so much like to know wouldn't you."

"Do you live with a man. Who supports you."

"Ha I support me. Me I support. But the rest is none of your damn business."

"Madam, let's make love."

"Make love. I am too, soaking fucking wet."

"No need Madam to get excited with such an unladylike expression."

"Well well. Out in zee middle of nowhere. What a thing to ask."

"I withdraw the request."

"Ah that is nice of you. Now get up."

"No. I shall I think Madam, just lie here. Casually let the rain drops fall, boom, bang, bing on my brow."

"They bloody fall on me too. My knee's in muck. And if you don't get up. I am."

"Madam if you leave me like this. I shall never never forgive you. Heavens my heart. And I do think one of my legs is gone."

"Ah my little broken bunny rabbit. Such an actor when you want to be, you are not that injured. With that little leg in your breeches bulging."

"Madam you are being uncommonly unrefined in your references."

"But is it not more that we are getting uncommonly fucking soaked and fucking muddy in this most unladylike and ungentlemanly fashion my darling in zee fucking wet grass."

"O dear, in spite of your vulgar Dublin parlance, I am smitten, Madam. That you will not make love."

"Ah my darling, it is not that I will not. But it is that certain time of the month."

"O no."

"O yes. But."

"But what."

"Ah but but. But."

154

"Tell me what but."

"It would be unladylike. As you say my expression has been. To tell you what but."

"That should not trouble you to be unladylike. For just the merest moment. To tell me something. That's clearly quite important."

"Tell. Who said tell. I shall do."

"What shall you do."

"Ah, I shall do as I am doing. While we are mad to be here in the rain. Try to get it out of these buttons. Mein Gott, like the locks on Colditz."

"What is Colditz Madam."

"It is an old castle with big thick walls and many locks like your buttons, impossible to open."

"O god Madam."

"Ah. Too funny. Just to think once that now again, it is suddenly like it was, my dear little darling."

"O please. Please. Say that to me once more."

"Mein lieber kleiner Liebling, das Glückskind. Ich liebe dich. Sometimes only. Ich liebe dich."

"Ah. Ah. Now tell me what but. I don't of course know exactly what beautiful words you are saying so softly beautifully. Only hope you're not calling me a little fucker or something."

"It is that I shall teach you a lesson you shall not forget. And suck your cock like it has never been sucked before, my dear little bog trotter."

The gates of Colditz unlocked, I did hear the banshees, the fairies, the poucas. Dancing all over the rainbow the bright side of one's brain. Her blond hair, the smooth locks of it netted and curled so neatly up underneath her bowler. And in that dark space underneath there must be the parting straight down the middle of her head. Bouncing up and down over me with the delicious sweet grabbing of her warm soft sucking mouth. Hands stealing up under my waist coat to squeeze pinching on the chill tips of my breasts. This woman. Comes to my rescue. Back into my pale cold world. Kneels between my legs. Akimbo. Strewn upon my back contused in adversity. Take me. So crushed those many months ago in my jealousy. Too shy to ever call you Gwendolene. Hide me somewhere in your life please. Lead me by the hand. Back to your tower. Where e'er it be. In

Dublin. To ring our bell. Whosoever shall clang my goolies. Resounding. Smashing all over the sky. Call me. On this darkening day. Who doth it be who hoots. Call me. To tell what death is. That stops the heart and the blood. That chills the lips to stillness. Melts eyes into darkness. Ah god now if that's death. I'll lead you to plenty that are alive and living. Who said that sound. Who spoke. As the seed gushes spurting. Sucked out of me. A fountain of life. In all this long stale celibacy. Scream at the top of one's lungs. To the ears of birds and beasts that go asleep now. Under the blankets of darkness, clouds close on this earth. Hurrying down over the hills. Sprinkling soft rain again. To wet the side of one's head, purring in bliss. One's cheek on the cold ground.

"Tally ho."

A cry. From the edge of the field. Grey strange bumps adorning an outcropping of rock. Where a face peeks up under a battered trilby hat. In the faded light the blood flooding up from her throat, blushing flagrant red across her cheeks. A flash of shy fear in her eyes. At the laughter and clapping. Shaking her fist. At the voice shouting bravo. And at least perhaps out of all the abysmal insolence all over this land, there is one less stupid fool among them. Saying not as much as Madam's mouthful.

> But bespeaking
> Poetical
> And intellectual
> Appreciations

12

Just over the hill. In the evening shadows. And alongside a mountainous ancient hedge of holly, briar, ash and whitethorn where one called to her, Petunia gave a neigh. And another. Of purring contentment one might say. And there on the opposite hill his great dark silhouette rearing and pawing as if in victory, the mad stallion. His thundering hoofs heard above the rising cold wind, striding out along the edge of the bog land.

"O those awful so ignorant people. Such idiots. I could choke their necks."

Miss von B still complaining, we mounted Petunia and I ferried us back. Miss von B's head occasionally resting on the back of my shoulder, her arms around my waist. I did have to remind her that it was I who continued to live in this countryside and whose name would be on every groom's, skivvy's and farmer's lips all over every parish.

Rashers ensconced in the library. Nervously jumping to his feet as I stuck my head in and nearly upsetting the drawer he held in his lap full of fishing flies tied by my grandfather. One did feel awfully conspicuous being watched by my ever suspicious sisters, past whom I hurried up the stairs. And following on the heels of Crooks showing Miss von B to a room. Having already, in the hall heaped more coals on my fires of jealousy, by again inviting the Mental Marquis to stay. Who was only a moment before to my relief excusing himself.

"Damn sorry, thanks all the same but think I've got to dash."

"O no please don't. You must stay."

"O well. It's a damn long way just to find out that one's groom has burned to a crisp, isn't it. Perhaps I would like to stay and sup as a matter of fact."

"O please do."

O god one had done it again. To invite new sufferings. Although one was feeling a signal relief between the legs. Crooks saying he took the liberty to dig out dinner togs for Rashers. And following my bath, a nap in the tub, dressing and a nice moment of well earned self pity on the down feathers of my mother's chaise longue, I journeyed back to the library door. Just ajar so that I could see in. And there he was sitting solitary. Staring into space. And again jumping to his feet at my appearance.

"Ah Kildare. Back and looking so splendid I see."

"And you too Rashers."

"I hope it's not asking too much but I do wish you might not call me by that name. Would you mind awfully. Somehow it makes me feel, how shall one put it, a little inappropriate in present company. But please call me Ronald."

"Of course. Ronald."

"Thank you, my dear chap. That's awfully good of you."

"Have a drink Ronald."

"O I've already got one thank you. I must say your man Crooks has been marvellously attentive. Had a nice little chat with him. Poor fellow seems a bit lonely in the country. Brought me that drawer of flies to look at. Says he does a bit of fishing. And if his eyes could only see straight he'd also do a bit of shooting."

"Yes, pity about Crooks' eyes. But he does manage to see a lot more with them than can be seen with ordinary eyes."

"You don't say. Hope you don't think I'm meddling my dear chap. I wouldn't want you to think that. But shouldn't you be looking for a wife."

"No. I don't think so."

"O well when one thinks of it, it is nice to simply sit here alone by oneself viewing these extensive volumes on the shelves. Puts one at a loss for words."

Rashers plumping himself down. His hands rubbing the worn shiny bright patches of the leather of the sofa chair. He seemed somewhat subdued but still at an effort to remind me even as bachelor, how well situated one was. As if a thousand or so neglected acres and thirty five or so mouldering rooms and fifteen or so layabouts, servants and staff, into whose hands outstretched every Friday, one deposited a packet of bank note and coin, were the absolute answer to all the problems in this life.

"Took a walk about my dear chap. It is simply quite magnificent. Not to mention how utterly glorious it will be come summer. And that splendid tunnel, like the Appian Way. Don't of course know what the latter thing looks like but nevertheless. In the rain it's a damn good place taking a morning constitutional. Why on earth were you ever in Dublin when you could be here. Making cider out of the apples. Watching the fattening of the damsons, artichokes, blackcurrants, raspberries and gooseberries. You know my dear chap, I should just love to bring my adored precious down to see it all. Keen keen gardener she is. I mean the towering walls surrounding your plethora of pleasure gardens. In the shade of which, come summer of course, one might take tea on the edge of the lawn where one plays croquet. I mean my dear chap, forgive me my trespassing. I wouldn't want to presume. I do sometimes feel as merely an ex Trinity College failed medical student at a disadvantage. I'm only sorry now I didn't take my botany more seriously. In those rather too debauched but nonetheless glorious uproarious undergraduate days."

One did pour oneself a stiff sherry. And nearly drink it back down like water. In this house getting fuller and fuller of inmates. Along with Rashers here whose constant reference to come summer did flash a vision of him still sitting there months hence, wielding a whisk brushing the flies away. And throwing a large bucket of awfully cold water on my spirits. Especially now as one notices that as well as being in my grandfather's dinner clothes and black tie, he is also wearing one of my silk shirts whose cuffs are clasped closed with my pearl inlaid platinum cufflinks bequeathed me by my grandmother. Plus a pair of my socks. Although he did retain his own brown shoes from which his own rather large feet bulged at the laces.

159

"You are aren't you. Kildare, looking at my shoes."

"Yes I believe I was. Sorry."

"Well they're damn hard to fall out of. And no need to apologise my dear chap. My own were stolen by some gurrier newsboy down the catacombs. Had to go barefoot to the pawnshop. Bought these second or third hand. I stupidly preferred their style to size. Damn it my dear Darcy, a man could sit and think in this room, couldn't he. You don't do you, mind my using your Christian name like that. After all I am a guest in your house. And I say this out of my heart. You will never know how grateful I am to you. I mean, the bound volumes of *Punch,* going back to the dawn of ages there on the shelves. You must be able to open one of those and get a jolly good antique laugh out of them."

"Upon occasion yes."

"And you know by god Darcy you've got a real looker in your household. But the glorious creature seemed to vanish like a ghost. Or was I indeed seeing one."

"No."

"Thank god for that. You know, one's mind is apt to play one up in these large country houses. My flat I was chucked out of was the size of a cheese box for an inferior cheese. And this extra space about one does rather let the imagination roam."

At the appearance of my sisters and Miss von B, Rashers did jump to his feet, tight shoes and all, clicking his heels in a military manner and bowing. Miss von B not unflatteringly attired in another one of my mother's gowns. A trifle too short and slightly illfittingly tight about the bosoms. But Rashers was far less military at the appearance of the Mental Marquis. To whom I was just about to introduce Rashers and Miss von B. When Rashers his mouth full of sherry spluttered it out all over the carpet. One thing of course one had learned in Dublin. That many a previous drama had befallen its citizen denizens. Between bar stools, beds and people. And one had that terrible feeling that something very awful was about to happen tonight. It wasn't long before his lordship, pretending to show me some porcelain in an issue of *Country Life,* had taken me aside and whispered.

"That ruddy fellow, Ronald Ronald or Rashers or Bashers or whatever he is called. That bloody bugger was in the Buttery drinking champagne out of a chalice, and did me for fifty quid. As a damn fee of membership to a casino in a basement in Fitzwilliam Square. And also the promise of an introduction to the most beautiful creature. Clarissa. Claimed she was his half sister. But more likely for whom he was pimping. Ruddy fellow did a disappearing act. What on earth is the fellow doing here. In the confines of your house Kildare."

"O him. Goodness. Yes. Well. He is rather here isn't he."

"Well I caught him up once on the street and he ran outright, left me holding his coat with not a blessed thing in it but dinched cigarettes out of the gutter and ruddy pawn tickets. I suppose you're going to ask me if I redeemed them. Of course I damn bloody well did. Quite an interesting place as a matter of fact. The damn bloke had pawned a ruddy toilet bowl, plus the baby's pram he pushed the ruddy thing to the pawn shop in. Suppose it does make you have to treat a chap like that with a certain respect I suppose."

Although in a get up defying domestic description which on scrutiny appeared to be my grandfather's hunting coat much too large for him, and the tails hanging below the backs of his knees, Crooks nonetheless absolutely in his element. But who my god should he have at his heels carrying the trays, and in my old school clothes, his hair plastered back and shifty eyed, but Foxy's brother.

"Master Reginald, begging your permission sir, I needed help you know, what with me knees and the lad here now, I can train him up. Sure half his life spent in the kitchen anyway and we'd make some use of him. And I'd like to be rid of that other one, our Dawn Beauty. Up there, won't answer to her door."

His lordship swallowing down more than a dram or two or three. Emptying the bottle specially got up from the cellar for the ladies. Necessitating Crooks sending Foxy's brother to unearthing yet another bottle. And clearly the little bloody bugger was bug eyed and swaying as he came back later to the door to receive Crooks' whispered growls of chastisement for his long delay. Which one was bloody sure meant having to check the cellar book and record the newly missing bottles, already nearing the very last of the precious few splendid ones remaining. The parsimony lurking in one's soul. As if I were English. But the fateful moment is coming. When Crooks will say, I am sorry sir, but there is no more Madeira, there is no more bloody nothing. And one did, knowing it was going fast, switch from sherry. Crooks murmuring to me as he filled the glass.

161

"Master Reginald this evening brings back memories of your mother my dear Antionette Delia Darcy Darcy Thormond. She would herself have taken pleasure at the company."

Rashers animatedly engaging Miss von B in conversation. Has her laughing. Still feel her lips between my legs still glowing. So comforting to have her here. Mine again. Maybe she wouldn't mind in the morning smartening things up. Go round as she used to with her keys and white gloves. Of course one is daydreaming. Put a log on the fire. In these flames. See Rashers walking bare foot to the pawn. His lordship pushing a pram down the street with a toilet bowl in it wearing a bonnet and bow of pink ribbon. And ah Crooks at the door. Waiting for a lull in the conversation, clearing his throat, bowing. Pursing his lips. And as if from a pulpit announcing.

"Master Reginald, ready whenever you are sir."

Crooks with a couple of extra candelabra had the hallway blazing. Showing perhaps just rather too much of the dilapidation for real delusions of grandeur but I must say in our little procession out the library door and up and around into the dining room, one did feel that nonetheless, the green faded brocaded wall fabric did lend itself well to the moment. With a distinct quickening of the pulse as the ladies' scents softened the sharpness of the hall's cold air. And making our way with perhaps just imagining for a moment, the ladies with tiaras. It all did look rather perfect. Andromeda Park suddenly the grandest of grand places. In the very height of fashion. Until of course, I chanced to see Rashers, who had departed to the toilet and thinking the rest of the guests had already turned the corner, was busy fingering a plate, upturning it to the candle to examine its underside. And even daring to handle a figurine off its plinth. O dear reminded again. That one is instead in the boggiest of the most bereft backwater. I mean damn it, he could ask one were it Meissen or not. Of course that piece is not. But back in the library I did think it strange, how his finger casually tipped up the flap of the silver topped water jug and suspended it as if to test the weight of the metal. I suppose poor chap his life is presently devoid of beautiful things and he wants to keep his finger in. No matter. He does at least help the evening along making it three ladies and three gentlemen. And he could not, no matter how bad he is, be all that bad. Having a friend and loving as he did. O god that name Clarissa. Comes back with tears into one's

162

world. Dropping from its every syllable. To make one shudder. For her beautiful silken pale white skin. Her gay flowing flood of laughter. Suddenly spilling out of her lips. Golden erupting glory. How could her body be pierced. How could she be impaled. Found by a milkman in the morning. On the coldest iron railings. On Stephen's Green. And forever now just a memory in Mr Arland's heart. And perhaps that is why. Rashers. When he did shed tears. For all their inappropriateness. May have shed them for Clarissa. For he too adored her. And yet how could she die. So alive in the minds of those who still live. And I must. Must go on the train. Find Mr Arland. Find him.

There is simply no denying Miss von B's aristocracy. The fluent way she included Rashers and Lavinia in conversation. While Christabel was busy trying to captivate his lordship into making her as soon as possible a marchioness. And before vacating the library, his lordship was giving Rashers the odd glance over Lavinia's shoulder, his alarm lessened considerably. And Rashers keeping very much to the sideline of his own conversation and instantly turning his attention to the forefront of his lordship's louder and most unfunny jokes.

"Ha, ha, ha, couldn't help hearing that in the corner of my ear. Damn funny."

During service of the soup one was all the time wondering where Leila was. As was his Lordship, looking up into the face of Norah, Kitty and Dingbats and hoping the next would be hers. And I was wondering whether she had broken the glass vase deliberately. Just to have reason to lock herself up in her room. With the Marquis' letter. A thought instantly discontinued, as Crooks was serving the wine, by a loud voice erupting in the pantry.

"Put that back away and take your hands this minute off me or I'll give you the hot gravy on top of it. You dirty little rooster."

A few minutes later Norah all red cheeked coming out with the carved slabs of lamb. And followed by equally red cheeked Kitty and Dingbats with bowls of sprouts. And the sound of Foxy's brother giggling in the pantry.

Dear me. All the fun is out there beyond the swing door. Miss von B listening politely to Lavinia get her day's outing off her chest. And talking about chests. In the furnishing sense. One noticed gone from my mother's dressing room, her toilet service. Not that it matters it was Louis the Sixteenth or that it was made in Paris by Boullier, or that I enjoyed to peruse my eye brows occasionally in the mirror and see if my teeth were still growing straight. But what matters is their continued bloody nerve to remove without my leave twenty pieces of silverware plus a pair of Louis Fifteenth silver gilt rocaille quatrefoil dishes by Jean Marie Jan de Villecler, from under my nose. With the both of them now spoutingly full of their own brands of very English foxhunting references.

"The scent was very sketchy today, wasn't it."

And Christabel throwing her tresses over her shoulder and affectedly sniffing at the air, as she tipped salt off the end of her knife, announcing her signal event.

"One does like to travel up front. And I would have but for coming off at that first double bank. Of course it was entirely my own fault."

Not that one is any kind of down to earth purist about foxhunting but I do confess that this latter comment of my sister's does make me utterly impatient. Being that one feels it a detestably phoney attempt to avoid saying. My effing stupid horse didn't watch where he was effing going and didn't know what he was effing doing and threw me off on my effing head. But of course one is lulled into a pleasant reverie listening to the same old hackneyed words.

"Vixen showed her mask twice."

"Yes they spoke to her line for nearly a mile."

"And my dear, did you see that green faced lady, whose horse rolled on her."

"Served her right for not bailing out."

This last remark emitted by his lordship. Now swirling the claret around in his glass before putting it under his nose and tipping it backwards gurgling down his throat. By the door slams Crooks must have seen to Foxy's brother in the pantry. As the food now appeared without the ladies bringing it being so red cheeked. Flushed all over the face like that did make the girls more attractive. And Dingbats was contusing her big tits ever so slightly against my shoulder. And smelling somewhat fusty, but not completely unpleasantly. One should make a household rule of at least one bath per fortnight per person. Or at least monthly. I'm sure they would figure some way to avoid such cleanliness. But Dingbats' reastiness did have a fumy musky quality which I was absolutely astonished provoked the most rigid erection under the table. Making me hesitate to rise to help Crooks prise open the cigar humidor. But one had to leap to action as the poor bugger was going to send the fucking thing skidding to kingdom come across the sideboard any second and knock over the decanters of port. And while I took hold of the snap ring on the humidor to gently prise it up, Crooks whispered to me in what I thought was a conspiratorially approving manner concerning the pantry altercation of Foxy's brother.

"Excuse me. But a bloody little bugger, sir. He had out his John Charles Thomas, stiff as a board, showing it to the girls and I assure you sir there will be no further nonsense of that kind while I'm in charge. You have my word on that."

Kitty now doing a curtsey with the bowl as she served his lordship seconds. Helping himself to about six potatoes, and even, if you please, fishing around underneath for the big ones. And as he did so, chewing upon a slab of lamb as thick as the top front door step. Not that I'm watching how much he drinks or counting how much he eats. But he does damn well quaff gallons and stuff down plenty. It's his fourth ruddy helping of lamb. As he attempts to address his remarks to Christabel across the table.

"Don't want to be an ill sport about it or ruin your appetite my dear but you also did rather come across my front you know at that double bank."

"O dear. Did I. But of course I did. Well I am sorry. But of course there were those loose ponies all over the place. But I do promise I hadn't in the least meant to inconvenience you."

"Ah not to worry my dear, not to worry. It was a wizard prang. And Kildare you missed it, where bloody hell were you."

"O I was searching for my lost horse."

"Well just so long as you weren't off in a copse with one of the ladies. Ha, ha. For a moment there, it was like a catastrophe at Beecher's brook in the National. Marvellous pile up. Too funny for words. With too many damn foolish out hunting without nerves or brakes. And the fisticuffs jolly disappointing."

Amazing how people quickly forget what really happened out on the hunt. Events reported to suit themselves. At any rate I wasn't going to tell him if he already didn't know that I nearly had my brains kicked out by Baptista and then had them blown out by Miss von B. But it seemed the perfect moment as Mr Arland had taught me, to raise my glass to the latter lady to skoal her in the Swedish manner.

"Your Highness, skoal."

"Skoal, Mr Kildare."

But Miss von B's eyes did not, as they should have, before replacing her glass to the table, linger for just that perfect length of time looking back into mine. Mostly perhaps because everyone reacted like scalded cats to my use of the title, your highness. Of course his lordship was more concerned with it not appearing that I might have one up on him in tableside manners albeit of the Arctic Circle variety. And he bloody well went most inappropriately skoaling everyone as if he were host. And in the process, putting away in his pot belly another three bottles of claret.

"Even though I don't know whether Stockholm or Oslo is the capital, I do think these Swedes a damn interesting race, don't you Kildare. Like the way they've rather chucked some of the tighter morals out of the cockpit. Not that loose morals should be everybody's cup of tea. But their endless stony silences with each other are to be admired. Wonderful the way a whole nation locks themselves away in huts up their fiords to be alone and to think. Listening to the trees falling down in the forest. Scratching their arses up there at the north pole. Damn interesting."

One could sense Miss von B utterly itching to say something to his lordship, not the least that fiords were ocean inlets and not forests, but each remark out of his mouth received such an approved reaction of hear hear from Rashers, that she never got the chance to speak. Or perhaps, better said, to jump down his throat. Anyway Crooks putting the port safely on the table. And after his lordship has polished it off one might reasonably contemplate its being not too long before bed. I've already nodded off twice asleep. Kitty now serving out the ice cream. Dingbats following with the sauce. And everyone unbelievably, except myself and Miss von B, taking a second helping. Perhaps coaxed by his lordship's comment.

"How jolly damn good. Best ice cream I've ever tasted."

Of course one was quite prepared to believe his lordship. That Catherine's ice cream was a dream. But doing as I most carefully always do, when I am about to eat in this household, I lean and sniff

166

first. And there was no doubt that upon my plate was ice cream. But one smelling of the distinct essence of lightly congealed giblets and other barnyard avian innard derivatives used for the making of gravy which one had liberally applied to the lamb, sprouts and potatoes from Dingbats' previous sauceboat. The others obviously thinking those nice little chunks floating in the creamy dark brown were chips of choicest chocolate to be savoured. Which the household had got its hands upon. His lordship having ladled it on liberally, continuing to shovel the whole concoction up.

"My kitchen should have this recipe Crooks. What about it."

"No trouble at all Your Grace. None whatever. Be pleased to accommodate you."

Amazingly how long one awaited some uproar or even slight question. Although after the first few mouthfuls, Rashers who continued eating, did start looking suspiciously up the table at me. And Dingbats coming round with seconds of sauce my sisters and Miss von B politely declined. As each mouthful went more and more slowly into each mouth and there got chewed or melted or whatever what. However my sisters finally were looking at each other and making not at all nice faces back down at their plates. But his Lordship, whatever is amiss with the man's taste bloody buds, even bloody well is on his third helping. As Crooks evaluates him to a dukedom.

An agitated Crooks bursting back into the dining room. Rubbing his hands together and then sweeping up the tails of his hunting coat. And frothing I thought the merest bit at the mouth. And licking his lips, his eyes neatly focused, one beaming each side of the Mental Marquis' head and at the most opposite angle to each other I have ever seen them achieve.

"Your Grace forgive us. I fear there has been a mistake. That is the gravy from the lamb sir. On your ice cream."

"Well get me the bloody recipe for the gravy then my dear man."

What's sauce
For the goose
Is bloody well
Damn savoury
For the gander

13

The poor ladies having withdrawn to the east parlour where they were rapidly freezing to death, gave up waiting upon us and retired to bed. Sending their apologies via Crooks. Who was, with his every syllable on the verge of laughter, only just able to get the words out of his mouth at the dining room door.

"Master Reginald, the ladies following the long day's hunt ask your respectful pardon to proceed to their bedchambers."

The news that the Mental Marquis wanted the recipe for the gravy for future ice cream sent Crooks into a state one had never before seen him enter and did not indeed think he would ever exit from. Before he withdrew his head back into the hall, paroxysms of mirth simply racked him bodily. And just as one spasm waned another succeeded it. Then while fetching port he let go of the two full decanters, his laughter now hysterical, sending his false teeth, upper and lower, flying out of his mouth, which he then crunched under foot. Holding his stomach and sides as if they were to be unhinged from him. Until I thought the man would become sick. Which would have been less expensive than his bumping into the side table and his full weight collapsing its delicate leg. The decanters through some miracle remained stoppered and unbroken. Crooks finding this additionally amusing, and totally out of control of himself, reeling out the door, where one found him doubled over in the hall.

"Good god, Crooks are you alright."

"Sir O I beg you excuse me. Sincerely excuse me. And forgive me. But that was funny enough about the gravy but when Catherine down the kitchen heard tell of it didn't she fall over the pig bucket and straight into the bucket full of eggs."

"I see. I suppose they were the eggs for breakfast."

"Well they were sir and won't they be well scrambled now by Catherine's backside."

Darcy Dancer leading Crooks off to bed. Up the main stairs. Crooks doubling up yet again. Hands cupping themselves over his stomach. Over his most recent and mercifully last little joke. As the damn man is drunk. Lame, footless and incapable. Heavier and heavier as one drags and pulls him forward in the dark. Down his lonely long hall. Up his own little steps into his anteroom. And wind and rain pouring in the open window of his chambers. Of course one had to just drop him like a sack of potatoes on the bed. And throw my grandfather's old leather motoring coat over him. Under which, between groans, he still spluttered and laughed.

"Ah Master Reginald, I'm done for. I'm finished. Sure I'm just an old butler who's sharpened his last knife. Look at me teeth. O dear O dear. Buggered they are. Buggered. Squashed like a beetle."

"You must not fuss Crooks. Mr Kelly the dentist will have them right as rain again."

"Don't I look a sight though in the meantime. With me cheeks caved in and me chin up near me nose. Ah god even with me eyes askew I am plenty handsome enough to attract the ladies."

"Of course you are Crooks."

"Cut a figure I do. When I have a mind. But now look at me. Sure what one of them decent ladies of this household would have even five minutes' time to spare now on an old butler minus his teeth. Sure it's only four paces there to that door. To hang myself inside from the rafter, like the two of me predecessors. Would you pass me now that bottle of the cough linctus medicine next to me clock on the mantel, Master Reginald."

One did stand momentarily trepidatory out in the hall wondering

169

if Crooks would string himself up. But the bottle of medicine, by its aromatics, clearly containing my best vintage Armagnac, would further assure Crooks not having the strength to stand up to get his neck properly in the noose. And one does rest quite assured that one will still have a butler albeit toothless in the morning. And perhaps even less than half dead.

Two candles burning in the dining room. Where I sensed much embarrassed silence may have ensued in the cigar smoke during my absence. But the fire still blazing a pleasant soft glow. Upon my reseating, his lordship sipping his port, wasting no time in getting on to the subject of ladies. Whether they were to be better enjoyed long before or shortly after dinner. And whether the Pope, to whom his lordship referred as the big guinea left footer in Rome, had the usual Neapolitan tart preferred by pontiffs as his main mistress or was the Vatican importing fluff and ecclesiastical arse from all over the kip including Sweden. Prompting the first real comment from Rashers all evening. Which he rather heatedly directed towards his lordship whose eyebrows did raise.

"I happen if you don't mind to be a left footer you know."

"Ah forgive me my dear chap. If I did tread on your toes. But it is to my astonished surprise that you have any religion at all. Never mind being a left footer. But as you are of that regrettable persuasion, let me fill you up with some good Protestant preserved port then, sir."

Clear consternation on his countenance, nevertheless Rashers pushing his glass forward under the flow of wine. His voice spluttering out.

"Should it concern you in the least, sir, the fact of the matter is I'm a left footer by virtue of my mother. I am however to the Protestant manner born. I know I deserve your remarks. And I do regret that your membership in the casino was not possible to effect on the night in question. It rather became difficult for the club when someone was found stabbed under the roulette table."

"I see. A knife probably in the back."

"Yes it was as a matter of fact. And I'm awfully sorry about your fifty quid. I have every intention of returning it. I'm a bit short at the moment."

"I see. Perhaps since you were unable to pay it into the hand of your club treasurer it temporarily went down your throat. Or I daresay if not that, on the back of a horse."

"Yes as a matter of fact, both. I drank ten and put forty on The Bug to win. But you may not know that the toilet bowl you redeemed from my pawn ticket is of a very high quality of pottery. And comes of a well known sanitary manufacturer."

"Well forgive me my dear chap if, just below Tara Street bridge, I ran both it and the pram off the quay into the Liffey thinking as I did so that a pity you weren't in it. Pram floated out to sea. But I'm sure your pottery's still there preserved in the mud."

In Rashers' hurt and subdued voice an angry edge was evident. In spite of what obviously his presently somewhat testy lordship represented in the way of a marvellous oasis of perhaps future invitations to hunt, shoot, fish, dine and drink on his estates. And his lordship was clearly gathering up his vowels to let Rashers have further what for in the solar plexus. Rashers suddenly getting up to rap the table with his glass.

"Pray silence. My lords, gentlemen. Permit me to recite some poetry. From the temporary depths of my dulcet toned Catholic testicles when they choose to chime and rhyme."

Rashers indeed was beginning to show for the first time his true form. I must confess I was spellbound as he then reeled off stanza after stanza of The Old Orange Flute. And to feel from his fervour that he might, standing up to his oxters in Catholic gore and papist's blood, have composed the damn words himself. But by god he did have his lordship's attention momentarily. Especially finally singing the last lines.

"So the ould flute was doomed, and its fate was pathetic. It was fastened and burned at the stake as a heretic. And while the flames roared they all heard a strange noise, 'twas the ould flute still playing the Protestant Boys."

But as Rashers rendered a further few risqué couplets of another ditty suggesting less than noble references to ladies in general, one sensed his lordship a little shocked. But he did clap rather politely and ask rather pointedly.

"Aside from reassuring us that the road to hell is paved with popery, what else can you do my dear chap, or to whom, perhaps one should say."

"As you may just have noticed from my divertissement I am a tenor sir."

171

"Ah so I did notice. And I'm sure our host will not mind your singing for your supper. Some other time. And dear chap do sit down. Surely you don't mean to curdle our port with a further medley of vocalized silly octaves. As you are sir, the most blatant mediocrity I think I have ever had the boredom to meet and your poetic pretensions are positively ludicrous and without the redeeming feature of being amusing."

Rashers' face flushed with fury, for a moment I thought he was about to swing the decanter of port crashing on his lordship's head. Or at least send a fist into the Marquis' gob. And by the way Rashers' hands were tightly knotted, Rashers must have thought he was too. But he stood rigidly silent. Taking into his lungs a long slow breath. And as the first shimmering tenor notes of Annie Laurie left Rashers' lips I shivered in awe as the hair stood up on the back of my neck. His lordship's hand loosened on the bowl of his glass and fell away on the table, his mouth open as he sat utterly transfixed. Not even the candle flame flickering. And in the dim light of the dining room, as the last note came vibrating from Rashers' throat, and was held shimmering in the air for what seemed a blissful heavenly eternity, the tears were tumbling down the Marquis' face.

"My god, I'm touched. My dear fellow. Touched. To the depths. To the marrow. The Count. The Count must be turning over in his grave. With envy. I retract my former most rude remarks. And sir if I were not so smitten here and so devilishly presently comfortable I would be upon my feet pumping your hand up and down in the utmost humble homage to your person. You are without doubt among the great tenors of this age."

Rashers' glowing eyes. His lips smiling. To see us both so stricken. Worshipping at his altar. Yet he remained so childlike in his joy at our appreciation. He was a dear man at this moment. So humbly eagerly delighted by our praise. Beaming at the Marquis. The Marquis beaming back. As if he had discovered both the north and south poles by flipping a coin backwards over the shoulder. And was now just back in the cozy fire lit confines of the Geographical Society. O dear one does conjure up ridiculous ideas. But I did think his lordship was carrying it just a little bit too far with his great long sighs and shakings back and forth of his head. But I must confess I did shiver right down to the bottom of one's limbs. And even though one knows not a fig about bloody singing in the professional sense, I could imagine awed gatherings of folks in village halls all over Ireland opening up their hearts and pocket books to this voice. And even on the Tara Street bridge, a hat, or ten dozen hats, being passed around to be filled with ten bob notes. And who knows what would happen in other more sophisticated capitals. With such accumulation of riches Rashers could return home to Eire. Buy himself a piece of land and raise, during summer grazing, sturdy young beef bullocks.

"Please do excuse me gentlemen, while I fetch more port."

Darcy Dancer a candle held aloft, proceeding along the hall. The footfalls echoing. Down to the cellars. Fingertips so cold. How sad it all is, somehow. That such beauty sung has lain unknown in another's breast. Perhaps one needs this evening over. This day done. For its non ending, utterly non ending sudden twists and turns draining of one's emotions. Living in the country should be quiet. Like in these cobwebbed stone vaults. Instead of dramatic. But dear me the sweetness of his dulcet vowels still weaves into one's senses. Filling one with such an awakened fervour. To indeed love. To cherish life. To wrap arms around and even kiss misfortune. It of course too does mean yet another trip down to fetch up more port. Carefully ferry it back. And in the precipitous process upset the lees in the bottom of the bottle. And her. Her soul. Up there. In that room. From whence she might fly and go away. And leave me. So totally distressful. And in this moment of sadness as I pull on this cork. The dining room door my god bursts open. Kitty and Norah. Kitty shouting.

"Come quick sir, come quick, it's Crooks, Crooks, he's hung himself sir. He's up there his feet kicking in the butler's hanging room."

At least one did wonder, while this nice brand new disaster was so typically unfolding, if the contorting rope around Crooks' neck would in some manner, as his eyes bulged out of their sockets, perhaps bring them back into alignment once more. Rashers, like a hound dog, eagerly awaiting me to show the way, and was indeed quite perturbed. No doubt contemplating a future absence of attendance being danced upon him. His lordship, however took a different view.

"O dear another servant's demise. Well Kildare, damn it, it does remind one I've left my groom roasted to a crisp. Do give a shout if you need help dear boy. I mean a decent butler is a damn sight harder to replace than a groom."

And the ruddy bunch of the rest of us skidding out the dining room door. Ruddy charging lickety split up the stairs. Rashers crashing into a side table on the way. The edge getting him in the lower stomach and doubling him up and one hopes not nearly castrating him.

"Sod it. Sod it. My dear man. Light the bloody way will you before I kill myself."

In the butler's suicide room, Crooks draped in my grandfather's motoring coat, a mauve scarf of my mother's at his throat. The hanging rope up over the rafter but the noose hopelessly under one armpit and only half around his neck. His rosary beads in his hand. But instead of mumbling his Hail Marys he was moaning and feebly kicking the wall, slowly turning and twisting in a circle, a chair turned on its side beneath him.

"Cut me down, cut me down. Let me die on me back in peace. Give me the viaticum. O Lord in thy greatest mercy release the spirit of this humble butler on this earth to join you in heaven and be eternally blessed."

Rashers on the chair severing the rope. As Crooks fell down into our arms, and between his religious outbursts, clearly adoring all the attention. But now demanding as he was carried back into his bedroom and laid out on the bed.

"Give me me teeth. I am without me teeth."

Crooks' room remarkably neat. Copies of *Tatler and Sketch* on a side table. His sofa chair with slippers parked in front of it and several dressing gowns hanging on the back of his door. But with his crushed teeth back in his mouth, and parts protruding between his lips, one cheek bulging, regrettably made him look like a vampire. Never mind, despite being drunk as a lord, he assumed the prostrate manner of a dying monarch on his bed, folded hands intertwined with his rosary, his body composed. Indeed with his crossed eyes closed and disregarding the disfigurement of a projecting point of one of his canine teeth, he did present a remarkably handsome countenance. And one could actually imagine the ladies giving him more than a tumble.

Darcy Dancer, Kitty, Rashers and Norah tiptoeing away out of the room. Leaving Crooks snoring asleep. Darcy Dancer excusing himself from Rashers on the landing. To head back up into this house. You might know that Crooks in his hopeless efforts to hang himself had most suitably dislocated his shoulder. And one chooses this moment to go back and find her door. Hesitating twice up the stairs. Racked with nerves. And even turning back. Until I was suddenly overwhelmed with anger. One had never before gone supplicatingly to knock on a servant's chamber. But there was light inside. Standing in the dark the toes of one's evening slippers illumined by the faint glow under the door.

"What do you want."

"I've come to enquire to see how you are. And if you were disturbed by the commotion."

Darcy Dancer standing in the silence. The cold draught blowing along this hall. Waiting. A vixen barking out in the frosty night. The squeaks and groans of the floorboards. O dear the poor lady, perhaps in there sick and ill. But the door opening. Her face. Quite magnificently beautiful in the shadow. And beyond, a candle lit on the black chimney piece. The low ceiling curving up over her narrow bed of this narrow room. Chill and damp. Strewn everywhere with bits of clothing. Torn pieces of paper. Two photographs propped up against the edge of a book. And next to them an envelope. Staring at me.

"May I. Please. Just come in."

"Suit yourself."

"You have no fire."

"No."

"But you must."

"I am alright as I am."

"But you might become sick and ill."

"Please do not worry about me."

"But have you eaten. You haven't have you. I will have something brought you."

"No please don't."

And all these terrible hours of agonizing jealousy spent. With her being all over my mind. Relieved only by the tribulations befalling me. As she sits on the edge of her narrow bed. Or stood that evening ghost like at the whim room window. All these scraps of paper on her floor. The room in such utter disarray. So unlike everything else she's so neatly done in this household. Including breaking a vase. Which may have been more precious than I dare to contemplate.

"Perhaps you ought to say why you really have come. It is isn't it, because I broke your vase and for that I can tell you I am most heartily sorry. And I will, no matter how long it takes, I will repay you for it."

"Please you mustn't say that. Every day crystal is broken, silver is scratched and bent, porcelain smashed. That vase is the merest of tragedies."

"You do say tragedy, don't you."

"That word merely slipped out. I really don't mean it in its sense applied to the vase but to you, that you might think it a tragedy."

"You can't get out of it. I know how valuable it was. And I will, and you must let me, pay you back."

"O god Madam. O god. You can, can't you, so distress me."

"Do I."

"Yes. When I don't see you. And haven't talked to you. And saw you at the whim room window as we rode off today."

"And why do you refer to me as Madam."

"I don't know. But somehow I must just feel the title is appropriate."

"I go there just to stand to look out. When I am upset. And I have to be alone then. I watched you once come up across the park on your horse one evening a while ago. I know it's presumptuous of me to go into that room at all."

"Please don't feel that."

"Mr Crooks has given me my notice."

"I'm the only one who can give you your notice. And I have not and do not choose yet to do so."

"But I may choose yet to do so."

"And for that I would be most heartily sorry. And where would you go and what would you do."

"There are so many places I could go. To Dublin. I could find work in a shop."

"But you would have to live on a mere pittance. A shop girl earns nothing."

"I would manage. I have managed before this."

"Please don't go. And we shall talk again, shan't we, like this. Perhaps somewhere alone. Would you mind. We could meet on a walk. Tomorrow. In the afternoon before tea. There is a little old boathouse on the lake about a mile along the old farm road through the forest.

Will you meet me. Please say yes. That you will. Now I must rush back to my guests. I know you know one of them quite well. Don't you."

"I don't wish to reply to your question, please. And if I am at the boathouse, I am there. And if not, I am not."

"Which may mean you won't be."

"It may not."

One did go on one's gloomy way down the stairs. The note of doubt in her voice. Sad and cold as the shadows of the beech grove trees were out in the wintry darkness as one passes on the landing back to the dining room. Where now sat my guests. And two greater pals it would be hard to find. That the Mental Marquis and Rashers had become in one's absence. One might have even thought they had fallen in love. Looking as they were beyond the purple ruby port into each other's blue eyes. The Marquis in some awe to find Rashers' father a distinguished General he had long admired. Who it would appear had won in the field of battle nearly every military distinction possible, including the Military Cross three times. And it would also appear that the Mental Marquis was nearly as distinguishingly entitled and decorated. Rashers quick to inform me in his lordship's momentary absence to take a piss.

"My dear fellow, the Marquis, don't you realise it, is a military hero. One of RAF's leading aces. Downed Germans all over the kip, rat tat tat tat tat, all over the sky. Isn't that wonderful. Don't you realise."

"Well Rashers, clearly I have no option as you seem to insist on it with some hysteria."

"I must. Absolutely must repatriate his fifty quid. And much sooner than pronto. You couldn't my dear man, could you, see it in your heart, in view of these circumstances of which I was absolutely unaware previously to give me the brief loan of the ten fivers required."

"I have already returned to you a previous loan of two fivers."

"Of course you have, my dear boy, of course you have."

"And that makes only forty pounds you require."

"Of course it is, my dear boy, of course it is. How silly of me not to realise. Of course. Forty will do. Of course it will. Good of you to point it out to me."

"But I have not said I shall give you forty."

"Of course you haven't my dear boy, of course you haven't."

"Or indeed said I even have such a sum."

"I shall never again ask of such a favour as I am doing upon this most desperate occasion. I promise you that my dear chap. Absolutely promise and cross my heart, not ever to do so again. If you can accommodate me on this moment of most desperate moments."

Of course there were now tears in Rashers' eyes. His lips were not perhaps trembling but it was interesting to find that I was in fact looking closely at them to see if they were. It was impossible to tell if one were confronting the biggest lying impostor of all time. In the soft candlelight. The pleading look. Of utter genuineness. And even reinforced somehow by the lurking smile that would steal on his face and carefully recede under his look of stricken abysmal disappointment and sorrow.

"O my dear boy. Recently and frequently, woe, trial and tribulation have been my lot. And I know. I simply absolutely know. You shall not on this most poignant occasion at least. Will you. Disappoint me."

Rashers' hand stealing out to place itself on my arm. And revealing my cufflinks under my nose. But his other hand firmly grasping his glass of port. His eye flicking towards the small amount remaining in the just recently refilled of the last of the two decanters. No question but that Rashers in his most soulful desperation was managing to keep an eye out for more mundane matters.

"It grieves me my dear Darcy that I cannot at this time bestow upon you equal favours. You must please realise that."

Rashers' fingers gently squeezing upon one's wrist. Yet there was some redeeming warmth in even his most extreme, crassest attempts at purloining some new favour of one and taking advantage of one's compassion. One does so want to be kind. Forgiving. Anoint tenderness to the suffering. But then from whom does one obtain it in return. To replenish that which one gives. Minor betrayals forgiven do seem to beget major ones in one awful hurry. Dear me, so much better to swear utter unrelenting revenge from the start. And present an implacability against blandishment and beseeching. For to give in seems only to have the effect of people looking for more. And my god just as the last of funds disappear. The once adequate stacks of five pound notes. Now a mere handful.

Darcy Dancer with a candlestick glowing, opening the safe in the estate office. The old rent table with its drawers worn with the coins that once filled it up so consistently. The tenants for miles around outside the door as they stood waiting, caps in hands to pay. Or as my grandfather said, were more likely waiting to spin a tissue of lies and fibs why they couldn't. But gone. Those days. Gone. More's the pity. We were kindly landlords. Despite the bullets fired at the walls and shutters which might indicate we were not.

Rashers there in the candlelight just as one had left him. And putting back down a pepper mill on the table. His fingers seemed to touch and feel the table ware. Perhaps he has, as does the Marquis, a vast knowledge of antiques. Certainly he bloody knows the sight of eight Irish five pound notes when he sees them.

"O my dear boy, thank you. Thank you. My dear fellow, you are, aren't you, a dear brick. You are. So many have been less than nice to me recently, not that it matters when such behaviour comes from people I would not normally associate with. His lordship will appreciate knowing that honourable standards are the unquestioned norm in your household."

"Rashers do please shut up. I cannot afford that. And I do want that money back. And it is the very last penny you will get from me."

"I shall be mum as you request. But must voice my feelings as I cannot be less than truly and utterly grateful to you my dear boy."

Darcy Dancer on yet another trip to the cellar. For yet another bottle of port. His lordship returned from peeing and feeding his horse. Back now purring in the company of Rashers. Listening to him discoursing on the subject of silver.

"The French do not exceed us in the purity of morals but they do in the purity of their silver. By three point three percent. To put a fine point on it. Now this rather nice sugar caster, made by Gabriel Sleuth I do believe seventeen nineteen."

"Upon my sweet smelling socks my dear man, not only the century's greatest tenor but you do don't you know your ruddy silver onions. You must join my London club. Isn't that right don't you think, Kildare. Skoal Kildare. Skoal."

The Mental Marquis his port aloft, turning his happy smiling and inebriated face towards Darcy Dancer. A gust of wind outside. Trembling the shutters, flickering the candle flame. One would think I was now on the election committee of the Marquis' club. And he's oblivious to the fact that as yet I have never even set foot in London. Must say one does feel a bit miffed. With his Lordship previously implying that the membership of his London club was small, discreet and très select. To put a French word on it. Albeit Rashers in proper footwear, does cut an acceptably fine figure. But one does think the Marquis is growing his hair far too long around the edges of his baldness. And by the look on his face clearly has another and different subject on his mind.

"Well chaps, I'm tight as a newt, should we let our hair down. Instead of precious metals, what about matters of the flesh. Ah Rashers I see you're listening attentively to this presently pissed peer. Well one shouldn't discuss one's old papa but that's how lessons in life are learnt. The Duke took up with an actress. Damn scandal's all over London. And damn all seems I can do about it. Very flighty but very beautiful young lady. Can't sing a note but a wonderful speaking voice she has. Is running the poor old goat ragged out of his mind. Getting her flowers to the theatre on time. Insisting he do errands for her. Even in restaurants she tries to turn the old Duke into a waiter. He set her up in an absolutely palatial flat in Mount Street. Four bloody bathrooms. And then the creature would lock him out. And when he did get in, ready to roger her with his semi annual erection, poor old devil, she'd be dead asleep snoring in bed. That's the thing about women isn't it. They want everything their own sweet way. Now what I want to know from you worldly chaps is how do I straighten the old devil out. I love my papa you know. But the poor old Duke, must occasionally give him his due. Third time the lady snored asleep, he had his chauffeur fetch a suitably wieldy fish from Billingsgate Market and he bloody well whacked her awake with slaps across the cheeks of the face and the arse. Bit of a struggle of course the lady being strong for her diminutive size. Duke's no slouch either. Outstanding huntsman, Master of Foxhounds. Keeps fit wood chopping. Left the lady at the time a bit smelly of course to climb on. But what the devil. I mean if he had daily or weekly erections, fine, but damn it, the poor old bugger deserved getting his rocks off. She maintains she gets her rocks off on stage. What about that chaps. You think that possible. I mean that we're there innocently in the stalls watching the mimes strutting on stage mouthing drama while they're coming in their drawers. Well gentlemen. Speak up. You're being of no damn help here. Rashers. What about it."

"Well it does rather make one think doesn't it."

"Damn right it does, sir. Damn right. Of course one thought matters would improve when the old Duke moved her diminutive ladyship within the Division Bell area. Into a big old mansion flat down the shadowy labyrinths of Westminster. Thought she'd get up to less mischief. In Mount Street. She threw flower pots at passers by. Then put all the bath taps on and flooded the building out. But of course the old Duke likes taking tea at the House of Lords. He'd walk her to the theatre. Pair of them could be seen crossing St James's Park hand in hand. And that sight I must say was rather touching. Of course gentlemen you both have the utter looks of ruddy astonishment on your faces. You're wondering how I know all this. Another story that. Suffice to say on this occasion I was actually following the poor old goat and her ladyship across the park trying to keep him out of trouble. Well in their usual manner they went sauntering out Queen Street at dusk and into the park. They'd crossed the bridge. Then the pair of them stopped the other side near the pond. And embraced. I thought how sublimely enviable. They truly are in love. I'd stopped to contemplate the ducks the other end of the bridge. And then the dear girl, just as the Duke seemed to be getting somewhat steamed up, suddenly shoved the old goat backwards flying off the shore into the pond. Water's not too deep but poor old bugger can't swim a stroke. He was left floundering and gasping. While she ran away laughing. I had to wade in and drag him to shore. It was ruddy attempted murder. I confronted her in her dressing room at the theatre and she denied the whole thing. Of course one doesn't want headlines ablaze in *The News of the World*. Duke Dunked by Saucy Star of West End Farce. Of course if I really felt the lady was malicious instead of mad, I'd damn certain inform the police. Now what I want to know from you two gentlemen being men of the world, don't you agree that the old Duke should give this lady up. What have you got to say Kildare. She professes lesbian tendencies as well. The Duke has more than once caught her with her tongue down some other lady's throat."

"Well, the Duke may in fact be having a good if surprising time of it."

"Well that's what I thought Kildare exactly. But is his old heart

going to stand up to it. Well I suppose, what's a chap to do sometimes. But get into his low cut gown and hack on as the braver of the
ladies do. As soon as the pair of them were back on terms again the
Duke planned a Sunday and Monday in Paris. The old fool waiting
in their carriage compartment at Victoria Station after the theatre.
She got the old bugger worked up and then just before the train left,
said she wanted to meditate a moment alone. And stepped off the
train just as it was leaving. Poor old Duke went trundling off by himself to Folkestone. I love my papa. Hate to see him suffer. Damn sad.
But damn if the old Duke didn't make the most of it. Somehow got
himself a doxy. Spent an agreeable two weeks with her at the Crillon.
With the actress screaming abuse at him down the long distance telephone. Hate to talk of one's old pops in this manner, but damn it,
I've got to look after the old fool. He sets one a lesson. Of course the
lady's a brilliant actress. When he got back from Paris she said she'd
meet him by the fountain in Sloane Square for tea. Then disguised as
a cockney waif she waylaid the poor old Duke, led him off into a side
street, revealed her identity and kicked him in the balls for his
infidelity. He adores her for it. That is of course what is somewhat
worrying. When he is so enthralled, you don't know what the old
Duke may suddenly do with his codicils in his final will and testa-
ment. Imagine he might even marry. The bloody lady actress could
end up mistress of his English and Scottish estates. Duke's been a wid-
ower now a long time. Once had a most beautiful mistress too. Got
killed in a hunting accident. For years he was mourning her, with his
hatchet faced housekeeper keeping every presentable lady away from
the Duke by one means or another. Now gentlemen is one better with
a steady lady of pleasure. Which only involves throwing the girl a
fiver or two now and again. I mean she would have sufficiently ad-
ministrated her charms with the punters to be even able occasionally
to agreeably pretend she was a faithful wife. For the novelty of course.
But I mean if the knot's tied. The actress lady will after all be a
Duchess. And if the old bugger ever expires, be my ruddy singular
parental step mother. Big difference you know, being right up there as
a Duchess. So many damn Barons and Earls around these days. I
think it's a mistake to be too blasé about one's title. Even if it's in
courtesy only. I do so love my Debrett handle so much. Even though
the damn thing shames me. Utterly shames me too, to adore it. Meet

these twits who pretend to find it a burden. Chaps, to me it's bliss. Gives one a bloody sense of belonging. Down the ages. I mean it takes ten minutes to change into rags. And that bloody well quicko teaches you a lesson. Old Duke does it from time to time. Took a leaf out of the actress's book. Stood in disguise one Sunday at Victoria Station with a placard proclaiming the wisdom of eating fresh fruit, nuts and fish. Smalls our butler, coming back that day down from visiting his elderly dying mom in the country, chanced upon him there and walked up and said. Is it you, your Grace. Of course it's me, Smalls. And can't you damn well read the sign. Go home and eat fresh fruit, nuts and fish as it says. What do you think I'm standing here for. Well chaps, a lot said tonight. Thing we must remember to love is a woman. Really love her. And from her we must require fidelity. Love her chaps. Love her. We must. We must. And you Rashers my dear chap are wearing brown bloody shoes sizes too small for you. But what, gentlemen are any of us ever ever going to do for humanity at large. Ah I see you Ronald, I'll call you that as Rashers seems to make you wince. I see a question burning upon your face."

"Well I really would like to know how you possibly know so much about your father's intimate life."

"I chanced upon the lady's locked up diary in the Westminster flat. Brought it to a locksmith and then to a typist. I have the voluminous volume on my bedside table. From time to time on matinee days I had it updated. Possibly the most disgusting document ever penned by a human being in history. Most of it unspeakable even by club after dinner standards. The Marquis de Sade, dear man could have learned something from these pages. I mean among the most mild references, a long long discourse on the amounts of sperm this lady has had discharged into her mouth. And remarking on the quality. Including damn it, the Duke's. You wouldn't think a woman could be so contemplative about such an intimately squeamish matter. And at what depth of penetration into that orifice discharge took place. I mean I don't want to be a prude gentlemen. But there are limits you know."

"But you are reading her diary."

"Of course I am Kildare. In the interests of my father whom I love dearly. And the cheeky lady informed him that she must remain celibate for six months. And in the next bloody sentence in the diary, she's picked up a raunchy, her word not mine, female member of the military she's met in the underwear department of Harrods and took her back to Westminster and had it off with the Naval lady for an entire night. Using bloody appliances including blessed left footer candles I might add, attached to their persons what's more. I mean that's morally fraudulent. The old Duke paying her medical and grocery bills. Although the old Duke never made it above Major he is an Army man. And of course she and the Naval lady who went absent without leave, are at it hammer and leather thongs and iron tongs and ruddy priapisms."

"But mournful as her infidelity may be, surely isn't that the lady's own business."

"Of course Rashers or rather Ronald, of course but I haven't said what my present dilemma is chaps. She's discovered I've copied the diary, and the bloody lady's now in correspondence with a filthy literature publisher in Paris and threatening to have it published. Word for bloody word. Names included. She wants five thousand quid. And the flat. And the furniture. Including a Gainsborough, two Turners and a Bonvicino. Not to mention the pair of French rouge marble and ormolu candelabra and torchères by Sormani in the bathing light of which she writes her diary. One does get awfully depressed you know. Damn lawyer's bills mounting up. I suppose it's all cheap at the price if we can chuck the lady but it's the feelings of my father I mind. She doesn't give a tinker's curse how she hurts the poor old gentleman. Taunting him. I mean, as genuine as a Duke's love is capable of being, which is not very, he does at least seem to feel it for this wretched lady. But dear me I do rave on. Of course now the bloody lady is trying to kill the Duke. Made him meet her in Sloane Square, in the freezing cold. Then steps out of a taxi in a sheer evening gown and says she wants to go for a walk to Victoria Station. And the Duke chivalrously removing his coat to put on her. Of course by the time the poor old shivering devil got into the safe warm confines of the Grosvenor Hotel at Victoria Station he was having pneumonia. He must have damn silly well said she'd hear something to her benefit from his lawyers when he popped off, what. I demanded to see her back stage, said what the devil do you mean pushing my old pop into the pond at St James's. She has these eyes, I don't know what they did to me but I could not say another word. And the very worst happened of course, I fell in love with her. I proffered an assignation and she said my dear, you're not the Duke yet, you know. And the damn old goat is still seeing the girl."

The Mental Marquis' hands were strangely delicate under their hairy exterior and clearly immensely strong. And somehow sad. One would never think he might have had these mournful occasions concerning his father. Or would protect the old gentleman so in his dotage. But he does get back on the subject of the actress and the Duke every time the port was passed to him.

"Of course we never think we ourselves will ever be old men one day, and we won't of course. Die young that's my motto. Drink to it, chaps, shall we. Welcome to the club, both of you. Ah we shall have many similar dinners, what. Grow old together, what. Man must have men to talk to you know. Every bloody thing you say to a woman can be taken the wrong way. Used bloody well against you. Damn nuisance in conversation. I'm not suggesting we have to be homosexuals about it but short of that, a man's company is the most satisfying thing in the world. You run a nice little squadron here, Kildare. Let's drink to it. And be damned hypocrisy, what."

After we had all taken a good long pee off the front steps his lordship did suggest we mount up again on fresh horses and ride the rest of the night away. However after a few miles I did suggest that one's dinner clothes were freezing me to death and that since the moon was hardly evident we were certain to be killed. Although there was no doubt that it cleared the port from one's brain. The damn Marquis however insisted we race the stretch up the front park lawn for a fiver, which I lost, the evening now having cost me on top of being a generous host an additional total of fifty five pounds.

"Thanks Kildare, for the fiver. And I wonder, does one ever seriously contemplate marrying a woman who can't ride a horse. Damn dilemma."

I watched his Lordship proceed ahead with Rashers who'd awaited our return, into the library. I reddened the fire embers with a few blows of the bellows. And there was no doubt that one had to regard the Marquis in another light. He seemed to have finer feelings which his bluff and blunt exterior hid. Even though he dredged up a mundane subject which indicated not one penny of my loan of forty pounds had been repaid the Marquis.

"Now Ronald my dear. Where did my fifty pounds go, would you

185

like to enlarge upon the reason. I'm sure you would. Come come now."

"Well as a matter of fact, my dear Marquis it was a horse. The first time The Bug ever lost a race. Which left the bloody streets around Duke, Anne, Dawson and Grafton and Stephen's Green empty, most having pawned everything decent off their backs. And were left naked all over Dublin."

"O my dear chap. How cruel. How cruel. And you know, whatever happened to that beautiful creature, Clarissa I believe was her name, that you were with that evening in the Buttery."

One watched Rashers' eyes fill with tears. And the Marquis leaning forward to see closer. And my god one is simply amazed at his stories and his turns of emotions. Who does he speak of. To love. O god. A flash of white, white, white of a wedding just blazed a second in one's mind. Terrible jealousy gives such painful visions. He won't. He wouldn't think of such a thing. But my god he is not above behaving in the most eccentric manner possible. Put his arm around Rashers' shoulders as if to comfort him. Rashers' voice stealing out upon the air. I went dozing off in the chair. At whatever it was that Rashers had chosen to tell him now. But woke, tears inexplicably dropping out of my eyes. For I had a dream in my sudden sleep. Of Stephen's Green. And the early morn upon which Clarissa died. I had come running out of the park. To her. Trying to tear from under her body the spears of fence. I loved her. So loved her. Because she loved him, Mr Arland. And the life he would have so lived with her. That dear man. A song singing, a choir raising their voices in a great cathedral. And then stirring distant drums and voices rising. And approaching from all the streets. A flooding procession of Dubliners. Candles aloft alight in the winter air. Singing, black hatted high priests in long emerald robes, their hands lifting her up above their heads. The swelling throb of choir voices as they came. Gliding so softly, so silently do they go.

> While her
> Bleeding
> Drops of red
> Fell
> Upon my hands

14

Hobbling to the shutters, in the dawn. Awakened by the sound of hoofs pounding out up the drive. The tips of one's toes frozen. One's senses smashed to smithereens this long night. To look down into the darkness and see the shadow of the Mental Marquis of Farranistic, insatiable man, aloft again flying on his poor horse, who will surely be dead before he gets half a parish away. And upon once more stretching out under my double layer of eiderdowns and passing into blissful unconsciousness one was awakened again at dawn. Out of a dream. And witnessing in awe, hoofs lashing, teeth snapping, as Midnight Shadow's shaft shoved deep up Petunia's quarters. A warm hand pressing hard on my cold arm to still my thrashing about. Stare up into these eyes. So pleasantly reassuring. Of Miss von B. In a tweed suit. Her bowler on top of her bag parked at the door.

"I am saying goodbye."

"O please, you must not go."

"Why not. I already wait for you. You do not even come to see me, the whole night. I am of course much miffed. In a freezing cold room. I am awake. Horses galloping around the house."

"The Mental Marquis, madam, who takes to the saddle in his sleep I think. And observing protocol, one could not depart while he was in the middle of his stories."

"Mein Gott. And also too, there is much noise and shouting and running."

"Crooks hung himself."

"Grosser Gott."

"In his intoxicated attempt, he did of course bungle it. But Madam please. Don't go. Nor make me plead with song, mirth, dance and gyration to make you stay. I'm far too fragile."

"I have responsibilities. I work."

"Then you too need calming redeeming sustenance. Please my pretty princess. Get with me cozy in bed."

"I should be angry with you."

"Ah Madam please don't be. Nor distress a poor exhausted farmer at this ungodly time of the morning. Be a good lady, and shut up. Strip off. And do in the interests of love, lay your good body by me I beg. Also lock the doors."

"Ah who is the exhausted little farmer boy. Maybe who is not so exhausted."

Miss von B, her sad face in the faint light, big baleful eyes hesitating. She sits so solemn on the edge of the bed. Strong fingers asplay on her skirt. Her shiny pale pink nails so neatly manicured. On her strong slender tapering fingers. Of those hands which can so gently touch. O god, will she get up. Go lock the doors. Please do, dear lady. On this day when a whole countryside will be alive with whispers. Of our embrace in the wet of a winter meadow. Nor can one take much comfort from Sexton's oft repeated remark. Liars, of course they're liars, Master Darcy, sure they're descended from liars, related to liars and lie to other liars, but by god when there's a scandalous rumour going the rounds you can bet on it that it's the gospel truth and that's a fact. Ah Miss von B. Removes her clothes so elegantly. Folding each garment. Laying them neatly upon the chair. Stepping out of her furry boots. She is really quite youthful. What pleasure to see such strappingly robust reliable thighs. What long dependable work one could get out of her. If one ended up without a pot to piss in. Or all the servants in this house hung themselves.

"Ah it is so good to see your splendid form again. And to warm my hands on your genial bosoms. So good to stick my chill knees between your thighs. So good to plunge my cold feet between your ankles. Ah this close clasped soothing warmth of you."

"I am not just a hot water bottle in the mattress for you."

"O no Madam, you are not, you are much, much more. But I cannot refrain from asking. Who was he."

"Who was who mister chilly boy."

"I must know. On moral principles. Before I can allow the passionate juices of our bodies to again unite."

"What. You utterly impossible little pup. Such heights of stupidity you reach."

"Who was he. That man with whom you sat to dinner in the Royal Hibernian Hotel. You put your hand on his."

"I do not even know what or who you are talking about. Now you have too much of the covers. I am cold."

"You sat adoring him. He had long flowing grey hair. And he bent to kiss your hand."

"There is much long flowing grey hair of gentlemen in Dublin. And at least more than a few who kiss occasionally the hands of ladies."

"And he looked like an aristocrat."

"Grosser Gott. That subject again. You are not jealous of me. You are jealous because you, bog trotter, think someone else is better socially than you are."

"That is positively, arrantly and totally untrue."

"Well I have sat with many in the Hibernian Hotel and who have long flowing grey hair. Please. I was beginning to enjoy here with you. Now I am not enjoying here with you. And now I am freezing. My feet are out."

"And I am not jealous. Nor care the least damn about anyone. But we may never have in this cozy household another peaceful moment like this together."

"Ah how dramatic you still are, my little poppet."

"And you Madam. You are distressing me. You can be immoral."

"Mein Gott. What immoral. You silly boy. About what immoral. There is anyway no such thing."

"Are you still in love with that man."

"My private life is not for you to know."

"Certainly if you so prefer, I shan't enquire further. And I shall stay this side of the bed. But you must have some morals. I think it would be most inconvenient for your soul, Madam, if you do not."

"But how stupid. Of course of women you expect that they have morals. But men, they need not. What woman for two seconds could afford such luxury of morals. When it takes one second for a man to be immoral. That is not what you want to hear. Is it."

"Well Madam, your English appears quite grammatically effective. But no. Perhaps that is not what I want to hear. But I think that women are capable of giving gentlemen damn shabby treatment, like pushing them into ponds, abandoning them on trains, conducting affairs behind their backs, taking their money, and even trying to kill them off. And then writing it all down in a book. Perhaps to gloat over the profits from publication or at least to amuse themselves with in their old age."

"This is now, bog trotter, your opinion of women, eh."

"It is quite."

"And so what do you want or expect me to say. To such Irish idiocy."

"What I want you to say is that perhaps you will come back again to this house. To live with me. As my officially recognised mistress. As you are with me in my bed now. Of course one shall be discreet, no one shall know you are my mistress."

"Who do you think you are."

"I think I am who I am. Madam."

"I should be your mistress. Official. But no one should know. Ha. Don't make me laugh. So that we lie together mister silly boy and have no morals."

"I intend that we shall have morals. I think that's how I should like it."

"You should like it huh."

"You will be faithful to me. In both body and spirit."

"And you, my Knave. What will you do."

"I have not yet perhaps become, because of a lack of foreign travel, a true man of the world. And I think that should be top of my priorities, so to speak. But I shall occasionally soon disport myself. At my London club. And you could do much worse than living here."

"London now is it."

"Yes as a matter of fact."

"And me. What would I do."

"You would regard me as being with you when I am not here and behave accordingly. Soon the electricity will be reaching us. And soon there will even be a telephone. And we shall occasionally travel abroad to Paris and stay in a suitable hotel."

"So in addition to the electrocution there is Paris now too. I suppose at the Crillon, the Meurice or zee Ritz. Ah it is so romantic to listen to you."

"You are, aren't you being uncommonly cynical. But yes Paris too. It has I believe one or two suitably wide boulevards for constitutionals where le grand monde display their haughtiness."

"Ah that would suit you. I suppose. In top hat. Zee silver knobbed cane rap tap tap upon zee pavement."

"Yes, as a matter of fact. I damn well intend to cut a figure."

"Ah to be among your betters. But it would not be le grand monde, my sweetie but distinctly the demi monde, whom you would be among."

"I abhor letting irritation get the better of me. But at this precise time I should be most pleased if you would dear lady please go and do fuck a duck."

"Ah duck fucking. That would be immoral."

"You are being inordinately most tiresome."

"Ah I am so sorry. Please what else. Tell me. I promise to listen."

"Well we shall go to the races at Chantilly. And I may indeed race there myself you know. I shall have by then bred up the fastest horses upon the face of the earth. Meanwhile you will enjoy the privileges of residing in a stately house with servants at your disposal."

"What a wonderful future. How gay. How exciting. Out in the bog. Servants. Stately house. Ha. Dust and dirt, rats and mice. Leaks and mildew. Chill and damp. Dat's what's at my disposal. And you breed racehorses eh. Ah dat's good."

"Is that all you have to say."

"Ya dat's all. But you should not stop. You should tell me more. And who is that dark beauty on zee staff who breaks things in the hall."

"I'd prefer not to discuss members of the staff for the moment if you don't mind. But if you didn't know Madam, I am now telling you. That I have some considerable acres of the best limestone land in the world. If you did ever trouble to take a look in any good encyclopaedia. It is just that I have with this place at this time quite a number of worries. And I know next time, completely by accident of course, Crooks in fact is going to succeed in hanging himself. I shall then be short of a butler. However, it's been a miserably long time since he has properly officiated as one."

"But why, should one butler more or less be a worry."

"Well for a start, undressing him last night after the hanging, he was wearing ladies' bright pink underwear. I think that in itself bespeaks present curiosities to be contended with and most certainly bodes uncertainty as to his behaviour for the future."

"Oooo la la, we have afoot how does one say zee wolf in sheep's pink pantaloon."

"One does not say anything Madam. And not that I want to flatter you unduly. But you were you know, rather wonderfully marvellous as a housekeeper. Everything shining, polished, folded. I did so enjoy my breakfast then. The neat way the cupboards were kept. Provisions stored. My socks darned, the laundry done. Floors so clean. Furniture so gleaming. Ouch Madam. What did you slap me for."

"You did want me to slap your face don't you for such impertinent ungallantry. I should like to hear such things said when I am not naked in the bed. Out of which you I should push. I will."

"Please Madam bloody well don't. Stop. Please."

"Because you like how I housekeep huh. And become your servant again huh. On your arse you go you little silly boy."

"Please. Stop bloody pushing. Bloody ruddy hell. Good heavens. Damn women anyway."

Darcy Dancer crashing out of the bed arse first on the floor. A beast mooing beyond somewhere under the winter sky. The cold damp wool pile of the carpet barely a cushion against the hard boards. One's erection so conspicuous. And now the door knob of one's mother's ablution room, turning, and the door opening. An aroma of reasty unwashed long worn socks filling the air. Good god. The face of the Dublin Poet peering around the door. A bottle of whisky in one hand. A sheepish utterly stupid look upon his countenance.

"Ah I thought I heard a noise."

"Would you mind, please. You're trespassing. Please get out of here and out of the room you've just come from."

"O I'm sorry for my inconvenience. Rashers Ronald said you were in need of some spoken verse."

"And you'll be in need of a new set of teeth, eyes and ears if you don't get out of here and this house this instant."

"Right you are your Eminence. But I can see there you're busy enough already. Very sorry to have troubled you in the least."

Door quietly closing. Feet tiptoeing away. And now heavier ones approaching pounding down the hall. And the tinkle of dishes. And knock on the door.

"Sir it would be your breakfast sir. The door is locked."

"Leave it outside the door, please, Mollie."

"I am wanting a word with you sir of a serious nature."

"Well please come back later, Mollie."

"It is this very moment urgent sir."

"What. Please. Is so urgent."

"Sir, the silverware, half of it is gone."

"Thank you for the information, Mollie. Just leave the tray."

Along with the silverware, listen to the footfalls disappear. Uninvited guests breakfasting on one's whisky, walking into one's bedroom. One would find more peace in the lobby of the Hibernian.

"Damn hell, Madam. That's what I mean about this household. And you Madam. Listen. Please. I was also going to say before you and that apparition rudely interrupted. That I adore your legs. And the firm yet lean muscles of your thighs. And now please, let me back into bed."

"And all I am now is legs. Thighs. Muscles."

"No you are much more than that, honestly. You sometimes have an attractive mind as well."

"Sometimes huh."

"No oft times in fact. Now just let me peacefully slide in. I'm desperately in need of warmth and rest. Really I am. Kept up as I've been nearly the whole night. Ah the feel of them. Your marvellous marvellous quarters. Like a large variety of grape indeed."

"Ja wohl, indeed."

"Ja wohl. That one might want to sink one's teeth into Madam. Or merely squeeze by hand. And your lean slender waist. And your so wonderful richly creamy pink budded breasts like spring primroses."

"Of course we are without zee primroses in the middle of winter, but that what you say is perhaps an improvement for my ear. I am not like a good quality brood mare, perhaps. To breed up your winners."

"Madam. Ah Madam, why not. Of course you are. Together we can as well as good colts and fillies breed up a great dynasty. Not only of horses but of little Darcy Dancers."

"What. When I am far older than you."

"But O Madam. I have missed you, you know. I have. Other ladies simply do not possess your elegance. Even though it's true I suppose, you really are nearly old enough to be my mother."

"You want I slap you again."

"But Madam our ages need not matter. It is how we can be helpful to one another. Isn't it that's how there is love, that it comes into being because of these mutually useful performances of chores. And it makes not a scrap of difference your getting the least little bit long in the tooth. Be a good little lady now and fetch in my breakfast tray. Why don't you say something Madam, why are you being so quiet."

"Tooth, breakfast, mein Gott. And whose tooth is long."

"Well perhaps I must wait till there is a little more light to have a look. Perhaps I am mistaken. But no need to get flustered and angry Madam."

"No fluster. I am not."

"Well your English is getting suddenly ungrammatical. And please, you must let me finish."

"You finish while you are telling me to serve you breakfast and perhaps with my long teeth I am finished. Yes."

"No no no, Madam. For god's sake. You do bloody well misconstrue. I just hate leaving a tray out there for someone to trip over. O god. Hear that. Exactly as has happened. And I mean you have, even though you are approaching middle age, such fine bags on you. That one would expect of a pedigree cow. A pair of the prettiest udders in the parish. Of a sort which promises a long, copious and dependable milk yield. These are the things which matter Madam. O god, what now have I said to make you go all rigid and silent again. What I am trying to tell you is, the important thing is that with the lineage you claim. Plus."

"I am some cow you would like in your herd to milk. And claim. What do you mean claim. It is bog trotters like you who claim. I do not claim."

"I see you have definitely taken to the continued unfortunate use of

194

that term bog trotter in your vocabulary. And it does not Madam, help in the improvement of your English. Please. Get the tray. There's a good sweet wonderful girl now."

Miss von B rising out of bed. An impatient sweep back of the eiderdowns. Going to one's mother's wardrobe for covering. God what a wonderful arse she has got. And such calf muscles. Merely the shadows across such contours send the heart thumping and prick twitching. Such a damn nuisance she's slow to take orders.

"Thank you so much Madam. I do appreciate it. Ah not too much damage. Little coffee spilled. But in any event I have plans for the future. Now that the sea lanes are open again to America, I shall be importing the modern exotics from that land."

"Vas exotics I may ask."

"Lavatory paper as a matter of fact. I understand they have a variety which is both soft and absorbent."

"Ah what problems you have."

"Do, have some coffee Madam. I indeed am going to build as well, a high tower to this house."

"What, to shit down from."

"Please Madam, do you think we could take up discussions of that architectural utility later. You see I am inclined to imitate that fascinating gentleman William Beckford as a matter of fact. Some accounts of his travels are in the library. Indeed as is the very desk which once belonged to him. I should like as he did, to travel widely and to return here winters to hunt. His tower was two hundred and sixty feet high. Mine will be a few feet shorter of course. There's much loose stone about. And it would be I think nice, cementing them together to have such an edifice."

"Such folly would fall down on your head."

"Bloody hell, you are, aren't you a barrel of enthusiasm this morning."

"Perhaps you would wish too by your edifice to pretend you are much high and mighty."

"Madam just shut up and put some honey on this barmbrack please. As a matter of fact from such a structure one could watch for poachers, trespassers and idlers."

"And also if commoners and peasants come too close who would not perhaps be schooled in the ways of court."

"You do Madam, don't you, seem to possess a rather jaundiced view of me. I think it is the duty of a landowner such as myself to set for the peasantry an example but not especially to encourage their closeness."

"No it is for you and your ancestors who bring yourselves here to this country to keep the land they steal from these people so that you can prance about with noses stuck up in the air. So precious. So refined. So superior. Thinking they are something grand. When all you are is parvenu and maybe not even deserving of zee word. Now you are silent and rigid."

"Yes, I am Madam. I am really hurt. To the quick. By your words. Which you say with a bitterness and almost hatred which would make me wonder who you consort with these days in Dublin. Here. Let me put your finger. To feel. That is my tear. That has come most genuinely out of my eye."

"Grosser Gott. You have, haven't you, with so much cunning, and still so stupidly charmingly stuck up, come back into my life."

"Madam, may I remind you, while you are still trouncing me spiritually in the balls, that it is you who have arrived here. And come back into mine. With not so much as a warning by your leave. But of course I do not complain of that. As you do bring with you so much elegant beauty and grace. And I do so need a housekeeper again. And you ought really to be glad of my putting such a proposition to you."

"Who do you think you are you insolent pup. And now I shall, I really shall. Hard. Slap your face."

Miss von B's slap landing on Darcy Dancer's jaw. Spinning his head around, sending coffee soaked chunks of chewed barmbrack across the room. Dishes clattering on the tray. The sting sinking deep in one's face. My how marvellously strong she is. Astonishing how in spite of seeing stars, it trembles one's prick into instant rigidity. With a desire flushed from scalp to toe to plunge it into her. And recall out upon yesterday's afternoon, looking up beyond her shoulder into the western sky. The grey clouds unloading their showers of rain. And then just above the horizon, the newest of new moons luminous white against a sliver of egg shell blue. Crescent of hope so needle sharp and bright. Perhaps amid catcalls and jeers not everything was to be continuous unglamorous gloom in one's life. That a world could begin all new again. After a war. Streets of cities to be walked. Arms held wide in joy. Singing. Windows opening to listen. Gwendolene. My Miss

196

von B. Are you now my first armful of supreme good luck. Grabbed and held. In the embrace of your glorious golden squirming body. Your so soft tongue darting, digging down against one's neck. Pressing between one's lips and down one's throat. And yet. Dear me, in the ways of women, one does sometimes feel like some filthy rich foxhunting novice arrived out in the field in the latest gear, and standing out like a sore thumb. A memorable monument to ostentation. And then on the most magnificently groomed horse, taking the first fence, and flying head over heels to splash spreadeagled in a drain full of the most moistly fresh cow flop. Face first. The Marquis did say his pop might sensibly now hang up his old testicles to dry. While one's own still moist balls have suffered such glooms. Hanging lonely. Waiting and waiting. In great yearning groans. To anoint in her silky loins some suitably desirous lady. Even the unsuitable. So desperate was one. Nearly chewing one's nails, which I don't, but pacing the carpet in front of the fire. Long months of one's flesh uncaressed by another hand. Mouldering untouched. And now feel her body. Rise up like a tide in an ocean. To deliriously drown. Enfolded in the musk of her. And in my brain holding Leila. Stretched upon thy body I lie crucified. And whom shall I ask. To walk with me. Upon the world's boulevards. If I asked you, Leila. To waltz with thee. Make thee laugh. Would you. The foreign streets. Hands tight entwined. Hearts alive with gaiety. Would you. Waltz with me. Leila. And yet. One does swear never again to make an assignation. To be there waiting. And that they might not come. Never to see one. Even by binoculars. So lonely crushed. Just before one stamps one's foot and says to hell with everybody. Yet you do. You do go seek them again. Her voice. And this voice. Gwendolene. O Darcy Dancer come into me. Push the prow of your ship deeper and deeper into these waters. Sail upon me. Tell me my name. Say your joy screaming aloud. Slap my palms upon your thighs. Say that you do.

Into all
My throats
You bring
A load
Of love
To pour

15

It was entirely sad with Miss von B gone. Seeming like a whole life-time ago, instead of this very morning. The feel of her breasts still on my chest. The sweet smells in under her hair. The warm cozy couch of her body. Making it so miserable to dislodge oneself from covers out into the cold. Legs still stiff from hunting. And Dingbats arriving to take away one's tray.

"Plus sir the gentleman Ronald had seven rashers, five cups of tea, six pieces of toast, sir, and a quarter pound of the butter and nearly half the pot of marmalade and kept saying, will ye bring pucks now of everything so's I won't have to keep asking for more. And he was asking for more before he was finished any of it."

While dressing, one could hear the wires pulled and clanking from my sisters' rooms, ringing down to the kitchens for their breakfasts. And where one wonders are the eggs coming from. Since Catherine smashed so many sitting on them. And since Rashers may still be bellowing for more. Which Dingbats echoed as she left, making an unprecedented curtsey at the door.

"Sir, an old nanny goat wouldn't be safe from the teeth of him."

Popping on my brown and most inconspicuous plus fours, one was not daring to even look down a hall or listen to a creak lest confronting Leila, who might then choose to tell me she had decided not to be at the boathouse. And I joined Rashers in the library for elevenses. Which he imbibed with as much relish as an Arab gobbling a goat. Nanny or otherwise. He had taken a turn about the gardens. And now, his tweeds as colourful as a vase full of wild flowers, he sits extremely comfortably, contentedly chuckling, and leafing through the more elderly volumes of *Punch*. But as one rattled off all the possibilities of the perpetrators of the silver theft, he seemed unconscionably sheepish and nervous.

"Damned bloody strange nasty fearsome and unpleasant thing Kildare, that's all I can say. But of course my dear chap, you did have a rather rum collection out here hunting you know. Of the lesser kind of the better people you might say."

With one's woe weighing hourly more heavily, one turned from Rashers sipping his coffee and chomping on oatmeal biscuits. Clearly and indubitably he was distinctly another mouth to feed. But before I reached the door he was bowing me out of the room and thanking me profusely for my continued hospitality.

"You have no idea my dear boy how wretched life can be in Dublin when one is a little short of the readies. This sojourn really has, you know, set me back on my feet again. Such kindness shall not be forgotten. Neither by me nor my heirs. Do believe me when I say that. I know you are going to adore meeting my betrothed. Dinner soon dear boy. Jammet's. My treat. Are you on."

"I should like very much Rashers to dine with you and your betrothed. But I couldn't help concluding from his Lordship's conversation last night that you, having borrowed from me, had not repatriated his fifty pounds."

"Ah. Ah. No indeed. You are quite absolutely and correctly right on that score as a matter of fact. Very astute of you to so observe. Very. But you see. Imagine. The expenses. My topper, tails extracted from pawn. And indeed I should like to have a night out with my dearest friends the day before the wedding."

Suitably armed with walking stick one did set off for the stables forgiving Rashers further for his trespasses. And checking the horses, and then climbing the hill to the fields beyond the wood, I felt Rashers really did mean sincerely what he said in spite of his always contradicting it the next minute. Perhaps one should have taken him along to spy that damn stallion, or at least help me generally count cattle

199

and attempt to cheer oneself with one's only remaining disposable assets. How could so much silver be gone. And months before I can fatten some cattle. O I do so hope that the cold dreary days will quick dawn a blazing glory of blue skied spring. When the swallows and swifts can come soaring and perch chirping and the larks rise singing in the scent of a blossoming land. Never mind the thefts. One so needs encouragement against wind, sleet and rain. Which so secretly seep in and lurk in the labyrinths of one's house. And cause some new rotting tribulation to quietly brew. And under Miss von B's assault, one's personal imperiousness does take a thwacking great thumping deflation. Watching her leave my bed, get dressed. That marvellous profile of her tit against the window light. And then brushing and combing her hair and setting so deliberately about her own life again. As if the pursuit of her daily business mattered so much more than me. As if, bloody hell, being manageress of the whole ground and basement floors of a Grafton Street shop was so important. When I could fit the place in one of my barns and have room left over to play soccer in. Dear me I should so love to pretend to be high powered. And damn it I am bloody sure I shall be. Soon enough.

Darcy Dancer walking back up the front lawn park land. Shoes soaking up moisture through the grass. Despite all. There it still stands. Through the accumulated generations. And two black bikes parked so neatly against the front steps. By the staid sombre look of them, dear me, they belong to the Guards who have wasted no time in coming to question the staff.

Darcy Dancer crossing the hall to the east front parlour. The door just ajar. The sound of Rashers. And clearly entertaining guests it would appear. From this arrival on Crooks' tray of a freshly opened whisky bottle.

"Ah Master Reginald sir, all these years, polished all them spoons, forks and knives. Like they were pieces of myself. Gone. And we need not look for the scoundrel. A leopard never changes its spots. Sure I knew by the sight of Foxy Slattery in the hall. That we were in for trouble."

From the previous glasses and the empty bottle of whisky in the library, one could tell there had been much and continuous imbibing. Rashers totally at home by the way he sits smiling, and not even bothering to announce me.

"Ah my dear Darcy I've just been discussing fingerprinting with these good gentlemen of law enforcement, and other of the most up to date inventions in the detection of crime. In turn I've been treated to a lurid tale of rural murder. And I took the liberty of telling a tall tale or two myself about the underworld of Dublin. They were just departing."

"Ah sir, Mr Kildare, we've got the facts and we'll have the culprit or culprits soon. Questioned the whole staff we have. As of this time we are keeping an open mind. But a suspicious character was reported seen struggling with two leather suitcases shortly after dawn and disappearing in a westerly direction. I'm sure under the mistaken misapprehension he was going east. For west he'll get nothing but up to his oxters in bog. Just back over there beyond the orchard this silver spoon was found in the vicinity of the wall which we here produce to you for an accurate identification. Do you recognize any identifying marks."

"Yes I do. The Thormond crest. It is my spoon."

"Ah you might say now you were born with it in your mouth, would that be a fact."

"Yes possibly."

"Proof enough then of ownership. Well the blackguard won't get far now, take it from me, I'm telling you. Not heading west he won't. But bedad we'd best now get after him, he could sink the lot plus himself in a bog hole. Good day now to you sir. We're about to be in a hurry about our serious business."

Darcy Dancer ushering the Guards out into the hall, following in their wafting aromas of Irish whisky. The two giant gentlemen pausing and turning round craning their necks peering at paintings, pilasters and pendentives, not to mention the numerous chipped, cracked and broken objets d'art. And hard to know if, as connoisseurs, they are admiring the art or like most neighbouring farmers who have got a foot in the door, are thinking what a grand place to winter a hundred head of cattle.

"Ah I'd venture to say it would be a thieves' paradise here. But not your worry Mr Kildare. We'll get the light fingers whoever he is. And we are not discounting the possibilities of a female being involved. As accessory before, during or by god even beyond the fact. Your friend, the interesting gentleman inside, has given us sufficient solid information to lead us to pursue a certain line of enquiry. And we hope it won't be long now till your silver cutlery is slipping the peas and carrots, never mind the caviar, back in again between your guests' lips. Crime detection these days is scientifically advanced. Sure I've heard tell of a theory now proving there is more room in a circle than in a square of the same area. And I'm not giving you statistics now. I'm giving you facts. As sure as Ireland is one nation, north and south."

"Well Guards, one might then say up the Republic. Sorry. Perhaps that should be up the whole Republic. Or even way up. In every geographical direction. And down too perhaps with crime. As well as in that general genealogical and geological direction."

"Ah now you've said it and as Aloysius Sexton, sir, your gardener out there with the Latin would say, it's all a matter of them semantics."

Darcy Dancer watching from the parlour window. Rashers at his shoulder. The Guards standing on the drive, brushing back their hair and putting on their caps. And mounting their cycles. Waving back at us as they unsteadily pedal over the gravel and knock off the edges of the grass verges as they weave and wobble away down the drive. They'll be lucky to get to the front gates, never mind leap frogging across a treacherous bog.

"Ah Darcy, my dear boy, what a pretty sight it is out there. That all of that is yours, as far as the eye can see. Cattle grazing among your ancient trees. Where you may take your spiritual ease without being disturbed by an interloper in the pursuit of your comfortable habits. And without some awful gurrier presuming upon one's presence. As in the case of my regrettable condition, to be endured back in Dublin. You wouldn't mind, would you my dear boy, if I just sort of catch my breath a day or two more before returning to town to face the flotsam and jetsam of human kind. Of course you know, disaster if it doesn't at first finish you, always then, goads one on. To tempt it again to do to one its utter worst. And then, what is appalling, it always does."

It was clear as one looked downwards, that Rashers had already made himself enough at home to commandeer a new and bigger pair of shoes. And I suppose if I told him he was no longer welcome, he would merely get up on his hind legs and sing a heart stopping aria. To reduce me to tears. And beg him not to go.

"Rashers but of course you may. Do please stay."

One's sisters appeared for lunch. Arriving in the library in tweeds and wrapped up with silk scarves at the throat. And very much sniffling, coughing and blowing their noses when they weren't very much daintily sipping at their sherries. Cross examining me for the umpteenth time on the Marquis. His ancestry, his entitlements, his ablution rooms, his horses, and the number of acres they grazed upon. Christabel especially. And very much pretending to be off hand.

"His father, the Duke has rather a lot of English and foreign estates, hasn't he."

Rashers wearing his most pleased grin exaggerating to the ladies about something he knew naught about. Volunteering to describe the Duke's chateaux in France and ranches in Canada. Crooks as he came and went, being very hang dog subdued. My sisters, so expert at it, ignoring him as he served them. And returning from the water closet I came upon him, just outside the door in the hall, his head hanging forward one hand pressed up against the wall. Putting a nicely etched handprint thereon and obviously making a remark meant for me to overhear.

"To spare you a bit of attention for merely a moment, a man has to go hang himself before they'd know you'd exist at all in this house."

Throughout lunch, Dingbats, blatantly staring at me from the sideboard, did manage to put one off one's feed. And despite the fact that Foxy's brother was wrestling with her in the hay, the rumour was going round reported to Sexton by Crooks, that she was planning to marry me. And obviously now had no time for the lovesick male staff who were moaning, I love thee Mollie, up the servants' stairwell. Must say her reastiness and fustiness which one found previously stimulating is, in the warmth of the blazing fire, reaching a most disagreeable pitch. As she leans in close, serving the cabbage, her armpit yawning near one's nose. And she has Lavinia and Christabel wincing in their turn. But one does admit it, that one did, more than betimes want to let her have it deep in the bifurcation. And now dear me wouldn't you know, there's Crooks, in the hall doorway. Good god. His fly is open. The big black buttons undone. And revealing not only a pink satiny fabric but the most particular darker pink part of his private as well.

"Sir, coffee is in the library whenever you are."

There was a small gasp from Kitty and she nearly did drop the seconds plate of mutton for Rashers but thank god no one else turned to notice. And one was much relieved to take a change of air in another room. While Lavinia was getting some ancient horse scrapbooks out for Rashers, I managed behind Christabel's back to indicate to Crooks' crossed eyes the need to attend to his dress. But then when casting his eyes downwards, and in the panicked effort to fish back in the exhibited portion of himself, he also managed quite promptly to spill the serving tray of coffee, sugar and cream straight over Christabel's knees.

"He did that deliberately, I know he did."

Crooks rushing from the room. Penis back in his trousers, head in his hands. Rashers jumping up, thought it all just too damn funny, and was much prolonged collecting up the crystals of sugar and dabbing up the moisture absorbed in the area of Christabel's thighs. When first they were all getting on so famously, how was one to know amid so many other domestic hostilities that such ill feeling had now developed between my sisters and the staff. Although one knew Leila refused even to be in the same room with them. Of course, when growing up, until I learned to bite them, they trounced me unmercifully. I later added a growl to my bite, which former often sufficed instead for having to sink my actual teeth into them. And a couple of roars from me would send them screaming running for their lives. They soon learned to stop tearing toys out of my hands, I can tell you. Of course I had to go and find Crooks, searching all over, down the cellars and parlours until finally finding him in the hall outside the ballroom doorway, crying beneath the portrait of my mother.

"O my dear Antoinette Delia Darcy Darcy Thormond, vouchsafe I implore thee to let me join thee out beyond under the slabs far from the unkindnesses, and humbly lie by thy side to serve thee all our days in the eternal next world."

"Crooks, Crooks please, you mustn't be so upset. Christabel was simply momentarily disconcerted."

"Spoke of me as she would a dog."

"Now now Crooks come with me. In here. Let's get you sitting down for a start. There, there."

"She could have at least sir, directed her remark directly at me. Such behaviour never has and never would come from you sir. You are a compassionate man. A kind man. A feeling man. Like your mother was before you. Leave the door open. So I may see her. There she is. The most precious beautiful and noble woman."

Of course in the ballroom, one ended up opening a shutter and taking the dust cloth off a settee. Beseating Crooks with his feet up and bringing him a large brandy. Poor old stick, clearly would like to be a raving transvestite. And meanwhile he certainly does know how to acquit himself to be waited upon hand and foot, a pillow under his ankles, his collar open. I nearly was tempted to get him a cigar. But in spite of my alleged compassion one did think it would be going a little bit too far. Back in the library Christabel was now giving Rashers sidelong glances as he sat puffing his own cigar and twirling his own very large brandy. My, how he can, at the drop of someone else's peacock feathered hat, so thoroughly enjoy life. Totally transforming the gloom. The pleased grin of his rabbit teeth flashing out under his moustache. One has never downright thought this before but he is quite a dashing figure. Sits there stretched out without rancour, regaling the ladies sipping their Drambuie, with risqué tales of last year's Galway Races, Puck Fair, and Dublin's night life. Hinting at the inhuman outrage committed down the depths of what appears to be a, by invitation only, midnight to midnight gathering in caves, cellars and tunnels located somewhere beneath one of the city's most exclusive and elegant thoroughfares. And it would appear, so aptly called the catacombs. Christabel pretending not to want to hear of such bestial shenanigans but clearly in her faint protest, perking her ears eager for more.

"You do don't you, Ronald, seem to know so many wild and unruly characters, quite putting off to normal people. Doing such appalling things. What do you suppose, apropos of common decency, makes them behave like that."

"Ah my dear ladies because they are, in a word, simply dreadfully disgusting. Illbred by moonlight or any light. Castigators of the good. Worshippers of evil. But you see that's the trouble with racing circles these days, embracing as they do rather too broad a class of jockeys, punters and owners."

One sensed the moment to be gone. And one's heart instantly beginning to pound walking down the park land. Soft mist of rain from clouds tumbling out of the west. One's silent voice already growing

tight in one's throat. Hidden by the deep grass, the little stream growing deeper and wider from other streams as it flows down through this
valley of tall trees. Breath blows white in the air. Along this long
unused path. Boots breaking through the thick crust of frost. No sign
of her feet. That one so hopes have preceded me. In bed with another, and dreaming it were her flesh I held. Her swelling smaller
quarters I pressed against. Her slenderer throat I kissed. Her spine I
felt. That she alone was the true lady of my dreams. Servant though
she is. And if only she were an aristocrat like Miss von B, she could,
with the merest of schooling, then so naturally fit into one's life. She
does at least already have acceptable Christian names. Not that caste
or status really matters. Even though it really desperately does. Due
prominent ranking in the parish calls for disporting oneself with the
dignity befitting the wife of a large landowner. As well as when up in
Dublin, to keep up proper appearances as one enters say, up the steps
and past the carved little monkeys on the sills of the Kildare Street
Club. Of course such as my grandfather a life long member, never
even entered the Club, not wanting to appear gauche and unknowl-
edgeable, having to ask of the location of the latrine. And if one were
passing through the lobbies of the Shelbourne or Hibernian, one
would want to appear to be very much at home. Or having returned
from a day's racing, to suitably arrive descending the stair into the
piquancies of sauces wafting about the main dining room of Jammet's
its hearth blazing. People knowing at the merest flick of a glance at the
back or front of you, exactly who you are. Where you have come from
and where you continue to go. Which are only to the most acceptable
places. Even though one is not titled I am at least a minor major
among the landed Irish gentry. Of course one might occasionally go
to unacceptable places after dark. Although certainly for the sake of
having a title, I should damn well not like to end up like the Marquis'
father, the Duke. And having in Dublin, to summon large fish from
McCabe's the fishmonger in Chatham Street. Which anyway is closed
in the dead of night. And then disagreeably and awfully smelly, have
to belt the insolence out of a difficult lady. Swish, splat, smack. But
then when one thinks of it a bit, why not. If such fishy corrective mea-
sures are deserved. It also could be such jolly peculiar excitement. The
Marquis did say that the benefit of occasional chastisement served
upon oneself, was equally well served upon ladies. He had personally

found that one should, while suffering what one thinks are the temporary blows of some women, attempt to rest comfortably, husbanding one's reserves of fortitude, for that same woman is usually planning, later on, something even far far worse. Dear me, he does paint an unpretty picture of scheming ladies who hold sway out in the stylish world. Ah but I shall upon my arrival in London avoid such femmes fatales. Or further afield. As my dear Mr Arland advised me go. To hear the great organs in the great churches. Of Chartres and St Sulpice. When you are of age Kildare you must to Vienna for opera. Moscow for ballet. And Sexton is quite right. One should sample the very latest philosophies being propounded in the cafés of the continental capital cities. Of course Mr Arland knew of whence he spoke but Sexton has never been to one of these places. Yet with both feet firmly in his potting shed he still unhesitatingly raves on about them as if he were there just yesterday. Master Darcy, ah by god you'll have about your ears such incredible intellectual delights. Sure the Prado will knock you sideways. And if I do ever reach such foreign parts I know the first damn thing such as Miss von B will say to me, is that I am trying to shake from one's heels the mud of the bog. Dear me, just murmuring Moscow, London, Vienna, Paris, Budapest. One feels a clutching thrill. Of course Miss von B made much of being a young lady in Vienna. Wearing her tiara and gown on the grand staircase of the Opera House, and betrothed to the grandest Count in the land. Waltzing her nights away under the chandeliers of only the very best of palaces and castles from Linz to Klagenfurt. Of course I will amply demonstrate soon my own ball in my own ballroom to make her previous grand evenings look like the awfully trumped up occasions they probably really were. Heavens. A nasty pigeon has just deposited on me. A most stupendous long white load straight down my lapel and even, bloody hell onto my knee. Shows you, in the moments when one is tempted to be at one's most eminent one is then most likely to be promptly besmirched. Of course, such shit does remind one that these foreign capitals are possessed of their debaucheries too. As are often required to sate one's pent up desires. Leaving one able to return with an equanimity of spirit, to Andromeda Park and not be feverishly desperate to put it up one's present or former domestic personnel. Ouch. What's this. A damn snare. Hidden in the middle of the footpath. God, one would so like for some prolonged moments not to suffer yet another bloody damn nuisance. While one has already enough with the seethings of staff plots, hangings, seditions, and the scheming craftiness of neighbouring farmers encroaching fences, plus the ruddy wiles of guests, and mad stallions. Not to mention now grand theft.

Darcy Dancer casting the snare away and striding near the deep channel of the brook. Now in spate from all the melting snows. Its racing current babbling beneath the thickets of fern in the darkness of the pine trees and the bare cold bark of great old elms soaring out into the sky. The stream slowed now from its winding way all through the wood, widening as it flowed into the lake. The little old wooden bridge which crossed it, now with its piers collapsed. Must take a jump.

Darcy Dancer stepping back into the ferns and running, leaping from the bank. One foot reaching the other side and one not. And sinking into the mud. Right over the top of my boot. And water damn it. Filling it up like a drain. As I grab plunging both fists and cuffs deep into the tufts of turf to pull myself out.

Darcy Dancer balancing on one foot, yanking off his boot. Spilling out the water. Wiping the mud from wrists. Straighten one's cap. Now just as it begins to pour rain. How appropriate, dreaming of my grand ball, while one has all the worst appearances of a drowned rat. Ah. The sound of the whirl and whirr of wings out over the lake. Two swans. Gleaming white against a dark sky. At least that is an uncontaminated splendour. Gliding down, ploughing up their silvery paths across the blackness of the lake. O god. The great old oak tree uprooted. And crashed to the ground. Mouldering in decay. Up in those massive branches. Once was our tree house. Built for my sisters. And where they said I should, blindfolded, merely pretend to walk the plank out over the lake and merely pretend to plunge to my doom. But then they suddenly pushed me from behind and as I held on struggling screaming as they were trying to bloody well throw me down into the water, I got my teeth sunk deep into Lavinia's arm. And I'm happy to say, in place of the chunk I nearly took out of it, there still remains to this day the little indentations of my fangs, pearly white scars like a bracelet on her skin. Badgers walk here at night. Rolling forward sniffing on their stumpy legs. All through these ancient trees. Owls hoot. Grab up the mice and rats. Hawks descend. Tear open the backs of pigeons. A bird house, put there by one of the men, was nestled up in the fork of that tree. So strange that little wooden house had been the most important thing in the world. Lying abed on stormy nights thinking I was a bird with a place safe to be. And will she be. There waiting. O god now even heavier rain beginning to fall. Run for it. Cold drops stinging my face. And she hasn't come. Couldn't have got here anyway. And will never be there. The soft satiny cheeks of her face. I so want to take between my hands and kiss. And kiss. Not that I bloody well am becoming suddenly religious. But Lord why doth thou so confound to send into my life such beauty. And yet keep it so untouchably far away.

Darcy Dancer vaulting over a vast fallen beech, uprooted and lying across the old boathouse path. Mushrooms and fungus sprouting on the decaying bark. Pushing further through the overgrown bramble. What an awful mistake, how could she ever find her way here. Mossy ground soft and muddy under foot. Boathouse door open. Hanging askew on its hinges. Scurry of a rat. The old boat my grandfather fished from, the sides broken and rotted through and half sunk in the water. Oars still in the rowlocks. And go out of this darkness, creaking up this stair. To where in this small room above, other trysts, and other rendezvous must have been kept.

Darcy Dancer standing. A shiver. The mirror cracked on the wicker table on the landing. The door ajar. Catch my breath back into my lungs. Push open the door. There. O god. Empty. Empty. Just as I thought. I've come late. And she's not come at all.

Darcy Dancer stepping into the room. Crossing to the bow front leaded window. The little piles of wood worm dust on the floor. The big sill I used to climb and lay upon as a child and watched out on the summer water. To the buzzing of bees and whines of flies. Memorized my first poem here. That Mr Arland bid me read for its celebration of lyric rural Irish beauty. All about the nobility of the nettle, the thistle and the dock. All weeds as it happens. But I suppose you would, if you were a hard put peasant without an Ardagh Chalice you found ploughing in the field or a rusty old tin to piss in, even compose a poem to ragwort.

"Hello."

Darcy Dancer spinning round. That soft voice. There. Seated in the wicker chair behind the door of this cobwebbed room. Under this ceiling. Under this roof. Under all these tall trees along the shore. In the darkened late afternoon rising wind. And the rattling of a shutter. And patter of rain on the tiny panes of window. She sits. Long black lashes of her moss green eyes. Nearly hidden in the shadows. The swans. Sound of their wings smacking the water. To go away. Taking their whiteness up into the sky again. Flying lonely to other lonely lakes.

"You came."

"Yes. I've come."

A black cloche hat on her black hair. The rough navy blue material of her skirt. Her hands folded whiter and softer looking now than when first I saw them red swollen as she carried dishes in the dining room. Thick brown woollen scarf around her neck. Her black coat buttoned tight. The alabaster silken skin of her face. A blush of red on her cheeks from the cold. A sudden chill sunshine sweeping across the lake. Comes in the window. Lights the dead leaves strewn on the floor. Brings the gleam of green back to her sombre eyes. The steam of my breath on the air. The sun goes. Room all grey again. Does she hear my voice caught back into my lungs. So demure she sits on the old wet stained broken wicker chair. So pale and slender thin in another bit of sunlight. Breaking out through the clouds and splashing on the broken legged table under the window. Her knees together. Black stockings above her boots.

"I didn't think you would come. Or that I'd already find you here. The paths are so overgrown."

"I've come here many times. By a way from around the other side of the lake."

"You've been here just alone."

"Yes. Now what do you want to say to me."

"I don't know. Except that I'm glad you're here."

"Please. Don't touch my hand. And please, don't be offended. It's not because I don't want you to. There's nothing more in this whole world than my wanting you to."

"Then why not."

"Because it is too late now."

"How can it be too late."

"You know nothing about me. And if you did, you would not any longer want to be with me. I am not pure and innocent as I appear. I know you have made something romantic of me. As all men seem to.

What has happened to me in my life perhaps does not show worn wrinkles yet on my face. But inside me there are the wounds and scars."

"But why cannot I hold you or touch you."

"Because I could not stop myself letting you make love to me. From the first moment you came in the front hall that bitter cold winter night, so shy and kindly. Your eyes without greed and without suspicion. From that moment, I knew if you wanted to have my body, that I would give it to you."

"And why now, can't you."

"Because I am leaving. And please, can't we just leave it at that. I saw how you were when the blond lady who is most attractive, came into the hall. Suddenly all the sad way you look sometimes seemed to lift. Almost as if you loved her. I feel you may have had many women and romances."

"But I do not. And have not."

"And I was angry. And jealous of her. And I hate being jealous. It makes me suddenly do things of which later I'm so ashamed."

"And you broke the vase."

"Yes. That is why. And why I must pay you for it."

"Of course you mustn't. This is so mournful. Leila. So very mournful."

"This is the first time you have ever used my name. And that is mournful."

"Could we not make love. Even sometime."

"Please. Don't ask me to do that."

"I must. Because I want to so much. And you say you are leaving. I must not let you go. And what would happen to you. Out in the world."

"But it is where I come from. Out in the world."

"But have you a job or somewhere to stay."

"When I go, you need not ever worry. I am well able to take care of myself. I've lived rough. I have run away many times from many places. I've been with travelling people on the side of the road. I went begging with them in the towns. And I could beg as much money in an afternoon than any ten of them could beg in a month. And they didn't want me to go away from them. They'd watch me day and night. Take any money off me. Even kept me short of food. It is how

I have this cough in my lungs. But to keep my teeth good I'd chew as much carrots and turnips as I could. I'm not complaining but the men would be forever pestering. And you'd never know whether they were more of a nuisance when they were drunk or when they were sober. But one day in Birr where we were begging I got away. I went as if I were begging at the station. I had extra shillings hid in my shoes and knew the time of the train. Asked the station master to let me use the bogs. He wouldn't let the rest of them come. I got on the train to Dublin."

"And what did you do in Dublin."

"I got a job. A waitress in a cinema café in Grafton Street. Ah but I must not just sit here telling the tale of my life."

"I ran away once. And was a waif too on the road. Why do you smile."

"Because I would like to believe you but I think that I shouldn't."

"I was found dying and delirious by some kindly monks. May I. Just to hold your hand. And I want so much to hold you close."

"No. Please. Please don't."

"Why. Surely just to touch you."

"I should tell you too. I have already had a child. Who was torn out of my arms. A little boy I shall never see again. And I have also sold myself on the street. And I have had diseases. You see. You are. Although you pretend not. You are shocked. You want to run away out of this room, don't you. Don't you."

"But I have not run out of this room."

"I cannot tell you more now than I've told you. But I have reasons now to go away. And you must not ask me what they are. But there is one more thing I want to say. With all my heart. With all my soul and with all my sins. Even as I know my already spoken words one by one have closed all the little gates that lead to the garden of your heart. And all I want to say.

Is
I
Love
You

16

Leaden skies above this morn. Flurries of snow swirling across the grey of the granite. A nosegay of heathers in one's overcoat buttonhole. Above the trees of the distant wood a flock of crows circling. Waiting here on the front steps of Andromeda Park. The clatter of hoofs from the stable yard. Up the road, Sexton driving the victoria. Wheeling it to stop precisely in front of one. Wield up to his hands my portmanteau. Step down one step and step up.

"It's not a bad old morning now, Master Darcy. There'd be a bit of kindness lurking in the air behind the present bitter bit of breeze."

Overgrown rhododendron leaves down the drive brushing against our faces. Out across the grey fields a momentary distant ray of sun. The only seldom brightness to come in one's life these many past days. Leila gone one morning. Departed as I still lay asleep. And woke nearly knowing when I heard the distant sound of the train whistle come in my open window on the chill silent air.

"And how are you Sexton. How is your back keeping."

"Ah a mite more than middling you'd say, if you had to say anything. But it would be me soul I'd be more worried about. I was, not long after dawn's early light, planning to say me Stations of the Cross around the garden."

"That's very commendable, Sexton."

213

"Ah by me prayer be exalting the humble and weak. And putting the Pharisee and the Philistine to flight. But wasn't that brazen butcher banging with his stick on me door. With a bill tabulating up two years he was collecting, he was."

"Awfully impromptu of him that hour Sexton."

"He said he wouldn't want to approach you himself in the big house direct. As you might not understand. Sure he knows quite right that you'd have blown him off the porch with a shotgun. Ah god now, they'll give you credit in the town Master Darcy. Up to your eyebrows. And you'd think with the slabs of bacon he'd be giving you a little extra, throwing in the offal and the dog bones and the like for nothing but by god when he's got the bill high enough giving you what he wants to get rid of and what you think is a good luck penny, then by god you'll get the bill counting up the whole lot of it. Deceit. Fraud. No other name for it."

The roar of a motor car. Horn beeping past. Petunia shying and Sexton reining her in along the verge. Wheel hitting a stone nearly upturning us. A wave out the window, exhaust smoke pouring out. Foxy Slattery, a smile across his face leaving consternation across Sexton's.

"Look at the like of that lout now. Driving a motor car no less."

"Foxy Slattery Sexton."

"Don't I know it's him. And now an even bigger lout than he was then. The country is sine dubio going to the dogs, I'm telling you. They're kicking in the teeth of the holy Roman Church that's protected the moral fibre of their souls all these centuries. While at the same time they're parading their vaingloriousness as members in good standing of Fatima and the Legion of Decency."

"You're taking a very poor view this morning Sexton. Don't we as a race and people have something to boast about."

"Well as a race we've never wasted time rushing anywhere. But no one can beat us at the speed with which we break up your grand piano into your anonymous atoms. Or at destroying your objet d'art into useless smithereens. Or your best architecture burned to the ground."

"I may remind you Sexton that soda water was invented in Dublin. And the bubbles are reputed to be of the highest quality."

"Well you could say too Master Darcy our lies are of the purest falsehood. Without one redeeming semblance of truth in them. We're a nation of champions at least in that I can tell you."

"We are waxing eloquent in anti Irish propaganda this morning Sexton."

"Well I caught your blind man Mick McGinty and his swamp trollop wife. Over in our bog stealing turf. You'd think the lesson I taught them when they attacked you when you were a lad would be enough. Sure they were rushing away to beat the band when they see me coming a mile away. But their old horse idling making a contrary fuss. Wouldn't get on pulling home his cart full of turf. Eager to be out of there. The pair of them. And doesn't the blind McGinty give the poor horse such a clatter of his fist. I could hear it where I stood. And didn't the eejit knock the poor horse dead in its tracks. And then didn't the wife attack him with the spade. Ah it was a great scene of justice. The pair of them running. And leaving of course the poor old horse there dead for us to bury. But now isn't the pair of them back to me now for the cart. Sure they're related to another whole slovenly family like themselves, beyond the edge of Thormondstown, brother, mother, sister, old father and sons and a more treacherous bunch never walked the face of the earth."

"You mustn't get so upset Sexton. We surely won't miss a cartload of turf."

"Sure who's upset. I put the turf and cart in our barn. Nor am I near yet like Crooks to dancing the Tyburn jig. But it took long enough to get anyone to stack the turf. No shortage on indolence. Sure your mother's father had signs posted up on the wall down in the servants' hall that lying down on the job or lying with words is strictly forbidden in this household. And Master Darcy I wouldn't mind so much either kind of lying. But it's the guile, cunning and duplicity of them. Sure some master thief among them would have got off with that silverware. If they could grab hold of it, they'd steal the very piece of sky you were standing under. Then tell you while you're staring at it that the colour of it was bright green. And not sky a'tall. The only time such a thing as the truth is spoken would be when it's a bit of scurrilous gossip. Then it would be gospel you can be sure of that. Didn't I catch that one Mollie with the young Slattery out in the hay. And more than once catch him pulling on himself out in the warmth of the greenhouse. Two of them said they were having a smoke of a cigarette. That one will have her belly as big as her tits, popping out a bastard soon I can tell you. Devoted loyalty is all fake and sham these days. Now I'll tell you the difference Master Darcy between a Protestant and a Catholic. And it's as much as if one was black and the other was white. One lies. The other tells the truth. One steals. The other is honest. One is dirty. The other is clean. One is treacherous. The other is loyal. And one would have to be a foreigner to think one was charming and the other dull."

"And which Sexton, pray, is the Protestant."

"Ah now, Master Darcy, that would be telling wouldn't it."

"Ah Sexton, you are indeed telling a good deal this morning."

Reaching the station up the little incline. Icicles hanging down from its roof gutters. Another flurry of snow. Two farmers huddled in their black coats, one with a pair of bright new shoes. Amid the pigeon droppings. There was no doubt as to the lighthearted attitude towards travellers this morning. Turf smoke smell of the fire in the ticket office. The station master saluting, with his ever cheery greeting.

"Ah up to town now is it Master Reginald Kildare. The metropolis of the east is your destination. Where there'd be them swanks now wouldn't there, as would have champagne delivered to their doors of a morning instead of milk."

Dear old Sexton carrying now my portmanteau. Lugging it ahead of me. And clearly taking exception to the station master's liberty. Which if I do say so myself is a damn good bloody suggestion. But you'd think I was heading off on the grand tour. Not to return for years. A tear in his eye. His massive hand opening my compartment door. And putting up my case. Suspiciously regarding another inmate.

"Goodbye Sexton."

"Goodbye Master Darcy. And while you're up in Dublin I'll be having a visit from the Professor Botanist from Trinity College. And it won't be long before we're up to our noses in the very latest horticultural exotics. Take heed now of the man who stepped out into the world liberally endowed with morals and money. And remember that as fast as your man lost the first he lost the second even faster."

The station master blowing his whistle. Sexton looming next to him, his breath chilled white on the air and waving that long arm. Dear man, through any bleakness, always seems to have his own hopeful world. And some beacon lighting up his future. As mine seethes with worries.

"Goodbye Sexton. I shall take heed."

"And by the way, Master Darcy. Petunia is in foal."

The train squealing, squeaking. Finally edging forward slowly slow. Moving, stopping. Moving again. Pulling past the grey little station. Sweet smell of turf burning. Past the station master's thatched cottage. Wash drying frozen stiff on a line over his little garden. Smoke curling out of the cottage chimney. The deep snows on the countryside when I came. All melted away on the fields grey green. Out there in the coverts, foxes long finished mating. Hope always arises with the days getting longer. Even out there on this passing bereft boggy emptiness. One only wishes one's fellow passenger wasn't reading *Stubbs' Gazette*. Roll call of the county's debtors. Clears his throat each time he turns a page and again as he writes something down. Looks so awfully like a solicitor. Wears same odious demeanour as one's former agent threatening a writ on me. Whose lawyers are still sending letters. I do believe I got a sound kick up the agent's arse when someone was trying to twist my testicles in the post hunt melee. Soon now south, will be the purple dark hills. The first signs of Dublin beyond the abandoned ditches over the heathery bog lands. Even as the cold ash branches shake by in the train's breeze, already feel the quickening pace of the city.

Darcy Dancer crossing the black and white tiles of the station. A porter leading the way and the people streaming everywhere.

"Sir just follow me now sir. To the entrance. I'll have a taxi for you. Not a bit of worry about that now."

Darcy Dancer stepping towards a motor taxi. Driver jumping round his vehicle to open up. Door falling off its hinges into the gutter.

"Ah I'd let you use the other door now sir only it's jammed shut. Get in now sir, only needs tying back on with a bit of string."

Porter tugging at the cover of the boot. Comes away in his hands. Of course in this vehicle one will be damn lucky to reach even the morgue just around the corner. Plus the window's cracked and the bottom of this seat is gone. Smells like a stable. Be safer taking a horse cab with a runaway horse between the shafts. As it is, one will oneself end up in the city morgue.

Taxi crossing the Liffey. Guinness boats waiting. Loading their big oak barrels. The heavy clip clop of the massive draught horses pulling more barrels on their clattering carts. Tara Street. Past the baths. Where Mr Arland said he had swum in its swimming pool. Wall and railings of Trinity College. Nosing out down Dame Street. Same massive red faced guard directing traffic with his white gloves as if he were conducting a Beethoven symphony. The Provost's House. Sits so elegantly in Protestant glory. Jammet's just there behind its so discreetly curtained front windows. As we head up this stylish boulevard of Grafton Street. Mitchell's grey granite monument to coffee cakes and tea. All of it still here just as I'd left it. There's where Miss von B works. Without zee dust, zee dirt and zee decayed mice stinking up her bathwater. Turn left at the Green. Ah, awaiting one. The canopy of the Shelbourne Hotel. O dear. The driver is now kicking at the bloody hinges to get me out. And now the doorman. Both tugging. O god. Off it comes. Landing them backwards right on top of a poor begging tinker.

"Ah jasus can't you give a decent ould woman minding her own business on the pavement, some peace, and fuck off the fool pair of you."

The doorman standing brushing himself off. And kicking out at the tinker lady. Sending her box of pennies flying into the gutter.

"Get out of the way you. Good day to you Mr Kildare. And don't mind the mayhem. Long time now since we've had the pleasure."

Darcy Dancer depositing himself on the pavement. Reaching into his pocket. Shilling tips for doorman and taxi driver. And handing over half a crown to the tinker lady.

"Ah sir you're a most decent and fine gentleman. God bless you. And may the sun never set on your glowing riches. And may you never back a losing horse."

Darcy Dancer led through the hotel door. Soft carpets. Late morning smell of coffee. Tinkle of cups. Scurrying porters dancing attendance. One must suppose they remember me with such welcome, having finally paid on my last visit the largest unpaid bill in their history. Massive debt has always been the fastest and surest way to achieve fame in the better places of Dublin.

"It is very good to have you back with us again Mr Kildare."

Past pillars in lobby, and preceded by this gentleman in his striped trousers, one is ushered into the lift. Such a nice comfortable feeling when one is followed by two pages, one carrying my portmanteau and the other transporting my selection of morning newspapers on a tray. So marvellous to ascend in this cage. The wires pulling us up through the well of the great staircase. Past the shiny mahogany balustrades. Alight at our floor. Maids in black quietly lurking in the carpeted corridor, watching my entourage enter into the quiet recess of this cozy comforting room.

"Now Mr Kildare we trust on short notice this apartment meets with your approval."

"Very satisfactory indeed."

"I suppose you're up in town to attend the theatre. Or is it to buy or sell a few cattle. Or would it be horses now."

"I sincerely hope it will be one or the other or indeed all three."

One of course stays at the Hibernian to attend theatre and at the Shelbourne to buy horses. Best anyway to supply an enigmatic answer that can be taken in the most number of numerous ways. Essential that one does not give the impression one is where one is for no damn good reason at all. And here so hauntingly ensconced in my crimson carpeted room for the mere fact it pleasantly presently pleases me. Out one's window over the tree tops. Seagulls softly sailing beneath the blue grey clouds, edges glowing pink. Ducks circling the sky to land on the pond in the Green. The whole city at one's feet. The roof tops and misty haze of smoking chimneys, spread all the way to the Wicklows rising purple in the distance. Mountain peak high with the Sugar Loaf. The tangy fermenting smell of the Guinness brew that keeps this whole metropolis alive and all its brains revived each day. Perhaps even fevered each night, putting them snoring asleep with their perishing dreams. Pubs with money pouring in and beer pouring out, makes every one of them a little bank. And the telephone ringing.

"Mr Kildare, your champagne is ready in the downstairs drawing room."

"Thank you. I shall be down shortly."

Could clonk someone unconscious with this telephone. It is, when one thinks of it, a marvellous instrument. If one had them installed all over the house. Imagine the nice new unbelievable confusion it would be possible to cause. Quick wash and brush up. Descend again from heaven on high down into the voices. Some of them nearly hysterically

219

snooty like my sisters. Eleven o'clock chiming the perfect time for having one's champagne. Aloof from the early Monday morning traffic out in the lobby. Sink back into this flowered sofa chair. Down here in the deserted quiet and peace of this room. God what bliss miles away from the turbulence of Andromeda Park. Beneath this comforting ceiling. And if one overlooked the cads, race course touts, amateur abortionists, mountebanks, medical students and gas meter readers, at least the few remaining would mostly be lords, ladies and squires, either heading in from the country or back out again. And now a hotel page intoning. Right into this very room.

"The Earl of Ronald Ronald please. Lord Ronald please."

My god, that cheeky bugger, Rashers. God he must be this city's biggest chancer. Sounds as if he's staying right in this hotel. Must confess I never thought I'd ever extricate him from Andromeda Park. Of course when they weren't dancing attendance upon him, he kept the whole staff idle with laughter. One had the guilty feeling that one would be kicking a great artiste out into the wet. Each morning confronting me in the library, reading yet another volume of *Punch*. Telling me yet again, how much the protracted comfort was healing his previous wounds of indignity. Further soothed now no doubt by his having clearly taken unto himself a title. And he no doubt is at this very moment planning some new coup. To help land his lady pub and tobacconist owner up the aisle. And not even at this moment is one safe from his depredations. As one carries this very last forgotten one hundred pound note. Miraculously stuffed away all these months. And dredged up from the very bottom seam of one's jacket's barrister's pocket. Designed so handily for either stuffing therein, torts or a stray pigeon or snipe one might shoot out walking. Such a welcome find, this big and sickly green coloured paper. A plentitude of ready, as Rashers would call it. Before one sinks instantly back into a nightmare of the unready. Unravel it. Bearded man's face on the back of this legal tender. Fish, swans' necks and sea shells hanging over his brow. A shawled lady, her chin in her hand, leaning on a harp. Her face the shape of Leila's.

"Sir you're ready are you for your champagne."

"I was expecting a guest. Who doesn't appear to be coming."

"Will you have some yourself sir while you wait."

"Please."

"It will do your elbow no harm, sir. And maybe you'd fancy a sliver of smoked salmon."

The waiter with his white hair combed flat back and parted in the middle of his red cheeked face. This high priest of his profession, taking his steps with his aloof dignity. A figure so familiar for so many years. Who brought us tea as I sat then waiting for Mr Arland trying to stop my eyes staring down between Clarissa's alabaster bosoms. Now he disappears away through the door and down into the great ample bowels of this hotel which one feels so reassured is so full of plenty.

"I trust sir, the Heidsieck is to your satisfaction."

"Excellent as a matter of fact."

"Shall I pour the other glass sir, for luck and for the welcome ghost that may be in it."

"I don't think I've heard that one before."

"Me old granny sir, down the country alone, never poured a cup of tea without a cup for the welcome ghost."

"I see. Well in that case do pour a glass in the hope that either my guest or the ghost may soon arrive."

"Pleasure's all mine."

One sits. Long and lonely. And sad. Mr Arland always so prompt. Wrote me back a fortnight ago. Only three days waiting for him to reply. To say he would come. Near where his beloved Clarissa died. And now he has not. One is tempted to venture down to his address. Mount Street. Not particularly salubrious as an area. Must be near Westland Row Station. Wait at least cozily quiet in here. Feeling no pain. He still may come. While one avoids the more desperate of Dublin's denizens. One or two of whom I see briefly creeping by. Among whom Rashers must be the king of chancers. Dispensing his endless charm. To even the beaten and broke. Who are always there to applaud one's largesse. Who seem never beaten, but always broke. Forever able to stick forth a hand to take to their lips a drink when someone else who can pay is buying their round. And now I count myself among the beaten. Walking away from the boathouse that day. A pall so great one was hardly able to bear it. She would not even go a few paces back with me. Our goodbyes are better this way, she said. Let us leave each other just as we do in this room. I hardly remembered returning back up the path. Oblivious to the briars scratching my hands and face. Through the wood and by the fields and meadows along where they joined the land of the great castle. Where the Mental Marquis was a guest. Imagining their making a tryst. During her hours off in the afternoon. Somewhere in the woods. That she would submit to the Mental Marquis' arms. He could touch her. Do other angering unspeakables. And then cast her back into the gutter again.

Darcy Dancer downing the last of the champagne. Rising from his chair. Stand over the ghost's glass with the tiny bubbles still arise in the pale light. The taste bud bliss in one's mouth of the soft slivers of salmon. Lunch bustle of waiters in the dining room. Blue flame of alcohol burners. Pleasant fume of sauces. My god, people actually speaking French are upon this doorstep. Mountains of very good quality luggage. Although the gentleman's tailoring is a trifle tight, the tall dark woman he is with has exquisite long slender legs, tapering wrists and ankles. Aloof beauty. Her dark eyes and satin soft skin. My god Miss von B is right, these clearly aristocratic people from the Continent do put us to shame. By their effortless casual elegance. Put my key to the porter. Must make an enquiry.

"Excuse me."

"Yes Mr Kildare. At your service."

"Ah, as a matter of fact I believe I heard the Earl of Ronald Ronald being paged."

"Yes sir, to be sure you did."

"Might I enquire if he is staying."

"Yes he is, sir."

"Ah, actually in the hotel."

"Would you like me to contact his apartments for you Mr Kildare."

"His apartments. Is that word actually plural."

"Yes, the royal Shamrock suite, sir. At the corner of the fourth floor. Two bedrooms, a drawing room, anteroom and two bathrooms."

"I see."

"Is there something wrong Mr Kildare."

"No. No. Just a momentary dizzy faint. I'm quite alright. Thank you for your help. But tell me. We are aren't we referring to the same gentleman, I think we both know."

"Yes. Indeed we are sir. Seems he was previously for private reasons under the incognito of a commoner. Isn't the father a big English General. Sure I remember him as Rashers if you'll excuse me now referring in that vernacular, in those days with his great friend Clarissa, the actress. May such a beauty rest in peace. The two of them now would be great gas together of an evening in there in the Shelbourne Rooms. Ah god she was lovely."

"Yes of course. Thank you so much."

I went out the Shelbourne. Popping a shilling in the tinker lady's hat. Her blessings crying out after me, one did lift one's heels to saunter along the Green. Clearly Rashers is a bigger mountebank than one had already conceived him to be. I must damn demand my money back. But I suppose he does keep one's mind off other dilemmas, even more irritating, attached to roof slates, livestock, plumbing and staff horrors which usually gloom over my life. And one does back in Dublin find a joy quickening and lightening one's step. The breeze milder with this bit of pale sunshine down Grafton Street. Past the smoky coffee smells of Roberts' café. Which Rashers said is forever full of perennially stalled first year medical students down from the College of Surgeons. Who maintained that if they ever got their first year exams they'd go flying through the rest. And then be in Fannin's with their window full of medical instruments, buying their scalpels, saws and stethoscopes.

"I say, hello, it is you Kildare."

"Why hello Kelly. Yes it's me."

"Well. You are looking well. How nice to see you, like this Kildare."

"Same to you Kelly, same to you."

"I suppose you're up in town on business."

"A little business, Kelly. That and some pleasure too I hope. And I suppose you want your fudge I borrowed that night at the school fire, back."

"I wish you wouldn't adhere to bringing that up again. That was all such a long time ago."

"Well you know Kelly, your horse, Tinkers Revenge saved my bloody life. I placed a bet on it at a hundred to one."

"Did you really, did you really."

"Yes I really did."

223

"Did you put a lot of money on him."

"Yes I did."

"You must have won a lot of money."

"Yes I did."

"I mean you could have won thousands."

"Yes I did. And as a matter of fact even planned to have Bewley's post you a weekly box of fudge. But didn't, thinking that it would make you extremely fat."

"I see. Well, it would have done. Of course you were extremely decent to me at school. I'm sorry you came down in your life as you did. But you do seem to be doing alright now."

"Yes I am. At least not having to work as a stable lad or an indoor servant."

"You must not hold that against me Kildare. I did everything possible to make your life reasonable when you were down on your luck."

"Yes you did Kelly. Yes you did."

"Well we have another similar horse running. With even greater prospects. At Phoenix Park. Ulidia Princess The Second."

"Are the brakes off Kelly."

"I hate that expression. It implies deceit."

"My goodness Kelly you are taking a moral view of racing aren't you."

"Well. Yes I do rather."

"Well I shall pop a moral bet on him, in memory of our school and previous squire and servant relationship."

"I don't find that at all funny, you know Kildare. Throughout I looked upon you as my friend and I so behaved."

"Ah so you did Kelly, so you did. Well I must rush on. And Kelly you know, you are not a'tall a badly turned out chap. Very smart. Yes."

"Well I'm part of my father's business now."

"Good."

"And what do you do, Kildare."

"Ah. Well. I may be breeding up a nag or two myself."

"Well Kildare, obviously you have improved yourself. This is my office right here."

"Ah."

224

"Please I should appreciate it, if you were to call in on me anytime. Really anytime. I should so like for us to keep in touch."

"I shall Kelly. I promise I shall. Ta ta."

"Goodbye Kildare."

Astonishing, one noticed actual tears in Kelly's eyes. Dear me. In spite of his awful parents he seems to have turned out decent enough. I suppose none of us really has to be as odious as our fathers. If the opportunity arises to be otherwise. Stand here a moment on the corner of Duke Street. Hard to know which way to turn in Dublin. There's the turf accountant's next to The Bailey. One must put something on old Kelly's horse. Meanwhile why not perhaps stroll through the Trinity College squares. Heavens who's poking me in the back.

"Grosser Gott. It is you."

"O my goodness, Miss von B, my countess."

"Why did you not say you were coming to Dublin."

"Well as a matter of fact, I didn't know myself. My you look awfully pretty."

"Thank you. I am just crossing here to go back to work after my quick coffee for lunch."

"Well won't you join me. Later. For an aperitif at the Shelbourne. What about six."

"Ah, my bog trotter, you are on."

"Ta ta."

My goodness, one is meeting folk today. Plus seeing an awful lot of old familiar faces. Even the Master of Foxhounds whose horse one stole. An occasion to carefully make one avert one's face. And turning in this gate way of Trinity College. One thinking of Mr Arland. Across the wooden blocks and out across the cobbles of the front square. And as I go closer and closer to the back gates. Past the green velvet lawns of the college squares. The sun coming out. The rugby pitch, churned up. Three gentlemen practising kicking goals in the mud. Why not go to Mr Arland's address. At least perhaps find if something may have befallen him. He could be sick. Injured or worse. Even as one knows that somehow his letter seemed not to encourage one to visit.

Darcy Dancer walking past the buildings, Zoology, Chemistry, Pathology, Anatomy. And towards the back college gates. Porter in

225

hunting cap outside the lodge, a watch chain across his waist coat. Saluting as if one were a respected student in good standing on the college books. This turreted emporium looming across the street looking like something out of Constantinople. It's said they were once Turkish baths. I suppose just one more desperate foreign innovation imported to hopelessly founder in the uncharted commercial seas of Dublin.

Sky darkening. Men just up the street, lurking in the doorway of the corner pub. Scarves wrapped up round their necks and eyeing me suspiciously from under their caps. One's heart nearly breaks standing here. On these ancient worn granite steps. This is the number. This is the door. Past Magennis Place. Down Mount Street and its bleak perspectives. The grime and the gloom. Pointing washed away between the bricks and the drain pipe from the roof gutter leaking down by the door. One's hand dare hardly reach to bang this knocker again. No sound inside. No sign. Not even his name. Yet must bang again. Wait. I may be mistaken. But his letter said he lived on the first floor of a Georgian house, with a broken iron balcony. Across from the back of Westland Row train station. And there it is, just as he said, the gentlemen's convenience tucked into the wall with a rather dignified arched cut stone elevation. Bang once more. A sound. Feet coming. Slowly. Now in the hall. Latch pulling back. Door opening.

"Kildare."

"Yes."

"Heavens I hardly expected to find you. I was expecting it to be the laundry man."

"I do apologise calling unbidden upon you like this."

"Well dear me, you have. And so you may as well come in. I was only at this very moment in the middle of a message to you."

"Mr Arland, you're limping."

"Yes. My hip. Went on me. Just as I was off to see you. Not as fit as you, Kildare, I'm sure. Come. Please don't expect a palace. Or indeed much more than a hovel."

Slowly up the stairs. In the musky odours. Laths showing through plaster broken on the walls. Around the landing past a sickly green door, a sign, The Trans World International Engineering Company, half scribbled and printed on a warped piece of cardboard hanging suspended under a rusted thumb tack. High up over the stairwell, a roof skylight throwing down pale gloomy light. On the head and back

226

of this man who so much by his kind words, his example, his advice and warm sympathies, bids me think that there was ahead in one's life a noble reason to live.

"Well Kildare, please forgive these conditions to which you are about to be exposed."

Key stuck in the door. Mr Arland pushing it open. A hand gesturing one in. His room. My god. This is awful. Unmade grey sheets on a narrow bed. A cooking stove. Frying pan full of grease. Clumps of wet turf smouldering in a tiny grate. A lone bare light bulb hanging by its cobwebbed wire from the ceiling. A steamer trunk. Lieut. N. P. Arland, R.N.V.R. in the corner. A warped cupboard, its panels cracked. A shirt by a bottle of milk. Sausages and two eggs next to a hair brush on his broken dresser. Sheets of paper strewn amid newspapers and books. A gnawed piece of bread.

"The condition of my room I fear is not exactly what one might expect of an ex naval officer, Kildare. And I do most abjectly apologise. Standing you up. I was coming to meet you. As you see I am still dressed for the occasion. But I fear my hip, when it goes like this, unless rested, only gets worse. As you see here on my College Historical Society note paper to which I helped myself copiously as an undergraduate, my message to you. A nuisance the time it takes me now to get up and down the stairs. Do. Sit there. Alas the only chair. I'll park here on the bed. Well dear me. It is good to see you. It is really. I wish it were in more auspicious surroundings."

"It is good to see you too. Mr Arland."

"Well we've got to stop that Mr Arland stuff."

"But you have never told me your Christian name."

"Alas with good reason, Kildare. And perhaps my middle one will better suit the purpose. My first Christian name being none other than Napoleon. It provokes endless inanities especially in Dublin. So therefore call me Patrick, please. And I shall call you Darcy if I may. Well you're about two feet taller. And clearly a man of the world. Did you come by taxi."

"I walked. By way of Westland Row."

"A smattering of one or two decent architectural features, aren't there, around this area, I think."

"Yes. One or two."

"Merrion Hall's not that far away with its Protestant elevations.

227

Does make one realise that there's hardly a Roman Catholic thing in Dublin to boast about. I mean the church by the station of course. Nice front pillars. Plinths plain at least. Inside, does have one interesting marble plaque to boast about. A viscountess who died in Paris in eighteen fifty. A County Meath family. Helps the soul to dwell on these little obscure antiquities. One attempts to cure one's injured spirit by any means. Ah, but I think the day comes when one has to rue the senseless pleasure in having been a romantic. Graviora quaedam sunt remedia periculis. Translate Kildare. Ah I see it's hard to change our use of names, isn't it."

"I do not believe there remains a single phrase of Latin left in my head, Mr Arland."

"Dear me. Have I also failed as a tutor then. Well in that case, some tea perhaps."

"Yes please."

"But how are you Kildare. And do tell me. How is Andromeda Park. I hear you have taken over. How is Sexton's Latin getting on. Or is it Greek nowadays. I did occasionally hear him rattling off the alphabet to himself. And Crooks, how is he."

Mr Arland, limping and disappearing out the door with his kettle. Returning with a smile. Striking a match. Turning on the gas ring. The blue flames licking out under the blackened aluminium. One does somehow feel it at least encouraging, Mr Arland keeps open his eyes to what is commendable in these streets of some squalour. Perhaps it reassures him he is not entirely removed from the civilised world. But as one tells him of Andromeda Park, a lost nostalgic sadder look grows on his face as he munches a cream cracker.

"Darcy, do have some brandy in your tea, I'm having it in mine."

"Thank you. But Mr Arland. Please do tell me now. How you really are."

"Kildare. Complaint is tiresome, you know. But I suppose it's been a long time since last we parted. Yes. I do put a brave face upon it. And must not bore you with what I'm sure is my transparent dishonesty."

"But please, it would so help to know if you are here like this through design or necessity."

"Not design Kildare. More necessity. But I simply found I could not work after Clarissa's death. I don't suppose there's any way of ever getting over it. As crushing as her dying by other circumstances would have been, it was doubly so to have been the cause oneself. Just from a glance through a window. And she was. Just innocently dining with someone else. A dreadful disease is jealousy. And what it has done to another out of one's own selfish pique. Had I only spoken. And not written. It's so easy to think all women flirts, and their interest in one, just their passing fancy. I suppose my letter revealed to her so much past hurt of mine. And then too late to find she loved me as much as I loved her."

"You mustn't talk further about it."

"No I mustn't. Not while I still can't hold back my tears. I came back here from London. Finding it there just as bleak and just as dark. If you look out the window. That street across there goes under the railway. Beneath the bridge there's an aperture through which one can peek and see a long series of arches supporting the tracks above. And like one's life. I've had to build each arch to carry one's burden. And I've managed to do that from day to day. Yet I do feel very under the weather sometimes. My steady if small emolument. At least allows survival. And occasionally I'm invited to dine on Commons. Rushing there like a hungry animal. To take a sherry in the Fellows' Common Room. Sit at high table. See the girls' sweating faces at the serving hatch having lugged up from the deep bowels of the kitchen the great roasts. The litany of grace. Scrape of chairs on the floor as we all sit down. The gowns. The swell of voices as the dishes clatter, the carvers carve and porters rush to serve. Those things keep one from entirely sinking. But I suppose living here is indeed like joining the lighthouse service, which I always said I might do. Keeping the flame going and the reflectors shined. Reading books as the seas pound. Yes, even to reading this strange volume I see you're casting your surprised eye at. Aptly called *Women, Love and Life*. Treating as it does of love and beauty. Love and courage. Love and tolerance. There's so much truth often found in the trite and sentimental. Anyway. Whiles away the solitude."

"But surely you don't propose to become a recluse."

"Ah Kildare not quite. I occasionally at least have in my life brighter patches now. Making me able to face the world and give it back an occasional kick in the backside."

229

"Sir I am glad. I think one must always be ready to rise by dawn's early light, shake the mud from one's heels and remount."

"Yes, Kildare, yes, remount. But I suppose one has meanwhile been taught one god awful agonizingly long lesson in loneliness."

"And you have, not even a wireless here, sir."

"No. I suppose if I did I could have found solace listening to the orchestral. Instead of pacing where it permits, on this awful green carpet. Turning again and again to look out the window for life somewhere down on the street. Only to see pathetic passing figures making their hunched cold way through the damp evening. Or see queer gentlemen in search of each other in the convenience across the road. Making one shrivel up even more in one's loneliness. Moments come when you feel that no one in the world wants your company. And what is worse, when you then see someone and think perhaps you could talk or get to know that person, and then, if you sense that he or she is lonely too, it makes you feel that their loneliness will only make your own more unable to bear. Leaving two people already so lonely, simply creeping cringing away from one another in their desperation."

"But you must, you must come and stay at Andromeda Park."

"Yes I must. One has got to know every inch nook crack and patch of this room, every spot on the wall. Stain or smudge on the carpet. The sound and squeak of every floorboard. Even know if a stranger's steps go by in the hall. All these things, if you let them, become drum beats of a dirge. Forgive me Kildare, I suppose it's the brandy talking now. But there were moments so wretched that time itself seemed to come and add to the crushing weight on one's soul. To be as if one were flung away as a discarded bandage. And not even accorded the minimal dignity of being deserving of some contempt, just merely the most utterly uncaring indifference. And all of one's own stupid making."

"But Mr Arland, we all must fight such things. Do them battle."

"Yes Kildare yes. But as much as one knew that one must soldier on, one could not crawl out from under the awful brooding gloom. The love one has for someone, left gnawing in one's vitals. Becoming such a sickly poisonous wretchedness that you wonder how the species could allow such to exist, except, yes, and I think this is why. It is to crush to dust the hopes such as I might ever have for fatherhood. For

230

sons being born like me, or daughters, who would be unruthless and loving, and sentimentally unwise like their father."

"No, no Mr Arland, that's not so."

"Yes it is Kildare, it is. And I have put far too much brandy in my tea. And what dreadful sophistic drivel I spill upon your kindly indulgent ears. The cure in my book of homeopathy is distillate from the bean of St Ignatius. Three globules, eighteenth dilution. Taken twice at intervals of three days when there is great moral depression consequent upon grief. But since no chemist Kildare seems able to make it up, I suffice to have just the brief joy one has of a visit to Bewley's Oriental Café for rasher, egg, toast and coffee and spice bun. Reading *The Times,* if it's arrived from London. One does take a little reassurance and some occasional amusement from the personal column. And yet having breakfasted well, paid my bill and visited Bewley's bogs, the best in Dublin by the way, and then going out to face the grim wet wooden cobbles of Grafton Street, one would still stand absolutely wondering, what to do next in order to further cope with the day. My only solace being, I suppose, knowing ahead of time that wherever one went one was still only somewhere where one's imagination allowed one to be."

"Sir, do I occasionally detect that your English grammar has gone completely to pot."

"Ha ha Kildare, you do rescue me from the glooms. You do. And it is so marvellous to see you. And I have I fear let myself be a bore."

"Mr Arland do you still take your snuff."

"Yes. I still take my snuff. And this is my same old cane. And I don't want you to abandon your Latin, you know. One does sometimes feel, what matter, Virgil, Horace, Juvenal, odes, satires and epistles. Yet sometimes a Latin proverb comes near to spelling the truth of life. Divitiae virum faciunt."

"Riches make the man."

"Good for you Kildare. Remember my privilege of dining on Commons free as an undergraduate came from one's ability to translate from the Greek and Latin authors."

A knock on the door. Mr Arland giving a start. His grey herringbone suit. His white shirt. The black, green, red and cerulean blue stripe of his Trinity tie. Slowly pulling himself up on his stick. Moving from the bed. Bent over as he unlatches and opens the door.

231

"Hi there. O gee I'm sorry. Didn't know you had anyone visiting. I'll come back, pardon me."

"Please, Clara. Do please come in."

"O gee no. I was only going to ask if I could get you something while I'm out to the store before they close."

"But please do meet Darcy Thormond Kildare. Clara Macventworth. Of the Michigan Macventworths. Or is it Minnesota Macventworths."

"Hi."

"How do you do."

"O I'm just fine. See you all later, nice meeting you Darcy Kildare. Bye bye Bonaparte."

Sound of her rapid footsteps pounding down the stairs, scrape of front door opening and banging shut. Mr Arland, some cheer on his face manoeuvring back to his seat on the bed. Pouring more brandy in his tea as I shake my head no.

"Of course Kildare, you see what I mean. But she is always one splendid blaze of colours. And totally mad. But she is one of the bigger bright spots in one's life. And lives upstairs. Seems such an awfully young lady, to be out globe trotting. She's doing, as they say over there across the water, a course and getting her credits, at Trinity. Americans seem to treat education like an abacus adding up numbers. She goes floating by my door in her dirndl skirts. Swirling round her knees like rainbows. Pity she nearly blots out her big saucer innocent eyes in mascara. She is dismayed by nothing. Least of all by living here. She's so kind and generous. Writes poetry. And staggering thing is, it's awfully good poetry. But coming back to you. Yes, you have, you've become a worthwhile member of society. Just as the destiny of Darcy Dancer, Gentleman, was foretold. Have more tea. And brandy."

"No. I must go thank you."

"Ah yes, you must, I can see."

"But you will won't you, soon, come and stay at Andromeda Park."

"It is kind of you to ask me, Kildare. I often thought of you. Knew you'd understand if I weren't in touch."

Down these gloomy stairs. In the damp reeking smells. I leave him. That dearest of men. His smile. Stealing out across his mouth, his del-

232

icate fingers. And his firm hand grasping mine to say goodbye. The soft warmth in his eyes. Perhaps there's hope in Mr Arland's life. A new love to take the place of that which he has so tragically lost. Spurned so abysmally as he was by Baptista Consuelo. One so hopes this is not another of such ladies. His old naval dress coat hung on the back of the battered door. One wonders if the love for a man cannot be far greater than that one can ever have for a woman. And one could not help recalling Mr Arland's long hard ascetic struggle through Trinity College. Gleaning his pennies by tutoring the thick skulled cramming for their exams. Plumbing the depths of his privileges as a sizar and later, scholar. His few lonely shillings always clutched always counted. Each quarter awaiting his emolument. His meagre breakfasts measuring out his flakes of porridge oats. But all the while popping into a large brown stone biscuit jar, any spare penny, a sixpence and sometimes half a crown. To be sure to finally save enough money to celebrate the conferring of his degree. A cold grey brooding Wednesday at two o'clock in the afternoon in Michaelmas Term. And at long last after all those four years, buying a barrel of Guinness it took four porters to lug up to his rooms. Excitedly issuing invitations to all his friends. And on that chill stormy eve he tremulously prepared for his splendid night of raucous rejoicing. Bustling about, keeping the fire in his previously empty grate, steeped high with glowing turf blazing. Listening for steps on the stairs and knocks on his door. His table covered with bottles, glasses. His skippery full of a reserve of sandwiches. Days previously spent scrubbing polishing and cleaning. And on this day, the final roasting of sausages at his fire. At seven p.m. prompt his tutor called. To sip a sherry. Shook his hand and was gone. And a rotund black African prince came. Puffing up the stairs. Just for a moment to stand in his tweeds smiling in the door, as he had a fleet of cars, engines revving, waiting in front square to take him and his retinue to the airport. And then the door closing on the big cheerful black face. The Campanile tolling the hour of eight. Then of nine. And there Mr Arland sat, after his long, four long years. Alone, solitary at his fire. The roar of an occasional tram passing out on College Green. Unused empty glasses agleam in the firelight. Slices of smoked salmon on a plate which he dared not think he could ever afford. The distant cry of the shoeless newsboys hawk-

ing their papers out through the wintry Dublin night. As he waited
and waited.

No knock
No sound
No pounding feet
Climbing up his stair

17

On the chill wet grimy granite pavements. From this bleak comfortless street behind the station. Look back. The dim yellow glow of his bulb burning from the ceiling of Mr Arland's room. Walk ahead under the train trestle. Carry a sorrow so close to despair. That makes the days ahead, deep black holes where one must step. This darkness here under the railway. The barred window. A light somewhere far within. Silhouetting the arches fading away into the gloom. Could be the bowels of death. Which so convolute in one's thoughts. And Leila. That envelope propped on her chimney piece. Secret words speaking from another heart.

"Hello."

Making a fist to unleash flying behind him, Darcy Dancer gasping back from the window. This high pitched voice behind his shoulder. And at this face all asmile in the cold evening air, drop one's arm in relief. A fur collared camel hair polo coat draped upon him. Golden buttons on a golden waist coat peeking agleam in the lamp light. Tight jodhpur cavalry twill trousers. Yellow shirt. A bright orange tweed tie. An emerald green silk scarf flying from his neck. Long blond locks back over his shoulders. Tiny tufts of auburn beard high on these spanking red cheeks. Of none other than the Count Brutus Blandus MacBuzuranti O'Biottus. Who has clearly just detached himself from a waving departing figure, whose rolling gait takes him disappearing around the corner at the end of the street.

"I must first blow a kiss goodbye to my sailor before I kiss you my dear. Ah but now my dear previous pupil. Who so make me furious to teach you from the tradition of the great days of the Medici to dance that I must tear my hair out in agony. But my pretty, it is so nice to find it is you. I hope you are not spying. Or might you be one of us. And you are letting your hair down. O dear. You blush. But of course you must my dear. And not be like me without a shame in the world. You come from the quays have you."

"No indeed. I mean I'm not. I have not. Nor am I letting my hair down."

"Ah but you must, you must let your hair down. Let me find for you a nice American sailor whom you would find delicious off the ship which is full of such nice boys as well as ten thousand tons of coal, my dear."

"As a matter of fact Count, I've just come from visiting. Mr Arland. My tutor."

"Ah but my such pretty boy. Regardez moi. I execute le grand jeté pour vous. You need not make excuses to me."

"It's not an excuse."

"But now. Let us see you. Do a simple pirouette en pointe. Ah but I embarrass you in the street my pretty. Watch. You see now arabesque penché en pointe."

"Count, if you don't mind I do not like to be referred to in that manner. And I'm afraid I cannot dance."

"Ah but of course, of course. I would not dream to offend you. But you must not call me Count. So cold. So unfriendly. Brutus, please. And yes. I do remember so well that dear sad man. And the such terrible sadness of his lady. That such wonderful wonderful Clarissa, so gay, so carefree. Such joy to laugh with her. I always laugh with her. So jolly. But then. We must not dwell on death. We must dwell on the delight of how nice we meet in this neck, how do you say, of the woods. But I tell you now my good news my dear fellow. From Milano Italy comes my inheritance. Of course I still keep my little school. But no longer must I teach. Now I am rich again. So you must come to my party. Only the best people. Of course do not take notice of that sailor. We will have new nicer sailors. I do not mind if

236

they are rough. I am stronger anyway. But I hate when they are too too coarse without the proper manners. And I do not invite him. But since you are not on your way to the gentlemen's convenience around the corner, we go together to the Buttery. And then you must come with me to my party. And we should not any longer stand here to freeze to death on the street."

Darcy Dancer keeping abreast of the rapidly striding feet of the Count MacBuzuranti. So lightfootedly gliding over the granite slabs. Executing attitudes allongées nearly en pointe à la Nijinsky off the curb stones. Passing again the turrets of the Turkish baths. And the closed back gates of Trinity College. The dental hospital. The recent Elizabethan windows of this pub, Lincoln's Inn. The big brass plate on the door, Mission to Lepers. Turn left up Kildare Street. The Count skipping up to the top step of my father's club. And diving in a heart stopping attitude croisée to the street again. Thank god the shutters are closed on the windows. Hiding away the big blazing coal fires inside as well as club members' eyes.

"But my Darcy, you see it is so simple. And I waste my genius to teach you to dance in the big castle in the country. It is not only good for the body but the mind as well. And now you are so elegant, so tall, and so much more attractive you have become. So many of us, as the time too fast flies, are ugh, so unattractive. You come on Monday. I give you free lessons at my school dear boy."

Darcy Dancer trotting to keep up. The Count O'Biottus, flying through his repertoire. His head snapping back to shout olé over his shoulder, his scarf waving and his coat flapping like wings in the breeze. As he goes en pointe down Molesworth Street. A gang following. Of barefoot newsboys. Their open torn shirts, the worn out seats of their short trousers. Green thick phlegm seeping from their nostrils. As they clap laugh and cheer and chant.

"Give us a penny mister. Do it again mister. Mister do it again. And give us a penny."

The urchins' awed ooos and ahs. The Count leaping from the porch of the Masonic Lodge. So Protestant and respectable. Doing a complete head over heels somersault through the air. Landing miraculously on his feet in front of his open mouthed audience. Thank god the Royal Hibernian Hotel is near ahead.

"Hey mister are you from a circus. Give us a penny will you mister."

"Now little boys of course, here are your pennies. Here are your shillings. And halfcrowns I scatter for you."

The Count throwing money back down the street. Towards the Dail Eireann. The newsboys fighting. Kicking and punching each other. Screams bites and scratches. As they chase and snatch at the coins.

"Ah Darcy, you see, how sad. They maim. They hurt. Come let us go. If they did not steal so I would invite all these little boys to my party. But like the colours of the rainbow, I invite the Black Widow. The White Prince. The Lemon Lady. The Purple Fucker, the Green Shit, Josintha, the musical sow. She grunts and squeals as she gets fucked standing on the head. And, my dear, did you know what Lois say about you all over Dublin. Ah you blush already before I tell you. She talk so much about your private part. O I do rush on don't I. Ah you blush again. She too shall be at my party."

"I am certainly not blushing."

"Ah but we know so much about you dear boy, much more than you think. Lois say you are well endowed. And of course I see her painting of you. In which is your prick, is flaccid of course. She knows better than anyone, the size of all the pricks in Dublin. She say when hard you have the second biggest. Not the biggest balls of course. But you would not expect God to be so kind to give you both. Would you. She adores to paint mine because I have myself so very wonderful, wonderful balls she says. Tending to be of the more aristocratic perfectly ellipsoidal instead of the more peasant rounder Irish variety. I admit my prick is not the very biggest. But if you come to my party you shall see my portrait. Ah but maybe now you wonder. Who it is who have a bigger prick than you. I tell you. His name is Harry. He is the aesthete. He is poetic. Harry comes to see me dance. Backstage I lock out the crowds. I say in the dressing room to Harry to show me your prick, Harry. But like you he is too shy. And the girls they are too many who push us boys away from Harry. He is so handsome. So I do not see his prick. I take him to Jammet's for dinner. He eats like a horse. So he must have a cock like a horse. Otherwise we must take such a big cock on trust. But who cares about such monsters. It is the little tiny beauties of the mind, my dear which matter so high above

238

all the long thick delicious cocks and balls like grapefruits. So perhaps if you show me your hard cock I shall know how big is the second biggest, my angel. Don't answer yet. Later I ask you again. Maybe then you answer yes. But always let us have ghiribizzo giocoso and grazia in all things."

The Count gathering in his scarves and coat as he goes sweeping across the black and white tiled front lobby of the Hibernian Hotel. That reassuring coal fire blazing in the grate. The porter nodding and smiling to see one. Girls behind the reception desk giggling, digging each other in the ribs. As I take off my cap. And the Count shakes his blond locks back over his ears. Sauntering by the grand staircase into the lounge. Pirouetting left and right past the little groups gathered about their tables. Under the faint cerulean blue skylight, conversation stopped. The Count casting upon the sudden silence merry and highly suggestive quips.

"Hello, hello, all you so nice people. Who are so nice to see you. Hello. Hello. Now that I am so unforgivably rich my dears. We shall later together all lift up our dresses, let down our hair and get to know each other better. All our lovely selves we shall unite in love n'est ce pas."

The Count waving his departure. Darcy Dancer following him down stairs. Thank god, into the darker cellar labyrinths of the Buttery. Where there won't be so many eyebrow raising gentry. But plenty of socially outcast untouchables. Whom one should avoid, if not to end up spending the entire rest of one's shortened life in besotted drunken debauch and penury. Not to mention being flung into a cauldron of the Count's friends unmercifully prodding each other with their pricks and gigglingly squeezing each other's balls. Already hear certain loud voices one knows only too well.

"Bash on regardless, all you damn nae hope commoners. And may I remind you that it is only through the fault of my stern handsome father and my beautiful mother who abandoned me to numerous doting nannies who overindulged me at an early age and set me upon the road to debauchery, that I am here among you. I know that my charm and unbearably good looks attract the many queers among you, drinking far too much of my excellent champagne, but would you please stop edging the women away out of my proximity. And do fuck off about your own bollocksing buggery."

Rashers. My god look at him. In tailcoated splendour, striped trousers. Red carnation. Amid this plethora of misfits. His Ardagh Chalice on the bar being stuffed with another magnum of champagne. As he hefts the aperture about and empties the bottle into the Black Widow's glass. The mirrors, the murmurs deep down in this Buttery. Rashers grinning with both bulging cheeks. Absolutely on top of his form. As if money were no object. Judging now from the new number of hands holding out glasses which he so readily fills.

"Drink up, nae hopers. Drink up. And let there be more dreams ahead of you upon which to sail your injured spirits."

Rashers cocking back his head under his own upended glass. And now he sees me. As his empty glass hits the bar. A distinct if brief apprehension flashing across his face. Disappearing in his welcoming smile. Dismounting his stool. Pushing his way towards me between the jam of shoulders. Of jockeys, trainers and ballroom dancers. And here at this end of the bar, right in front of me, bloody hell, is the Poet. Whose first terrified sight of me strangely turns to a most sickly ingratiating grin. His brand new shiny regrettably blue suit. And thoroughly inappropriate red white and blue striped tie. And taking his cigarettes, not out of a pack of ten, but from a whole pack of twenty. And who suddenly appears to be surrounded by doting admirers instead of the usual indifferent habitués who normally would take great pleasure in shoving his sheets of poetry back in his face and kicking in his teeth or slowly lowering their heels crushingly on his balls.

"Ah my dearest friend Darcy, my dear Kildare. The noble Marquis of Delgany. Let the man pass. Let him pass through to me. My most triumphant and honoured fellow. Forgive these about among whom one must momentarily rub elbows. But how are you my dear boy. The soul comforting pleasure of your great country house lives still in my heart. Come. Let me lead you. You are of course to drink some champagne. For any moment soon, we shall sadly be hearing our host behind this bar singing last orders now, and time ladies and gentlemen please. From *Gray's Anatomy* let me recite for you the muscles of the throat and neck. But O dear, in a gathering such as this, perhaps it is more appropriate to treat of the muscles of the pelvic outlet. The corrugator curtis ani. The external and internal sphincter ani."

"Rashers. I believe you are staying at the Shelbourne Hotel."

"Good lord. Am I. How do you know. O dear you do know. But

ah not so loud dear boy, not so loud. Although I am in partial incognito up there, there are those still about whose ears I should not like that personally pleasant information to sink into. At least not quite yet. But damn, it is such a nice relief to shake from one's person the indignities of low life."

"I believe you are occupying a suite. And also, so it appears, assuming a title. You do seem suddenly awfully prosperous."

"Well yes, but don't you think it suits me. A few winners at the races dear boy. But heavens above, am I to assume by these questions that you are being shirtily aggrieved in some manner. Pray not be. All is to be well. Of course you shall meet soon my nearest and dearest. She's bought another pub. Dear girl. And would you believe it her accountants have agreed to her acquiring, at my suggestion, also a turf accountant's shop. Where I shall in future credit my bets. These are times for acting one's true role in life. Do taste, my dear boy from this plate. The brown breads and the orange pink of this smoked salmon. Our dear Count Brutus MacBuzuranti is giving one of his soirees tonight. As he did last night and the previous night. And the night before that. You're coming of course. To frolic among the folk singers and authentic Aran islanders in their pampooties, not to numerously mention the lesbians, nymphomaniacs, literati, the nancy boys and lepidopterists."

In a turf smoke scented drizzle of rain, a procession of little groups arriving outside this narrow red brick Georgian building down Duke Street. A brass sign over the letter opening. The MacBuzuranti School of Ballet. Red curtains drawn over the lighted windows. Sound of throbbing music. Climbing up these narrow stairs. The walls ashake and bannister trembling. The voice of the Count O'Biottus himself on the top landing receiving.

"Come, come up my dear nice people. And into my office. One and all. Welcome."

Into the small sea of old familiar faces. Squeezed tight against each other. The wheaty fragrance of Irish whisky. The musky smell of hemp. Stout bottles upending pouring down the throats. The Count's portraits of the Popes one remembers from another address near Molesworth Street. And smack between these supreme pontiffs of the holy Roman Catholic Church, Lois's massive stark raving nude portrait of the Count.

241

"Take no notice my dear nice people of me in the altogether. Even though my body is so beautiful."

Drunken eyes welcoming one back. My god. There is Lois. Her hair braided in a long blond pigtail. The far end of the room gossiping in her loud Bloomsbury voice. With an even longer cigarette holder. And seeing me. Beckoning to me across the heads. As one's suddenly hardening prick points the way through the turned backs, bent elbows and indeed one or two open flies and gleaming white stiff pricks exposed.

"Darling dear boy, how nice to see you again. You're shaving your face. But you mustn't. Let a little hair grow which I so adore on pretty young men. Of course you are still a callow youth. While my pubic hair is going rapidly grey. You do, don't you, I understand, have a very adequate place in the countryside. A very very large house. To which, may I say, I am extremely chagrined not to have been invited. How dare you not invite me. I don't foxhunt but surely you have room somewhere for me to paint by northern light. I've just come down from the Dawson Lounge. Been all by myself the entire evening in a most boring corner. Having to smoke my own cigarettes and buy my own drinks. Don't people know I am poor. And that I must get on with my etchings. Where tell me, are the serious patrons of the arts. Have they no feelings for the artist. Allowing me to subsist on simply nothing at all. But I don't want to complain."

"Lois do forgive me. But you are, aren't you, totally full of shit."

"I say, how dare you. Damn you. Be so bloody rude. I've been suffering. Do you know what it is to truly suffer. How would you know in your big house. That I am freezing to death in my own studio. Not even enough milk to feed my cats. Both of whom have recently died."

"I am sorry to hear that."

"And you clearly are a very rich young man. While I haven't had a holiday by the seaside for years. I can't afford it. Nor can I afford tubes of paint."

"Here please, take this Lois."

"What. Take money from you. How dare you attempt to bribe me. I have no intention to compromise myself or my art."

"Bloody hell, I'm not bribing or compromising you. I'm just trying

242

to shut you up a moment in your complaining. And you can buy your tubes of paint."

"In that case, I shall shut up and take it. But insist I give you an etching. It may not be signed of course. And dear boy even though you have become quite rude, it is quite nice to see you. Come closer. I shall stick my tongue deeply in your ear."

"Thank you. I am as a matter of fact more than rather mildly randy."

"You poor dear lecherous boy. You may come home with me. But you do realise I can't promise you anything. In fact you may have to masturbate. Since this is my celibate period. One must be celibate to exact from one's inner spirit the full use of the self in the creation of one's work. Without the emotional havoc pricks inside one can cause. It is a contradiction in terms but my celibate period is my most fertile. I'm sure any number of our dear friends here will gladly accommodate you."

"O god. I am not a homosexual."

"Why O god. So despairingly. Most of my nicest friends are homosexual."

"I'd rather go home with you."

"That's nice to know. But as I've just told you, there's to be no hanky panky."

"You have you know considerably steamed me up by your tongue."

"Well I appreciate your telling me. I should hate to bring you back to my studio and have you then attempt to rape me."

"Why are you then arousing me kissing me like this."

"I shall immediately stop then."

"Please don't."

"Well I shall. You see. You are so utterly indifferent to the requirements of my life. I am not saying I am not quite glad you have given me five pounds. Please don't misunderstand me. But it is so simple for you to find another outlet for the erection I may have given you. And if you remember I haven't completed your portrait yet. It's there in my studio gathering dust. Of course if you can manage another payment on account, I shall prepare another sitting for you and get a bag of coal for my stove."

More arrivals up the stairs. Gas meter readers. Stars of stage and radio. Deafening noise of voices. All the louder now that Lois's tongue is no longer plunging deep in one's ear. At least it did shut up her complaining. My god, what a mob. The floor is quaking with the weight. Whole damn building could fall Georgian faced flat down into the street. The Poet smirking across there in the corner. And goodness. How sad. Clara the poetess. With about four macintoshed, battered trilby hatted, criminal looking, doting men in tow. Poor Mr Arland. It was at such a party as this, he first met Clarissa. She laughed at his jokes. Now not another inch to stand in this room. Smoke smarting one's eyes as the grinning face of Rashers comes near. And Lois with a haughty sneer and snake like lick around her lips, turning away. As one recalls Rashers' remark about her paintings. The insane ravings of an alley cat in heat. Now of course they'll be the wild deliriums of one in celibacy.

"My dear Darcy. Please. Just allow me to contemplate you a moment. Just to see you is like music reigning in the bright key of E major. Come spring. Come Ascot. Tea at the Paddock Bar. Gentle goosings up the best arses in the Royal Enclosure. But meanwhile of course, you will, won't you, join me in my pilgrimage. Back to the sacred evil confines of the catacombs. From whence I have finally escaped. The stench. The gurriers. I hid my best cufflinks in the wall. And must retrieve them. Well dear Darcy, I see Lois has your trousers sticking out. Most women pretend they're mad. And I think perhaps the only charming thing about Lois is, that she really is mad."

"I just heard what you said, you awful man. And you're not, Darcy Kildare, leaving me for that dreadful fortune hunting philistine person are you. Well go then and don't you ever speak to me again."

One did think sadly as one departed with Rashers that a piece of arse in the hand in the Count's dancing institution might be worth two in the rumoured underground tunnels of where one was going. However, hardly a moment to dwell on such problems as other matters were quickly afoot. Just as one was coming down the last flight of stairs of the MacBuzuranti School of Ballet. An almighty sound of a crash. Screams coming up from the front hallway. Where the Poet had just landed showered in plaster and rotted lumps of wood, prick in his hands and peeing right upon the hysterical legs of two of the Count's refined female ballet patrons who must have been loitering too shy to advance up the stairs into the thick of things.

"How dare you do that upon us."

The Poet continuing to indiscriminately piss on them. Puffing on a cigarette still hanging out of his mouth with a look of only slight amazement on his face. Having just two floors above in a water closet, his pockets weighted down, suddenly gone straight through the lavish and constantly pissed upon purple thick carpet covering the totally disguised rotted floor and the force of his descent taking him through the next rotted floor to deposit him where the ballet patrons stood now brushing themselves off as they looked up at the hole the Poet had just come through and underneath which he was now trying to hold his water and get his penis back in his fly as the ladies were, with their patent leather handbags, taking swipes at his face. Rashers shouting from the front door.

"That's it, dear ladies. Smite him. He is a well known disgusting pervert."

The jarvey leaping down to open the horse cab door. Tipping his cap as he slammed it shut. Rashers taking a flask from his coat pocket. Filling the cap with brandy.

"Let justice triumph. Of course your man's only a minor poet. Clearly Darcy the entire building is suspect. At least in the catacombs my dear fellow, if one goes downwards, it's only on the way to hell."

Hoofs clip clopping through the empty Dublin streets. Shiny and wet under the glowing pale light of the gas lamps. The mist and fog along St Stephen's Green. Bells over the city tolling midnight. We go, mid the shadows passing. By the gloomy great old skulls of these houses. The musky dampness inside this unhandsome cab. Ancient broken leather cushions covered in old rugs and remnants of an overcoat. Awful reek of stale cat smells. Rashers, eyes burning like coals in his head. As he lowers his flask, his teeth smiling out his lips. Hands planted upon each of his stripe trousered knees. Cuffs of his coat sleeves drawn back. Veins standing out on his wrists.

"Let us Darcy bash on regardless. To the catacombs. The cellars of nae hope. Although the class of people shall not be much improved, they do at least make abject attempts at being odiously revolting which one takes as cautionary as to whom and what one should avoid in life. Darcy we must remain friends. You see before you a man who for a brief but devastating period of his youth was thrust into an insti-this time of night. Still trying to sell a paper. Suppose it would be to a

245

better word. In a trice those sadists turned me from a pure stainless spirit into an instant and unhappy reluctant masochist and liar. Slamming rulers down on my pathetic upraised innocent palms. Ridiculing me. Elegant as I was with my nice clothes and brave little British accent. Beating the poor pathetic bejesus out of me. Heroic sanctity one needed in abundance to sustain against their poisoned souls and brutally evil ways. Of course before it was too late, one did escape back to the civilised safety, albeit highly homosexual, world of an English public school. But those brief months of my tender youth in Dublin left their scars. I know I have been upon occasion a very bad boy since. But all done in pursuit of what I desperately require in life. Merely a modest simple detached house with a wee bit of lawn front and back. Perhaps a little garden too. Is that too much to ask for. With a non leaking jade or even pewter pot to piss in. Some decent bloodstock at a nearby training establishment to which I might venture after breakfast to watch them being ridden out of a morning. And my dearly beloved near. You see, I should not want to straight off reside on her very adequate acres until I have some of my very own wherewithal. Although she's getting on, the dear girl does have a passably resilient pair of decent bosoms. Legs like a refectory table. And nipples not awfully attractive but then, I do find there are variations one can indulge upon them which are adequately exciting in pitch blackness. But Darcy, in what I say to you now, you must dear man believe me. There are many shameful deeds one has done. And I ask please pray accept my contrition. Pray accept. Will you."

"But Rashers of course. But I don't quite know what on earth you're talking about."

"Darcy. It was I. Me. Who is responsible for the theft of your silver."

"Good heavens."

"Find it in your heart to forgive me. Please. You see these tears. Coming out of my eyes. Don't you. It is simply that I can not bear to perpetrate the deceit any longer. I beg you. Do have it in your heart to forgive me. I'm so close now to ushering my dear one up the aisle. Do remain silent if you wish. I do understand that you may feel our friendship has been fatally breeched. Darcy there does, in all of us, exist some little semblance of worthiness. Even too, in me. Though I may have at times stooped unbelievably low. And done things which utterly rack me with shame. This silk hanky upon which my tears now fall. I give to you. Take it. Darcy, my dear Darcy. Take it with you. Through your life. Keep warm from the cold of the world. Keep aloof from its brash noise and fashion. Keep safe from its betrayal."

And
Never forsake
Your sweet
Compassion

18

Up past the little park and terrace of bright doored houses around Fitzwilliam Square, the horse cab stopping in this shadowy street. Soft misty rain falling. A black cat stepping down from the curb stone. Shaking its paws as it steps in a puddle of water. Rashers alighting, popping on his top hat and sweeping his cloak around him and holding up his hand to Darcy Dancer.

"We are here, dear boy. And you'd never know it, would you, from this rather presumptuously refined and respectable street. Do follow me. And don't be appalled."

The driver, his whip left stuck like a fishing rod over the quarters of his nag, climbing down with his blanket to wrap himself in. A greasy parcel of potato chips tucked under his arm as he steps up into the back of his cab to wait.

"That's a good chap my jarvey. We shall be presently back."

"Right you are, no hurry your Lordship. Sure catching ten winks or forty winks is all the same to me."

"Dear me, Darcy, what do we see over there. A damsel. Perhaps in distress."

Rashers walking away on the pavement towards an alley, a lone figure of a girl against a wall. Her head hanging down watching a puddle gather between her broken high heeled shoes as she stands peeing down her legs. Rashers putting a pound note in front of her face which she grabs clutching in her fingers.

"Is it a short time you want."

"No my dear girl. I simply want you as desirable company. And who knows I may have a promising future for you. Come there'll be another pound or two later."

Rashers taking the girl by the elbow. Leading her with him to a gate he opens in the stone railings. Making his steep way down the steps in front of us.

"Where are you taking me a'tall."

"Dear girl, your mother must have been a sensible lady to have christened you Sheena. Sheena you don't know your luck, do you. You happen to be momentarily in the refined company of two gentlemen who wish you much profit and no harm. You see, if later we have a moment to talk to you, we would like to put the question for which I was banished when putting it to the Philosophical Society of Trinity College Dublin, that this house moves to find the greater truth in the statements, deep in every woman's heart is a whore, or deep in every whore's heart is a woman."

"Don't youse be wasting me time. And how do you know me name. Why is youse dressed like that. Youse is students."

"Ah we are Sheena, of a sort, students of fucking, that's how we know. And down here is the night school of comparative anatomy we attend. For spiritual autopsies on the mind."

"Would there be any rashers, eggs and chips."

"Quite possibly my dear, quite possibly. A spud or two at least."

Rashers pressing a button and knocking on the big black door. Piles of empty stout bottles. Rancid smell of cats. Bars on a large window. Light inside and voices shouting and singing. A rat scurrying into a coal cellar under the pavement. The door opening. Behind a whisky bottle, Binky's face at the end of a long cigarette holder, peeking out the door.

"Ah it's you my dear. Welcome back. Even though you still owe me last month's rent. Come in and bring your nice friends. Whose bodies I'm sure someone will be interested in. And who is this male lovely with you I'm sure I've seen somewhere before. And I do love the way you are attired. So many of my tenants go walking out of here in the morning in their pyjamas to return by evening in their opera cloaks. But instead of arias of course, you'll hear nothing but a lot of choking croaking. Of pricks my dear, down the throats. Ah. That's very nice. Thank you for the six pounds. And my girl do pardon my nudity."

Binky's thin shanks and arse disappearing with a mincing skip. Through another door and out into the light of this large stone paved room. Figures in little groups around the walls. A kettle steaming on a great cooking range. A copper tank in the corner. A table covered in grey parcels full of bottles. Drawn corks and broken crockery strewn everywhere. A man huddled over an egg stained plate stuffing bacon rinds in his mouth.

"My dears, do make yourselves at home among the other dears. Too many of whom tonight I'm afraid resemble condoms full of custard. Then of course there are so many among us with arse holes like deck quoits that the two can easily fit together."

A man rearing up out of a corner. Collar up on his coat. Hat pulled down on his head. And waving his arms.

"Ah you're making a great attempt at originality you poofta whore, you. But them's all platitudes and clichés."

Rashers leading Darcy Dancer aside. A burlap bag of potatoes and one of cabbages. A pile of wet turf stinking of cat shit.

"Dear boy we stand next to what did keep me alive. And slightly unfrozen for miserable weeks. A sack full of Wicklow potatoes. And these mouldering cabbage leaves. And dear boy, you won't. In this dungeon of nae hope. Promise me you won't. Lose your faith in human nature. I do know in the present circumstances that that does sound rather sham coming from me."

"And I suppose too Rashers, one should keep the safe locked in which one keeps one's silver, to prevent the thefts perpetrated by one's friends."

"I deserve that, dear Darcy. I do. But borrowing is such a better word. Can't you see looking about you in this place how one was driven to it. All the long months during which one hardly had said to one, a single endearing thing. And even now, having managed a new start, when nice things are said to one, one simply does not believe them to be true. Just look at these wretches. From whence I have torn myself. Of course I was led into temptation by that pissing poet chap.

Spouting his awful impertinent verse. I mean there he was, an utterly uninvited guest at Andromeda Park. Helping himself greedily to your hospitality. Stuffing his face at your expense. I did give him a piece of my mind. I said to him, I said, how dare you arrive here, creeping sneakily about and eating from my esteemed friend's table when you have not earned the remotest right to be referred to as a friend. Fuck off out of my sight, I said. Before your arse gets kicked into the shape of your face and makes you less ugly than you are. I really did say that Darcy, you know. Of course the wretched chap paused a microsecond in chomping down his fistful of greasy sausages and glass of brandy, and suddenly turned on me to say the only thing he has ever said that has impressed me. He said, ah jesus now, wouldn't you at least be letting me be treated as well as the horses that's out there in the stables of this place. It did make me think Darcy. That all over Ireland, even in the worst stables, horses live better than most of the humans. It was in fact his heartfelt words which incited me to procure him as intermediary in the temporary taking of a loan of your silver. And I absolutely shall return all. Even the leather suitcases I took the liberty of borrowing in which the Poet lugged away the less valuable Sheffield plate, spoons and knives. Of course I took the most precious silver back with me on the train."

"However, you did Rashers, despite this long elaborate tale behave like a common thief."

"Please Darcy, don't use such language. I mean I have already suffered such spiritual agony over it all. That's how the wretched poet fell through the floor. Still loaded down with some of your poorer quality cutlery."

"Are you bloody well now telling me my silverware is of poor quality."

"No. No. Never. And I assure you the better stuff is with the most reputable pawn merchant. Whose ticket I shall be at any moment placing in your hand. You see I did successfully bet the proceeds but I fear previous debt and recent expenditure have been high and I regret that I do not have sufficient funds left to repatriate the silver items back into your hopefully forgiving hands."

"Are you now attempting to perpetrate a further spiv con upon me."

"Darcy you do take such a poor view of my person. When I shall in

251

only a moment now place in your hands my cufflinks as collateral. Each has a diamond as big as a decent sized petit pois. Also hidden in the wall is the pawn ticket that I shall also give you. I mean your continued friendship is everything to me. Everything. I know I have done the unforgivable. But who but me would have confessed to your face. Here have a nip of brandy. Do you like my flask. I've had it emblazoned with the escutcheon of the Earls of Ronald Ronald. You see. Two stallions rampant. With crossed erections."

In this battered Hessian draped cavernous room, Rashers his opera cloak thrown back from his shoulders, its crimson lining blazing in the bleakness as he turns in each direction bowing and smiling to faces he has clearly bowed and smiled to before. Of course one's compassion was also to the fore, even though between his heart rending profundities, he spoke such utter tripe and onions. But it is I suppose the way one says things which matters. And even if morally fraudulent he does have such a warmly effusive manner.

"Of course, Darcy that stench you are noticeably recoiling from is the odour of yearly unwashed bodies. Utterly appalling isn't it. If they didn't assemble in these little groups, the smell of one big group would simply asphyxiate. Imagine having to face one's breakfast every morning in such a fume. But such woe happily shall no longer assail me. As you notice by the graphic priapic and testicular designs, my dear Darcy, Lois has done the wall decor. Some of the best known pricks in Dublin. She complains of course that Binky who commissioned her has not paid her. But ah now let me a moment Darcy point out to you the various habitués. Driven by their poverty here. Valentine, that balding chap with the well rounded gut there is from that important provincial town Mullingar on the Grand Canal. You'd never know now would you that he is the former whistling champion of Ireland. Ruddy chap can polish off a stone of raw steak at a sitting. He has an equally fat sister with a pair of tits the size of the Atlantic shelf who is a champion bridge player. Regard him lecherously eyeing Sheena, poor sad whoring girl, her name is about the only distinctive thing she possesses. I don't know why on earth I didn't simply leave her up there on the street pissing in her knickers. Except that I plan to wash and brush her up. Put her back on the road to respectability as a much more highly paid whore. And of course our whistling champion thinks she is free of charge."

A cauldron of potatoes boiling on a cooking range. Rancid smells fuming variously in the fug of steam and smoke. Children's eyes peeking in from behind a coal scuttle door. A fearful tiny auburn headed girl standing shrinking back under a water tank in the corner. Perhaps Crooks in his spare time might emulate Binky, the Black Widow's butler. Binky his fist full of pound and ten shilling notes he collects, nakedly rushing back and forth with drinks for three terrified wide eyed American tourists.

"Now my dears, the black mass presently in progress in the first wine cellar is being said by the Rev. MacNamara, Bishop of Kilburn. It's all very cheap at the price my dears. You won't see anything like it in Milwaukee, Wisconsin. This additional admission price, not included at the front door does entitle you to entry into the back passage, no pun intended, nevertheless it is where you might do anything to anybody my dears and anybody may, if you are pretty enough, do something to you too. Then you can tell everyone back in Dayton, Ohio how excitingly devout you found holy Catholic Ireland to be."

A bull like figure with long black cascades of hair, the hump of a broken nose jutting on his face, waddling out into the middle of the room. His shirt torn open over his belly and stumpy fingers clutching an overflowing pint glass. Tongues bent forward out his shoes, their worn sides turning over as he walked. Whites of his feet and ankles showing through the tatters of his trousers. Like some tiny king. He licks his lips smiling. Standing contentedly surveying his kingdom. Crouched by his elbow, a mild little man in a grey suit, with bottles in each hand replenishing his drink. Pouring port, and poteen every time he took a swallow. And nodding a smiling yes every time he throws back his head to sing.

Our father
Who art in bliss
Down here in hell
Hallowed be thine orgasm
Thy kingdom come
Like we have lately done
All over his
Or her fucking face

253

"That's disgusting the song he's singing."

"Did I hear you say disgusting, madam. Sure your name must be Eeena. The female insult to humanity. Peeking out from behind the aspidistra. Deigning to come among us. To take your filthy gossip notes to flog to the British gutter press. Now madam if you'll keep your emotions to a minimum for a moment I'll give you a taste of the low and scurrilous to fill your fucking column to the full. For a start report this. Bang. The most unfragrant fart laid this century."

"You're a most dreadful person."

"And how Madam would you like to be sentenced to the horrible tragedy of marrying me. With me life an intoxicated celebration devoted to the constant and relentless protest against death. I sang for you the liturgical plain song of the catacombs. In order that you wouldn't give up hope in your suburban desperation for catharsis. Did you know that by day right above me head is a chair screwed to the floor where a reputable dentist drills and yanks out rotted teeth. And the screams up there drown out the calls for help down here. Did you know that. Now Madam, the next time I make my annual speech to the members of the royal society of coprophagists anonymous, I'd like if you would demonstrate how you gamarouched the last bit of rusty old sperm out that bollocks of a husband you married for his few miserable quid."

"How dare you say such things to me. Hit him somebody."

"Madam, don't please encourage unnecessary violence before the necessary violence commences. Instead now meet me at the pawn shop and kiss me under the balls. Sure I was baptised in a money lender's. And remember that as a dirty filthy Catholic you're among clean pure Orangemen down here. And may the beatific light sparkling from the pontiff's ring, shine upon the sins you've committed in your commodious and semi detached residence in Rathgar. With its one and a half water closets, where the gombeen likes of you and your mean bollocks of a husband are over your soufflé supper giving blessed thanks for your safe deliverance from socialism. While the noble illustrious likes of me is having to kip down in the Dublin shelter for men at thirty one Tara Street if I'm not over at me Iveagh House address in Bride Street, having to take me daily morning walks in fucking working class infamy up and down Grafton Street looking to quell me pangs of thirst and find a few bob for the few bottles of Mountjoy

Nourishing Stout served over the north side in Madigan's of Earl Street at a penny cheaper than the Guinness variety so that when I'd have six drunk you'd have the price of a seventh free. While the fucking likes of you bred in hypocrisy are on your rayon smooth arse on your imitation Louis the cat's torts chaise longue drinking your Rathgar pink gin pinched delicately between your manicured fingers in front of your three bar electric fire. Fuck off then back there if you don't want to listen to the likes of me rearing up out of the gutter in your face. Sure what would the sham cultured likes of you know of black shawled and bare foot women coming a wintry wet night shivering with death into shops to buy a pennyworth to eat, or a single rasher or egg or small pat of butter or a quarter a loaf of bread to take back to give the tiny crumbs to a dozen childer clutched together on the same rotted mattress up the fucking freezing stairs of some Georgian rat hole. Who the fuck are you to say I'm dreadful. Don't I know as well as you do, that my redeemer liveth. And when he has a moment free from making his personal appearances, getting his pucks of publicity all over the kip, you may be sure that the first fucking thing he'll tell you is that he fucking well loveth me. For the tiny bit of honesty that passes me lips once in a while, more than he fucking well loveth you, for your phoney pose of Irish female sincerity. Here come kiss this. The pale priestly skin of my prick. Take thou a sip of this spit from this holy horn most high. And may the red star in the east, shine like the star of Bethlehem. Up the Republic. And may the good Lord bless me while defenceless I sleep."

"You are the most filthy disgusting person."

"Ah with me hands in prayer, close me eyes now, and I will seek the intercession of the Blessed Gainor Stephen Crist, who one day soon will be canonized as the patron saint of those driven to drink when the bedevilment of the fucking significance of life makes them think it has no meaning better than that found in another jar of stout."

"Can't someone stop him blaspheming."

"Of course I am Madam all those things you mention. But as to what I do in my diabolism, is me own fucking business. Sure, the letter E beginning as it does your name, would give you a bad start in life. Being as it is the first letter of such words as evil not to mention ebb, eczema, edema and electrocution. But eftsoons, egad, if you give us the velocity of your viscosity of your bifurcation, madam and get out your big pair of bosoms. I'd get out my cock. And during my premature ejaculation spattering your purity you could beat me to death with your bound copies of the *Catholic Herald*."

"Why doesn't someone kick him flying."

"Madam, I'm flying already. Wait while I take a read of me altimeter. Meanwhile did you hear what the toilet bowl said to the arse. Thank you for dropping that in. Give me Vat Sixty Nine now. And it's not the Pope's telephone number I'm after. And while I put my yarmulka on give the woman in bed more petroleum. And would someone ever divulge to me this instant the fucking melting point of tungsten."

"Three thousand degrees centigrade."

"Give the Phi Beta Kappa man who knew that a bottle of stout. And Madam that's about the likes of the heat that it would take to melt you into a decent piece of arse."

"Someone please take me home out of here."

Eeena in her big black hat, hands up to her face, rushing for the door. Two men in attendance upon her turning to look back. A bottle smashing on the wall next to one of their heads as they hasten their departure. Buster The Beastly putting his pint glass to his lips, his adam's apple going up and down in his throat gulping down the contents in one long swallow. Murmurs of disapproval. Growls of objection. A man, arms folded across his chest, grey weather beaten hat clamped down on his skull, looks round as he shouts.

"Now the evil likes of you is nothing but a treacherous gurrier only fit to be a rat down in the likes of this vile place."

Buster The Beastly rocking back on his heels, face contorted in a snarl and jutting his head towards the man in the battered grey hat.

"With your phoney quaint innocent verse dotted with primroses, go back and piss on the soil from which your refreshingly natural rhymes grow. You fucking bog peasant. Sure aren't you cricking your neck kissing the arse of the visiting London intelligentsia, and still up to your bollocks in nettles and wiping your own arse with dock leaves."

The man tearing off his grey battered hat throwing it to the stone floor and jumping up and down on it. Wagging his fists around his balding skull.

"I won't be insulted by the likes of worthless trash. Scum you are. Nothing but the worst slandering vicious wickedness, a poison so foul it would kill an oak tree standing a mile away from you."

"So long as you drop dead with it, you cunt, I'd be content."

Rashers coming to the side of Darcy Dancer. His hand gently on his shoulder and smiling into his face. The sound of a fist socking flesh. And of a skull thumping and cracking on the floor.

"I do apologise my dear Darcy for the unseemly unfeeling sentiments you're hearing expressed. The world of art. Nothing but a nest of vipers of course. But soon a better class of café society will be arriving. But I see you're just quietly here watching and listening. And even a little bemused. Ah but I see our big bellied champion whistler is joining us who's long been a fellow tenant of mine down here. Ah my dear Valentine allow me to introduce you to Marquis of Delgany and Kilquade. I was just explaining to his Lordship how you and I, products of good schools and families have had to incarcerate here in this malevolent homespun condition."

"And a worse place for barbarians you couldn't find. And you whore you, don't know your old friends now, over there in the Shelbourne stretching your legs out over an entire floor."

"Ah now Val, that may be temporarily true. But you see what I've brought for you. Sheena, over there. Price is usually a tenner. But as she's a little laggards tonight there is a fifty per cent reduction. For you of course there is a further discount of a quid making four pounds and only requiring two pounds and ten shillings in advance if you please."

"You'd sell the pubic hairs off your mother in her coffin, you whore you. I'll pay you two and a half thumps in the gob. And have the lady for nothing."

"Please Valentine, I can see you've already shocked his Lordship here. That's the type of uncalled for vulgar intransigence that really does try one's patience. Don't please fuck up my little enterprise now, which has been such a long time organizing. Sheena needs some sprucing up, one admits, but you'll find beneath her rags an awfully curvaceous creature. And there's more where she came from. Her mother who presides over an assorted vegetable barrow in Henry Street is from a long line of genuine Mecklenburg Street whores, her poor dear father, a Guinness barrel having fallen upon his toe, is now an incorrigible invalid drinking to excess the very thing that crippled him in the first place."

"O.K. you awful whore you, here's thirty bob and even that's too much. Goodbye now, you bloody awful chancer."

"Ah Darcy, see what a brilliant ponce I am. I've sold Sheena not only to the whistling champ, but to four other insanely sexually frustrated chaps who I hope will all have the patient decency to peacefully wait in a row."

"That's absolutely disgraceful."

"Ah I knew dear boy you'd disapprove. But you know, strange fact of life, the least expense is often involved in the making of the most profit. You do, don't you, find this place unfitting. O dear. So do I. But take heart. There in the dark suits the far side of the room, stand gentlemen members of the Legion of Decency. Who are also on the government censorship board. Indeed I think I also spy militant members of the Legion of Mary. Dear me. I actually do. They are, bless their hearts, a most deadly serious intentioned people dedicated to stamping out Dublin vice. And although you may not believe it, these catacombs have produced more than their share of candidates for sainthood. In fact the Legion are here in such force, to investigate an apparition. Seen by four of the children. Yes. Happened one morning. I was the other side of that wall. Playing as it would unseemly happen, with my very lonely prick. While a miraculous and beautiful vision took place right in that corner where the water tank stands, and where you now see the statue of the Blessed Virgin in front of which burn those votive lights and candles. It appears that she said she had come to dispense hope to those most without hope. Indeed my dear boy, this hellish hole of Calcutta is now the Lourdes of Dublin. And take no notice of that gesticulating chap in front of the statue of Our Lady. He is, from the end of his foreskinless prick to the top of his red curly head, entirely Hebrew. From a good Jewish Clanbrassil Street family. Those are merely his traffic signals which he frequently employs directing Dublin traffic in the evening rush. Without him the whole city would be a nightmare of entangled bicycles and horsecarts not to mention motor vehicles. You don't believe a single word I'm saying, do you Darcy. Think I'm spinning a fantastic yarn, don't you."

"No, not actually."

"Ah I worship you dear boy. For your tolerant understanding. May I interject then the merest bit of fantasy. One of my former professors in Senior Freshman physics is actually over there, incognito of course, among that strange lot discussing astro nuclear quirks and quarks. He maintains that the atmosphere of this dungeon of despair allows them to reach the very heights of their theoretical explorations."

"And who is that next to them, talking to himself in the mirror."

"Ah dear boy, I'm entirely glad you noticed a lost soul. He is Horatio Macbeth. Sundays past, when both he and I were often low and lonely he visited for tea in my college rooms. Poor devil, banished to Dublin by his rich mill owning family, albeit with a very nice little private income. Fellow couldn't restrain himself pinching ladies' bottoms all over the better parts of Manchester. His great ambition, like us all, to be an actor. You will see him just before pub closing time mouthing his lines into any nearby mirror. Most impressively too. Frequently an entire jammed pub has ended up shouting bravo. He rehearses late at night confronting his reflection in the better shop windows up and down Grafton Street. Dear boy. I must but I must leave you here a moment. Do have another bottle of stout. While I slip away to see if Sheena is earning her keep. And also to collect for you the pawn ticket and my cufflinks. Despite this being the new Lourdes, arguments do appear to continue to rage in a blaze of insult and blame. And dear me, neither souls, morals, principles and especially chattels, are safe."

Rashers disappearing under the arch of the passageway. The stench of bodies, smoke, and fumes thickening. A cold swirl of air around the ankles as the doors to anteroom and the street open and shut. Corks popping, songs singing, and one stands here a sore thumb. In this conflagration of discontent. The cold country night would have long settled now on Andromeda Park. My head on my pillow. Frost white over the fields. Beasts lonely mooing. And O my god, as I stand here deceived and thieved from, I've also stood up Miss von B. A girl grins from across the room. And Leila. Could she have once been someone like Sheena. Women must do anything, anything at all, for money. And now who's this slipping up next to me. Leaning in close to one's ear to whisper.

"Excuse me now. I'm a bit of a nut. Been nineteen years in Grangegorman. Let out an odd weekend now and again to be enjoying a

259

pint of stout among nomal people like yourself. But I was once meself a gas meter reader. And a devout Catholic. And if you don't mind me saying it's a disgrace that the likes of that Buster and a worse friend of his, Danno, should be allowed down here in the vicinity of the holy happening of the apparition. I'm reformed now. And haven't made an impure suggestion to any mother superiors on the doorsteps of their convents when I'd come a calling in me guise as a monk. And that's a fact. And hear that roaring and drum pounding now. That's Danno. And he's coming in here by the sound. And I can tell you sir, I'm going. Goodbye to you. And thanks for your kindness to me."

Emerging from the dark passage, a massive figure, sweat pouring from his brow. Yellow and black rotted teeth in his yawning open jaws. As he grins and holds up a half full whisky bottle in one hand and beats his other in a fist on a great drum strapped to his shoulders. Lurching in to stand next to Buster The Beastly.

"Me name is Danno, when I'm not abroad under me nom de plume of the Reverend Felix De Gascoigne Dilettante, blessing nuns up the bifurcation with me genuine beeswax candles. Shut up now. The bunch of youse. I am here waiting for your emotional attention. And youse now, with a belch out his arse, just heard me friend here in the shoes too short for him give you a fucking valuable piece of his mind. Give us your wet kiss of fealty youse whore British debutantes. While I'd be playing football with the preserved head of Cromwell youse would be playing football with the head of the Blessed Oliver Plunkett off his altar in Drogheda and kicking the last dry old tooth hanging from his cheek out of him. Dehumanized now he may be. But by god he'll be canonized yet. And if any of youse don't have faith in me predictions or so much as mildly offend me friend Buster here doing his fucking utmost to entertain you, I'll stuff the lot of your heads in the fucking Wicklow gap. Listen now while I beat me Lambeg drum I took off an Orangeman. I'm a mental and physical demolitionist. To the animate and inanimate. Pull the fucking lead pipes out of houses. And before pawning them would wrap them around youse necks who don't pay attention and listen to me while I'm telling you. I have just come from singing Ave Maria up there at the top of Nelson's Pillar. With a pint of stout in one hand, me prick in the other. Pissing down one hundred and thirty eight feet on top of the populace waiting for the tram to Dalkey and them all thinking it was a spot of rain. That will give you just an introduction to the fact that I am the most evil scoundrel that any of youse ever met. I am an itinerant. And betimes I am a hospital porter. Humping the female corpses. The breath out of some of them would kill you. When I don't like the look of someone dying in the bed, I give the undertaker measurements six inches too short for the coffin so's the legs have to be broken to get the dead bugger in. When it comes to living and breathing women I am mad on them graduates of the higher institutions of learning. When I am not fucking a woman in peace then I am at war and am given to violence of a violent nature. I am an unreformed informer. Sentenced to death in the absence of my presence, by the high command of the Irish Republican Army. I would beat an old defenceless lady out of two pence. Ah, you'd ask, what is there good about me, I'll tell you. As a true example of the native treachery and viciousness I could be a great tourist attraction. And a living warning of the villain that you'd do well to keep well away from."

"You should be put in a cage."

"Who said that. Sure behind me drum with this bit of chain now I'd undo round me waist I would remove the head off the fucker in this room who said that. That's a threat. I am only just after lifting a publican up by the scruff down there on the Aston Quay and stuffing his grey old head in his own brown old shit bowl. No one will tell me I'm barred from a premises. And don't any of youse use the wrong tone of voice with me."

"Now Danno, I'm Buster your friend. Put away your chain, give us a beat on the drum and tell us about the holy revelation you encountered down there on the quay."

"Me friend here now in that suggestion stated a fact. Never mind the apparition in this place. Didn't I down there on the quays a June summer evening passing a tree look up in the branches to see the Blessed Virgin herself. She said hello Danno. Instead of saying hello or praying back up to her asking for a fucking miracle on the spot, didn't I look up her sky blue habit instead. By god by the look of youse faces listening, if I said she had no knickers on you'd dance out of your minds with rage at the blasphemy. And be next asking me to swear on a stack of bibles the height of Nelson's Pillar, that the immaculate lady had no cunt. And that I swear. She did not have one. And she said, go Danno from this holy spot and spread the news from

Inchicore to Sandymount. And now here's a recent poem now I wrote meself."

> Sure as
> Me name is Danno
> I'm a fucking terror
> To trust me an inch
> Is a mile of error
> While some ladies love me
> I'm still held in dread
> For the rest of the hypocritical bunch of you
> Would fucking love to see me dead

A figure emerging from the shadows of the passage. Stepping up behind Danno with a bottle raised and swinging it downwards smashing on the back of Danno's head.

"And that's the way you'll be by god you disgusting insult to religion."

A fist flying catching Danno mid nose as he falls forward like a giant tree. His face crunching and bouncing off the side of his drum. Whisky splashing and broken glass scattering across the floor. Buster The Beastly rising slowly on his toes and turning to look down over his shoulder upon the horizontal unconscious body.

"Ah me flattened friend, most prostrate. Sucked every sup your mother had to give you from her breasts. The poor woman in her consternation watching you grow from a babe in arms swinging from her apron strings, into the big violent whore you are lying there. I will give you another poem now, an epitaph commemorating you in case you are coffin stretched ready for Glasnevin cemetery where they'd have to deconsecrate the ground to lie you in it."

> Behold
> Many times and oft
> In the course of his life
> Was he sad
> But it was nothing
> Compared to the times
> He was mad

And absolutely nothing compared
To the times
He was fucking bad

Sound of bagpipes outside. The door opening. A voice calling attention. Six tweed capped macintoshed gentlemen, their coats bulging, stepping in. Another shout of command. And the platoon taking up positions over the prostrate Danno. A hand reaching to turn over the unconscious face.

"Commandant, he's in no fit state now to be executed."

A seventh gentleman appearing in the doorway. Wavy curly hair above a domed forehead, taking a butt of a cigarette from his lips and crushing it on the floor.

"In that case remove that fucking criminal's body from the room and if he wakes up, keep him under close arrest."

The body of Danno carried disappearing into the back passage. Conversation and voices seeping back into the hushed gathering. O my god, that broad skulled curly haired visage, the very gunman whose kinky head I baptised with the leg of some piece of furniture one night in Lois's studio as he was waving both his prick and his Polish nine millimeter Parabellum about the room. Still wearing the same mustard coloured sweater I remember so well. And he's walking straight towards me.

"And what have the tweedy likes of you got to say for yourself. Is it nothing. Well keep it that fucking way. Now the rest of you bunch of British homosexual bollocks here gathered, hear this. Ireland integral is Ireland free. And no one is to touch another bottle of stout on that table which is of this moment commandeered until my men have had their fill. Pass me a bottle of stout, put out that electricity and let's have a candle or two."

"Don't you dare."

Naked Binky shouting from the passageway. A man jumping to pull the light out of the ceiling. A flash of blue flame and in the darkness cigarettes and candles lighting up. Buster The Beastly now disappeared down the passageway, and the Mild Man in the grey suit, previously in attendance, raising up his own bottle of stout among the newly arrived.

"Ah it's grand by this candlelight to see patriots of the purification

263

squad in action. Up the Republic lads. And will someone sing us Stephen Foster's My Old Kentucky Home."

The commandant lowering his bottle from his mouth and wiping his lips, shouting above the heads.

"Sing the man his song, and that's a fucking order."

"Never mind the old kip in Kentucky, sing us, would you live on woman's earnings."

"Who said that."

"It wasn't me."

A voice yodeling. The platoon of patriots in close order drill. Corks pulled out and their bottles at the ready. As their elbows bend to the commands called out.

"Bottles to the lips. Drink."

The squad in clockwork unison. As the foaming black beer pours down the stretched back throats. And their arms lift over their heads to throw the empty bottles whistling across the room to smash against the sackcloth draped wall. Strains of a violin coming from the dark passageway. The feet of more arrivals on the steps outside. The door opening. The Mild Man in the grey suit shouting.

"Begorra it's the socialites."

Binky stepping over the supine figures, as he crosses the room. An apron tented out over his erection. His wiry arms outstretched towards the newcomers.

"Just so long my dears that you are not the gobshites, you are my sweetie pies welcome to my little tea party."

Beads of perspiration on Rashers' brow returning to Darcy Dancer's side. A nervous smile on his face. His fingers gently touching Darcy Dancer's arm.

"Darcy it's so good of you to remain so silently patient. Road's not yet quite clear back there. I fear the dangerous atmosphere down here grows even more dangerous by the second. Some awful gin and lime spivs have just come in the door whom one occasionally encounters in the gilded cage of Davy Byrne's when one is imbibing one's Black Velvet. And dear me, they are in the company of a chap from your neck of the woods, a Master of foxhounds. That lady likes being fucked standing on her head, and is the wife of a top government minister. The chap in cowboy boots and hat, armed with two revolvers, with her is mad, as well as being a damn good bridge player. O dear I do apologise for having brought you here."

"Well I am about to leave."

"But dear Darcy, you mustn't yet. I so need your reassuring company you know. I am a fragile person, really. Among such as this lot. There's the Sober Judge, his inebriation on the bench is legendary. Just behind him, the Royal Rat, my erstwhile associate who runs our little casino. Pawned his own mother's sick bed. While she was still in it. Imagine he was pushing her on a handcart down the road when the heavy rain woke her up. You wouldn't believe such a hunched decrepit figure could also be the brother of Clarissa and the Black Widow. And that man with the hanky is the Mourner. Never without a tear or sob. Très lugubre, mélancolique, funèbre, to put a French word on it. Attends funerals by day. And wakes such as this, at night. A sad evening to be made even sadder. He'll bring this entire room sobbing uncontrollably to their knees. Tiresome of course if one had more randy things on one's mind. You mustn't go."

"Rashers, I really do feel one wants to return to the Shelbourne to bed."

"But ah wait, here's the very chap now, getting on the table with his contraption. The vacuum cleaner salesman. As to who would have use of such in Ireland one will never know. Under the suction most carpets would vaporise in dust anyway. You mustn't miss this demonstration. Ignorant or clever man, one doesn't know which, but I suppose in our backward way of life, having the end of a vacuum cleaner to stick one's organ into would help relieve the nationwide celibacy. Summer time he demonstrates how it catches flies. Dear me, he's engorged already."

A single candle left lighting the room. Jeering and cheering. Fist shaking and laughter. The salesman on the table entangled with his vacuum hose, tripping and landing bare arsed among the parcels of unopened bottles.

"There are ladies present."

"As a decent Catholic and native born Irishman I object."

"Dear me, Darcy it would seem there are prigs present. And I sincerely hope the root of his penis is firmly connected to the rami of the os pubis and ischium. Else his organ will end up in his dust bag. Of

265

course so many demonstrations have distorted the obtuse cone of his extremity. But by the look of that copious substance coming out of the orifice of his urethra, everything is working. I think I'll have him deliver me a vacuum at the Shelbourne."

Rashers pulling the cork and handing Darcy Dancer a bottle of stout. Smiling as he puts one to his own lips. And reaching to squeeze Darcy Dancer on the arm.

"Dear boy this may I know be the sort of environment you abhor. But you see. We are this moment to be joined by dear friends."

In the semi darkness, a commotion at the front door. Binky waving a horse whip, riding on the shoulders of another naked gentleman, plunging their way through the ever tightening throng. Shouting over the heads.

"No more please allowed tonight into Binky's royal enclosure. O but yes. We do make an exception for my most esteemed and most worshipped employer. Forgive me Madam, my perch up here. And welcome too, to distinguished members of the aristocracy. Of course we all know your Lordship that you were previously a Major in the Army before joining the Royal Air Force. And that you are also titled in the French peerage. So pleased to have you, and your particularly pretty lady friend."

Blowing a kiss to Binky, the Black Widow sweeping in. Followed by the Mental Marquis in his kilt. Someone at his side, a lady in an elegant black coat and black gloves, her black hair shadowed by a hat. And she turns her head. And the faint candlelight throws a shadow across her face.

Rashers turning to Darcy Dancer who groans and shrinks backwards, his heels banging against a crate on the floor. The preliminary insults of a fight, concerning the colour of the sky, erupting nearby.

"Darcy, what's the matter dear boy. You have haven't you, found the present company too appalling. You've gone completely pale white. Even in this light. Here, sit down. On this soda water crate. I'll only be the briefest instant nipping again into my hara kiri room. To put pawn ticket and cufflinks into your possession. And take you away. I promise. I absolutely promise."

Rashers pushing through the shrieking laughter, tears and growls. His intrepid head, beyond the smoke, disappearing into the dark passage. And across this room. It is. I know. Standing by the Marquis' shoulder. Beneath the wide brimmed hat, that satin skinned exquisite face. Luscious lips crimson soft. Your purple ribbon. The flash of your eyes. Which have already seen so much woe of the world. With their green that looks so black. So full of mellow sympathy. He dare. Bring your gentle demeanour, your silent presence here. The neck of your coat open, a jewel sparkling at your throat. I crouch. I cower. Hide away from you. Tremble and shake. Heart crushed and damned. Utterly betrayed. As Mr Arland must have felt. When he thought his preciously beloved. Was severed from him by another man. Are you now Leila to be from me. After all the months you seemed so safely waiting in my mind. While I did nothing. To reach and touch you. Before any other should say. Be mine. How late is it now. To plead and pray. Please leave open all the little gates. That lead to the garden of your heart. That once I heard you say. Out of all your sins. And with all your soul.

Would
Never
Close

19

Darcy Dancer, through the jostling and stumbling drunken figures, making his way away in the semi darkness. Water dripping in the cold damp smell of this long corridor. Past these vaulted caverns. And shadows. Go by this sallow sad faced blond gentleman. A violin held to his face, bow delicately drawn across the strings as he plays. Hair like the Count's, nearly to his shoulders. Sorrow instead of lust in his eyes. A naval great coat like Mr Arland's across his shoulders. A long Trinity College scarf wrapped again and again around his neck. One shivers at his sound. Even in one's despair. He does so play so beautifully. To a man in tears listening. In pyjamas and slippers. Blood trickling from a cut on his brow.

A hand reaching out to grab Darcy Dancer by the arm. A figure in an arched doorway, drinking a bottle of stout. Pulling him into a dank cellar. Piles of strewn bottles. Broken crates. A mouldering mattress on the floor.

"If you've nothing better to do comrade, come now have a closer look in here. At the sight of that. There's concupiscence for you."

Beyond this man inside this dungeon interior. Two naked men. One bent over, his hand grasping a sheaf of bank notes, and propped against the wall. While another stands only in spectacles. Buggering him. Darcy Dancer pulling his arm away. The man pulling him back.

"Now what's your hurry. Passing up this bit of anthropology. Look at them. N mind given to the cold. Nor was a kindness ever given by that mean ıcking eejit, who's humping. Fist full of pound notes. From profits out of his electrical appliance shop. Putting his horn up that bollocks naked apprentice seaman there charging him a pound a thrust paid prior to execution. And behold the sweaty face on him to get his money's worth. Up the Republic comrade. And if it wasn't so funny it would be the most diabolical piece of revolting uncircumcised heathenish commercialism I've ever had the displeasure of seeing. But jesus now I'd grease up me own arse and give up socialism for good, if someone were pushing pounds like that into me fist."

Darcy Dancer retreating further along the corridor. To stop. Listen. Hear back there in that crowded room. A balalaika playing. Hands clapping. Must now be the Count MacBuzuranti has arrived. Bursting into this subterranean nightmare with a Russian dance. How does one escape. Neither forward nor back. Peeking past more archways leading into other caves, tunnels and cellars. More supine entangled groaning and heaving bodies on more mattresses. Or am I merely standing dizzily turning in a desperate circle. To find my way out of here. Mouth dry. Throat tasting of vomit. A crash. A sound of a struggle. A shout. Of help. Rashers' voice. This door ajar to this room behind me. Which has a window. Which I'm sure does not open out on heaven. But to the red bleak darkness of hell. My god, two on top of him. In violence instead of lust. A third trying to prise open his fingers. As they hold him down. Pinned over a bed. Knocking over the candle. Which is putting a pile of newspapers alight. To bring us all more bright cheery news.

"Darcy, the buggers, by god. The buggers."

One large flame illumined silhouette spinning round turning to confront Darcy Dancer. Pausing to look for a wieldy weapon. And none to hand, his head lowering to charge. To butt me like a bull. Hands reach up to grab. To drag me down. As I let fly with every ounce of one's might behind a fist, arching up from my bent knee in an upper cut. Connecting to the side of his face.

"Cream the buggers, Darcy."

Like an apple squashed on granite. The man's head rising up. Blood bursting from a great gash across his cheek under his eye. His feet leaving the floor. Upwards he goes over a crate. Falling crashing to the other side. Growls and curses. A struggling shout from Rashers unpinioning himself from the bed.

"Marvellous Darcy. We'll soon put paid to you damn thieves."

Rashers' feet kicking out throwing the second man flying backwards across the room. Crackling sound of breaking gramophone records. Just as one now suddenly remembers. In the middle of all this. So clear and distinct. That my god I had an appointment. That one has so rudely forgotten. To meet Miss von B. For social intercourse.

"Darcy, the damn bugger has crashed into my McCormack records. Kill him."

Man's hands grabbing at the Hessian drape to pull himself up. Fittings tearing out of the plaster. The fabric falling, covering his head. Rashers landing a kick between the third man's legs. Doubling him up in a squeal of agony to the floor. As he rolls back and forth clutching his goolies. The smoke billowing over the room. The man holding his split face together at the door, blood pouring out between his fingers. His two associates crawling towards him gasping. And shouting out into the hall.

"Hit us with axes, the fuckers. Slashed him with an axe down the face."

Rashers, his tailcoat torn and tie tightened into a tiny knot. Throws a blanket over the flames. Stamping out the burning newspaper. And turning to loose from a clenched fist, cufflinks and a pawn ticket into Darcy Dancer's hand.

"Here take these, my dear fellow, the whole place is being incited against us. Every one of those evil bastards whose prick is not securely plunged up something or someone, will want to bathe themselves in our Anglo Irish blood."

Rashers tugging and pulling up the bottom of the window. Lifting up his foot and smashing out the panes. And up on his knees on the sill and disappearing out into the darkness. As one feels something stuck in one's back.

"This is a Schmeisser, you fucker. And I'll blow your spine to pieces if you move."

Darcy Dancer shoved with the barrel of a gun. Out the door. Along the corridor into another dungeon room. Gathered faces in the candlelight.

"Here he is. He's yours."

Gunman pushing the long barrel of the pistol back in under his coat, hunching up his collar and disappearing. Face this crowd of baleful faces leaning against this wall. Staring at me. As this man malevolently stands with his sour breath accosting my nostrils.

"Did you hit that man with an axe."

"He was hit with my fist."

"You hit him with an axe, or keys or something, no fist could do that damage."

Other faces gathering ominously closer. Moving. As I move. My back closer against the wall. While the man with the gun is gone. I may only have to face gouging hands, kicking feet, kneeings and butting heads. My demise in all their eyes. Rashers to whose rescue one goes. Also gone. At least his cufflinks and pawn ticket are unsafely in my pocket. To whom does one shout for help. And have even the merest hope of being heard from this dungeon room. All I can do. Is fight. Foot and fist. At least make one die with me. Smash in this first nearest face. Kick the goolies of the smirking man behind him. Send them splattering on the ceiling. And distinctly announce my intentions.

"If you so much as move a hair to touch me, I will part your face in two with the same fist that demolished your associate."

A furtive sheepish grin stealing over the lips of the interrogator, uneasily shifting his weight from foot to foot. Eyes slowly believing what I'm saying. But still smiling, knowing half a dozen pair of hands stand safely behind his back. Ready to beat me to a pulp. But my fist will reach his jaw before I die. Now. Here. Within steps of her touch. As the silence shivers. The interrogator has just given some signal. And one of them now. I spy. Moving sideways along the wall. But at least this interrogator is going to go down dead in front of me. Before this chilling sound is over. The end smashed off a bottle. A voice. Firmly loud. Word by slow word announcing.

"Anyone here who is interested to know. Better know that I'm on the side of Darcy Thormond Dancer Kildare. And that the end of this will have your jugular cut before it's jammed deep in your face. Just any of you make one move to put a hand on him."

The candlelight flickering. Distant sound of singing. The Old Orange Flute. And in the doorway. The broken dark green thick jagged glass of a champagne bottle held up. Glinting in the fist of Foxy Slattery. Full of courage just as his smaller brother is full of cunning. And here. An ally. Braving all this assembled brawn. Just as he did in the battles of our childhood. When he taught me how to fight the world. In the uneasy silence. His voice speaking so sure and solemn.

"Now that that's understood. One by one, each of you. Vacate out of here."

Out the brick arched entrance, the figures slowly departing past Foxy. Off up the passage back into the melee of this bleak underground jungle. The last one, the interrogator. Stopping. Looking back.

"We're not finished with you yet."

Darcy Dancer putting out his hand. To clamp it gratefully hard upon that of the Foxy Slattery as his brow furrows and he noddingly grins.

"Foxy you saved my life."

"You can bet I did and all. And if it wasn't for the man with his face pouring blood, coming out front there where I nearly had a horse and car sold, and hearing them say they were stringing up a man called Dancer who did it, named after the racehorse, I wouldn't have bothered coming back here. But follow me, we'd be as well to wander out of this place as fast as our feet can take us. And you can be bloody sure they'd be this second gathering up a bigger gang. There's a way by the back we can go."

Past more dungeon rooms. Opening a door. Out into the misty night. Soft rain still falling. Darcy Dancer and Foxy clambering over broken bottles, dead rats and a dead cat. Vaulting up on the roof of a water closet. A woman inside screaming, as the toilet flushes.

"Don't mind the lady in distress now boss, she'd be that way anyway when she gets back inside."

Climbing a wall, jumping down the other side into an alley. Foxy shimmying up a drain pipe. Darcy Dancer following. Past a window. And higher onto a roof. Hands scratching clawing crawling up the wet slippery slates splitting under their weight. Clambering over the ridge tiles. Knocking one loose to tumble clattering down. A voice from a window shouting.

"Call the Guards that's the second of them tonight from out that bloody sewer over there and breaking this place down."

Darcy Dancer and Foxy lowering on another drain pipe to the pavement. And running along an alley and out another. To emerge on the street. And cross over to slowly walk along the banks of the canal. Its still water flowing past under the flecks of lamp light. Catching their breath.

"Well that's a nice little bit of exercise boss I don't mind telling you."

"It was Foxy. And I can't thank you enough."

"Well you just remember that I've not ever forgot. Your own footsteps coming once. When I was huddled cold up hid hardly with shelter saying the act of contrition thinking I was already dead from starvation when you brought me the bit of a bite to eat that saved my life. And it's only just and fitting that I had at last the chance to save yours. I'll be going now boss. Can I drop you anywhere. My car's not that far."

"No thank you, Foxy. I'll walk here a bit by the canal."

"Slán agat go fóill, boss. See you again."

"Goodbye Foxy. And thank you."

The great heavy timbers of the canal locks, over which the water pours. Two gleaming white swans cruise. A dead bloated dog floats. The weeds and rushes. There goes Foxy. A moment of brief kindness given once, repaid this day with my life itself. Walk now under this lamp light. Take out Rashers' cufflinks and the pawn ticket to redeem my own silverware. Stare at them in my hand. And wouldn't you believe it. A bloody punched tram ticket to Dalkey. And as for priceless cufflinks. These trinkets, aside from being most awfully garish, are clearly nothing but imitation jewelry.

Darcy Dancer walking the path along the canal. Houses the other side with big gardens up to their entrance doors. A light on in a window. Only sign of life. Man standing in dressing gown in the middle of the room looking at a book held open in his hand. And out here. Wet. Cold. Bereft. My trousers torn. Shoes scuffed. One hears Sexton's voice. Telling of when he was a little boy, often without a shoe. Up at two in the morning to drive his dead father's cattle ten miles over the hilly winding roads to the market in the town. Arriving at dawn, waiting soaked and chilled by his scrawny hungry bullocks for a buyer. And sometimes no one would even look at him, never mind

273

the cattle. And then drive the beasts home again unsold. Many a sad time that happened Master Darcy, many a sad time. It would drain your heart of blood, but it would never stop you doing it again.

Darcy Dancer walking north across the empty city. Past shop fronts. The mist lifting. The air chilling. A star or two blinking in the sky. One does miss loyal old Sexton. With his razor sharp hedge hook, he'd have been a help down in the catacombs. If he weren't shocked rigid by the goings on. Knuckle of my thumb swollen where my fist landed. Stood up Miss von B. A heart searing glimpse of Leila, I walk with. As I go from one sadness to another. The damp penetrating one's bones. Nearly hear the huntsman's horn calling to the hounds. Out there westwards on the wild lonely land. And without a horse, quicken my steps back to the Shelbourne and a warm bed. What bleak desolation through these streets. One has no one at all. And is it, that all anyone really wants in this world, is just each other. One body enfolding another in comfort when it carries so much pain. Turn now. North. Charlemont Street. At least a name bespeaking some elegance out of the past.

The sky widening with more stars. A faint moon lighting clouds. Darcy Dancer stopping to stand on a corner. Where this road divides. Look up. A sign over a pub. The Bleeding Horse. Such a name, Mr Arland mentioned once. Said he came here to buy cheap vegetables, haggling with the barrow women. Took him from the walled safety of college out into the harsh world. Sexton used to say, know about horses and you know all there is to know about the rest of life. A cinema over there. Camden Street. Must go on. Just as I feel I am bleeding. And need someone. With whom to console. A friendly voice to hear. While the whole city is asleep. Eggs, butter and cheese in this glass front. Nice nourishing name on the sign, Monument Creamery. Down this way somewhere is Lois's street. Am I hearing things. A voice. This utterly ancient hour of the morning. O my god. There's Horatio Macbeth. Declaiming at his reflection in a shop front window. I suppose I'm not that lonely that one feels the need to pass the time of night with him. But what a convenient way to amuse oneself. And avoid thinking how sad life is. I know no lines to orate. To put alive again my hopes and dreams. I had that night as Leila stood in my mother's room. When I should have reached out for her. Gathered her into my arms. Without fear of rebuff. Even with all the household's spying and listening behind doors. Not let her have escaped. As my mother's admirers had let her in her scrapbook. Their love poems. I worship thee from afar. And had one of them worshipped my mother from near, she would not have married a gambling waster called my father. With his whisky reddened face, mean and pinched. And shall I now. Sell land. Go away forever somewhere. Preferably sophisticated. Rid one's mind of Leila. Of mad stallions, butlers, rot, falling slates, dying cattle and other troublesome servants. To London. Where I shall of course avoid the Marquis' most stupid sounding club. Go instead to one of those hotels where during the season, my mother stayed. A suitable one I remember called Claridge's. Yet is there anywhere or time when one can ever be safe from grave injury to the spirit. Or the more mortal of embarrassments. Such as one, once befallen my mother's mother. Gone bald in bereavement over my great grandfather's death. The scarves she wore over her pate often blown off by the wind. Till family members insisted she get a wig. Which, the first time she wore it out hunting, was knocked off with her hat. And there her red tinged hair lay against the green grass. And as it resembled a fox, it was instantly set upon and eaten by the hounds. She did however jovially say to the huntsman. O dear, little left isn't there, not even the tail.

Darcy Dancer walking along this shadowy dingy street. An undertaker's. Can smell the stables. Black horses who pull the carriages. A church. Outside a statue to the Blessed Virgin. Inside it must have walls lined with boxy wooden confessionals where the whole city pours out their sins. Now every Dubliner will be rushing down into the dungeons of the catacombs instead. And I've not yet come to Lois's street. Gone the wrong way. Remember looming a big grey granite hospital on the corner. Perhaps if I turn right now instead of left. Vaguely recognise this shoemaker's. A grocery. A timber merchant's. And here. At last is the alley. God it's as late as one is desperate. No street lamp to see by. Hers is the only door. A green one numbered four. Knock. Or better bang on it. Peer in the letterbox. Not a sign of life inside. She may tell me to go away. I must be waking her. Wait for her to dress and come to the door. Just sit a moment on this box. So tired. Intended tomorrow to have my hair cut. Go to the chiropodists to have my toe nails trimmed. Then to the races. And I may instead in my present state, leave Dublin altogether. Go home. Back across the lonely flat bogs. Let my life live and die out there on that rolling hunting land. Away from the sordid world. Out where the banks of earth, streams and the boughs of beech are friends one knows. And not these bereft pavements. Down those dungeons, tonight someone shouted that when Adam and Eve left the Garden of Eden it became the Garden of Evil called the catacombs.

Darcy Dancer slumped asleep back against the stone wall. Suddenly awakening, shivering and cold. Sound of footsteps approaching up the alley. A voice whispering and calling to a cat.

"Here pussy puss. Here here pussy puss."

A shadow. A figure. Stopping. Looking down. Two feet in black Wellington boots. Her face in the hood of her duffle coat, one, she said, her husband wore on the bridge of his ship during the war.

"Good god, it's you. What are you doing here like this."

"I'm afraid I called upon you to collect my etching and fell asleep."

"This time of night. How dare you assume you can arrive like this. Just whom do you think you are to take such prerogative."

"I do apologise."

"Well I should think so. Just because I am an artist does not mean you can take for granted that I am a bohemian whose privacy can be invaded willy nilly. I happen to be of a distinguished family. With admirality and foreign office connections."

"But you did invite me earlier at the Count's party. However I am sorry to have given you vexation. Goodbye Madam."

"You did earlier of course ignore me. For the company of that fortune hunting very aptly named philistine called Rashers. Well of course if you wish to say goodbye, do. I won't stop you. But you are you know, practically shivering with cold. Why aren't you more warmly dressed foolish boy. And I of course am not so inhospitable as to not at least offer you a cup of tea or cocoa. As little of that as I may still possess."

"Thank you, that would be very kind."

"Well come in. Don't stand there making a draught. And just remember I am now celibate."

Church bells. Tolling three over the city. Climbing up these stairs. Where once I had convulsions of laughter. With Lois tripping and falling on her arse over bottles. And now one is utterly embarrassed at her mercy. Her so British nasal voice. Her age. From which one suddenly wants to run. Despite her lack of wrinkles, she must be nearly thirty eight. Or in her god forsaken forties. She does have a certain smoothness to her skin. But O god, she does so damn moan on. Ought to be bloody glad someone's calling upon her. She is of course considerably more ancient than even Miss von B. O god. This big grim room. How cold. The black of night above on the skylight. And dear me. A wash line hung with her personal underthings. Smell of turpentine. The sweeter smell of linseed oil. Her bookcase crammed with books.

"If it weren't for the fact that I had to remain late at the Count's conferring over some ballet sets I've been asked to design, I should have been soundly asleep. Or at the very least, having one of my nightmares. And I should not like dear boy since I'm inviting you in, for you to ever get the idea that if you call upon me at this hour of the night again that you will be welcome. It does make one think that beneath your English exterior, you may be just like the Irish."

"I do wish, since you are now in fact having me in, that you did not continue to complain about my not making an appointment to call upon you."

"Well I shall stop. But I also think with that cruel edge to your voice, that you can be hurtful when you choose to be, can't you."

"Perhaps yes. I can be."

"Spoilt I think as well. However at least you are not obnoxious."

"Thank you."

"And you are young and beautiful. I do like young and beautiful men, and if they are extremely young and extremely beautiful, I like sucking their cocks."

"I hope then, Madam, that being just merely young and beautiful does not exclude me from your latter category."

"It most certainly does. No matter how enticingly beautiful. I must make it quite clear in case you're getting ideas that my celibacy most certainly excludes sucking your cock."

"O dear. Well I hope the youth and beauty you refer to does not also imply you're preferring too, lack of brains."

"I regard beauty as being part of intelligence. However without wanting to sound trite, intelligence makes an ugly face beautiful. Put those drawings on the chair on the floor and do sit down."

277

Lois vigorously riddling her stove. Sparks flying up from the dying embers as she throws in pieces of turf. Taking off her duffle coat. Scratching herself under both bosoms through several layers of sweaters. Pours milk and puts it on a gas ring. Her little world here. Fewer balls and pricks on display than I previously remember. Must be her celibacy. Even has a sketch or two of country scenes.

"I like that watercolour very much Lois."

"O that. That's nothing. Done on an excursion. Enniskerry village."

"But it's very attractive."

"Thank you. Well at least I can tell you something nice did come of our previous brief little association. An awfully cultivated American at Trinity College came and bought an entire portfolio of washes of the male nude. Choosing as it happens all those I did of you. If you can recall your being somewhat difficult when you posed, ruining the tension of line with your constant erection. Actually, although I thought at the time your erections an artistic imbalance he was enthralled by what he called the refreshing tumesced quality the drawings had. I do wish there were more cultivated Americans like him. Of course Count MacBuzuranti could so easily be my patron now, since he has come into his inheritance. Having bought his previous portrait at such a reduced price, you'd think he'd now have the courtesy to commission me to do another. I am so continually being exploited by people. Now what about you. Surely you can commission. I've heard all about your stately home, you know. And your extravagant dinner parties. And balls. And I just wonder. I really do, why I am not invited. I feel quite put out. After all, we have previously at least been in the same bed together. And there. Just look. It's leaking from the skylight right on top of my stove. And O god, did you see that. Right in the corner. A rat. O no. He's gone under the bed. O god, not that, I don't think I shall be able to stand being in here with a rat. O dear with my cats dead."

"I'll get him Madam for you."

Darcy Dancer taking a broom. Shoving it under the bed. The rat scurrying out. Lois screaming. The rat running along the baseboard. Darcy Dancer grabbing an empty wine bottle and flinging it. The bottle missing and smashing on the wall.

"Good lord, don't. Don't. You're breaking up my studio."

278

"Well Madam, you want me to kill it, don't you."

"Yes I do."

"Well then you must be prepared for a little mayhem. Rats are deucedly clever and almost impossible to corner and kill."

"But does that require for you to wreak absolute havoc."

"Well a little havoc at least. You would not enjoy for it to bite you in bed."

Darcy Dancer grabbing another bottle. Rat scurrying out from behind paintings and heading across the open floor. Lois screaming and jumping on the table. Darcy Dancer unleashing his missile. End over end. Bouncing as it glances off the stove. And flies across the room smashing into the bookcase. Knocking over a little group of ceramic figures standing between books on the shelves.

"O god, O god, you Irish. No matter what you do, you somehow always manage to be destructive don't you."

"Damn it Madam, do please try to control your ethnic slurs when I am in fact doing my damnedest best to kill a bloody rat here for you."

"Well I would appreciate at least if you would leave me a place to live in afterwards."

"Well, you go kill him then. He's right behind your painting pallet leaning there."

"I shall attempt to do no such thing. I am mortally terrified of rats. Here's your cocoa."

"Thank you."

"O dear. My trials. My tribulations. Now I shan't sleep a wink the entire night. When indeed tomorrow I shall need to be at my most productive."

"Well the rat should cause no difficulty, if you treat him as you did one of your cats and feed him properly."

"I'll do no such thing. He must be got rid of."

"Why Madam."

"Why. I'll tell you why. To conserve my creative energy. I'll have you know I am in the middle of my blue spheroid period if you must know. And also have an important commission to undertake. You see, occasionally some fortune does at least show promise of soon coming into my life."

"Well I'm delighted. What is it."

"I shan't say who, as the matter is only exploratory at this stage.

279

But I have been offered, by someone who can afford, one rather large portrait commission. And if it in fact happens I shall be at least temporarily quite well off. And I always find those things one talks about too much have the habit of not happening. O god, there's the rat again."

"Madam for god's sake don't bloody panic like that."

Darcy Dancer spilling the hot cocoa on his fist jumping to his feet. The rat running in behind canvasses propped against the wall. Darcy Dancer grabbing the broom. Hot on its heels. Lois shrieking as her canvasses overturn. And O god I feel something soft under foot. A long tube. With its distinctly wrong end splitting open. Flake white it says on the label. Jetting out a long wiggling fat worm of paint. And whoops. The cap's off this, alizarine crimson. And O shit, burnt sienna too. And cobalt bloody blue, squeezed out everywhere under my feet.

"Stop. Stop. For god's sake stop. You're ruining me. You're stepping on top of my paint, squeezing out all my tubes."

"Damn it Madam, why do you leave them here on the floor where they can't be seen."

"Stop. Stand still. Now you're trampling it all over. O my god, you've got it on to my Afghan rug. The only precious thing I possess in the world. On my very good only single heirloom. Which lay in front of my father's desk at the Admiralty and upon which some of England's most distinguished feet have stood. I'm ruined."

"Do shut up Madam. Don't be so obtuse. Please."

"Obtuse. Whomever do you think you're speaking to, you little upstart. I could outwit you in any endeavour you care to mention."

"Except killing rats of course."

"How utterly pretentious. You haven't, have you, changed. Assuming superiority. O god, the rat. There he is. Peering at me. He's stalking me."

"Just stay where you are and don't move."

"I'm not."

"Rats can jump at your throat."

"O god do something. But don't have the paint go everywhere."

"I've got paint all over my shoes."

"Well dear stupid boy take them off."

"O christ. Now I've got bloody paint all over my socks."

"You fool you fool, take them off."

"O shit now I have paint all over my feet."

"O god. O dear god. Hit the rat, hit him, he's crouched going to jump at me."

"This should put paid to him. Soon as I take aim."

"O my god don't throw my very last full tube of flake white at him when you've already squeezed out the others. Do you know how much a tube costs. Do you."

"But I hit him. Did you see that. I bloody well sent that footling rat for six."

"Yes. And now he's right back under this bed. O god, this is worse than being bombed in Bloomsbury by the bloody Germans."

"Watch it, Lois he's after you. There he is again. The rat."

"O god, god for heaven's sake do something. I think he's growling and snarling at me. This is absolutely the most wretched night of my absolutely entire life. And you're back on my Afghan rug again. Get off."

"Blithering hell, I could have clonked him one just then if you'd only calm down and let me."

"I was to hang that as a backdrop for my large commission which I haven't even got yet. O how wretched. O how cruel. I shall just lie here now in a heap and die. Please go home. Go away. At least a rat will not destroy my entire professional life."

"Certainly, Madam if you feel that way."

"No rat however awful can be as hideously horrifying as what you have wrought upon my future as an artist."

"Well damn you Madam as an artist. I was trying to save you as a human being. From possible bubonic plague. I will of course leave you with the rat, since you prefer."

Lois, legs in Wellington boots hanging over the edge of her bed. Hands up clutched covering her face, as she lies crumpled in a heap. Church bell ringing the half hour. A shudder of wind across the skylight. And a moan down the stove chimney.

"O god. Blackmail. Sheer absolute cruel blackmail. Ruin me. Run off. Leave me. Go ahead. After making you cocoa with the milk I intended for breakfast. After I've put turf in my stove to be hospitable. And opened up my chimney flue. You cruel wretched creature. I might have known."

"Madam I think you're absolutely nuts."

281

"Nuts am I. Nuts. You call me nuts. I am not nuts. I have never been nuts. That's one of those stupid American expressions."

"Clearly you know what it means."

"Of course I know what it stupidly well means."

"Well do you or don't you want me to go. I am perfectly content not to go on attempting to kill your rat. And of course I shall see to your carpet being cleaned."

"Cleaned. Are you mad. Absolutely raving mad. How. Do you expect me to entrust a precious heirloom to an Irish cleaner's. Where I've already had my one and only tweed suit washed and boiled by imbeciles and given back to me to wear. Shrunken so dreadfully that it is fit only for a midget or to use as rags to wipe my brushes. Cleaned. My god."

"Madam, I sigh. My socks and shoes of course are also discoloured. Honestly I simply don't know what to do. Or suggest. Aside from hoping that you would accede to painting my portrait on my horse and in hunting clothes and that this might be considered as some form of tiny restitution."

"Well, at least at last you're thinking in the right direction."

"Shall we agree then. To a full portrait. On my horse."

"Of course a canvas that size must be specially made and is frightfully expensive. And indeed to include your horse. Not to mention the amount of paint required."

"I assure you Madam."

"Please do stop calling me Madam. Surely you can accept that we are familiar enough now for Christian names."

"Lois, I assure you money is no object."

"Well, you're showing promise as a patron. My other commission permitting, I shall try to fit you in."

"Thank you. I am so grateful. And of course one hopes you will do it while I am in residence at Andromeda Park. One will put at your disposal the necessary room or rooms in which to paint. Ah the rat seems quiet. Now do you think Lois we might please, retire together to bed."

"It doesn't take you long to change from your role as patron. Does it."

"I beg your pardon."

"I'm not some sort of nymphomaniac. I've already said four times.

I'm celibate. Why prey on me. Why not find some pure little innocent girl your own age. Although she may not suck your cock, you might terminate her virginity for her. I can't believe you're now inviting yourself into my bed."

"Well I don't see any other beds in the room."

"Ha ha, that is awfully funny."

"Well one is rather tired. And it would keep you protected. Rats are vicious creatures. Especially ones as large as that."

"This is utter blackmail. Is your commission blackmail too. You do this to me. Are you desperate."

"Well yes I'm equally as desperate as perhaps you hopefully might be."

"Don't you dare call me desperate. And don't start removing your clothes. You are the most exasperatingly presumptuous young man aren't you. I certainly think you are. And as bourgeois as it may sound, you're clearly exhibiting the result of a long lack of proper parental influence and control. One hates to bring up personalities but I had heard your father did seem to desert you."

"What he did do Madam, was to sell off cattle, land and go off with certain valuable furnishings, not his property and set up with a mistress here in Dublin."

"You did though didn't you have the care and counsel of that goose stepping phoney Austrian nazi Princess Miss von B who it appears is again about town."

"That remark I think is highly uncalled for. She was a brilliant housekeeper and is a genuine aristocrat."

"Yes who gave you genuine love bites if I remember correctly. Yet you do seem to remain so naïvely innocent."

"Exactly why Madam, your company helps acquaint me with the ways of the world. Perhaps as a philistine imperialist member of the squirearchy, you can help cultivate in me a true artistic spirit."

"I doubt it very much. But you do, don't you possess the most astonishing nerve. Taking off your clothes like this. And waving that in my face in that manner. I still think your face is so Flemish. And you are callous, don't you know how hard it is for me to resist wanting your very well endowed cock inside me. Don't you. Making me face temptation like this. And how difficult it makes it for me."

"Madam you think it's difficult for you. You're not the only one.

Country gentlemen suffer. I've had months of celibacy too. When before one's very eyes one's very own bulls and stallions not to mention roosters, are, to put it in the vulgar vernacular, freely fucking my heifers, fillies and hens."

"What. How could celibacy be a hardship. In your thousands of acres. Snap your fingers for breakfast, just summon, and tea served you. Butler, cook, maids. Suffer. I'll go suffer there. Quite gladly."

"It's not quite a snap of the fingers, Lois. It's a pull on the servants' bell and often one has to dislodge to rise from one's chair to do it."

"O dear, poor you. My family were never quite large country house owners, but I would certainly not consider it dislodgment to get out of my chair to pull on the servants' bell. If you invite me, I shall gladly do it for you. And speaking of pulling. I mean can't you pull yourself off. You've got rather big and strong hands to masturbate with. I'll watch you if you like. I mean it's just like milking a cow. But do not dear boy ejaculate on my floor. Where I think you've already done enough."

"Lois don't you understand. That you are a beautiful and desirable woman. Are you oblivious to that. And this. Just look at it. Nearly twice the size of my normal erections. The mere presence of you exciting this extra length and breadth."

"Dear boy. Did anyone ever tell you, you should be an actor. You do give quite an incredible performance. Are you in fact larger than usual. You wouldn't be pulling my leg would you. And you are I must confess, so well endowed. Do pull your foreskin further back. Pity I don't have my gouache and brushes to hand. One could capture the marvellous cone shape the end of your cock has. My American patron I'm sure would be enthralled."

"Wouldn't that be what is commonly referred to as a dirty picture."

"Dear boy, I'll have you know I have never compromised my artistic integrity. And I am in no way being pornographic or obscene. But I do have this awfully uncomfortable sneaking suspicion, that behind your affected innocence, you are laughing at me. Are you."

"No no Madam, sincerely I am not."

"O god. I am defeated. Get into bed, will you. And damn you anyway. I shall take off my clothes. But only on the understanding that it is for the sharing of our bodily warmth."

284

"But yes, of course. Heavens. One. Two. Three sweaters."

"Yes. And my long johns."

"You know Madam, I have always admired the stunningly beautiful breasts you have. They are the most exquisite I have ever seen. I mean they are astonishing."

"Don't you dare ruin that remark by saying for my age."

"No no. For any age. Ageless."

"Well they are I suppose among my few prized possessions."

"Why are you smiling Madam."

"Just recalling the last time you were here. And instead of making love, you had to hit that awful I.R.A. man over the head with a hammer or something, clonked senseless while he was raping me."

"It was in fact with a big pole. That monster one over there as a matter of fact. And indeed Madam, you see, I have returned yet again. To save you from yet another rat."

"O god. Alright. Stop waving it in my face. You have without intending a pun, made your point. You may. Get in bed."

"May I make love to you."

"No."

"Then I shan't get into bed. I shall instead say thank you so much for the cocoa, get dressed and say goodbye. To both you and the rat."

"O god. You are a spoilt brat. Blackmailing me. Alright. Yes you may make love to me. Now let me by to light a candle. I just hope to god it's not the wrong time of the month. I am the most silly stupid creature on god's earth. To chuck out the window as I am doing. All the accumulated precious months of my celibacy. Don't you know that such conservation of the sexual emotion gives succour to the frisson necessary to create."

"O dear I had no idea, Lois, honestly."

"Self denial is the treasury from which one draws the golden thread of truth from one's inner spirit. Is the world now to be denied the possibility of my producing some of my greatest work. And whose fault shall it be. Whose."

"O dear. Mine Madam. Utterly and solely mine. Please might I just squeeze in the bed. Move over please."

"Just so long as you understand the implications of what you are compelling me to do."

"I do. I so absolutely do understand. But can't you immediately reimpose your sanction and catch up with your stored up celibacy when I entrain back to the country."

"Don't you continue to be so damn smart, you."

"I'm really not. I mean it is after all, the fact of the matter is it not."

"No it's not. And do you know what I think dear boy."

"What do you think Lois."

"Someone should take you in hand. Before you become one of these horse racing playboys. I think you would selfishly say or selfishly do just about anything just to get what you want."

"Well even as a racing enthusiast and modest horse breeder, there do exist some gentlemanly limits beyond which I'd consider it highly improper to go."

"O god I would like music and my gramophone is broken, and I can't afford to have it shipped back to England to be fixed."

"Ah but Lois I shall play the solo part in a D minor symphony on top of you. Call it a horn concerto, if you like."

"You shall certainly not. I shall be on top if you don't mind. You may be funny but you are also being extremely unromantic. And while you are exercising your gentlemanly inclinations also include a thought for when my arthritis prevents me from painting. I may need in the not too distant future, a small perhaps semi grace and favour residence. I certainly think you should have regard for the long term aspect of being a patron."

"Well there are unoccupied cottages. Indeed that I do have. Outlying perhaps. In need of renovation. I mean a new thatch and a patch and window pane or two. Could make one of them quite livable."

"I see. Chuck me into some damp labourer's hovel. Exactly what my arthritis needs."

"No no. It could be smartened up and prettified. My gardener is a marvellous hand at such things. I have a cemetery as well."

"You what."

"I mean it is ancient. And nearly full. But so attractive. Has a ninth century ruin of a church."

"I said I had arthritis. I did not say I was dying."

"No of course you didn't, Lois. But we all must go sometime. And I suggest it only in the interests of providing you with a final resting place."

"Do you simply think that because I am older than you. That I am at death's door. Is that what you think."

"No no. Not. Never. Nein, nao, nu, nyet, nie, nae, ne, nem."

"And what are you mumbling."

"I am just saying no in a few other languages. My tutor frequently set me various exercises in comparative linguistics. And the word no happens to be one I still remember."

"O god. Here one is. Selling off my body to you, for some protection against a heinous rodent. Compromising my soul. And in return, instead of dignified retirement one day, I am being offered burial."

"Lois, please. I think you're a long way off from finally packing it in. I really do. You have such a marvellous figure and you do feel so marvellously naked in my arms."

"This is just a blatant exploitation of my body."

"Well if it is, why don't we really make the most of it. Sorry I didn't quite mean to say that."

"You said it. O god, get it over with, you brazen bold boy."

Lois squeezing, digging in her fingernails into Darcy Dancer's back. As she writhes and sticks her tongue in his ear and rolls over on top of him. Her arms pinning him down as she shakes her braided long pigtails loose. A cat wailing outside. That should keep the rat quiet. And one supposes, what does it matter. Another bit of land, a cottage, a fraction of one's birthright. Slap a little lime wash on the walls, sweep out the cobwebs. After all in spite of all her high falutin intellectual flights of fancy she is a decent enough sort. One simply cannot understand how she retains such a splendid physique. If it weren't for the sometimes utterly mad expression worn on her face, she could, be classed as quite beautiful. And in spite of making no effort as she does to look in the least smart or feminine. Her tongue darting out her mouth and licking around her lips does resemble some sort of lizard. Even so I don't suppose she deserves to have heaped upon her one lie on top of another. How can one ever afford, broke as one is, to commission a painting. One's staff's last fortnight's wages unpaid. The resounding loud scraping sounds at the bottom of all one's barrels. My mother's jewels. I see sparkling and glowing in a great iron chest which becomes a nightmare when I wake up. Her pearls. Long gone black without a woman's skin to give them life. Her rings, bracelets. Where do they lie. To be unearthed and bring one back to solvency.

287

And one must remind oneself yet again. That so much of my mother's family riches came from an act of kindness. Of one's great great grandfather. Who one hot summer's day came riding cross country on his horse to the flooded ford of a wide stream. To there find an old gentleman stranded, wheels stuck in the mud trying to get his pair of horses and carriage across. And my great great grandfather dismounted and after an hour or two's digging, pushing, shoving and tying and adding his own horse to tugging, finally pulled the old gentleman's carriage across the stream. The old gentleman tipped his hat and thanked him. And my ancestor bowed and smiled. Till many years later he was one day summoned up to Dublin. To climb the stairs of a big old house to an office. Whose windows overlooked the green velvet lawns of Trinity College's Provost's garden. And to there find an agent and a lawyer with deeds and papers and to learn from them that he'd been bequeathed by the old gentleman two great tracts of land of two thousand Irish acres. On one tract stood nearly the whole of a midlands town. And on another, part of Dublin. No wonder one rushes to every little old lady's elbow to safely usher her across the roadway. Such compassion as a forebear had, I suppose still flows in my veins. But my god, administering such similar kindness. Help Lois to reimpose her celibacy. Kill her rat. Would only get me bequeathed her obscene pictures swirling with male private parts. Which in turn would get me arrested and imprisoned. And she'll no doubt strangle me for all the crimson, blue and green paint she finds my feet are presently wiping off all over her sheets. Taste her saliva. She does have such sweet breath. To sniff back comfortingly into one's nostrils. Makes all sorts of contorted gyrations and groans. Getting up on top of me. Which duly reminds that I must my god, win at the races. Borrow or beg to bet on Awfully Stupid Kelly's Ulidia Princess The Second. So much has happened can't remember where he said it was running. Leopardstown or Phoenix Park. My god, she's finally got down. Changing from one orifice to another. And biting and painfully chewing one's balls in between. Now feels as if she's nearly swallowing me up. Shaking my prick in her mouth from one cheek to the other, teeth sawing back and forth. Pigtails flying like an autogyro. And O my god, licking her chops sucking out the last single drop. Must be her improverished condition.

"Are you tired already darling."

"Lois for someone whose recent regime was celibacy you do demonstrate an uncommonly explosive enthusiasm. Which is also if I may say so, entirely unarthritic."

"Well there is little point darling in not being wholehearted. And I'm not a cripple you know. Shall I try to get it up for you again."

"Well seemingly, for the time being at least, it does appear to be down, doesn't it."

"Yes darling. Let us kiss it more. But what a lot of work you're being dear boy. It's still down and my jaw muscles are getting quite painfully tired."

"Is it your arthritis."

"I shall slap you. Of course it isn't."

"Well can't you get it in the jaw joints."

"No you can't."

"Why. If you get it in other joints."

"I simply don't know why, but I distinctly haven't got it in my jaw joints anyway. You do don't you, masquerading under your little boy innocence, possess a rather cynical impertinence. You who wanted to jump in bed with me. With this quite flaccid thing in an entirely unusable state."

Lois on her hands and knees hovering over the prostrate Darcy Dancer. Kissing deep in the ears, at his throat, over the breasts, over the belly. Swaying biting like a hound tearing at a fox. Church bells again ringing. While one is hidden in here under Lois. Briefly away from the world. And far out over the city. Where somewhere Leila may be. O my god my love I clutch thee. Why is it not your white slender body. To which I cling. Your purple beribboned hair into which my fingers entwine. Your softly smiling lips upon which my mouth can press. Hold you grasped I still do, so bereft. And yet could hardly wait to get my mouth and hands to Lois's breasts. And watch her ribs breathe on her so muscularly lean chest. But sounds as if instead of a simple cottage she wants me to supply a whole ruddy house. Suppose she could if she didn't require wages, be my artist in residence. Get her to lend a hand in odd jobs. Lime wash the boxes in the stables. Plenty of hay about upon which she can throw an artistic fit at the thought. My god she really is desperate. Tasting one's cool goolies in her warm mouth. Climbing on top again. Before it's even semi hard. Bending it. Heavens above. Riding me like she was in the Grand National. Over Beecher's brook for the last time. And one jump to go. And fancy that, she's switching to my knee. Grinding it up into her bifurcation. Growling. And screeching out. What a mad creature. She'd fuck the end of a carriage shaft. And she'll put the fear of God into the poor old rodent. Throwing the bloody covers back. Slapping me on the thighs. Freezing the bloody hell out of both of us. Grunting. O my goodness where did they come from. She's got her castanets. Her nipples bouncing up and down to their clack. Ah. But what magic. Miraculously getting me instantly as hard as an oak fence post. Quite wonderfully astonishing. Under starter's orders again. The flag's down. We're off. Good lord the rat's out. In the middle of the ruddy studio. On the Afghan rug. Ruddy well sitting back upon his hind legs. And bloody well eyes popping, his tiny ears twitching, watching us.

And
Clearly
Wanting
To join in
Too

290

20

An occasional tread of a foot on the crimson carpet over some loose board out in the hall as one awakes these Dublin mornings. To peek out of a half open eye. Find the brass lamp at my bedside. The mellow shiny chestnut colour of the dresser among the darker mahoganies. The glass panelled and curtained wardrobe doors. Flowered curtains and writing desk. Toggle switches at the door for light and ivory button for servants. And that morn, following the rat battle at Lois's studio, there were stronger foot steps, and a pounding knock with the door sweeping open.

"Good morning, my dear boy, good morning. Let us put forever behind us the sordidness of last evening."

"Rashers you ran off leaving me to be executed by a gang of thugs."

"Forgive me, dear boy. Once more I must abjectly put myself to ask of you amnesty if not your total amnesia. It wasn't until I was streets away that I realised the person behind me was not you and was in fact a man in his pyjamas hysterically waving his umbrella, whose drain pipe I wrenched off his house. Honestly. And you know I was beside myself. My McCormack records shattered. But look. The sun's up and out beaming down there over the Green. In fact it is well past twelve o'clock. Don't you catch the fragrance of coffee and newly baked spice buns wafting across the city. The squeal and clang of

291

trams. To and from Donnybrook. The bustle down there of people malcontent at work. Peerage being paged in the lobby. Dowagers, duchesses arriving to lunch at the ladies' entrance down there at the Kildare Street Club. And tinker ladies already on the pavements with their bunches of violets for sale."

"O god, do come in Rashers. And if I am not quite at my best this morning you will of course please forgive me. I've not had that much sleep. Fire brigade wouldn't let me in for an hour at dawn this morning."

"My precious dear boy, but how wonderful it is to have you so close by like this. Down the hall, pop up some steps two at a time and there you are. Ah isn't this awfully nice in here. Shall I ring down for a spot of breakfast for you. We mustn't miss the first race. I might myself have a tipple of white sparkling wine, if you don't mind. Glorious out. Just look. Here let me open your curtains a bit. Aren't you dear boy, delighted to be alive. To see out there. Our purple hills arise beyond our gracious city."

"No. It appears the pawn ticket you gave me is an already punched tram ticket to Dalkey. And your diamond cufflinks happen to be genuine imitation jewelry."

"O my dear boy, I know, I know what a dismal awful mistake that was for me to have made. Only noticed it later. I am so damn sorry. You see it was my way of tricking those catacomb denizen bastards into thinking they'd stumbled on the real McCoy."

"They would certainly have known a bloody Dalkey tram ticket when they saw it."

"Not in the semi dark, dear boy. Of course it was careless of me. Of course near dawn a riot finally broke forth wrecking the catacombs, Binky having made most unwisely a derogatory remark about the wife of one of his tenants. The husband returned from his nightly philandering jumped upon Binky just as he was asleep. Compressed poor queer devil's throat into a shoelace. Then picked him up, threw him through a door, closed at the time. And finally chased Binky as he ran stark naked down the street for his life. The milkman delivering milk, fell off his horsecart and broke his arm laughing. Saved Binky's life as his adversary also fell into the gutter laughing at the milkman. The catacombs are an utter shambles. Broke every bottle in the place. But ah. Here we are. Within these safe plush confines. Just lift the receiver. Or would you rather come join me in my neck of the woods. Lots more elbow room in my little suite you know for a spot of breakfast. No I see you wouldn't. Another morning perhaps. But last night or rather very early morning my dear boy. I waltzed back into the lobby. To find an inebriated doctor in pursuit of a female guest. A well known surgeon no less. Crawled after her up the main stair from the lobby. Got to the top, stood up asking the lady for directions to her room. That he would in a short time when he had regathered his equilibrium, find her. And then he fell backwards nearly into but alas just beyond my arms, and down the entire flight of stairs. And I did myself, suppressing my laughter of course, escort the lady to her room. Thinking I was on to a damn good thing. And look at my swollen fingers. She was an utter and complete maniac. Out of some Galway heap of rubble they call castles these days. She had actually pushed the doctor. And then the creature slammed the door on me. And safely inside her locked room started screaming rape. It was I who rang the fire alarm. Thought it the only sensible and humane thing to do. She'd have a ladder at least exiting her window. Ah but now. I have it all planned. The entire day ahead. An ancient but reliable vehicle is calling for us. The only Daimler in town as a matter of fact. Shall I ring for your bath to be drawn."

"Please give me a few minutes Rashers. To face life."

"Racing dear boy. We must motor countrywards. An abomination to be late. Must be quicko now, my dear chap. We shall have much jolly conversation and champagne in the various privileged enclosures. Then back to town. Black Velvet in the gilded cage. Then dispossessing ourselves of parvenus, we shall then oyster and Heidsieck in Jammet's. And sup at the Dolphin Hotel upon a slab of haunch of a Mullingar heifer, blue rare, with some sappy rich grand cru of the Côte de Nuits. And please, dear boy, I humbly put to you don't forget I am incognito. And remember at all times my present cognomen of the Earl of Ronald Ronald."

Of course, from the moment one returned at dawn from Lois's bed, and woke that fatal noon, one lost just about every single penny at the races over such ensuing days. And spent the rest of one's zero remaining pounds running up vast accounts with the help of Rashers, all over town. And still came the daily insistent hammering on one's hotel door. Rashers striding in. Racing journals under arm. Radiantly outfitted in morning suit. A carnation in his buttonhole. And my awaking spirits already squashed by the previous days' totally dismal losses. Rashers always somehow managing to come back to town a winner. Giving a good luck pound to any tinker lady at the course near enough to hand us a flower through the Daimler limousine door. And even unbelievably, albeit piecemeal, making restitution of my previous loan to him. But not ever again explaining the whereabouts of the real pawn ticket.

"Now dear boy. Here you are. Another fiver owed you. And I shall the moment the moment is ripe, dump at your feet, polished and gleaming and straight from Dublin's best silversmiths, every item of your temporarily borrowed silver."

"Rashers, does that mean in future, that should one have you as a guest again, my spoons upon your departure, shall have to be counted."

"O dear. Deserve I do. But that is rather below the belt this crucial time of the morning you know. Especially as my emotive perception must devote itself entirely to estimating form for the day's racing. Have you no heart dear boy. Do remember it was not my fingers but those light ones of the Poet who actually purloined or rather took a loan of your valuable utensils. I am crushed that you should take that attitude. And here I am with my humble little offering. A bottle of the best gents' toilet water to be found in London. To give you."

"Thank you Rashers. Nice of you to think of me. And my apologies. But the moment is overripe for the return of my silver. I am in deep financial difficulties."

"The status quo dear boy, merely the status quo."

"Well my personal state of things Rashers, is not being improved by this hotel bill mounting precipitously by the hour. And the haberdashery you persuaded me to purchase. And the fact that I lie here, temporarily at least, beholden to you."

"Nae. O friend. Speak not so."

"Rashers, I bloody well speak so."

"Dear boy, you just haven't fancied my choice of nags. Now. I'll give you the following tips for today."

"Rashers I did take, if you remember, one or two of your tips and lost a packet."

"O dear. But such condition of which you speak so disconsolately merely requires to bring off a coup dear boy. A master stroke. Which shall even eventually lead to one of an international dimension. I mean, for a local start, there is our friendly little stock exchange just a hop skip and jump away over there on Anglesea Street. Indeed seven six eight four one is the telephone number. Buy up barley. Rubber. Tin."

"There is Rashers, also *Stubbs' Gazette* in which I have just prominently been published."

"Dear boy, my name is there for all to see each week of the year. Admittedly one does appear frequently under pseudonyms. Take no notice of such small and infinitely trifling matters. The grand coup is what you must put your mind to. For which right now you must make yourself ready. Keeping your options open as it were."

"Was borrowing my silver one of your coups and master strokes."

"Darcy, please. Haven't we now been through so much together. At least I am happy to know you recognise that I have merely borrowed. A much better frame shall be upon you once you have breakfasted dear boy and taken your bath. Now you just relax."

A black uniformed smiling maid assisted by two impressively self important page boys quick about their business wheeling in one's table. Sausages still sizzling on a hot plate. Egg yolks glistening in their shiny fat. Rashers downing the rinds I cut from one's bacon. Even having half my coffee. Munching down three pieces of soda bread toast and honey. And without interlude switching to the champagne next wheeled in the door.

"Darcy. Now listen. We must corner the market in some desperately needed commodity."

"I suppose something like Guinness stout for instance."

"Darcy there is no need to be funny about such a deadly serious matter. Now what about becoming a major shareholder in our little casino. Now that the matter of the gent who was stabbed under our roulette table has blown over. Gala reopening soon. The Royal Rat will of course still preside as front man. Of course having had to return the bed he tried to pawn with his mother still in it, he then unfastened the stove and took that with the poor lady's potatoes still boiling on it. Now I don't want you to think we do not have pots to piss in. How about a modest investment."

"No."

"Ah pity. Well then. What about a small dance hall we might open. Or can we interest you in say some choice little restaurant operation. O dear. Well then some shares. Gilt edge. Also know a chap anxious to vend his tea plantations in Ceylon."

"Rashers, you are flogging a dead horse. I haven't even got enough seed potatoes for spring. No grass. And hardly enough hay even to last till next week. An agent suing me. Trees being cut and stolen. My entire staff as I lie here are fattening themselves upon their gargantuan lunch. The only reason this hotel isn't demanding payment is because I settled an even larger bill previously."

"Darcy. Never take that appalling attitude. Positiveness, belief in the future. No doubting. Somewhere, somehow, there is always a profit flowering for someone. Let there be no bewilderment. No nonplus or quandary. Never allow the self to dwell in the regions of nae hope."

Breakfasting with Rashers did undeniably cheer one up. Just as quickly as his meal and champagne being listed on my bill, did then depress me. Each morning warmed in the bath one did lie deeply thinking. And remembering all too vividly my departure that dawn from Lois. One of the most harrowing events of my entire life. As she crawled on hands and knees across her studio floor after me, oblivious to the smears of paint or lurking rat. Clutching at my garments as I attempted to put them on. Wailing and sobbing for me not to go and leave her. Without a husband in the future. Long divorced as she was. Without her cats. Her nipples shrunken hard by the cold. Her breasts wagging nakedly on her chest. Her face looking up beseeching. She did with the tears streaming down her face suddenly look like an ancient crone. Don't leave me. I beg of you don't leave me. And I left. Saying I must. I must. Lois following me step by step down her stairs. And as I ran away down her alley. I could hear her fists behind me pounding feebly inside her front door. But what she did not know. Was that I had fallen asleep into a dream. Of Leila on a rack. In a damp dungeon room. Being drawn and quartered. A blade cutting into her. Her stomach lying open. Entrails reddened as she squealed in pain. A white coffin carrying her body on tinker men's shoulders through the evening mist and smoke of a bitter Dublin slum street. And I could hardly catch my breath as I woke, shaking in the coldest of sweats. And I could not stay. Could not comfort. For all I could see ahead in my life was an endless lonely tundra, icy cold, a wind chasing me. A name calling. Leila.

"Darcy, a promising nag or two I perceive here this morning. Yes. Deserving of at least a fiver. On Sweet Sixteen in the first race should start matters off nicely enough. Little lady had a notable run recently. Only beaten by a neck."

Rashers shouting to me in the tub. And in my room, feet propped up. Tucking in once more to his innumerable eggs, bacon, stacks of soda bread, dishes of butter balls, and washing it all down with replacement pots of hot coffee. And not that many minutes later, rustling his racing journals open under his cigar, was deeply into his first bottle of the day's champagne.

"Join me Darcy. Very nicely fruity this. Dry too. But fruity."

Rashers did set one's mind to thinking. Why should one not become enormously rich. Go out into the world beyond this world. Not have to each day wake up wondering where one's fivers were to come from. Or to contemplate going off deep into the oak forest at Andromeda Park and put a barrel of one's best Purdey to one's head. Meanwhile Rashers did see me to one or two meals at Jammet's. And one unforgettable one in the company of his beloved. Blond dyed lady on the verge of being what one might charitably refer to as pudgy. Whose middle structure was clearly the same circumference as her rather voluminous bosoms decorated by the neckline of plunging sequined fabric. Her legs equally misproportioned, at least in terms of good equine conformation. Her very high heels making her very upright in the pasterns. Rashers uncustomarily becoming so becomingly shy. Nervously putting his hand on top of hers following the serving of each course. Throughout the evening watching her eagerly as she deposited a first mouthful in her mouth. Always smiling, and jumping to do her merest bidding. Lighting her cigarettes. Even adoring as it dangled from her lip, and the smoke she let rise into her eyes making them water. Fetching her opera glasses from her nearly ankle length muskrat fur coat. Which she said she planned, as soon as one appeared in Dublin, to replace with mink. And then for her to rudely peer at other, albeit and thank god, distant guests. And the most astonishing thing of all. I do not believe I shall ever encounter anyone who has ever loved anyone else in the world as much as Rashers seemed to love her. She did keep rather silent in my company. But was appreciatively more talkative as we brought up the subject of horses. And one was astonished she knew exactly my family racing colours and the names and pedigrees of many of my mother's fillies and colts running long before I was even born. She kept staring out into the middle distance. As another name would come to mind. Rashers grinning approvingly from ear to ear. But I could see him wince as she snapped her fingers at the waiter which I found frightfully embarrassing. And poor Rashers equally so as he did slump more than slightly in his chair. But he was treating one extremely handsomely. To an utterly incredible enrapturing rare magnum of Pommard, with which I washed down my roast wild duckling a l'orange. And Rashers at evening's end smiling elatedly and bowing across the room to three gentlemen. All of whom grinned happily back.

"My former professor of Bacteriology and Preventive Medicine, Dr Bigger dear boy. Indeed that's my actual tutor in the corner. He was as well my King's Professor of Materia Medica and Pharmacy. You see Darcy practically across the street is a private gate through Trinity's wall through which properly entitled College Fellows may discreetly slip out of college to dine."

The flames of the blazing fire dying over brandy and cigars. Tears in Rashers' eyes lifting his glass as we toasted his beloved. Who'd excused herself to retire to the ladies. She was I am certain not a moment younger than an entire forty five or even more years.

"You do like her, don't you Darcy. You do find her acceptable. You are enamoured of her, even a wee bit."

"O my god Rashers, not to put too fine a point on it, your lady is a trifle on the robust side. But she does have a remarkably pretty complexion and rather nice ringlets of blond curls."

"There is no need for you to go on. I know she is not the most beautiful lady in Dublin and that she is what is commonly referred to as of stout build. But you do not have to be so hurtfully euphemistic about it, do you. You don't do you, believe I love her. Do you."

One could see the pleading in his eyes. So desperate for one's approval. And somehow I could not restrain myself from remarking.

"Well as a matter of fact Rashers, no, I don't believe you love her. I rather think you find her attractive for perhaps a few other not insubstantial reasons."

"Well I'll tell you. I'm not after her pubs, tobacconist's shops and her country house as you may think. I respect her too much for that. How would you know what a fine noble person she is. And from a damn decent family too. You do don't you attribute to me only the crassest of motives. I'm sorry now I made the mistake of having you meet her."

No amount of insistence would dissuade Rashers that I had not meant a word I said. Arriving at the race course, I attempted to refer to her in my most off handed manner, as such a cheerfully buxom girl who would make a fine wife.

"There is no necessity for false praise of her. I know you think I am sulking. And I was deeply hurt. But may I remind you, I am born under the planet Jupiter. And as a jovialist, the depths of despair is simply not my cup of tea."

At the paddock Rashers hardly glanced in my direction from his race card. And continued to behave in this fashion till the last race. When I saw Awfully Stupid Kelly in a natty brown trilby and what he must imagine is an extremely well cut suit, giving his jockey a leg up on Ulidia Princess The Second. Which Rashers already has as a hot tip to win. Kelly popping the handle of a tightly rolled brolly over an arm and holding his race card aside as he lifted his jockey's knee with his free hand. One spied Baptista Consuelo attempting to look glamorous with a party of friends including some of the bastards descended upon me in my own front hall. She's just the sort of female with whom one would open up one's dinner conversation by announcing, that when one was in Egypt one was attacked by wild dogs. And always my eyes wherever they looked, hoping for a sight of Leila, that I might speak with her. That she must be somewhere, hopefully not in the company of the Mental Marquis. That she had come to Dublin and found employment. Then I saw through the heads one's once mean old stable boss, Matt. When I, a runaway from school and home was an itinerant like Leila. Exploited and shunned. And Matt watching from the paling and looking much down on his luck again. How quickly the world forgets you were once on top of it. How soon the hounds howl out in their long moans heralding death. His shabby clothes, his cheeks sunken on his face. Just as he was when one came to his rescue before. And from whom, in exchange for my compassion, came the biggest racing win of my life. So strange now to see other familiar faces in this passing parade, and to even think that I could have been a stable lad in Kelly's stables. Even Foxy Slattery with an owner in the paddock. And seeing me. To wave. Shaking his head up and down yes and nodding at his horse. Must mean the brakes are off. And someone is nudging me in the back.

"Hello Matt."

"Hello sir, I saw you from across the paddock there."

"How are you."

"Ah not great. There used to be a decent time when no one could be unknown in Dublin and now by god people are forgotten all over the place. But I can still judge a good horse. And I've come to give you a tip. Those mean gombeen Kellys have a winner there, again."

"But I've just got a tip on number six, Rumoured Ghost."

"Not a chance."

"Thanks Matt."

"Would you have a pound now sir to spare."

"Not to spare. But certainly Matt."

"Goodbye and thanks sir."

So sad. Matt goes. As Rashers comes. Jovial again. Grinningly puffing his cigar. Known by all around him. Like some kind of king. But I suppose jollier than most monarchs. His binocular case flying myriad colours of his many private club enclosure tickets. And finally his cognomen ringing out on the public address.

"Will Lord Ronald Ronald come to the Steward's Office please."

"Excuse me a jiff dear boy. The chaps must require my assistance, or there awaits a hot tip."

"But I have a hot tip for you Rashers. Number six, Rumoured Ghost."

"No thank you."

"Rashers I'm sure."

"Dear boy. Word from my trusted inner sanctum is Ulidia Princess The Second. Just look at her. Like a coiled steel spring. But of course don't let me dissuade you from promptly doubling or even tripling your stakes on your choice dear boy. Be right back."

"Rashers. I haven't a bloody cent but this fiver left."

"Now now not to worry. You always know, don't you that your banker stands right in front of you, ready to lend. Give that fiver to me. I'll pop it on for you with a little something extra. And apropos of nothing at all dear boy. Did you know that it requires a tart to be a first rate actress, and it requires a wife to be only second rate. Ta ta."

Rashers irrepressible, as well as being a ready philosopher, did of course over the days, back more than a few no hopers. But undeniably did, every few races, return again with an enormous fist full of fivers. And one's heart was more than a little in dilemma over his certainty of Ulidia Princess. And back in the enclosure, just at the off, as one tapped one's cold toes up and down, he steamed up beside me effusively confident as well as overjoyed.

"Dear boy. Do you know what that was all about. Honestly today is my day. It utterly is. I've just been asked to become a member of the Jockey Club."

"How wonderful Rashers."

"Yes isn't it. And I have my sad chap placed your bet for you. Pity you're missing such a damn good thing at thirty five to one dear boy."

"But Rumoured Ghost is fifty to one."

"Of course it is. Surprised it's not a hundred to one. Out of an unknown stable, trained by a trainer no one's heard of. Like this nag, nine, Knocknamuck. Imagine, such a downtrodden name for a horse. You did however didn't you, see what a lovely muscled, lean in the loins filly Ulidia Princess is. Her balletic dainty feet actually thrive in heavy ground. Turf is riding very dead today dear boy. An up and coming jockey upon her. Of course the very hush hush news that the brakes are well and truly off was only out at the very last second. Had only two previous leisurely outings. And she is out of the stable dear boy that bred Tinkers Revenge. Won at a hundred to one last year."

"Which I backed with an enormous bet, Rashers."

"What. O my god did you."

"Yes I did. And from such winnings I also loaned you a fiver."

"Did you."

"Yes I did."

"Ah dear boy, it shows you doesn't it. How much I have to thank you for, doesn't it. But please don't answer that too provocative a reflection. But you know one does find it irritating if we look about us that far too many are wearing emblems associated with the hound and fox. You would think, wouldn't you that they would need a breather from adorning as they do their scarves, cars, lapels, ties with such creatures. Ah but we must pay attention to the race. Here's your ticket dear boy. And it's not one to Dalkey. Sad for you, but I've put your fiver on your fifty to one shot."

"Thank you Rashers."

"Please remember, Earl of Ronald Ronald. Soon to be a member of an august body."

"Sorry your Lordship."

"Ah isn't it good to be alive. At the start of a race. As the heart pounds hopefully. One's life now free from gurriers, vandals and galoots. And all other disgraceful contretemps. No longer having to crucify one's spirit in the catacombs or besmirch one's day by cowering in under those three golden balls."

"To pawn someone else's silver."

"O dear, dear boy. Must you. Yes yes. I did. I did. But please instead let me draw your attention to this race. They're just rounding the first turn. All over the first jump. Ah the field nicely sorting themselves out a little."

Rashers temporarily silent, nearly taking one's arm off. As he was clearly having a heart attack. Especially at each jump. His filly from the off, was running last. Despite his shouting, grabbing and tugging me.

"Don't dismay dear boy. Ulidia Princess is keeping a sedate pace. Won't make her move till a jump to go. Saves every ounce of energy for those coiled steel quarters of hers. We shall see her dainty pasterns stretching over the emerald grass blades in the final furlong, her hoofs bombarding the nags distantly following with a veritable plethora of wet sods."

"She's last Rashers."

"May be. But the Princess took that jump foot perfect. Any moment, just watch, she'll leave the rest of the field well and truly stranded. I mean your old nag's not doing badly up fourth, Darcy."

"Third, Rashers, according to the announcer's voice. And if my own eyes don't deceive me."

As one cheerfully reminded his present Lordship that Rumoured Ghost was in the thick of the leaders, one's heart began sinking as Ulidia Princess began coming. Unbelievably from last. Way way out on the outside.

"Like a rocket dear boy. You see. Like a veritable bloody rocket is she blazing towards the post."

Each momentary second he put his binoculars aside, Rashers socking me so hard on the shoulder, nearly knocking me over. Getting more and more hysterical with the Princess overtaking the field with three furlongs to go.

"My one hundred quid dear boy, rides flying upon her. One hundred bloody wonderful magnificent quid. Come on you Princess namesake of the bloody north. Show your ruddy bloody elegant heels. Look at that. Whoopee hooray."

"Rashers, please. You've got me by the collar and throat."

Rashers was, his binoculars momentarily dropped on his chest, actually throttling me. His face grinning ear to ear at my dismay. And two furlongs to go. With the announcer now bellowing.

"Out in front now. Last to first in a furlong. Ulidia Princess. Six lengths ahead of the field. And Rumoured Ghost. Coming fast. It's still Ulidia Princess. A length on Rumoured Ghost who's gaining ground. Every stride. It's Rumoured Ghost now, neck and neck with Ulidia Princess."

Rashers' jaw more than slightly dropping open. His mouth suddenly chewing air. His head craning forward behind his binoculars. As I chose now to give him a good bloody solid punch on the arm. The announcer quite utterly hoarse, shouting, screaming, nearly out of his mind.

"No one else in it now. This is a sensation. Two rank outsiders now. Seven lengths in front of the field. A furlong to go. Stride for stride. Leaving two Ascot winners, and a winner of the Arc de Triomphe in their wake. Nothing between them. One hundred yards to go. Still neck and neck. Ear to ear. Nostril to nostril. Fifty yards. Twenty. It is. It is. Rumoured Ghost. Yes it is. It's Rumoured Ghost. Over the line. By a whisker, if not a nose. Rumoured Ghost the winner."

Rashers putting his binoculars slowly down. As one let out one's own whoopee and hooray. Beaming all one's teeth for a change in his direction. And perhaps cheer up his ruddy face paler than pale, drained of blood. Even the flecks of bright colour in his tweed coat seemed to fade. As one's own mind conjured warmth. Hope. As one

303

might have, making hay under the summer sultry skies. And a red sun, redder, sinking in the west.

"Ah your Lordship, so sorry you sad chap. For you to have lost. Didn't I tell you I had a hot tip. Don't you know I'm an old friend and true horseman who can tell speed and stamina in the glint of an equine eye. O what relief. God. How many bloody days. Finally a winner. Not only pay one's hotel bill but wages for a fortnight. Lime a hundred acres of pasture. See my tailor, too. I am highly cheered up. Come. No glum jaw now."

"Darcy, I think I am about to incur your final lifelong wrath."

"Nonsense. Sad chap. Come with me. To collect one's winnings. I'll need all your extra pockets. And thence to the champagne bar where you may incur my hospitality."

"O my dear boy, I cannot bear to continue to somehow bedevil your life."

"Rashers at this very particular moment, believe me you are, for a change, certainly not."

"Darcy, I don't quite know how to put it."

"Put what."

"Put what seems just to be one more of my very good intentions, which I fear has gone absolutely awry."

"What on earth are you talking about Rashers."

"Darcy I placed your bet."

"And thank you very much. And what pray is troubling you your Lordship, aside from your very unfortunate loss, of course."

"Darcy, to make up for my little committed indiscretions in our friendship, I was so eager for you to win. Deeply and sincerely."

"Ah were you. How nice."

"Darcy, so deeply and sincerely. And you must forgive me. I placed your bet on Ulidia Princess."

"You what."

"Yes. On Ulidia Princess to win. I am. I am most heartily sorry. I'm a dead loss. No help to myself. Nor to my dearest of friends."

The enclosure emptied. Race cards, betting tickets strewn on the stand steps and the enclosure grass. Bookmakers their signs down, their little black boards packed away. Departing with their bags stuffed with bank notes. My feet rooted still to the porch upon which one stood. And Rashers one step beneath me, taking from his side coat a massive roll of notes. Peeling them off.

"Darcy, here. I'm making your bet good."

"No you're not. Absolutely not. To dare insult me in this way. On top of what you've already done. Please."

"Then you please for god's sake strike me. Please. Take a swing at least. Don't leave me standing here like this. I will of course try to duck."

Westwards, clouds edged with pink out over the thickets of tree branches. Back towards Dublin. The skies brooding their strange cold blue grey and black. The breeze chill on the back of my neck. My clenched hands plunged cold in my pockets. Rashers' eyes glancing up.

"But dear boy, you're not, as I can see, going to strike me, are you."

"No. I am not."

"Well can I then offer you solace. You see. I am leaving Ireland. At any moment."

His checked cap removed, Rashers who invites one's fist. A gust of wind blowing an auburn tinted lock of hair across his brow. A big freckle at the corner of his right eye one never noticed before. Groundsmen now arriving. To clean up the debris. And apropos of nothing at all, one's own eyes looked down. For some reason at Rashers' shoes. At their wrinkled cracks, polished a thousand times. An ancient leather of a military boot. And one was somehow certain they had once belonged to his father. A hero of wars. An army General, celebrated, decorated, feted and respected. In command of thousands and thousands of men. And this one man here. His errant son. Fortunate hunter, con man, chancer, thief. Author of my demise. Who devil may care, forever seems to frequent my life. And now suddenly in one's anger. Hopelessness comes. As I remember once. Dressing in my room at Andromeda Park. Ready to order the men to harness up the horses to the rakes. As the rain hit the windows. In a pouring drenching squall. My heart sinking with the hay cut. Cured under the day's previous lucky skies, and ready for cocking out across the acres and acres of meadows. I drew the curtains across the tinted pink glass panes. And beat and beat the walls with my fists. But as a certain horse may have character for hunting.

> So must it be
> That one has
> A soul
> For despair

21

On that miserable eve in the smoky noisy fug of the packed bar, one did take a subdued funereal champagne. Amid the bubbling voices. The greetings. The plans for parties, hunt balls and other race meetings. Rashers buying a magnum. Pouring the grapey ash white delicious fluid, refilling and refilling my glass. And again attempting to shove fifty pound notes in my pocket. And as I would push his hand away, I would catch a glimpse of the treasury script's etched purple woman and her harp. Like Leila. And me. Like the back of the note. A sad green bearded face. And a three pronged spear sticking up from oak leaves. A bowl of wheat sheaves and fruit. All of Ireland's plenty. For the rich few who lord luckily over all the impoverished many. Of whom Foxy Slattery, grinningly coming in, is no longer one of them. One did try desperately to hide the disaster on one's face. And pretend that he was yet again saver of one's life.

"Boss what did I tell you."

"Thank you Foxy. Thank you. You're the maker of my fortune. Please join us in a glass of champagne."

"And boss maybe I can sell you a car now on the riches."

"Perhaps Foxy. Perhaps."

One simply did not have the heart to disappoint him. To tell him one's best asinine friend bare faced took one's last bloody money and lost it on a losing nag. But I could see the cheer on Foxy's face vanish in a second. Beyond his shoulder, Baptista Consuelo, her mink coat sweeping open revealing a tight plunging neckline. And just at the moment I was about to effect his introduction to her, she promptly turned her wide backside on him.

"Ah boss, I may not be good enough for some people, but we did it again now didn't we. Never get a repeat of odds like that till Rumoured Ghost's ready for the knacker's yard."

Motoring back the country lanes to town and finally across the Liffey, one was, astonishingly at the moment sporting an erection. And had the uncontrollably strange urge. To fuck Baptista Consuelo straight up her big stuck up arse. With one's present prick that could just bloody well do the job. For her sake, sand in the lubricant. Plunging it in her dog style till she went barking across the floor on her naked hands and knees with a suitably dumb and entertained look on her overly pretty face. Rashers humming. The Lark In The Clear Air. And one had to admit, in one's champagne swirling mind, to being soothed by the sound. But to know that one was feeling again somehow, the same shattering shock that one always feels poor and skint. Making one avoid taking any notice, as one steps out of the warm confines of the Shelbourne, of the resentful passing faces of discontent. As one's own face goes displeased in this dear desecrated dirty Dublin. But at least presently insulated by the soft upholstery and shiny elegant fittings of this Daimler. John, Rashers' endlessly patient chauffeur, changing gear to pull us up the cobble stone narrow hill. Past these gates of Steevens' Hospital. Rashers again nervously pushing towards my hand another sheaf, this time of big white English fivers instead of Irish fifties, as if the brand or denomination of currency made a difference.

"But then I proffer you this by way of interest dear boy. On the loan of your family heirlooms."

"Rashers I'm sorry. But I've already made it eminently clear I cannot accept money from you in this fashion. It's just a bit of bloody bad luck that's all. The same I've already had on innumerable previous races. And you could, just as easily, have been quite right. Ulidia Princess might have won by a whisker instead."

"Dear boy but I was wrong. Not to abide by your instruction. Life itself is lost by such whiskers. Are you trying to break my heart. You are. Of course you can take a few measly old crumpled fivers. And of course you must. Never could I have been bankrolled into my modest present prosperity without the assistance of your august family's silverware. You will never have faith in me again will you. Well at least tell me you had some previous faith in me."

"Yes. I had. For a few minutes after we first met. And you thought I was a promising con man. And I nearly believed it."

"Well dear boy. You were. The way you took a fiver from the Mental Marquis. But see in there. Those gates we presently pass by. As a medical student, I took post mortem notes down in the basement over dead cold Dubliners' cadavers. Sorrowful work. When it's children. But I would have I think in the end, lacked dedication. To spend the rest of one's life listening to rumbling rotted lungs or up to one's elbows in guts. But did you ever wonder why I ceased my studies and took my detour in life out of the professional classes."

"No. Actually I haven't."

"Well I suppose, why should you. But I'll tell you why. I did have many girlfriends I'll admit. But there was a fellow student, a very tweedy slender pretty lady with most wonderful legs, of whom I became much enamoured. For her shy and strange ways. Never would she join me for tea or coffee at Johnston, Mooney and O'Brien's out the back gate. And try as I did she would take but little notice of my attentions. I knew there was something much wrong with her hair. She constantly wore cloche hats. And one afternoon. Which one cannot ever forget. At a pathology lecture. She sat without her hat on the tier directly in front and below me. And I took my fountain pen just to tease. And reached down and devilishly poked in her hair. The clip got caught in the strands. And as she turned, pulling away to look back up, a wig came off her bald head. Darcy."

"For heaven's sake Rashers."

"Darcy. Yes. There are tears in my eyes. Because she ran from lecture hall. Tripping and squeezing past her fellow students' knees. There were no jeers but there was cruel involuntary laughter chasing her. And from the hall window. She jumped. And was found lying dead on the steps. The brains shattered out of her skull."

Our car heading in the direction of the Coombe back streets. Passing the shadowy great elevations of Guinness's brewery walls. The smell of hops. Up Robert Street. Into Marrowbone Lane. The prolonging silence. I turned to look at Rashers. Sitting but a hand's touch away. Tears dropping down his cheeks. His chest heaved once.

"Not my happiest day Darcy I can tell you. I never returned to college. And I am grateful to you. For at least not severely dressing me down all this ride back to town as you have, even sportingly, every reason to do. Would you in the very near future contemplate catching the mail boat with me. Sometimes the sound of steerage passengers drunkenly vomiting, does require the company of pleasant distraction. One doesn't want to pitch and roll across the Irish Sea completely alone even in the safe confines of one's state room."

"But surely my god Rashers, you're not really leaving Dublin are you."

"Yes. I shall be. Not hard to do. Uncomfortable yes, but following a good breakfast in the one and only palatial hotel in Liverpool, one slips on a train from Lime Street. To whisk hopefully at speed through those midland industrial slag heaps. Deposit oneself at journey's end in one of the better London hotels. And I shall thence to Paris. And thence, dear boy, entrain from the Gare d'Austerlitz to Monte Carlo."

"But Rashers this is madness. It's not because of that silly old bet."

"No. It's not. It is my dear boy, because one must occasionally shake from one's heels this unfortunate broken city's tatters and grime. And its even more broken and tattered citizens. Minions who grimly drag feet back and forth, to and from their malingering toil. Whose hearts daily beg St Jude or somebody for the impossible. To hide somewhere to escape their thankless lives. But don't think me on the side of socialism, dear boy. I'm all for exploiting people. But I have you know, been turning over in my mind your remarks. I am a fortune hunter. No. Say nothing dear boy. It's true. But believe me too when I say I do not seek from my beloved her goods. Even as I admit I am a con man. You know, before the advent of your silverware I actually had presented myself to the Association for the Relief of Distressed Protestants in Molesworth Street, and did as a left footer, without shame or nervous quiver, prise three quid out of them."

"You're not a con man Rashers."

"I am. And so kind of you to say that I am not. Nor do I presume, despite my reasonable good birth and acceptable demeanour, to regard myself as a gentleman."

"You are Rashers. A gentleman. You are at least that. Most of the time."

"No I am a cad. Albeit of a sporting nature. But you see Darcy, the real fact of the matter is, and I know you will laugh as I tell you. That I did so much want to be an Admiral. That broad band of gold braid upon my cuff. Gold upon the peak of my cap. My flotilla of ships. And my father's army pushed by the enemy to the edge of the sea. But ah perhaps I wouldn't, as I dream that I would, weigh anchor to sail my fleet away and to leave the pompous bugger and his army trapped there on the shore. Just a thought, dear boy. But a more important thought. The greatest of casinos calls. My portmanteau is fairly filled with fivers. To manoeuvre there. There is a hotel on a hill where one takes one's calm, comfortable and pleasant refuge. One's window shall look out and down over the yacht filled harbour. And conveniently one merely strolls across a verdured street or two to mount the wide imposing steps of the casino. You see Darcy the moment for my coup has arrived. Which shall be wrought into reality under those enormously high glorious ceilings. And I shall not return unless it is to pull my own true weight with my beloved."

"Yes I can understand Rashers. Hers would be considerable. To pull."

Rashers sulked until we arrived in front of the Shelbourne and he whispered a message to John. Handing him a fiver. But he hardly spoke another word to me. Just polite nods and grunts. I was merely after one's own dismal disappointment, trying to be somehow amusing. As one does at such times. My heart now utterly sinking at the thought of Rashers' departure. And not entirely because it meant not ever seeing one's silverware again. Which one was certain somehow, he had in fact sold. But he did for all his endless faults and presumptions upon my good will, at least encourage one to bolster against the dismal chilling winds whirling round one's soul. And as we alighted to the pavement John the chauffeur had to push a way clear for us to pass. Rashers assuming his best aristocratic poise as a gang of newsboys clustered around him, their hoarse voices calling out.

"Give us a penny mister Rashers. Give us a penny."

"I beg your pardon boys, but please, it's Lord Ronald Ronald to you."

Clanging bell. And a crowded tram roaring by. Through its

steamed up windows, shadows of heads and newspapers within. The bare foot newsboys, clutching their papers under arm. Rheumy eyed, scabbed and scratched. Their faces streaked with phlegm. Torn garments hardly covering their chests. Hands and feet blue with cold. As grimy fingers touched upon one's sleeve.

"Come on mister, give us a penny."

The smoky mists swirling over the wet glistening granite. Rashers scattering a handful of coins into the gutter. Newsboys rushing after them. Kicking, punching and pushing each other. Amid the furtive faced pedestrians hurrying home. And a voice shouting to Rashers as he entered in under the glass canopy.

"Rashers, give us a song, will you, Rashers."

In the lobby's warm smells, of coffee, whisky and perfume. Folk in from the country still in hunting clothes, throwing their weight about, proudly mud spattered, recently scratched. Rashers collecting his key, attended by two page boy acolytes, one carrying his binoculars the other his newspapers. And I watched him move on quickly between the pillars, entering the lift. And as I looked up, his feet and trouser legs disappearing from sight, a strange sad shudder went through me. That I had grievously offended him. But just around the corner, who should one nearly bump into, her large arse conspicuously present, and her loud voice haughtily demanding.

"I must have at least three hot water bottles in my bed. And my hot toddy was cold last night. And please haven't you got anyone available who knows how to lay out clothes. I don't want to be late for the theatre again tonight."

Baptista Consuelo sweeping her fur up to drape it over her shoulders. Hardly wasting a second to breeze past me with her most withering look. The soft silken lustre of her breasts in the light. Heading for the lift where she waited for it to descend again. Making, as she turned around, rather too large an effort to ignore me.

Next morning on my breakfast table a note, compliments of the Manager to communicate with him. Wouldn't one know it was time to be evicted for non payment of my bill. And following my bath and a long look out at the mountains, I thought why not go out into the elements before Rashers appeared and purloined me off to the races. Or the glooms descend as I think of Leila, not knowing where she is and in whose arms she may lie clutched. Go instead to mend some social fences. And in a moment of sunshine one strode through the busy morning pedestrians down Grafton Street. A time of day when a hint of prosperity seemed afoot. Through these shop doors. But Miss von B, she was so bloody icy. Making me speechless trying to expiate my unpardonable rudeness. In fact it's exactly how I put it.

"Please I do beg you forgive me for my unpardonable rudeness. I am quite speechless attempting an apology. But I was waylaid by the Count on my way back from visiting Mr Arland whose plight in an appalling room the worst end of Mount Street is desperate."

She did not exactly snub me but entertained the first opportunity of a customer taking her attention. Leaving me standing there far too close to the edge of the ladies' lingerie department. With one fat female acting as if one were focusing binoculars on her while she was being measured up for her monster sized whale bone corsets. I ventured for a quick reconnoitre of the delft department and returned after I thought Miss von B might have got her little revenge out of her system. I even attempted to impress her.

"Lois the accomplished and very fashionable artist is to do my full portrait. Mounted."

"Vas mounted."

"On my horse of course."

"Ha ha vas a good joke. That you should keep quiet about. She has been mounted. By all zee pricks in Dublin. And I suppose of course she is taking up residence in Andromeda Park to do it."

"What an awfully vulgar thing of you to asperse. She happens to be a very fine artist whose work is much sought after by Americans. And I think you are just jealous."

One was of course planning to invite Miss von B for coffee at the Oriental Café up the street. And to find out where she lived. And if she had a bowl we could both eat out of, and a bed we could both get into. But instead, worried out of my mind, that indeed if Lois was mounted by everyone in Dublin, as indeed I really knew she must be, one was bound to have a grave social disease. I went back up to the Green. Imagining my shrivelled testicles dropping off down my trouser leg and being squashed on the wooden street blocks by a motor vehicle. With no one to pass the time of day with, one realised one needed swift distraction. And I did present myself into one's grocer. Stepping over the well worn granite step. Pushing on the brass handle.

Open these mahogany and glass gleaming doors. To be greeted by the white coated, smiling manager.

"Good morning sir. How nice to see you. My it's been a considerable time since we had the pleasure."

"Yes. Indeed I think it has, hasn't it. I'm just popping in rather to peek about, as it were."

"But of course, please. We're getting now many of what one might refer to as some very nice exotics indeed. And your order including the bananas and pineapples just in this morning is entirely ready. Ah you'd nearly think it was her Ladyship herself back at Andromeda Park. Shall I add another tin of the caviar, our very last. There'd be every bit of two pounds of the best Beluga in it. First we've had for years. Two were sent last week."

"I don't believe I have in fact ordered anything. Certainly not caviar."

"O but you have sir. But of course please do let me check. Yes. Now there was last week's. Here we are, Andromeda Park. I knew I was not mistaken on the caviar. Even in such a substantial order. Ready to be taken to the station to be sent down on the afternoon train. Now just among some of the items, sir. Four charcoal cooked hams. Three dozen tins of our terrine of goose liver with truffles. Three dozen tins of our pâté maison with green peppercorns, petit fours, toffee assortments, mint humbugs, selection of marmalades, our own apricot and almond. Four dozen of our own jars of chicken breasts in aspic."

"Good lord."

"Is there something wrong sir. We've even succeeded in getting some double Devon fudge for you."

"I think more than possibly yes there is something wrong. I most certainly haven't ordered one of those items including double Devon fudge."

"O dear sir. But I myself spoke with your Mr Crooks."

"Spoke."

"Yes on the telephone."

"I don't have a telephone."

"Might he have called from the town. I know his voice, Mr Kildare."

Tears in Mr Hamilton's eyes. Of course no need to get one's grocer as alarmed as oneself. And certainly one could not give him offence. Nor could one make him think I was a ninny and one's butler a nut. Better to promptly reel out of Smyth's of the Green. Attempt to erase from one's mind the columns upon columns of itemized figures in the flowing embellished script. Fancy victuals listed as long as your arm. Click clacking on the train to Andromeda Park. In my utter absence. Extravagances behind my back. Seeing with one's own eyes, caviar, smoked salmon, even wines, port, even bloody hams and bacon sides which at least could have been provided from one's own bloody pig pens. It only confirms, as one was already convinced, that the whole world is against one. And one always did, with the exception of Sexton, Leila, and old Edna Annie, suspect the worst malingering whenever one saw a member of the household or estate not with their hands actively on some tool in violent motion. Impoverishment does deepen loneliness. Now nearly reaching a pitch where I'll soon be street dramatizing like Horatio the actor. Screaming incoherently at baskets of brown eggs in shop windows. Instead of walking smack into Rashers, equine journals under his arm, a bright crimson carnation in his buttonhole, his black silk tie decorated with tiny white diamond shapes, and his mouth grinning from ear to ear.

"Ah my dear Darcy, missed you for breakfast. Dear me you do look a mite peakedly poorly."

"I am."

One thing had to be said for Rashers. His mind was certainly alert to savouring mention of a long list of fancy edibles, his eyes sparkling and his tongue licking his lips. And he listened to one with such sympathy, one was nearly sorry one had only one disaster to unfold.

"Ah but calm dear boy, calm. Your grocery bill I'm sure can last a year or two on credit. But there is one wonderful aspect your complaint has from which you should take much comfort."

"I would certainly like to know what it is."

"Ah hasn't it dawned on you."

"No. It has not."

"Well, for a distinct change, it is not I who is responsible."

Of course I immediately did conjure up Rashers imitating Crooks into his hotel phone. But one's suspicions waned as I could sense his mind was miles away. And towards the top of Dawson Street, strolling through the coffee bound mid morning stream of solicitors, bank clerks, and accountants, Rashers stopped to purchase a bouquet of red roses. And one was nearly too embarrassed to enquire of him if an utter nymphomaniac like Lois could have lodged up one's urethra a fatal long simmering microbe. But I did ask.

"Rashers. I think I may have the dreaded pox."

"You what dear boy."

"Syphilis."

"Come directly with me this instant into the basement gents of the Dawson Lounge."

It was an appalling embarrassment to have to present one's prick to Rashers in this lavatorial manner especially as someone in the next cubicle had already got the wrong idea seeing two pairs of feet and the trousers of one pair around its ankles. But after careful perusement he pronounced.

"Dear chap you are quite free of the pox. Not a chancre for miles. But if you must plunge into love, you must also say to hell with venereal disease."

We did pause to take morning refreshment down these dark confines. And in order to change the subject from medical to cultural matters I enquired of Rashers over his armful of roses.

"Rashers why don't you sing. You really do you know, have a voice which I'm sure would bring you riches on the concert stage."

"So kind of you to say dear boy. That is nice to hear this tender time of morn. But you see the answer is as surprising as it is simple. My voice is the only thing I have never compromised, sold, bartered or prostituted. Well dear boy. Shall it be down with betrayal. Shall it be down with back stabbers. Put the begrudgers and unfaithful to the sword. And on to Monte Carlo. And Darcy. You are my good friend. And even in the debacle of your fear of the dreaded pox, always a joy to meet. Let's make another appointment soon shall we. Ta ta."

Standing on the pavement of Dawson Street in front of a ladies' hat shop Rashers threw a kiss in at a most pretty lady arranging a hat in the window and then waved goodbye to me and strutting off, seemed to disappear into the entrance of the Royal Automobile Club. Not to be outdone by Rashers' seemingly lofty principle. I foolishly opened an account in the flower shop and extravagantly charged my own bouquet of a dozen red roses. And I proceeded to Lois. Still

terrified out of my wits. That if I did not have the pox, I may, as
Rashers suggested, have the gleet.

"So it's you. Well come in."

"These are for you."

"Well thank you very much. And it's not that I am not appreciative but I hope you don't think I am putty in your hands. It just so
happened I was having a low moment when I asked you to stay."

Going up her steep stairs. Ushered into an actually warm studio.
Two eggs simmering in a pan on her stove in the middle of the room.
Her Afghan rug hanging where she'd been cleaning it. Of course Lois
was now out of her mind, preparing for her secret commission. And
one must suppose the rug would be a backdrop. As clearly she had
borrowed a rather regal chair from the Count's School of Ballet.
Much gilt, gold and satin, which stood up on the dais. Such whoo
haaa you never heard or saw. Actually sweating in her four or so thick
sweaters. But one did make the whole thing suddenly even more hysterical, accosting her with my worry. Just as she'd put the roses in her
one and only vase.

"I think Lois it is entirely possible for you to have given me a
venereal disease. Which I meant to ask if you had one before we went
to bed. Heavens. I am putting this rather badly."

Astonishingly in a corner behind Lois, the rat peeked out, then ventured out. And sat amusedly back on his haunches, his nose, whiskers
and even ears twitching in the much ensuing silence. Lois pale with
shock. And slowly growing red with anger.

"You most certainly are putting it badly. You mean to say dear
boy, that you would go willingly to bed with someone you thought
might have a venereal disease. How dare you, having abandoned me,
how utterly dare you, accuse me of giving you a venereal disease. It is
more likely that you are the one who might have given a venereal disease to me."

"But I've been told you've been mounted by everyone in Dublin.
And perhaps I should go to the doctor's."

"How heinous. How dare you. I should slap your face. You stupid
Irish boy. And if you think you have such a thing, you had it before
you slept with me and I should be the one to go to the doctor's."

"But Rashers has told me I have no sign of the pox."

"That dreadful philistine rascal told you did he. Well I'm telling you. Get out. Out of my studio."

Dear me. How quick one's social life becomes a shambles. In the very middle of my discussion of the possible pox. Here I am being shown the door. And of course Lois screamed at the sight of Mr Rat. Whose own social life was clearly recently much improved. I did my usual tripping over her bloody pictures and paints, and I must say, deliberately squashed one tube beautifully under heel. The contents squirting out like a calf plopping from a good old cow. But mindful of chivalry one did seriously try to put paid to the rat. And flung her pan of simmering eggs at the rodent. You never heard such an insane outburst.

"My eggs. My only eggs for luncheon. O my god. Splattered. Right on my watercolours. You slanderous little monster. For the final time. Get out."

"Lois I am most awfully frightfully sorry. I thought the eggs were hardboiled."

"Well they weren't. Please don't ever ever again come back."

Well of course Mr Rat could nibble up the yolk for a midnight snack. But I did go to the doctor's. For a second opinion. Another agonizing wait. Looking out his waiting room window at the bare trees and green lawns one could see stretched across to the amber brick the other side of Merrion Square. Asking the highly sceptical physician if one could have caught something from a door knob or lavatory seat.

"I'm afraid not. But all I can see is evidence of perhaps a trifling bruising and contusion. The result perhaps of a little too energetic activity. But we certainly can if you prefer get laboratory results. And send specimens straight over to Trinity College for a quick report."

One was mortified to find the doctor occasionally hunted and even knew my Uncle Willie. The whole of next afternoon I spent at the Grafton Street Cinema. Safe momentarily in the dark, viewing two westerns and the usual tropical travelogues. Afterwards relishing to be as those people were, on their great cruise ship, just delighting in the flora and fauna of exotic foreign lands. Instead of taking a tasty tea reading the matrimonial column of the evening paper. Of serious minded bog trotting farmers wanting ladies under sixty of stout build to be mutually suited with a view to marriage. But at least one did sit utterly alone in some baronial splendour upstairs in the Cinema Cafe.

Dreaming and thinking every moment of Leila. She worked here. Touched these cups. Fetched back and forth these trays to the kitchen lift there behind the screen across the room. Where the waitresses bringing me endless supplies of bread and tea all peek out to watch me eat.

I returned alone to my room. And I found myself for some reason, writing my last will and terrified testicle so to speak. Then in sleep having a desperately violent erotic dream about Leila. Who was nakedly running from me chased by Baptista Consuelo who with a whip, was lashing red weals across her white slender body. Next morning feeling no pain in one's prick but needing a breath of fresh air in one's brain, it was I who went to knock at Rashers' suite. Trying to invent something to thank him for or even to pay my apologies for dragging him down the bowels of a pub to examine my prick. And not least, to request his medical advice for my amorous future. I banged and even kicked his door. And with no one answering, stopped to enquire of him at the lobby desk.

"Ah yes Mr Kildare. His Lordship departed last night. His car collected him for the mail boat. Exactly following supper in his apartments with the Countess, Lady Ronald Ronald. No forwarding address. Is there something we can do."

"No thank you."

"Ah but isn't the Earl one of the great singers. Did you ever hear him now render O Danny Boy."

"No. I regret I haven't."

One never imagined to take Rashers seriously. Always expecting to find his joyful knock on my door in the morning. Or that he would be any more than just amusing one with his bizarre plan. But clearly now he is dislodged from Dublin. Where he enlivened every block of granite his heels clicked upon. Lit up the lobbies, made the Buttery and Jammet's glow with life. Not to mention, I suppose, some darker pawn shops and catacombs. But nevertheless a comfort like a familiar field or horse one knew so well. And here I am stranded having somehow to busy about one's life.

The days of Wednesday, Thursday and Friday. Attempting to dislodge from one's own trough of despair. Searching every street, peeking in every shop for a sign of Leila. Just hoping to meet her. As one finally pauses conspicuous on a street corner. Watching the bicycles, the trams and hooting motor cars go by. Do as Rashers said. Keep my options open. Have one's hair cut. Attend fittings at one's tailor. Shoes at one's shoemaker. Order cartridges at the gunsmith's. Keep moving lively in the world. Yet one did so miss him. Waking waiting, soul submerged, for his jovial momentum to take him in the door. And his entrepreneurial endeavours lugging my family silver, all the blue cloth wrapped little bags, in another door under three balls to the pawn.

Now as I walk wandering lonely still on the utter verge of utter complete and absolute despair. One's butler should make one glad to be alive instead of making one think one is dying in bankruptcy. Eaten out of house and home by staff. How can I return. To find at every little strong breeze, the great slates crashing from the roof. Rot in floors, walls and ceilings. What tools there are, disappearing. Machinery rusted and broken. Rashers said take the long term view. Dear boy, the land isn't going to get up and run away. My god. No. Instead one will, with worry, drop dead on it and melt away to one's bones. Leaving them white and criss crossed on a meadow's emerald soft bosom. Having no way to find my love I loved. From whose loins my sons and daughters could have come. And do I now go searching for my mother's jewels, so long rumoured hidden somewhere out on that land. Do I flog the paintings. The delft. Now as I go around the Green. In this Dublin. Up past the College of Surgeons. Its thick giant fortress walls. Throw this tinker lady a penny. Cross the street. Go into the park. Sit on a bench. Watch the seagulls. And the ducks glide in. A hawk high up chasing some large slowly flapping bird across the sky. The grounds keeper sweeping up the wet leaves clinging to the paths. A softness falling. Shall I westwards homewards depart. On the train. Await an end of winter at Andromeda Park while still a small ember of hope within me burns. That reassuring sign of spring is sure to come. The first swallow zooming over the orchard. Or hang on. And the operative word. Being I suppose. Hang.

Darcy Dancer emerging from the park. Walk by the fence, cross into the strange streets. Sound of engines puffing. Trains. Harcourt Street Station. Something cold, alone and wretched along these pavements. Go in this archway down this alley. Stout and whisky inside. One feels so many of these Dubliners leave their dead dreams on the smoke stained walls of a pub. Turn left, turn next right. A timber merchant's. What on earth do all these people do in there behind all these twitching curtains. This blank day. When no fox is found. Ride on to another covert. I suppose in adversity I must continue to hold my head up high. Be worthy of my acreage. Even now one remembers. The day as a child I was sick and dying. All one's servants led one by one into my room to hover their spooky heads above my bed. Sexton placing his plaster statue of the Blessed Virgin on the dresser. A Catholic candle burning. For my Protestant soul. I could, out in the country, be hunting today. Hear Foxy Slattery telling me when we were boys, as he gave me a leg up. Ah now this would be a horse so safe if it would throw you sky high in a jump it would run and catch you squarely as you somersaulted down from the clouds. And now tacked up, this little unprepossessing sign, stuck on this doorway as one passes here in some foot discomfort, is exactly what one presently requires. Carefully hand printed. Footcare Specialist. Late of London. At least one's presence in Dublin can be occasioned by a visit to the chiropodist's. And indeed by all indications of this foot note ha ha, a sophisticated big city one at that. At this lonely three o'clock in the afternoon.

Darcy Dancer proceeding up the stairs and to the end of a cold bereft hallway. Flowered wet wallpaper peeling. Knock and enter it says. A chair. A table. Shiny waxed linoleum squeaking under foot. And ah. A most ancient and dog eared copy of *Tatler and Sketch*. A lady's voice in the next room saying come in.

"Is this the chiropodist's."

"Yes."

"I'm sorry I don't have an appointment."

A white coated chilled lady creature getting up from writing what appears to be a letter. Steps to look in a book whose pages are clearly congealed closed by the damp. Rubbing her hands together. Obviously hasn't had a previous customer for years.

"Yes. I think we can just fit you in."

"Thank you so much."

And sitting in her rickety chair, as she switched on a bar of an electric fire, it was rather nice having someone take off one's shoes. Drag down one's socks. Listening to her. Begin talking nearly a mile a minute. As if I were going to run away. Telling how she spent the war in

England. Saved to take a course. Now returned to set up professionally in her native land. Where the rent was cheap. But from whence she planned to expand to Grafton or Nassau Street soon. In the tiny windowless room, she did take the longest time to trim a corn on my toe, and then ages to clip and file my nails. Pushing back the cuticle exposing the moons. As if one were entered in a beauty contest. Then she did rather deliciously massage my considerably chilly feet. With a nice, very nice circular motion applied to the instep. And then one's ankles. Asked if one went skiing. And I lied. With two little words. Yes. Frequently. And even added. Down the Matterhorn. When wartime travel permitted of course. Then asking me rather leading questions. Where I was from. Was I English. Of course I had the incredible notion to say I was an Austrian. But thought being French might give a more pleasant impression. And yes of course one was educated in England. Harrow as a matter of fact. I was astonished how lies could so easily spill out of one. But as it was fast appearing I would soon have to be a con man it was as well to start practising. I used the word chateau just as she remarked on my elegant bone structure which she said was especially apparent about the inferior tibio fibular articulation. At least it was evident she knew her anatomy. Indeed she was beginning to sound like Rashers.

"You have an extremely fine ankle. This is the external malleolus of the fibula. And this muscle I am rubbing is the flexor brevis digitorum."

One really didn't give a fig about what muscle any muscle was, for at the moment going through one's mind was a vision of Lois, stark naked at the top of her narrow steep stairs, a line of men waiting out her front door and down her alley. And she wore a sign around her neck. Which said. One at a time only. Of course the vision completely vanished as the chiropodist's hands having nicely massaged my Achilles' tendons, were now venturing upwards upon the back of my legs. And one was slowly but surely becoming utterly transfixed with this albeit most embarrassingly bizarre but rapidly increasing enjoyable frisson. As she had now both her hands deep up my trouser legs. All ten of her brightly crimson nail varnished fingers, five to the left, five to the right, engaged caressing my calf muscles.

"Skiing has made your legs strong. And you do don't you, do a lot of walking."

"Yes as a matter of fact I do."

"Yes I can feel. In your soleus. And especially along here in your gastrocnemius. Only one tendon actually reaches the sole of the foot."

"O does it really, that's considerably interesting."

"People don't really pay enough attention to their leg muscles these days."

"No I'm sure they don't."

A lot more awfully Latin sounding words erupted from her as her hands fondled between two prominent ligaments at the back of my knee. Of course the creature was beginning to tremble like a leaf. I certainly was not exactly as calm as any old cucumber either. With her actually tickling down the sides of my legs in among my hairs with her fingertips. My trousers now conspicuously bulging.

"At the tarsal and tarso metatarsal articulations there's so much that can go wrong."

"I entirely agree."

I took Rashers' silk hanky upon which his tears had fallen and wiped my brow. Around her neck a silver chain with a gold cross hanging forward out her open white coat. Surely she's not intending to do anything irreligious. Or break her vows as a chiropodist. But her lungs are distinctly heaving under her brown sweater. While her fingers, my goodness gracious me, are, good lord, unbuttoning my fly. I must say one is on the verge of saying something utterly daft. As to whether, in dealing with one's ligaments higher up, to which naturally one's leg is attached, did this still comprise part of the foot treatment. Involving one hopes, no additional charge. But as, at the presently awfully awkward moment, she cannot find the entrance to my complicated drawers, one does not ask niggling questions. Particularly now her fingers have finally got into the confines of my underwear. Where I am bulging so madly that bloody hell even with both of our pairs of cold hands, it is going to be a major engineering feat to get my member free of its clothed encumbrances. Especially as these drawers, also embarrassingly a dim shade of white, happen to have also been once my grandfather's. And nearly of woven metal made traditionally by a Manx mill specially for farmers shepherding their sheep on their wintry windy moors. And I did only last night have such a severely erotic dream. Involving of all people, Dingbats and her big hefty red tinged tits. Nakedly serving me supper in my apartments. A late summer dish of mushrooms. She danced around showing off her fine points. And Sexton came bursting into the room. Pointing an accusing finger at my plate. Ah I wouldn't Master Darcy touch that fungi or be caught dead eating a mushroom that one would pick. Sure she's here in the house, with murder on her mind for the inhabitants. With a bag full of toadstools collected as deadly as a dozen cobras keeping warm in your bed. Them's death caps and destroying angels in that sauce. O god will she never get it out.

"I hope I'm not hurting you."

"No no. My undergarments are a little old fashioned that's all."

Ah at last. In now this cool afternoon air, one's regenerative organ is out. And instead of Dingbats one is looking down on this chiropodist's dark reddish brown roots of her dyed blond hair. With nothing but an unprotesting groan blurting out my lips. Her warm mouth. Is indeed nothing but a welcome bit of bliss on my mind. As she does rather hungrily suck. Her hair parted down the middle. Her head bumping up and down like the old ram pump used to do, before it conked out, down in the cleft of the meadow in the rushy field by the oak wood. My goodness what treatment would she give one for a sprained foot. Daren't read her surname. But her Christian name is Cloadagh, it says on her diploma on the wall. More to this chiropody business than meets the eye. Certainly much more to it than can be said in a mouthful. Has an orange bow tied at the back of her hair. And Leila's purple one. Of which Crooks once said. Youse will take that bow out of your hair, or youse will be terminated in this employment. O god. I nearly had apoplexy when first I saw Leila's pretty legs. Not believing the beauty which started at the top of her head could go all the way down to the tip of her toes. Which talking about toes, this foot specialist's hand is presently wrapped squeezing upon my goolies. As her mouth is gobbling and sucking like a starved pig in a swill of molasses. Teetering me exactly on that knife edge of pleasure verging on pain. O my god, I'm exploding.

Darcy Dancer's head flying back, his feet upwards. One foot kicking over her whole tray of instruments. Bottles and scalpels and talcum powder scattering across the floor. Footsteps out in the next room. The door opening. And a high pitched bark. Behind my busy chiropodist's back. As I groaningly stiffen in terrified delirium. And sit bolt upright. Staring straight at this grey headed lady. In a blue tweed coat and crimson cloche hat speckled with rain drops and sporting several flowers. Each petal of which along with the expression of her pug dog's sniffling yapping face will be, I am absolutely sure, forever emblazoned on my mind. The lady's eyes saucer round looking up at me. Her half open umbrella dripping rain.

"Is this, is this, is this, the chiropodist's."

Of course the visiting lady, poor dear, having seen over my foot specialist's shoulder the full treatment in progress, was with a leash, hysterically choking back her equally hysterical tiny squashed faced pug dog from biting the chiropodist's heels. And lifting the canine into her arms she backed rapidly out the door. Which some wind from somewhere unmercifully blew further open. And another breeze mercifully then slammed shut. But good lord, the door opening again. The pug face mutt, his claws scrabbling on the shiny linoleum, snarling. The lady craning her head in, this time with a lorgnette held poised tiptoe on her nose.

"I didn't think I could believe my eyes. I have a good mind to summon the police."

My poor chiropodist creature, her one hand still absolutely stuck caught entangled in my grandfather's inpenetrable Manx drawers as I sprang up. Both of us yanking and pulling and skating on the talcum powder, and falling. The two of us crashing on the cold slippery floor. The chiropodist ashen faced ready to faint, but with her other hand still unfortunately firmly holding my obvious penis. And the awful ruddy bloody pug mutt snapping and growling at the lumps of cotton wool and finally sneezing uncontrollably in the raised dust of white powder. Having listened so often to Rashers dispense quips to quell all kinds of ignoble faux pas, I simply could not, racking one's brain, venture what I thought might be practical as well as reassuring information. Which might allay the lady's concern in requiring the attention of law enforcement. And exaggerating one's refined English I opened my mouth.

"Yes, Madam, it is the chiropodist's, but my condition requires me to have massaging of the musculature."

"You disgusting disgusting people."

Should the Garda Siochána come charging in the downstairs hall, there is no exit out these windowless walls. Nor any room to retreat. For the lady lowering her lorgnette, merely had to raise her umbrella to easily clonk my poor chiropodist on her head. But the angry way my foot specialist eyed her scalpel on the floor, she obviously had a sense of life preservation. And indeed murder. As she grabbed the sharp blade. Various evening newspaper headlines already flashing across one's brain. Member of landed gentry indecently found concerned in stabbing of elderly blue stocking by prostitute chiropodist. Rashers anyway could take comfort that this is yet another disaster he is not responsible for.

"Don't you dare raise that knife to me young lady. As a devout Protestant I object to this absolutely shockingly beastly sight. I happen to have come all the way in on the train from Greystones. And if you don't mind I shall take my custom elsewhere. Since the war's been over, Dublin simply isn't safe anymore. And you in your notoriously Catholic profession in this place, should be reported to the appropriate parish priest."

Without taking any notice whatever of what her pug mutt was doing, which was lifting its stumpy leg on the skirting board, the lady from Greystones gave the door such an unmerciful slamming that plaster fell from the ceiling and the bare light bulb swung back and forth on its flex. And in a delayed action the diploma already hanging askew, plummeted to the floor, the glass in the frame smashing. Good god. At Lois's it was the stink of turpentine and squishy paint tubes, and now it's scalpels and the stink of alcohol. Out on a bloody innocent walk. I have just time to flee this sorry mess and get to the barber to have my non pubic hair cut for tea. An alarm clock loudly ticking on a shelf among her bottles. If one can diplomatically get my damn fly buttons done up, my socks on, shoes laced. I will ruddy well gallop out of here. And join the rest of the field who must by now, have roused a fox. As my chiropodist friend is now bent over against her damp wall. Hair falling forward around her face. Her thumb going back and forth on her red fingernails.

"O god. I was so lonely. I've never done a thing like this before. I'll be driven out. Into the streets. The likes of her will have the scourge of the tongues upon me."

"Well hypocrisy being what it is these days it isn't exactly the type of tootsy wootsy treatment of which a member of an older generation, I think would approve."

"Are you trying to make a joke of this."

"No. Certainly not."

"And you don't sound French. You're English. And the likes of you will be gone by the mail boat. How would you know what could happen to me."

"Well the likes of me thinks you do have a very good point there. Yes. I am very very English. But please don't think I can't appreciate your difficulty."

"And don't you think that I do this all the time."

"O no. Of course not. But perhaps, please, you might tell me how much it is please."

"The treatment is four shillings a single foot. And seven and six for both."

"I mean, I fear madam, that I must at least ask, in view of the situation, is there an extra charge or something to that effect."

"Are you trying to insult me. I'm a real chiropodist."

"Yes of course you are. And I assure you."

I am
A very
Satisfied
Customer

22

Shoelaces still loose, one reeled out of the chiropodist's quite apoplectic. And totally unprepared for what was about to unfold. With the lady of Greystones lurking in a doorway. And then as I innocently passed and stopped to put up a foot to tie a bow in one's footwear, she jumped out shouting, and with her mutt growling and barking, both hurried after me down the street. Clearly she and her ugly yapping canine were together criminally insane. Her umbrella pointing. Everyone hearing her extremely well enunciated shouts.

"That gentleman is a debauché. He is unchaste. He is licentious."

The use of the term gentleman attracted much more attention than the simple word man would have done. And I found myself actually running outright across the Green. The park bloody attendant choosing this moment to tell me it was against the rules to run. Somehow one didn't want to discourteously ignore his very polite good intentioned caution. And as I slowed to a rapid walk the bloody mad lady catching up once more.

"I saw you. Don't think I didn't. You Catholic. All you filthy Catholics."

Of course not even a Protestant could flee back into the Shelbourne with this diatribe following. Especially right in the bloody thick of the afternoon teatime swarm. I skipped over Dawson Street nearly being run down by a tram. And still unable to shake off my pursuers. Thought I might duck down the steps to the Country Shop for tea but it was just the bloody sort of place, such as the better bred insane might choose to hang out in, amid the Aran Island sweaters and socks and good nourishing cakes and scones.

"There he goes. That's him who thinks he will escape the wrath of the gods. And I vouchsafe, as my redeemer liveth, that he shall not."

On the pavement one did make a spurt. In and out folk, until of course knocking a little old lady flat. Tears were on the verge of descending my cheeks. There I was. Lifting the poor dear up to her feet. And my adversary again close up pointing her umbrella.

"Rid us of evil."

Had one had one's Purdey barrels handy I do honestly think I would, quite without hesitation, rid the earth of her and her mutt. But just as one was despairing, a begging gang of newsboys collected. And I pointed to my adversary.

"She, my dear fellows, is the richest lady in Dublin chock full of halfcrowns."

Hurrying another forty paces. I finally escaped from her sight. Nipping into an auction room. And there the other side the gathering, was Horatio the actor. A beaming young auctioneer calling out the bids. Horatio waving up his catalogue to rather adamantly signal his purchase. Then another. And another. My god he must be furnishing an entire large house. Ah he smiles at me. As he appears to be doing at everyone watching him. And now that I've again come back to my senses momentarily, I do think it is absolutely ruddy time to escape round the corner for a haircut, shampoo and scalp massage. But as I paused to examine close up some of the auction items for sale, the young auctioneer down from his dais, suddenly literally was reeling in a state of near collapse against the wall. As I manoeuvred over closer. To overhear his hysterical conversation with Horatio.

"But sir, you did, you clearly did bid."

"I was declaiming sir, as I rehearsed my Macbeth and was merely signalling my words with my arm."

"Good grief. But I've knocked down everything to you. I'm ruined. The entire auction will have to be held over again."

It was reassuring to find that others were having their troubles too. But as one looked about, O dear god. She's found me. Just as I am to go out she's come in. To denounce me.

"There he is. I point him out for you all to see. The wicked. The unvirtuous. The evil doer, accursed."

Of course her words were taken in the present situation to mean poor old Horatio, who was already in some hot water. With even some pushing and shoving taking place. Which thank god was causing someone to take a humourous view. Crashing about the place laughing. And in the melee someone did step on her damn mutt. Who let out such a yowl. And coupled with the heated debate going on with the auctioneer and Horatio and the lady from Greystones loudly summoning the president of the league for the prevention of cruelty to Protestant animals, I slipped out back into the street. Darkness having fallen. Hopping as quick as I could around the corner into Kildare Street and smartly doing a turn on my left articulated ankle into the barber's. Who I must say seemed happy to see me.

"How would you like it styled this time Mr Kildare, sir, the usual. Or the latest."

Of course I couldn't remember for the life of me what my usual was. Nor did one much care for the latest. Which, recent accusations being what they were, might make me look like a rapist. And one suggested merely a tidying up. And as my barber clipped me carefully about the ears and brought down the big whirling brushes from the ceiling to spin upon my head, I was regaining my senses. I opened a recent edition of *The Field* and was actually staring at a photograph of the hunt gathered in front of, of all places, Andromeda Park. And just as I was lapsing into some delicious reverie that here in front of me was evidence of one's status in the world, lo and bloody behold. A tap tapping came a knocking on the barber's street window. There she was. Her hat lopsided on her head. Rapping her umbrella. Staring and pointing and audible enough.

"There sits he. Wallower in carnality."

Only Rashers would know what to do at a time like this. This bloody woman is not only in the process of ruining my haircut but the bloody rest of my ruddy life. She seemed reasonably sane enough when barging into the throes of my convulsively writhing intensive foot care. But obviously pondering that piquancy has thrown her for a ninny noodled loony loop. Being as she has now decided to pursue a lifelong career of hounding me with some crazy bee in her bloody bonnet. Which can only be put to rest by wrapping her mutt's leash around her neck and stringing them both up to the nearest lamp post. Or introduce her to Horatio. Pair of them avec canine could go round the Dublin auctions bidding for everything in sight.

"That's him, guilty of concupiscence."

The lucky thing of course is, with all five chairs occupied I am midway in the row. Each chap thinking that it was he at which she pointed. And you've never seen such a cowering collection of guilty looks in all your life. One having to laugh into one's towel as the chap in the next chair enquired of his barber.

"Is there a back way out of here."

"Yes sir, as there happens. But I fear it does require scaling a wall or two and even perhaps breaking and entering. Unless of course you are a member of the club around the corner on the Green. Then all you have to do is climb the first wall."

My own barber liberally pouring on the best of smell juices to massage my scalp, found the matter of this looming shadowy lady, part of his daily entertainment and chose to confidentially inform my ear.

"Ah sir we get them all the time. Shouters. Harmless enough."

One stole a look at the window. Just darkness out there. The figure gone. Lie back in the hot towels wrapped about one's head. Well into teatime on this late afternoon. One is so abysmally sad. Here in Dublin. Think and think so much about death. Voices singing. Slowly marching across one's brain. A figure on a catafalque. Mr Arland's Clarissa. Tinkers carrying her. And those long black tresses of hair hanging down. And not Clarissa's. Leila's. Small white flower either side of her brow, tied with a bow of purple ribbon. Cold alabaster skin of her face. Make tears well in my eyes. O god. Is she dead. The winds in requiem over her. Can one ever hope to have another woman in one's life to make me completely forget her. Today I could have been at Punchestown. Racing. Amid the gently rising hills. The distant horses across the green striding in their blur of colours. Bookies standing on their boxes. All the names up on their signs. Little trays for chalk and rags for wiping. As they await the next runners. Rashers gone. Just like these late winter afternoons die so soon, fading in the sun. And leave a cold cold chill to blow. As the last races are run.

More and more losing faces getting longer. In the smoky bars, the crowd thickened. Drink flushing down their throats. And there was a moment when I thought I saw Leila. Just a fraction of her face. Thought I saw her exquisite teeth and a corner of her soft eye when she turned to smile. And I pushed through to reach her. Shoving and nearly punching. No one budging or getting out of the way. Till at last I came to where she stood and she was nowhere to be found.

"Now sir, Mr Kildare. Are we right now. Do you find yourself tonsorially suited for the evening."

"Yes. Thank you so much."

Darcy Dancer departing the warm perfumed air of the barber's. Out in the cold damp, looking left and right up and down the street. Staring back over the shoulder for signs of the lady from Greystones. In this darkness. Safety. But even so. One does not want to be followed into the side entrance of the Shelbourne. Best to detour down into Molesworth Street. Go right past the door where Rashers prised his three quid out of the Association for the Relief of Distressed Protestants. And where, in the few minutes I have to spare from my debacles, I have a good mind now to present myself. Clearly Rashers' toilet water he gave me which he said was direct from London, smells just like that from my ruddy own barber. O my god. Can I believe this. There she is, passing under the lamplight, coming directly at me, dragging her mutt behind, as if she has been reading my mind.

"You who are not pure. Who are not unblemished. Who are not immaculate. Repent."

"Holy and immaculate shit lady, I'm not going to repent. I'm going to bloody well run."

Darcy Dancer reversing course charging past the Masonic Lodge. Feet pounding on the pavement. Guard in front of Dail Eireann leaving the big gates and giving chase. As the two pairs of feet went sprinting down Kildare Street. Flying around the corner along by Trinity. Into Merrion Square. Past the doctor's waiting room window. Poor Guard left in the mist. He doesn't even know why he's chasing me. But now he is about to know that no one has ever run a faster mile than this in Ireland. The Zoological Museum. Past the government buildings. Turn right. Keep up the speed. Unless he gets a bicycle and she a racing car, I'll be at last home and dry. Shoot past the Huguenot cemetery. Don't even pause a second as one usually does to peek in on these peacefully deceased Protestants. Past the steps to the Shelbourne Rooms. At last now, through the newsboys.

"Mister, mister where's your man Rashers. Give us a penny, mister."

Scatter behind at least a threepenny bit or two as I go in the door of the Shelbourne. Panting, sweating, and hopefully at last safe. Get up to my room into the bath. Don't wait for the lift, two at a time up the stairs. And of course the nation's parliament has no doubt all this time been left completely unguarded.

Darcy Dancer stretched out in the bath. Paddling the warm waters. What a day. Through no fault of my own, turned into nearly a permanent nightmare. At last it's at least now seven o'clock. And the final last bloody train will have left Westland Row for Greystones. Such bliss privacy. And by god I shall not cower in poverty. In spite of yet another note with the compliments of the Manager. I think, not think, I shall, with a total change from my grandpapa's underwear, repair down to the Shelbourne Rooms where I shall request for myself an entire bottle of champagne.

Darcy Dancer in black thorn proof tweed wearing Mr Arland's Trinity College graduate's tie, descending into the front lobby hall. Clink of glass and cutlery coming out the door of the dining room. A long triple barrelled name being paged. Folk departing and arriving to dine. Many monocles everywhere. Ah what nice fragrant fumes doth tempt the nostrils. Makes one nearly as famished as Rashers. Dear me it is nice to feel free. With not a sign of any accusers. For the moment at least. Unwatched. Unwitnessed. Bathed. Soothed. Night of pleasant contemplative champagne induced reverie ahead. Must purchase a copy of *The Field*. And peruse further and better particulars of the hunt reported therein.

"*The Field* please."

"Sorry copies all gone sir."

"O dear."

That is a sure sign. That a lawn meet at Andromeda Park is the very tops. Everyone rushing to buy. To scan with a microscope their identities. O well. Detour through the always empty residents' lounge here. Go up the stairs. Along the hall. Down the stairs. So comforting the white splendour of Georgian medallions on these egg shell blue walls. Ah quite a little bit of activity this evening. Amid the wicker chairs and glass topped tables. Redolent of some romantic verandah somewhere on the banks of the Nile. Only eighty five degrees cooler. Ah a nice empty table left in a peaceful corner. Just go over here and sit down. Ah someone has left a book behind on this chair.

"Good evening Mr Kildare. We haven't had this pleasure for donkey's years."

"No indeed. It's been rather rush rush rush. Out there in the country. And equally rush rush in town."

"Ah now that hardly allows for a little healthy recreation."

"Well as a matter of fact I fear that's what the rush has been all about. Recreation."

"And I'm sure well deserved. Why wouldn't it be. What's it to be sir."

"A bottle please. Of champagne. Heidsieck. Charles."

"Ah I see what you mean now about the recreation. Very good sir. How many glasses sir."

"Just one."

Never in all one's too brief life has one ever savoured one's semi anonymous loneliness so much. Pity watching these ears here, that they do not, as a horse's might, tell you what they are thinking. My god that waiter would do as butler at Andromeda Park next time Crooks hangs himself. Dear me. What have we here. A book. Heavens someone's erudite. Ah a novel. Light reading. Clearly that is what it is. Someone then wants to be entertained. Flick open the pages. Dear me. Do one's eyes set upon the obscene. Threw her down with his mouth eagerly hard upon hers. How did this ruddy piece of saucy literature get into the country.

"Do you mind. That happens to be my book."

Hardly dare look up. In fact. I won't. No. It can't be. But if it is. That ruddy bloody woman from Greystones. I shall commit murder. Steal just a peek. Ah these are rather elegant high heeled shoes. Attached very pleasantly to a distinctly young and trim ankle. Pretty skirt. O my god. It's even worse. Baptista. Consuelo.

"I am sorry. The book simply happened to be here on the chair."

"Well I was in fact sitting at this table."

"I am frightfully awfully sorry. But of course I shall move."

"Well you needn't do a song and dance, not on my account."

Darcy Dancer getting to his feet. Handing the red bound book across the table. Into this rather surprisingly long fingered bejeweled hand, with an absolutely monumentally large diamond sported on one of her phalanges. Thick gold bracelet on her right wrist. And an equally thick one on her left. Each set with three acorn sized rubies. This bloody bitch kicked me in the head. Spurned my Mr Arland. Was even whipped in the nude across an hotel floor by the Mental Marquis. And now has the unmitigated gall to pretend that I was trying to steal her filthy disgusting book. And now with every table occupied I shall have to decamp. Ah. The waiter. Have him serve me on another surface as many miles away as possible. Even out on the stair steps in the hall will do.

"Sorry Madam, I thought you had left."

"No, I was just getting my reading glasses I forgot in my room. Perhaps you can find me another table. I'll sit over there at the bar and wait till a table's free."

"Very good Madam."

"There's no need to you know, I'll move. I've clearly taken your place."

"No. That won't be at all necessary I'll move over there. I see at least a chair free. Or it was free."

"No I insist. I'll move."

"Well pardon me ladies and gentlemen, may I as the servant at your disposal, do the Solomon here. Since there is nowhere else to sit for the time being. Would it solve the problem now, if you both sat down, right here with the four chairs available, and two extra for an arriving guest if need be. Now if I may make so bold it isn't as if you were cat and dog is it."

"No it isn't. Do you mind, Mr Kildare then if I sit down."

"Do please sit down if you wish."

"Ah now ladies and gentlemen that's better now isn't it. Sure if the big world out there worked as well we wouldn't have had a war. And what may I now get for you Madam. Or are you waiting."

"No I'm not waiting. As a matter of pleasure I'll have the same as Mr Kildare is having. Only a snipe will do."

"Well, do please. Then. That's a whole bottle. Have some of mine."

"Are you sure you don't mind if I do."

"No not at all, please do."

"Then I shall."

Our immaculately white coated waiter having safely placed one's ice bucket, now flourishing his tray as if he were throwing the discus, and bowing deeply.

"Ah there's now a satisfactory solution to a dilemma. Requiring as it merely does. Just one more glass."

God. What a day. Here I am. Seated with the last person in the world I could imagine I'd ever be saddled with. At least her voice seems to have slight overtones of friendliness in it. Suppose one merely starts off with some utterly inane non leading question. Avoiding all and any mention of hunting of course. Since I'm supposed to have attempted to have raped her or something. When in fact I nearly killed myself saving her life. Astonishing how such an upstart from a small country town, just because she is pretty, can put on such airs to float all by herself into the Shelbourne Rooms and even pretend to include me in the same social bracket as if she were a member as one is oneself of the landed gentry. I suppose she could just scrape by as an adherent of the professional classes, having as she has, a monkey tree growing in her front garden. In spite of rumours of her father owning a butcher's, chemist's and haberdashery. All one knows is her mother threw tantrums merely to get her dancing lessons from the Count when he was teaching us in the great castle, and has since been taking her to every bloody race meeting in Ireland in the biggest hats in order to get her picture in the papers.

"And what are you doing up in town Baptista. If one might enquire."

"You might. I am here because my husband is not here."

"I see."

"No you don't actually. It so happens my husband is a bit of a pompous ass."

"I see."

"Do you really see, or are you being like everyone of those people one meets, full of their ad nauseam euphemisms. My husband who used to absorb all his time playing rugby, now absorbs all his time at his mills in Bradford, Manchester and Leeds, and is mostly interested in the weft and warp of his cloth. Less than a fortnight after our wedding, his bolts of gabardine plus a certain piece of fluff, seemed to take up far more of his attention than I did."

"Why don't you divorce him then."

"He may be an ass, but I'm not exactly one. There are as it happens, considerable compensations. Which we won't go into here and now."

The champagne poured into our glasses. One had somehow, in distaste of her, forgotten how spectacular her golden hair and blue eyes could be, albeit so slightly marred by an overly upturned nose. As she sits, highly perfumed, sleeves pulled back from her rather nice wrists. As well as all the conspicuous jewelry, she is actually wearing a smile on her lips. My god she doesn't sound like the Baptista I so recently pulled by her legs and hair up out of the muddy ditch. Or when she was so full of her priggish social climbing snobberies and far too good for my Mr Arland. Sucking up to her betters all over the parish.

"I suppose Darcy Dancer you're sitting there thinking I'm still full of my former priggish snobberies."

"O no. No. Of course I'm not."

"Well that's exactly the look you're wearing on your face, changed now of course to your one of utter amazement. You see I've found something which replaces my snobberies entirely."

"I'm not amazed, but I would like to know what it is new you've found. Sorry. I didn't quite mean that."

"Of course you meant it. But what I've found in a word. Is money. And you are amazed aren't you. Money simply buys people. Buys them anywhere, anyplace, anytime. And one no longer need ride on one's high horse. But I think you should come down off yours. Or do you prefer instead we bore each other with stupid little bits of contrived small talk."

"Well, the champagne, I hope, if you pause to taste it, is not the least contrived."

"Ha ha, touché. Well perhaps you are not then, completely the stuck up little gallant one has come to regard you as."

"Heavens. You don't appear to entertain a very high opinion of me."

"Nor, wouldn't you admit, do you entertain one of me. But then, really when you look into it close enough, we're nothing but a pair of

Irish country yokels, up in town behaving as if we weren't. But at least you do, I must say, have rather good taste in your choice of champagne."

"I really don't, except for the champagne, feel as if your description aptly applies to me as a matter of fact."

"O dear, you see. Because you happen to have some modestly good paintings and statuary in your house, you want so much to pretend that your taste in champagne is merely natural to you. That your grandfather and his grandfather drank it. It's been in your cellar for years."

"Certain vintages of champagne can vary considerably. And even the best champagne can fade after a generation."

"Well I did notice how democratic of you to have been drinking with your previous sergeant at arms. Or whatever that Foxy Slattery did or was, at Andromeda Park. He certainly had a filthy gossiping mouth."

"Madam, would you rather I leave you to your racy novel and move to another part of this building."

"No I would not rather you did. As a matter of fact I'm thoroughly enjoying giving you a piece of my mind."

"I see. But one does sense I think a slight embitteredness somehow, perhaps not mitigated by our previous somewhat embarrassing encounters."

"You allude of course to your fancying the cut and fit of my breeches. Which I hope you haven't entirely forgotten all about. Well I didn't take you up on the occasion because, since gentlemen seem frequently to prefer being on top, I didn't exactly relish being rolled about in a field where one's backside is likely to get awfully wet and muddy. And quite possibly too, people after the fox, might come jumping over one. Now. Has the cat got your tongue darling."

"No the cat has not."

"Am I scaring you out of your wits. Pour me please, more champagne. You see. Truth of the matter is. I think you hold it against me ever since I had a whipping match with that now shop assistant and former whore housekeeper of yours, and spurned your poor Mr Arland. As a matter of fact. Although I did spurn him. I did think he was sweet to come kneeling with his posies on my front stoop trying to sing his love songs."

338

"My Mr Arland never knelt to do that."

"Well. Whether he did or not is not the problem. But I have a mother. Who I admit is utterly raddled with her small town ambitions, and who nearly killed herself in her attempts to make me a Marchioness. And of course we both know the Marquis I speak of. I was forced. Forced. To do every rotten low cruel deceitful toadying and contemptible thing to become what would probably be the thirteenth or is it now fourteenth Marchioness. And for my pains. I got as the vulgar expression has it, royally buggered. And ended up still a commoner but without perhaps a commoner's bugger all. And then again, had I ever become a Marchioness, I could have, as was one of the Marquis' grooms, been burned to a crisp in his horsebox. But don't you realize people like your Mr Arland have not a chance in this world."

"I do not think that's entirely so. People of high principles do occasionally rise to the top."

"Do they."

"Yes they do."

"Well blow me down. At times, you do sound quite righteous. Perhaps then I should not ask will you dine with me. I could pretend of course I'm not at a loose end. As in fact I am. I have absolutely nowhere to go this evening. In spite of these various men earlier making their goggle eyes at me. Well, will you dine with me. That's an invitation."

"Yes. Yes. That would be entirely."

"Entirely what."

"Entirely enjoyable."

"Ha, you weren't were you, because of your slight tendency to pusillanimity, not saying it would be entirely a pain in the arse."

"No I certainly was not."

"Well then. We dine together. Provided of course it's absolutely on me. If you don't mind."

"Well I would rather it weren't you know."

"Well I would rather it were. Do you mind, awfully."

"No. Indeed. If you insist."

"May I tell you something."

"Do please."

"You are a bit of a con man."

"I beg your pardon."

"You and that Rashers practically make a pair."

"Madam I really don't feel it necessary for me to take up defence of myself against such a ridiculous aspersion."

"O come on. You're forgetting I've long been a lady of the world. And you do take me too seriously. Can't we have some fun. The pair of us."

Following smoked salmon, and more champagne, I had duck. Yet again. We both had duck. A l'orange. Sprouts. Baked potato. And a fairly splendid bottle of burgundy. And one was becoming aware of her quite excellent palate for wine as she ordered another half. One's formerly achingly hungry stomach filling, my limbs glowing. And one had to admit to absolutely thoroughly enjoying oneself. So marvellous a feeling the expense was not to be branded upon one's bill. Had a slight moment of alarm as I caught sight of the Manager at the door, who instantly bowed and smiled. Clearly it was time for compliments.

"I do like what you're wearing Baptista, you do dress beautifully you know. That fabric is quite exquisite."

"Thank you. Well I suppose being the wife of a mill owner does allow one a rather large field of the very best cloth to choose from."

Although largish in the quarters, Baptista was surprisingly slender in the joints. And getting by the minute more quite spectacularly beautiful in her candlelit face. Seated as we were away quietly in the corner of the dining room. The blue of her eyes fading to an exquisite grey at the edges. But one could notice sprinkled about, what one was fast realising was nearly every whispering gossip in Dublin. Not to mention those from the open countryside as far away as Galway. All sneaking their glances each time Baptista laughed. Which was getting quite frequent as I stopped trying my utter damnedest to be funny as hell, and then, relating an odd tale of previous childhood woe, became quite hysterically amusing. And when my hand was on the way to pour another spot of wine in her glass, she touched my metacarpal.

"Darcy, no, you finish it. I've already had far more than my share."

Her hand lingered. Mine holding the basket lingered. And following the afternoon's imbroglios, I did not think that one could again get explosively stimulated between the legs. But my old pole absolutely shot bolt upright and nearly turned the ruddy table over. And god, one really was having such a great good old time. Right up to the moment when I felt a distinct vast barrel of ice water being dumped upon one.

"Of course, my husband should be here any moment now. He's flying in. In his own airplane. His name is Harold. You know, I think the two of you would get on marvellously together."

"Do you."

"Yes. I do. You could go together to rugby matches."

"I see. Could we."

"Yes. He shoots. You could shoot together."

"I suppose too, he fishes."

"Yes. You could fish together. But you don't at all sound enthusiastic."

"As a matter of fact, actually I'm not."

"Ah. False alarm. Darling. I just wanted to see how far I could make your jaw drop."

"What do you mean."

"I mean my husband's not coming."

"I don't think I quite like playing this charade."

"Ah well he is in fact coming. But in a week or so. And he did play rugby you know. For quite a good team. O dear I haven't have I ruined what a nice little evening we were having together. Two old friends aren't we now. Well now. What do you think I should do. Now that we've finished off the burgundy and Brie. To entice you."

"Baptista, my dear. I do hope you will forgive me if I suggest that, should you continue what appears to be your idea of a little innocent fun at the expense of my easy excitability, that I may sock your bloody damn jaw across this table."

"O dear. Horror of horrors. Please don't do that. Remember you are a Darcy Thormond you know. And we rather haven't even had our brandy yet. Which let us please request is the very best in the house. And you will won't you. Have a cigar."

She did with her first douche make one's pole go down. And as equally quickly, merely by purringly lowering the octave of her voice, make my pole go up again. Just as one was recalling her stallion she hunted who once during an attempted gallop across a bog, actually tried to shaft my little mare Molly. And of course I was totally

341

unprepared for what she did next. As I felt a nudging at my crotch under the table. From her shoeless toes. Whose incredible prehensibility actually enabled them to enfold the spheroid shape of my delighted goolies. I of course trying to focus on the arrival of the exquisitely ancient brandy, was rapidly going more than slightly out of my mind. And she, leaving all chiropody and other musculature entirely out of it, absolutely pretended as if nothing at all was happening. God one can really end up paying even when it goes on someone else's bill. The dust of the brandy bottle could have smothered us. And now uncorked and poured in our snifters it did no help for my heart pounding all over my chest as I nearly swooned. No question, the damn girl is damn lavish. And god. If she said she could buy people. I had just put myself up for sale.

"Darling."

"You are, ha ha, speaking to me Baptista."

"Yes. I like calling you darling. Better than dearie, or you old fart, isn't it."

"Yes. I suppose."

"Well. Do you suppose that we can make, when we arise from this table, a conspicuous departure from one another."

"I see."

"No, perhaps you don't yet. I'll go alone to the lift."

"Certainly. Do."

"I haven't finished yet. And you. You darling have another brandy in the lounge."

"Thank you."

"My you are uncontrollably pessimistic. Then dear, when you have finished it. Go up the stairs. To number three nineteen. Don't knock. The door will be open."

> And I
> Trust madam
> It will be
> To enter
> Much more
> Than your
> Room

23

Centre lobby, Baptista and I quite formally and conspicuously put out our hands to shake. The Manager coming out of the lounge nearly made me nip behind a pillar. But again nodding benignly in my direction. And bowing to Baptista. Who did stick me for the bill for dinner. Conveniently forgetting at the opportune time it was she who invited me.

"Hello there Baptista."

"O hello."

Dear me she does attract much attention from the gentlemen. Batting her eyes as she smiles looks of vague recognition in various directions and at those who one imagines must be the late night revelling members of Dublin's smart set. Playing her little role so well, one was on the verge of believing her words.

"Do call on us, won't you, if you come to England. We are positively infected with snipe and Harold would so like to see you."

We parted. And on this, the advent of the greatest carnal conviviality one could ever conjure in one's wildest randiest dreams, I portrayed a glacial calm. Busying myself with the porter, pretending one was interested in a tip for the next day's races. One wasn't listening as he reeled off a series of possible winners. But I certainly was looking and not wanting to believe my eyes. To suddenly see. Over the porter's shoulder and just pushing her way in the door, to plant herself squarely in the middle of the lobby with her mutt. None other than the lady from Greystones. And one had to believe one's ears. She had of course already called me everything under the sun, but she further loudly announced.

"So there you are. I've finally caught up with you at last, haven't I. The wicked shall be inflicted with their just punishment."

Holding her umbrella like a lance, her dog clutched under one arm, she charged. As an American lady screamed. The lance digging me straight in the solar plexus. But happily making no progress whatever through my black thorn proof Manx tweed waist coat. But nevertheless what a bloody nice how do you do. I was about to pretend to faint, which wasn't too difficult as I was in fact fainting. But I retained enough vestige of sensibility to put hands over my stomach, as I went down. Groaning. Holding to the tip of the umbrella so that it could better appear speared deeply into me. Closed my eyes. Let a sigh of breath from my lips. To sound distinctly like my last. As the porter, quite uncharacteristically, got quite overexcited.

"Good god. She's kilt him dead. And Mr Kildare is private secretary and equerry emeritus to the Earl of Ronald Ronald. Sure he'll have a fit to hear of this in Monte Carlo."

I lay as dead as I possibly could. In spite of my tendency to want to get up and correct this ridiculous role one was being given by that unbelievable bastard Rashers. But at least the two porters were busy escorting the lady from Greystones out of my vicinity, and thankfully, to just the other side of the front doors. One just barely hearing her voice.

"I've been wanting to do that to that heinous gentleman all afternoon."

I did play the role of murder victim so perfectly that I had to jump up from the surprisingly comfortable carpet to stop the porter telephoning an ambulance and the Garda.

"I'm alright I assure you. Just winded me. I only ask you return her umbrella and please, don't let that lady back in. Thank you so much. Goodnight."

Collecting my key. Jumping three at a time up the stairs. Till naturally I had to pull a ligament. And limp the rest of the way to the

344

third floor. O god. Dare I. Now do what I've actually wanted to do. For years previous. And for these last hours especially. To mount upon her quarters which mounds one can pound till dawn do us part. Giddyyap dear girl. Could have used another brandy. Feel now limping in these empty halls that one is the only one left awake in this entire hotel. If I can only make it. Discreetly over this bright crimson carpet. Without being seen. Or shouted at. Or assaulted. Or collapsing in leg pain. Can you imagine. What if that maniac from Greystones ever finds out where I live. Lead an entire fife and drum band up the front drive. Placards aloft.

REPENT THOSE WHO SIN IN CHIROPODY

Darcy Dancer stopping outside the shiny brass numerals on the door of number three one nine. Facing out the back of the hotel, Baptista must require a noiseless night. My private, dear me, is engorged like a crowbar that could splinter straight through this mahogany door. Don't knock. She said. The door would be open. Turn the knob. And it is. Open. And now it's pitch black closing it behind me. What a bloody strange smell. Horses and stables. After the marvellous fragrance of her perfume. My god she must have all her saddlery and equipage ready for being whipped back and forth across her floor. I say. Damn strange sort of snort she's making. Must mean we get down to basics straight off. As equines do. My god she must be insatiably randy. I'm about to sample some real debauchery. Can hear Rashers say. Keep your morals up dear boy, never let your psyche sink into this Dublin abyss of iniquity, get thee Satan behind me is the catchword.

"Baptista. Baptista."

O jesus. What is she trying to do. Making that bloody noise. But my god this is exciting. In the pitch black. And even in the slight aroma of horse piss. Just feel my way to enough free space. Get off my jacket, waist coat, tie. And drop my trousers. To the utter relief of my explosive penis. Ah. Jetzt ist das besser or something to that German effect as Miss von B used to say.

Darcy Dancer feeling his way towards the bed across the soft carpet. Distant sounds of newsboys shouting *Herald* and *Mail*. Imagine this time of night. Still trying to sell a paper. Suppose it would be to a drunk, lurching his way across the forlorn midnight wastes of the city. I'm close. Whatever has happened to her marvellous perfume. I distinctly sniff snuff on the air. Or is it that her saddles need cleaning.

"Baptista. Baptista. Holy heavens. This damn bloody chair. Put on the bloody light. Baptista, where are you. Is it you. I've fractured a foot."

"It damn well is not sir, Baptista or any damn remote resemblance. Who the devil are you sir. In my room."

"My god. I am most awfully frightfully sorry. I do believe I am in the wrong room."

"Damn bloody right you are sir. And I'll appreciate your getting the damn hell out."

"Yes indeed. I do beg your pardon. I'm just trying to find my way. My garments, I'm just looking for them."

"Garments. What exactly are you at sir."

"Don't turn on the light please."

"I bloody well shall turn on the light and call the Manager if necessary."

"I promise you it's not necessary."

"I'll be the damn judge of that sir."

The bedside lamp throwing soft bathing rays upon Darcy Dancer, one sock in hand hanging down over a rapidly subsiding recently tumesced penis. The figure in bed bolt upright. Like a gleaming sabre. Which speaking of sabres. Plus the tasselled nightcap gold embellished with heraldic arms atop his head. As well as his fitting a ruddy monocle in his eye. It is. O my god. The highly decorated ex Indian Army cavalry Colonel, and once our former Master of Foxhounds, equally famous for shooting poachers out of his trees and then as they fell with their teeth still sunk in the apples, chasing them slashing a sabre at their disappearing backsides hysterically escaping over his high walls. And god, there is a stack of saddles and what looks like a scabbard. Got to keep my back to him or he may recognise me. Equally risky if he doesn't. Because I may then get a sabre up the arse.

"Who the hell are you sir. Turn around."

"I'm trying to put on my socks."

"I said turn around or I shall make a citizen's arrest. And come out from behind that chair. I say sir. You're damn naked. And don't I know your face. Isn't your father a member of my club."

"No. I'm sure not. I'm an orphan."

"Don't come the hound with me sir. By jove, I know who you are, you're that Kildare. Andromeda Park. What the bloody damn hell are you doing coming in my damn door, this hour of the night. And knocking over my damn snuff."

"I really am most awfully frightfully sorry. I'm afraid I've mistaken my floor."

"Number's plain enough. Damn woke me up out of my sleep. I should have stayed tonight at the club. Are you becoming some kind of damn sodomite. If you are, do bloody well see to it you find your own bloody right room for that kind of caper."

"I am not, as a matter of fact, sir, of that persuasion but if I may say so, perhaps you shouldn't leave your door open."

"Don't you tell me not to leave my door open. When there was a bloody damn fire alarm the other morning. With the door stuck. Damn unreliable locks. Damn prefer a trespasser to being burned to a crisp. By the by, are you hunting Friday."

"Yes indeed in fact."

"Good show. Scent's never perfect in this bloody weather, but we'll have some fair sport. Now don't bloody well barge in again will you. There's a good chap. Goodnight to you."

"Goodnight Master."

Darcy Dancer standing at the window of his room. The wind blowing hard. The skies clear and pinpoints of stars sparkling. As one again dismantles one's clothes to a state of undress. And one does sometimes wonder, when certain days will ever come to an end. That bitch Baptista. It's the last bloody damn low trick that she will ever play. The price of the bottle of Cognac from the vintagetime of Charlemagne. That alone on the bill for dinner could have bought ten calves. Stupid silly girl. My god if I ever get the chance. I'll get even. One should beware of anyone who hunts a stallion for a start. Make abysmally bad jumpers. Absolutely dislike having their balls scratched by briars and other hedgerow sharpnesses. And she had the gall to tickle mine own goolies with her toes. Knew bloody exactly where she was sending me. At least I can creep now into my own bed. Try to sleep. Jump the women one has slept with, like sheep over a hurdle in one's mind. Till their buttocks fade away. That's one, that's two. Maybe that's the third. And one has hardly any more to count. No

347

debauchery. And this as well, is going to be a night without sleep. Bleary eyed to face another day of struggle. Bloody Baptista. She's like the bite of a horse. Striking out with its teeth. As you stand at what you fatefully thought was a safe distance. One did on the way back from the Colonel, Master of Foxhounds, angrily kick, with one of my better legs, the door of some innocent Americans who were having a middle of the night chat. It really got them terrified out of bed. One simply has to take one's rage out on someone. And it may as well be on those from a country whose culture could never be regarded as in the least refined. Porters no doubt creeping about still searching for the culprit. Thought I heard a floorboard squeak. A seagull still awake out on the roof gutter. And I know exactly the thing I should like to see. Right at this moment. Her whole big fat behind. Enclosed firmly by my ancient man trap, too long hidden down in its old cellar cupboard. God. Just to see that superior smile wiped off her face with those massive spiked clutches clamped on her big bloody arse. Another squeak. Christ the porters may have tracked my footprints on the carpet. My god am I imagining it, or is there female laughing right outside this door. O god. Could it ever be. Yet again. The ruddy lady. From bloody ruddy Greystones. Go away. Hasn't enough already happened to me on this day. Is that my name. Whispered. Damn it. My god there is someone out there. Giggling.

"I say. Who is that."

"It's me. Baptista. Open up please."

"No. Leave me bloody well alone, will you."

"Don't be such a dismal sport. Well if you don't open you're in for a ruckus. I shall kick the door."

Darcy Dancer opening the door. In ancient albeit silk pyjamas. Frayed to a transparency at the crotch. Worn by one's mother's father. And Baptista still in her clothes, a black peasant shawl over her shoulders. Waltzes in my bloody door. And nearly falls over holding her ruddy stomach, laughing. Lurching as if crippled and guffawing around the room. And going into even more paroxysms enjoying the look on my face.

"O dear. Dear. O forgive me. I can't, simply can't help it. That was the funniest thing I have ever heard. Imagine asking if you were hunting on Friday."

"You bloody well were listening."

"Of course."

"Now what do you want."

"You of course."

"You plotted that deliberately."

"You know, Darcy, darling, you do surprise me. You are, as a person, really not as bad as I have always imagined."

"I think you really should shut up you know."

"Darling there's absolutely nothing to complain about. You should be cheering that I'm here. O dear. You're not. I am so sad, that you're sad."

"And I have damn good reason. Everything in my life is collapsing."

"O you poor poor darling. Can I do something."

"Well you could have for a start, and one is not being in the least niggardly, nor making I assure you, an ungentlemanly issue of it, but you did invite me to dinner."

"O dear is that monumental bill weighing upon your conscience."

"No, upon my head."

"But darling why didn't you say something. I would have put it on my bill."

"Well you didn't."

"Surely you're not that hard up."

"I am. In fact, if you must know, I am now wondering how I am ever going to get out of this hotel."

"Well stop wondering. Or you'll put me to wonder if I'm going to get a chance to commit adultery. Turn out the light. And do tell me. Was our former Master of Foxhounds wearing his five hunt buttons on his pink and white striped pyjamas. You no doubt interrupted him chasing a fox in his sleep. Now watch darling. I'm taking off my clothes, if you don't mind. Can you see. And darling, the Colonel also once laughed so much at a huntsman who splashed head first into a drink, that he himself toppled like an ancient monument off his horse. Top hat first. And when he regained his feet up to his knees in the black silt, he had the most marvellous long green tresses of watercress hanging like hair over each ear. Hunting does break one's neck, arm or leg but it does so help uphold one's sense of humour."

"Well madam you've certainly thoroughly destroyed mine."

"O dear. I hope you're not that upset. Or shy. Not to look this

349

way. And you will won't you, since I'm quite without clothes, let me get in that awfully narrow bed. And not let me freeze. It's a frosty night out. I am a little, if perhaps, more than a trifle strongly made in my quarters. But even in this light, doesn't what you see cheer you up. And put your mind to more pleasurable things. Now my dear darling shove over."

Nice to get horse piss out of the nostrils. And feel warm flesh and sniff marvellous perfume. Rid of the fear of a sabre up the rear. One was beginning to feel like the Mental Marquis' father, the Duke. As well as being some kind of Count MacBuzuranti paederast creeping around hotel bedrooms. This arse upon which I now clutch my sinking fingers seems nearly to have been the bane of my entire life. And may, by its firm if over generous rotundity disturb the balance of my mind for all time. Her hands run up and down my back. Her open mouth she puts on mine. Tongue wagging and digging against my tongue all the way to my back teeth. Nearly down my throat. Grabs me tight by the cock. And god. Ouch. Squeezes, twisting my balls. Won't be able to tell one from the other now. She bites. Married to someone in trade. So considerably below my rank in life. And here in our mutual loneliness we are joined in this present increasingly sweaty endeavour. Crack open one lid. Look up. Can't believe my eye. When carriages came to Andromeda Park. Cook would look up. And out from between the basement window bars and would draw attention to anyone whose higher station in life was not befitted by their conveyance. And she took no notice whatever of those whose lower station was embellished by their grander vehicle. And Baptista. Throwing the covers back. Lowering ample quarters right down over my pole. Wastes not a second to sit on top. In the shadows. Perched pretty. Like a swallow tucked up under a barn rafter. Ready to fly in the first light of dawn. To snap from the sky insects like me. And be as ominous as any shark in the sea. Comes swiftly devouring. Wagging her breasts. Cantering. Bed springs squealing. Galloping. Slapping me stingingly on the thighs. Giddyyap boyo. She has her nerve. Giddyyap boyo. And no modesty. And thank god, no whip. Or I'd be lashed senseless. Hear swan wings. Great groaning strokes they make on the wind. Wolfhound howls. Who doth it be who hoots. Beyond. Where's Leila. She is somewhere under some space of sky. Whose hair dark as night goes agleam shining through my mind. Were only these your noises of love. Hear Rashers' voice. Degradation. That's what I want to be saved from, dear boy. Sound of a heavy footfall in hall. I hear. In the middle of her groaning gyrations. A pounding heavy thump shaking mahogany door. O my god. What on earth now. Is this new most awful event. The Manager. Could be in force. All the page boys. Waiters. Bartenders. And the Society of Dublin Laity for the Stamping Out of Adultery.

"Damn it, you in there, Kildare."

That voice. Out there. Of which blissfully groaning Baptista is so utterly oblivious, belongs to the Colonel, Master of Foxhounds.

"Sir do you hear me in there."

O my god. Now what have I done to bring him charging down hotel hallways in search of me with his sabre. His head streaming tresses of watercress. Happily, by the sound of Baptista, he'll already think I'm in throes of death. And no further bloody cuts and thrusts are needed. Good heavens, the lady from Greystones might be commandeering him. To ensure I've had the very last private orgasm of my life.

"I say in there, what's all that commotion. Sir. I demand an answer."

"Please go away."

"I shall be glad to. As soon as you sir return my property."

"What property."

"You sir, have gone off in my socks and damn shoes and I am sir returning yours."

As I did my shoe and sock transaction between a crack in the door with the Colonel, Baptista laughed her head off into the pillow. Bloody damn girl is easily amused. In the morning a seagull perched crying on the window sill. Dreamt my ancient man trap was clamped firmly on Baptista's arse. But wakened by her snores, my fingers were gripped there instead. A soft fuzz at the back of her neck. Long blond tresses aflow over her shoulder. Roar of trams. Cars honk down the street. Sun through the curtains. Now the mortification to face Baptista awake, naked and sober, a skin's breadth away. And here I am already prodding her with an erection as she lolls like a log. One felt the pleasure one might get out of her in bed, that her sort would soon see how the bloody hell she could make you pay for it. And dearly. And miserably. And if anyone in Ireland gets wind of

351

this night, such news will go twitching lace curtain to lace curtain around Thormondstown out the relishing lips of the butcher's, chemist's not to mention the ironmonger's wife. Women in terms of guile and cunning can and do, I suppose, make mincemeat out of men. And now at stroke of twelve noon the phone is ringing. Just as one attempts some sodomy.

"Sorry to disturb you Mr Kildare, this is the Manager. I have left several notes to ask you to stop into my office. Might you be available before lunch this morning. It is in fact a rather large sum concerned."

Baptista rolling over. Her ample breasts with two dark tipped hardened nipples. Slight alarm on her face, as she slowly wakes and pulls up the blankets. The bottle of brandy. Manager seeing that appear listed under wines, spirits, beers and mineral waters and brought forward on my account, must think I've decided so long as I'm going to leave an unpaid bill, I may as well ensure it is whoppingly astronomical. By now room service instructed to be stopped. Better rush to have one's last bath. Before they cut off the hot water as well. Perhaps they wouldn't dare. And one might order a morsel or two of breakfast. Before being published with banner headlines in *Stubbs' Gazette*. And every creditor in the country. Including Smyth's of the Green closes in. Suggest to the Manager I work off my indebtedness washing dishes in the kitchen. Or butlering for the cavalry Colonel. I suppose it's always worse to worry about something. Better to just face it head on. Hide Baptista under the bed as they wheel in my tea, toast, sausages and eggs. The sun's beaming. A beautiful day out. And god, with the erection I've got. One may as well have one last insertion and exertion. Wrapped now, in a towel propped out like a nomad's tent. Pitched in a damn big desert. And she's so nonchalantly yawning at the back of her hand. Must say her face looks more than slightly older than it did last night. And her arse much younger.

"What's the matter, my dear boy. You've got such a look of concern on your pretty face."

"Just a matter I must attend to."

"Is there anything I can do. You seem quite upset."

"That was the Manager on the telephone. He wants me to pay my bill. Right now. It appears."

"O dear. But you mustn't get upset over such a trifling matter. Why not just pay it."

352

"Because I'm bloody well broke, that's why."

"Well you need only need get my chequebook."

"What do you mean."

"I'll pay it for you. Or are you too proud for that perhaps."

"If you must know, I am, as a matter of fact."

"Dear me this does make it such a nice little predicament for you doesn't it. Your prick itching for years and now you've at last made love to me. Do please don't stop your grooming. Or had I not to use that romantic word love. Reminds me of a story of my childhood. Just in case dear boy you'd like to know of my growing up among the gentry as a little innocent girl. Of course this is before foxhunting became finally my entrée, if one can call it that, into the fringes of county society. And you were hardly then out of your layette. It was on a beautiful warm sunny summer's day that your sisters were holding a dansant at Andromeda Park. A tea dance of course but so described in French on one of the engraved invitations which I was not sent. Of course my mother insisted it was an oversight. That I had every right to present myself to the Darcy Thormond Kildares. And so, unbidden, having come all the way out from town, in my best frilly party dress and party shoes and pushed by our handyman up your front steps, and quite trembling in terror already, your sister Christabel saw me, and imperiously levelling her arm and pointing her finger in my direction, said, in about the loudest voice I shall ever hear for the rest of my life. I did not invite her. Of course someone did come after me. But I had already run in hysterics. Right out across your front lawn. I even had a present to present. I ended up being found in the bog unconscious with exhaustion. My gift still clutched to my breast. And which I still carry with me. Wherever I go in this world. You will find it there. In my toiletry purse. And next to my chequebook."

A scribble
Upon which
Can buy
You now

353

24

The pair of Americans descending in the lift. My god, one can't possibly conceive of an entire nation just like them. Preparing for an excursion to Glendalough. From which by the uncertain tone of their voices they think they might never return. Little do they know of course that they are highly unlikely to ever get there in the first place. As the bus due to leave, has by my reckoning, already left from outside the gentlemen's convenience in St Stephen's Green.

Rashers in a trice would have counselled me in this moment of spiritual dread. I've been bought. Dear boy but of course you have. Take her money as a temporary emolument enabling you to keep both your head and prick up while you regain your financial feet. Baptista sitting up in bed signed the cheque on the desk blotter. Her breasts hovering over the pink tinged slip of paper like the most formidable mountain range. I suggested that perhaps it was time she decamped to her own apartments, before we became the subject of gossip.

"Pity it worries you. But I don't give a damn what anyone thinks and certainly not nosey little skivvies running around an hotel. And of course you are coming to Paris with me."

"Am I."

"Yes. You are. I'm having some riding boots and some dresses made."

354

"And if I don't."

"Well, shall I tear this up."

Severe lobby traffic for lunch. Count MacBuzuranti not even noticing me, sweeping by in his flowing scarf and polo coat. Champagne corks already popping. Parties preparing to depart for the races. And whoops. The cavalry Colonel. Growling at tourists in his way. Monocle glinting. As I disappear. To come rapping at this Manager's door. Without even a cup of coffee to cheer up an empty stomach. Carrying Baptista's massive revenge. A tiny piece of paper in my pocket. Her childhood gift a small silver spoon. Come in. Compelled to enter in here. As if facing a headmaster. Or worse, like a common travelling salesman. Desperately in need of chiropody.

"So sorry to have had to ask you to call in Mr Kildare."

The Manager still smiling. Perhaps I should be sporting a red polka dot bow tie. And a tight shiny suit. Befitting my new station of kept man. He is even getting up from behind his desk. My god it almost seems as if, were I to reach out he would shake my hand. Suppose when one's bill is big enough, it requires of him to exhibit a certain pretence of happy calm. My previous planned story was to simply tell him I was soon selling prime cattle mooing already on their way in on the train. Now must in the most casual tones present this blatant cheque, which risks painting me as a professional male paid fornicator, and even unmitigated cad. Not to mention gigolo, fancy man and other rankings much lower than gent. Explain the cheque as the signatory's part payment on the price of a horse. Ha ha, rather convenient to pay my bill with it, you understand. My god he does have a monstrously fat envelope to hand me. Obviously detailing everything but ladies' hairdressing and including all Rashers' enormous breakfasts and pre lunch champagnes, cigars and lunch and god knows what else.

"O. No need yet, ha ha Mr Kildare to settle your account. Ha ha. Plenty of time enough now for that. But as you see, I dare not entrust this to you in any other way. As given me, it was attached together with a rubber band. Hope you don't mind that we've enclosed it in this envelope. But it is a rather large sum of money."

"I see."

Of course I didn't actually see or know what on earth he was talking about. However as one does at such moments, I tried to show as

355

much of my nervous teeth as possible. Reached to take the heavy envelope and did with the left hand quietly lower Baptista's cheque previously tendered, stuffing it deeply into one's pocket. While listening avidly.

"It was delivered some considerable days ago with this letter by a young lady who left no name. If I may perhaps take the liberty to say, an extremely beautiful and charming young lady. Would you mind just signing this receipt for me please, Mr Kildare."

"Yes of course."

"Do hope that in spite of last night's incident in the hall, that you are enjoying your stay here with us. And that you are entirely comfortable."

"Yes I am thank you."

"As ridiculous as it sounds I believe the lady in the lobby was simply agitated by some phenomenon she said she'd seen. At a chiropodist's of all places. Can you imagine anything so daft. Suppose it's what we must expect these days."

"Yes quite."

"We could if you like, still keep that in our safe but I thought you might want to get it to the bank."

"Yes, I may in fact pop it in there."

Darcy Dancer hurrying away. Out the hall. After the nods and smiles. Back into the lobby. Stop. Take a deep breath. Dear me. This place is a rogue's gallery. My former sneaky agent just in the door. Plus Major Bottom, the hunt secretary heading into the dining room. And the damn sanitary supplier who assaulted me in my own front hall. Even the Poet is skulking around. Whom I should have had arrested. Turn quick left. Left again. Secrete myself in the privacy of the residents' lounge. Good god. This is a stack of bloody fivers. Some tens. Even fifties. And this letter. Here in my hand trembling. Such a lifetime ago that I first saw this neat fine penmanship so carefully propped up on my dressing table. Open it.

My dearest friend,

I wanted so much to talk to you before I did what I've done. And it was not to rob a bank, but I did win at the races. I thought I saw you there but when I finally pushed my way through the crowd towards you, you had gone. I

356

looked around town and even went into pubs and places. Till I heard too late, you were here. And I am leaving this as partial payment for the vase. Please never let us not be friends. I will always love you as I always have. And will always be there should you ever need me.

Leila

P.S. In haste now on my way to the country.

She said. In her cold small little room. When a vixen barked out in the frosty night. She did say. Sitting on the edge of her bed. Her dark stockinged slender legs. Shadows of her exquisite shy face in candlelight. That she would pay me for the broken vase. That has now saved more than my life. Ballast for a sinking soul. Find her. If ever I could. Take her body close to mine. Worship at her shrine. Never let her go. No stupid snobbery. No sin. Ever to stand between us.

"Good morning. Or is it more properly good afternoon, Darcy Dancer, Gentleman. May I sit down."

Baptista Consuelo. Traps me. In her flowing tweeds, silk scarves. Twin rows of pearls on the grey cashmere softnesses of her bosom. As she plops down in a flowered sofa chair.

"Ah I see, not only paid your bill but you cashed my cheque as well. Shades of your ancestors. That was rum of you if I might say. Judging by the amount of money that appears to be in your hand. Of course, if it is a ridiculously large sum I simply shall stop payment on the cheque. Now darling. Here are your orders for the afternoon. Three saddles to be fetched from Callaghan's down Dame Street. Do take a taxi. They are quite heavy. We shall meet for tea in my rooms at four. Please be packed for the mail boat by nine. We'll dine on board. En route of course for Paris. Is that all agreeable, my darling boy. Now exactly what amount have you attempted to defraud me of."

Darcy Dancer taking the creased and folded piece of paper from his pocket. Opening it up and smoothing it out in his hand. Seizing it by a tiny corner, the pink slip of paper hanging from two tweezing fingers, and handed across to Baptista.

"O I see. What's this."

"Your cheque. The truth is I certainly would have cashed it. And become your fancy man. But the fact is, I suddenly had no need to. And so shall not now be, my dear sow, your fancy man. Perhaps we can have tea and go to Paris another time."

"I suppose now you're going home to play squire lording it over your peasants. And when you do please just remember you walked out of that bedroom this morning with my cheque."

"And do I as a result Madam, now know how to accommodate your kind of lady."

"You are, aren't you, in fact a rather cruel, mean conceited contemptible little son of a bitch. And believe me, there's no shortage of your kind of young man."

"Do Madam please then let me say upon parting, that I think you are quite a bit more marvellous than I ever thought you were previously. Goodbye."

Darcy Dancer in the Shelbourne lobby. The din of voices swelling from dining room and public lounge. Side step out of any possible sight of any possible ladies from Greystones. And these three prowling figures. The Royal Rat hunched forward in his baggy grey tweeds. Followed by Buster The Beastly and Danno The Damned. Purchase a London newspaper. Hide behind the pillar. Concentrate on the well bred agony of the personal column of *The Times*. And be no longer myself unpleasantly haunted by my hotel bill. Tiptoe in and around the narrow pillar to avoid the more familiar faces in the lobby. In the middle of her insults, Baptista suddenly had tears in her eyes. Black kid skin gloves on her folded hands. Sitting so alone in her chair. My prick suddenly aswell rigid in one's trousers. Wanting to make love to her. Could be my mistress without too many attachments or ties. Fetch her a bunch of violets from a tinker lady at the door. Take insult. But I suppose one does not, no matter how deserving insult a lady. Following the performance of a few chores, she was after all, inviting me to stroll with her on easy street. Temporarily allowing respite from having to sell household paintings and objets d'art. Waltz up or is it down the Champs Elysées in Paris. Do what Sexton so many times said I should. Ah now you would broaden the vistas of the brain you would, hobnobbing with the very latest in intellectuals. Baptista can stew a moment in her own highly perfumed juice, blatantly betraying her husband Harold. Seems quite a popular trend these days not to give a tinker's damn about loyalty. Ah but perhaps

358

that moral question on this noonday is best left back in the bedroom. Especially while my person is insulated with quids. Which one merely unpeels to pay my bill.

"Mr Kildare."

"Yes."

"There's a letter for you. Just arrived sir."

This envelope, soiled and battered. My god. Monaco. Gracious me, rip it open. A picture postcard of chandeliers ablaze over a roulette table. In a vast empty Salle des Jeux du Casino.

> The Cathedral Steps
> The Old Town
> Monaco.

Darcy my dear boy, hope this reaches you still comfortably ensconced in that so pleasantly homespun elevation of mellow red brick on the Green. Having embarrassingly outstayed my welcome here on earth and in the elsewheres, I have decided in my state of nae hope to do the decent thing. By all accounts in the fish museum and aquarium here from which I have just emerged, there are predatory pisces nearby in the waters. By the time you read this I shall have heaved myself off these steep cliffs and down into the thrashing waves of a presently raging Mediterranean Sea. Jockey Club members do enjoy a full two minute silence of remembrance held by other members. And so no need for you to mourn. Although I hope you bloody well will, a tiny little bit. A cheaper final departure cannot be got. But more sad because I had for two nights straight practically won a fortune. And on the third, distracted unduly by an awfully nice and pleasantly rich lady and basking in her flattery my concentration wavered, and as one should have known one would, I lost all. Including the lady who turned out not to be so rich and departed on the train for Paris. I did croon for coins in the Market Place and alas on the steps of the Casino, thereby compromising my only remaining dearly held principle, till the police intervened. They were quite civil about it, but following this social if not spiritual disgrace, only enough coin was collected for a decent meal, bottle of champagne and cigar. I was however, offered a job to butler on a yacht moored in the harbour and to sing after dinner, but can you believe it, I was finally turned down on my handsome looks being too much a temptation to the ladies. I suppose this more than anything convinced me it was time to put an end to it all. Please believe me. When I say. How sorry I am about your silver. Herewith pawn ticket. I am and shall be always your undoubted friend. Ta ta,

Rashers.

One's tear fell plop upon the word sorry. Smearing the letters S and O and R. And he once said. My dear boy. If ever I did die. It would be so nice to have been an admiral. Bared heads would be bowed. My cocked hat unworn. Boots reversed in the stirrups of my riderless charger. A piper's lament. To the slow throbbing drums. And folding the letter. My eye caught sight of a further scrawl.

P.S. Alas dear boy, pride is the energy of survival just as it is the substance of defeat.

Beyond veils dark
Mourn for me
Buried in the deep

25

One walked the dismal empty streets. Saw Sheena, Rashers' whore from the catacombs, plying for trade under the railway trestle. Called on Mr Arland, no answer, his window dark and I went down the quays. Past ships. One sailing out silent in the swell. Port and starboard lights. Red and green like Christmas. Crossed over the canal lock. Walked by the great coal bunkers and gas works as I had once before on such a night of sorrow.

"Ah yes. The note will be delivered to await the gentleman's next arrival in the Common Room."

At Trinity College's front gate, I had stopped at the Porter's Lodge, a fire aglow in the cozy interior. And suddenly approaching, limping from under the gas lamp, there was Mr Arland. We went to sit for a coffee in the wicker chairs and under palm fronds in the welcome warmth of Jury's Hotel down Dame Street. He spoke of the American girl, Clara Macventworth, and I could see he was again so sad.

"Kildare, I suppose I never knew it possible even to remotely fall in love again. Especially as she seemed forever going off somewhere. To Rome, Madrid or the South of France. Now she's moved out of my building to another address. The appointments we make to meet, either she turns up hours late to rush away, or turns up not at all. Said she was ill and needed an urgent operation and was leaving to go to the American Hospital in Paris. And then I saw her, only yesterday, arm in arm with another man, laughing and gay on the steps of the Gresham Hotel."

Sorrow looming in the world everywhere. Somehow there upon Mr Arland's face, the same resigned anguish one had seen with Baptista. And the crushing sorrow with Clarissa. Women. Pretty women do, when they want to, demolish men. As he stared down at his cup of coffee.

"Mr Arland, I do think this lady has done you an injustice."

"No Kildare. One does that to oneself. And even when one expects little, it is always prudent to expect much less."

"Mr Arland now you promise, you will, won't you, come and stay with me at Andromeda Park."

"I promise, Kildare. I promise. But I wonder if it is not for some men to always stub their toes on women and make asses and fools of themselves."

"In that case, I shall, when you come, provide ladies galore."

"Kildare ah, you do cheer one up. I truly sense you've become now in your destiny, a man of the world who will outflank his adversities."

Returned to my room back in the Shelbourne. Took a solitary supper. As I lay abed, listened to a concert on the wireless. Staring through the shadows out my window. Towards the night clouds. My own voice pleading. Don't be dead. Rashers. Help peel back these fingers agrip squeezing all joy out of one's heart. Please come back. Rashers please. To the land where even if we waste all our time in hope, at least some of our laughter is not in vain.

Next morning under the squawk of seagulls, I stood on the summit of the little stone bridge in the Green. In memory of Rashers, threw down a carnation in the water which floated slowly away pushed by the breeze. Then took a taxi to alight under three golden balls. Of this dark shuttered shop. An ancient toothless crone pawning clothes beckoning me ahead of her. The proprietor summoning me past a woman, her young thick black hair streaked with grey, three tiny shoeless children in tow.

"Ah after you sir, please now. He'd have us know there's plenty of time for the likes of us."

Into a private cubby hole. For the attentions of the gentry. Funereally suited broker lifting up the suitcase of one's silver on the counter. Could hear Sexton's voice. Ah an Irishman would do anything for ready money, sell his birthright as quick as spit. So that he could take his ease at Dublin's crustacean counters, feasting his life away, with destiny behind him instead of in front, Master Darcy keep away from bad company.

"Ah it's fine stuff that is now sir. The very finest of the very best. Heirlooms, generations in his family, escutcheon engraved on them handles. Deposited by the peer himself, Ronald Ronald, the Earl of Rashers. Who said his equerry in waiting might be calling, which I assume is your distinguished self."

One did manage to smile. At the pawn broker's so appropriate title. Of that bloody lovable impostor. Never missing an opportunity as he ascended in his self styled nobility to reduce his victims in rank. And now sadden me further to hand over nearly the remainder of Leila's money. To retrieve my own property. Helped by the taxi man to load it in his desperately soiled boot. The whole rear of his vehicle swaying as the rear wheel verged on wobbling off.

Then how swift the darkening afternoon came. Like a great strange thunderclap. Exploding in my life. Hotel bill paid, decamping from the Shelbourne. Amid the late teatime lobby bustle.

"All packed sir ready whenever you are."

Getting back in my taxi, one could not believe one's eyes. To look out the departing back window in case the lady from Greystones was chasing us and instead see the Royal Rat, Buster The Beastly and Danno The Damned, all escorting a fur coated Baptista out the front door of the Shelbourne Hotel. And as we pulled past the small Huguenot cemetery gate, Horatio the actor, an arm stuck through the bars, was declaiming to the long dead buried inside.

"Will you look at that crazy nut sir, isn't he everywhere in town, speaking his mind to no one in particular."

The whole of this city. Its crazy carnival. Leave it to its fog lowering on this rotten cold Dublin winter night. Leila. Every moment to think of her. So gone. Mists coming up the Liffey. Approach up the long grey ramp. Rough blocks of stone topping the wall. Up to the station. Porter flickering me suspicious glances with clank and weight of my luggage. A solitary cattle dealer buying a ticket in front of one.

The last train of the day out to the country. And whispers that coal was firing the boiler of the train. At the barrier my ticket being punched.

"Ah god you're on the Meteorite, it's going to be a fast trip west tonight sir."

Then the long wait, as the Meteorite and its creaking squealing cars, waved ahead by a lantern, finally backed their way into the station platform. How dim the lights glow. Grey sacks of mail. Wind sweeps along the platform. Stamp one's feet waiting in the chill. The sweet smell of turf in the air. Nun climbing in ahead of me to the first class compartment. A woman wrapped up in her tweeds in the corner. Beckoning the nun.

"Ah there's plenty of room. Come sit here beside me, sure I had a sister worked for the nuns and I know all about them."

The train slowly pulling out. Pale yellow light flickers in the carriage. A farmer and his wife jumping aboard. Nearly look like tinkers. Sitting roaring and raging in the corner that there was no drink to be had on the train. The wife listening in stoic silence wrapping her ancient tatty fur coat tighter around her as they both puff cigarettes. The farmer continuing to curse and blather. Finally asking me.

"Hey boss give us the time on your watch boss."

Halfway chugging in the darkness across the final bog lands. A boom. The train lurched. I had fallen asleep. Head against the cold glass of the window. Clanks and squeals and screech of wheels. Sparks flying. As we slowly came to a stop. The conductor with a lantern announcing.

"All disembark."

The boiler blown up. Right out here in the bog. So much for the Meteorite. At a standstill. Could not now see the time on my watch. Nor the hand in front of my face. Out of a nearby cottage, a civil old farmer insisting he carry my case, led us knee deep through the muck and water, scaring up the snipe across the bog. Finally taking the nun, tweedy lady and myself on his donkey and cart out to the main road. Where we stood in wind and drizzle. My arms nearly broken carrying the silver. Till a travelling salesman stopped and took us in his car to the main street of the town. And I went to knock up a taxi. Visiting three doors before I could find one which happened to be on its way from the west through the town and actually had petrol in its tanks, not to mention wheels and an engine that worked. And appropriately enough. A hearse. The eager to please gombeen man from the town of Sligo, putting my bags up on the catafalque. He was also a butcher, an ironmonger, a publican and an undertaker. One learned a thing or two about the quality of coffins.

"Ah now sir, believe me when I tell you to your surprise, no better coffin was ever made than one of the American oak."

On the road passing a horse and carriage. A whiff of candle fume in the air from its lights. Driving up through the rhododendrons. A motor car ahead and now the lights of another behind. My god. In front of the house, myriad vehicles. As well as lurking members of the Garda Siochána. The front lawn fence down and cars parked. And more being directed. Doors opening and closing. Lights beyond the cracks in the shutters of nearly every window. People in top hats, tails and tiaras packed at the door. And in my soiled appearance, actually shoving and pushing me out of the way. From entering my own house, as one went nearly backwards down the ruddy steps again. And then to face a commissionaire inside the door.

"And who shall I say sir."

"Say."

"Yes the name sir. To announce you sir."

"You are not announcing me."

"I'm sorry but have you an invitation sir."

"I have not an invitation. And do please get out of my way."

"Sir I must please have your name sir."

"The name is Reginald Darcy Thormond Dancer Kildare. And this is my ruddy bloody house."

The Gardai did leap to my aid. And Crooks one spotted. Looking astonishingly regal, but something like a dissatisfied host among all these myriad strangers. As his eyes surveyed in their three different directions.

"Ah Master Reginald. What an utter relief to see you. Imagine a hired commissionaire. A bloody Brit, forgive the expression. From bloody England. With them false epaulettes. Ersatz is the word. After all the years of me faithful service. I am disgusted."

"Please calm down Crooks and tell me what on earth is going on."

"It's the ball sir."

"What bloody ball."

365

"I respectfully submit the ladies, Christabel and Lavinia, your sisters sir. The cream of the land have been invited but by the look of it already, it will be an assemblage of gatecrashers and interlopers before the night's done."

"Good heavens Crooks what's that music."

"The orchestra sir."

"That's Haydn's symphony number forty in F major."

"Well Master Reginald it could be his fiftieth for all I know. They have even got the old organ opened up from in behind the wall in the ballroom. And the pipes hooting with that lad down in the basement, pumping the bellows for the pressure."

"Damn thing's out of tune."

"Exactly what I was thinking sir."

"And what lad."

"Ah a lad that's been living rough down the cellars for months sir. Caught him when you were gone. He'd do polishing a boot here and there now and again. Train him up, I will."

Chandeliers lit. On every console table, candelabra that had not seen the light of day for many a year. Damask white, the tables. Crystal. Tureens. The great punch bowl. The old lead lined caskets full of ice and bottles of champagne. Strangers everywhere. Except for the hunt secretary with his brimful glass. My god I am about to be eaten, drunk, and waltzed out of house and home. And into utter destitution.

"This is a mighty damn good show Kildare. Nice to see the right sort all back together again. And see the old place looking its best. Didn't I see you up in Dublin, having a chat with Baptista."

"I'm sure you're mistaken. Excuse me. I must, as you can see, dress."

Out of the rapidly increasing din of voices, candle smell and smoke, to mount the stairs. Past Dingbats coming down. One arm bandaged. Beads of sweat uncharacteristically on her brow. As she is actually going right by me without a sign of recognition.

"I say Mollie."

"O god. It's you sir. Forgive me."

"Where's the fire."

"If I may say so sir, in every bedroom. In the sitting rooms. In the bathrooms. And I am kilt with the running back and forth. 'Tis good to see you back. This place has never seen the like. With old Pete and Willie dead as well. I am just after hearing that the boiler for the hot water is blown up in the kitchen. And I am to get the other boiler going. And I have been this very night again assaulted. Interfering up me, by him, Crooks."

"Ah Mollie, my dear. Well, so nice to be reminded so soon that by the sound of things, one is home."

Old Pete and Willie, one's ancient retired pair of tack room habitués. Sitting puffing on their pipes. Like old pieces of furniture in one's life, always there. Now gone. And clearly one of my sisters was taking her final step to displace me out of my mother's apartments. A new wardrobe shoved into the dressing room. Peach silk sheets emblazoned with coronets on the bed. And following my cold bath, shivering in front of my fire in my dressing gown, Sexton arriving at the door. In his Sunday best.

"Master Darcy, welcome home, I'm glad you're back. Ah god they come at us, the guests, s'il vous plait like a thousand horsemen. A line of them nearly now down to the front gates. And a bit of sad news. Pete and Willie sir, both have had it. Happened in the orchard. Wasn't I watching Pete in a beam of sunshine him taking relief of his bladder against the wall. On one of my prize roses. And he keeled over. Sure I knew it wasn't an act by the way he fell. I rushed to him. And old Willie came in the gate. And as soon as I said to him. Pete's gone. He's gone Willie. Says I. I turn then. At the thump beside me. Willie too. Fell. In his tracks. Stone dead when I put my hand to him."

"Have we coffins."

"There's one spare alright. Over in the old mill house. Gave it a few last belts of the hammer. And both boxes are ready to rest comfortably their mortal contents. Wake the corpses tonight each in his cottage. Neither of them have kin. Ah all they had, the pair of them. Was each other. And another little piece of poor news now as well. The garden wall, forty yards of it, all twelve feet high fell like the slap of a hand out into the meadow."

"O god Sexton. Poor news. That's disastrous news."

"Ah but now sir, with the good advices of the Professor Botanist of Trinity College Dublin, a plan is drawn for the expansion of the conservatory, and the new gardens, the greatest ever seen on this island."

367

"Sexton, for god's sake, I know this is all meant well, but I am I fear, aided and abetted by what is happening in this house this very night, about to have to dismiss all of you save those who still stay on and go bankrupt into starvation with me. We are in short all finished."

"Now how do you figure that now sir."

"Am I to put it more succinctly than that, Sexton. Would the word destitute help. My venture to Dublin produced nothing more than an expensive recovery of our silverware. And simply resulted in the further inclination in the steepness of the slope upon which I now find myself sliding at an ever increasing speed. I may hold out an impecunious week or two more."

"Now sir."

"No Sexton, there can be no argument. Even the agent is taking me to court. There's not enough fodder for the cattle. And if there were, there's no market for them anyway. No wages. I have exactly those few fivers you see there on that dresser left. And that is, I assure you Sexton, nothing to smile about."

"Ah now, in a minute, Master Darcy, in a minute. I can tell you something. If you'd like to continue with the roll call of misfortune."

"It's simply too long."

"Well now I've examined my conscience Master Darcy. And the moment I think has arrived."

"What moment."

"Ah now, a particular moment. And we need go no further with this discussion. You're to come with me in the morning. I can say no further than that. Other than you might bring a witness."

"Good lord Sexton, O jesus, not another blasted writ that someone is serving upon me or something."

"Hop not with anger now. Nothing of the kind. And I'll forgive you your little slip of blasphemy in the meantime. We'll meet in the morning. If it's appropriate to you, I'll knock at the library. Would before lunch do."

"O god Sexton, I don't think I can sleep upon another bloody mystery."

"Ah, you will and your dreams should not be nightmares."

In the front hall. Barrels of Guinness stout and cider. Not a soul one knows. As here one is, in a distinctly makeshift variety of grandpapa's white tie and tails. Wandering towards the ballroom, orchestra thundering the rafters blasting out a lightning polka. Step through the open double doors. Even the brass hinges shined. One looks. And a more ruinous sight one could never see. Kitty, Norah and Dingbats ferrying trays. Couples swirling upon the waxed gleaming floor. Crinoline satin and silks. The conductor fanning the air with a baton. Streamers flying from the ceiling. Beneath the great black marble chimney piece, a massive log fire blazing. Every flower Andromeda Park possesses, obviously wrested in from the hot house. And the dusty bottles up from the cellar. With their rat nibbled labels of what could be my very last most precious irreplaceable, Madeira, port, claret. Not to mention rum and brandy. The four charcoal cooked hams from Smyth's of the Green, the goose liver pâté, caviar. All already quickly disappearing. Buns being thrown. Hand clapping me on the back. A face I have never seen before.

"You're Kildare I understand. All this is jolly nice of you."

Even though a total stranger, at least one single someone being pleasantly politic. And then the grand finale entrance of Lavinia and Christabel. Both in my mother's gowns. A trumpet voluntary of the orchestra blasting as they swept in the door. Nearly expected the pair of them in American neon lighted tiaras. With Crooks white gloved behind them his arms wide as if he were presenting them at the Court of St James. Surprised the whole staff of Andromeda Park weren't laying rose petals before them.

"I say there, do you mind, if we squeeze by. There's a good fellow, waiter. Thank you."

My god. That passing imbecile. One now not only squeezed but nearly crushed out of the limelight. And referred to as a servant. In my own ballroom. Relegated to a corner. Picking up a glass. And then having to find a discarded bottle of champagne to fill it with. I suppose if one must sink. Best to go down in the deep in one continuous swallow. Quaff this in memory of Rashers. This is the way to do it. A grand finale. Instead of like a nearby neighbour who set off for a day's hunting, leaving his magnifying glass on his freshly pressed *Times* newspaper from London. And on the particular rare sunny afternoon, the paper ignited and burned his house to the ground. And before being in a similar circumstance, one will make oneself heard in this throbbing din.

"I should like to know the entire meaning of this entire night, Lavinia."

"It's absolutely none of my business, ask Christabel."

"I have just asked her. And she said it was none of her business. And rudely suggested I shut up."

"Well shut up then, why don't you."

Amazing. To have to grit one's teeth wanting to strangle them. Even as I forthrightly accosted them both in the centre of their toadying clusters of admirers. Neither one of them even deigned so much as to introduce me. To what they imagined were clearly their superior friends. One could hear the commissionaire still reverberating announcing the arrivals. Which would clearly go on till past midnight. Even the occupants of the great castle, noteworthy intellectuals, turning up. Whom one had not ever met oneself, as they were always on their world travels. Even heard this whole bloody ruddy financial debacle referred to as a social coup.

"I do think, don't you that Lavinia and Christabel have rather pulled it off. All in aid of finding husbands of course."

Could spot the faces of Catherine the cook, Henry and Thomas, the herds, peeking in at the ballroom serving staircase. One suddenly remembering a nice little game my sisters taught me as a toddler. Go Darcy dear, to the barrels in the hall, turn the tap as we showed you. Rush I would, to reach, and struggle to finally twist the tap, and stand marvelling at the dark brew flooding down over my knees and creeping out making an enormous black shiny lake in the hall. To then get, as my sisters rejoiced in laughter, a furious chastisement from an angry nanny. And so strange now. To feel so utterly alone. At least I shall munch on a thick slice of ham. In a house that hardly any longer seems my own. Where, were Rashers here, at least, even with his perpetrations of diabolical liberties upon my basic good nature, I would be cheered. Instead of gloomily despondent. Amid the perfumes. The plethora of ladies' flesh. The pop of corks. And even this nearby debutante, not at all unpretty, giving me an inviting eye, as the musicians finish playing what she refers to as a foxtrot.

Darcy Dancer walking from the ballroom. Orchestra striking up the Blue Danube Waltz. Passing the still arriving couples. A crowded front hall. Coats hats now stacked everywhere. Ladies' loud giggles. Men's laughter. Shouts of greetings. My hand to be put upon the bannister. To climb these stairs. Wait till the morrow to pay my last respects to Pete and Willie. Retreat now and retire asleep. Sexton in the morning will probably demonstrate to me some brand new winter flower he's invented to make our fortunes. Heard someone say the stars were out. Take a tired step up. One at a time. To stop. And shudder. Heart pounding in my chest. The commissionaire's voice. So loud. So utterly clear. Echoing in the hall.

"The Marquis and Marchioness of Farranistic."

Turn. Step back down. Just one two three steps. Near where my grandmother's portrait hangs. So solemnly watching. Look out into the bright candlelit hall. That face shyly smiling. Her fur taken from her white shoulders. Her slender elegant figure in a clinging shimmery black satin gown. A tiara of diamonds sparkling on her black hair. The Mental Marquis' flushed face beaming above his white tie. Making an introduction. To all those who would listen nearby. Who I knew heard him saying. Allow me to introduce you to the fourteenth Marchioness.

My wife
Leila

26

All one could remember were snatches of oblivion. And wondering how one would die. Ireland to sink. Covered in a tidal wave. Last night instead of to bed, I went down and out of the house. By the back servants' stairs. Through the stable yard. The tunnel. And up out across the fields in the bright cold night to where Pete and Willie were being waked, each in their tiny adjoining cottages.

"Welcome, come in, Master Darcy. Sure there's room for one more sardine."

In Pete's a hooley in progress. Tearing corks out of the bottles of stout. A fiddler playing. Songs singing. Say hello to your Uncle Finn me boy. Feet thumping round the cottage's hard earthen floor, a dance called the whicheverway jump. The ancient turf fire aglow in the grate. Poteen poured. Fresh from a still hidden right in the confines of Andromeda Park. The voices appearing at the door.

"Friend of the corpse, I am."

"Come in then, and welcome, friend of the corpse."

Johnny Gearoid, his red face blazing out of his greasy coat. Asking, where was the whisky and where was the deceased, in that order. Kitty and Norah arriving with Dingbats. The latter entirely drunk. Hiking up her skirts. Unbuttoning her blouse. Whirling her reasty amplitude about. Making mock curtseys to Kitty and Norah taking turns to be the Marchioness of Farranistic. Until stopped by my angry glare.

"Ah give us a tune there and I'll show you a nifty pair of heels to cut ruts in the dust."

Sexton, the patch fallen off his missing eye, doing a jig. And Pete, the deceased yet to be put in his waiting coffin, was propped up sitting in bed. Kitty and Norah playing noughts and crosses on his bald head with bits of charcoal. Until others of the inebriate, pulled Pete in his white chemise out of the bed and bedroom entirely, struggling in the middle of the cottage floor to hold up the corpse by the armpits to dance.

A white stiff frost on the ground. Passing under one's eyes. Somewhere in the course of events Midnight Shadow put chauffeurs, nags and guests to rout. Galloping around and nearly up into the house, through the orchard and over the fallen wall. As I was carried halfway back to the front steps over Sexton's shoulder. To finally rest in one's bed. Top hat on one's head. The guests departed. But the not at all unpretty debutante, accosted getting her coat in the darkened hall, tarried to listen to my drunken implorements that she could keep warm in my arms from the freezing cold.

"Darling, you're taking the first prelude deplorably slow."

Of course I didn't know what on earth she was talking about. And in the morning in the first sunshine. The debutante departed. In a huff, that I would not immediately agree to marry her. Which of course one would have done should she have suggested she had a staggeringly enormous dowry. Head clearing as I sat in the rising silvery vapours of steam up from my bath. Recount the nightmare dreams. An unreachable queen upon her throne. As I knelt begging to some god, I beseech thee, in the bowels of Christ to consider it possible that you may be mistaken that I deserve the fate to which you sentence me. Whither now Leila goes. From my life. Like an autumn swallow. To fly away out into the highest circles far beyond this land. Taking with her, her loyalty. She said was her love. Kept my hope alive. The only future left now is that I still live. Kneeling on this silk bright carpet of my mother's. Pumping the bellows on the embers of the smoky fire in my room. A knock. Crooks entering. As I step the other side of the screen to dress. In my black thorn proof Manx tweed, silk shirt and black silk tie.

"Master Reginald, I have been asked to convey to you the confidential information that a surprise awaits you sir below in a state room. And may I make a most humble request of you. So many of us now on the place are dying. And I don't mind saying I take it hard, very hard. And worse is it that former lowly staff, so far below myself, should think themselves better than me now and come back here to spite me, to cut me dead in my tracks. You know of whom I speak. I wept myself to sleep last night. And I've had it up to here sir, right up to here."

"Where Crooks, I can't see from behind the screen."

"To the very top of my throat sir and I am giving my notice. I simply can't stomach the ladies Lavinia and Christabel one further moment. Fetch this fetch that. Hiring interlopers. Run me off my feet, countermand my authority. Without your courtesy Master Reginald."

"I see Crooks."

"I hope you do sir, because it just so happens I caught the pair of them in the blue east parlour firing olive pips from the recently ordered jars from Smyth's of the Green and hitting your photographic portraiture with remarks such as, ah I got brother precisely between the eyes that time. And Master Reginald I have but one most humble request to make of you. You who have treated me nobly. Would you spare an evening to dine with me, sir prior to my leaving.

"Of course I should be most happy to Crooks. Just as I should be entirely sad if you left. Do please say when."

"In my quarters sir, at eight tomorrow night if convenient. The new lad I'm putting through his paces will be in attendance upon us."

The silence. Tiptoe along the hall. Like the awfully well bred person one hoped to remain, in spite of all threatening doom. That one would tread lightly as one does in a house where somewhere there might be a baby sleeping. A pause on the landing. Look out there. From such an empty house as this is now. Suppose, as well as the enormous bill, some tiny good came out of the ball. My sisters setting their caps for the Marquis. And a former servant putting them in their place, with their noses permanently out of joint. And the preening pair of them departed for today's hunting. Pursuing their own damn selfish pleasures with no respect for the dead. This morning thought I heard Rashers' voice. Singing, It's a Long Way to Tipperary. The first signs of going mad. To be hearing things. If there is any encouraging comfort left, at least the beauty of the beech grove still stands. Silvery and shining. Jackdaws screaming up in the heights of the branches. Could not find my proper cufflinks. Or indeed the needy appurtenance of my crimson braces. However there are certain manners in dress preparing for the extremes of outdoors, when it is acceptable to appear slightly incorrect. Especially when previous to such an excursion one is only momentarily repairing to the confines of one's library.

"Ah Sexton. Sorry to keep you waiting."

"Ah Master Darcy isn't there such a weight of erudition stacked around these walls. And wasn't it a great night rejoicing had by all to put old Willie and Pete to rest in peace."

"I wish I could include myself Sexton. But I am rather hungover. And I haven't brought a witness."

"Ah I have a witness. Just excused himself a moment to visit the gentlemen's water closet."

"Well what is our mystery Sexton. Do I suppose as I suspect, that we get out our treasure maps, our picks and shovels."

"Well you've nearly put your finger on it now. And the time has come that has been entrusted to me. But no need now for even a toothpick. For your mother's jewels, Master Darcy, sit as dry as any bone. Down in the stone bowels, safe as houses, under the Bank of Ireland, there in College Green."

"Good god, Sexton, is this really true."

"As true as an intertwinement of necklaces, bracelets, earrings, brooches can be. And never mind the topazes and rubies. There are pearls, diamonds, emeralds. Fit for the crown jewels of France, from which more than one of them gems came. Needing only two little slips of paper to put them into your possession. And here's one of them. And you take this to the manager. And he has the other."

A floorboard squeaking, a rap of a knuckle on the corner of the library book shelf just inside the door. This head stretching forward, grinning at me in my joy. A voice one recognises clearing its throat. And a body one recognises in its morning suit.

"Is it time I am required, by any chance."

"Rashers."

"Ah Darcy my dear boy, how good it is to see you. I do apologise popping in upon you in this way. But I took the liberty as I knew you would want me to, to come by the first taxi I could flag down in Dublin, as one hobbled down the gangway of the mail boat to dear old Erin's isle. And as I am a trifle short of change, would you

375

mind awfully awfully, paying him off. He's down I believe presently late breakfasting or perhaps early lunching in your kitchen."

Rashers signed as a witness. Under both real and assumed names. Bowing clicking his heels and chuckling as he nearly skipped out of the library. And later one actually waltzed after him along the hall. As if borne by the sweetest of balmy breezes. Light footed to a minuet. Reciting a prayer. Of utter thanksgiving singing from one's lips. I actually embraced old Sexton. Dear man. Who could use his finger like a crowbar and his hand to comfort a tiny wren. And he let drop more than one tear or two out of his eye.

"Ah and don't think sir, I was unaware of your little Leila. And that I didn't know you were sweet on her. As we all were in our own ways. Too good for him. But who are we to go charging to slay him who has stolen away our women. But she'll make a great aristocrat for Ireland. And when the time comes she'll be the most beautiful duchess in England. And leave her ghost here to haunt us, she will too."

Darcy Dancer heading for the dining room. The damp cold chill. The loud click one's heels make. Past this painting Leila admired, with her so soft black green eyes. A small figure flits across, way down at the end of the hall. A boy's head peeks back out and now disappears. Having a look at me. Must be our cellar stowaway. To be soon trained up to be our new assistant butler. To trip over trays down the stairs as our top butler does. If our top butler doesn't strangle himself or depart. Take with me this precious piece of paper deep in my barrister's pocket. Before someone kindles it into fire. Cable Lois. Bring palette, paints and canvas. Paint my portrait to hang and haunt this house. And there beyond this door he enthrones, my confidential surprise, tinged red hair bent over a vast breakfast. All the mahoganies and silver sauceboats shimmering in the red blazing firelight. Crooks departing in the pantry door. The scent of Irish whisky. And that hand. Gripped around a glass of that distillate.

"Dear Darcy may we avenge our slights. Kick up dust again in the face of our begrudgers."

"My god Rashers. I really did believe you popped into the Mediterranean."

"Well yes I did, in a manner of speaking. Pop. To the top of my shoelaces perhaps. And let us sincerely hope such rumour persists in making itself sufficiently felt for one's creditors to believe before I make my triumphant reappearance in Dublin with the wherewithal to meet my unpleasantly accumulated commitments. Ah, but what a wonderful occasion today is for you my dear boy. You see. Ancient lineage and lands do, if one but ferrets about, produce their welcome surprises. But as for me, I really did fling myself off the cliffs of Monaco. Executed what I thought was quite a decent dive. But in the dark I did not realise I was already on the beach and the water I chose was only ankle deep. I was however really ready to drown like a man. At dawn I was stranded at the cliff bottom. Listening to myself release a series of those terrible farts one suffers on the Continent. And lo and behold a pair of insistent fishermen whose French I simply could not make head nor tail of, and who I simply could not convince to throw me back in, returned me with them into the harbour and safe to shore. As you can see my usually impeccable garments are in a poor state. My dear Darcy, you won't mind if I stay a wee bit. I simply can't face the catacombs again. Or trying to earn my keep from the idle likes of Sheena the whore. Catch my breath so to speak."

"But not I hope, to pawn my silver."

"Nae dear boy nae. I am forever chastened. I want you to know you can rely on me as your prudhomme. In this your moment of riches. I shall be at your elbow beck and call. You see, the fact of the matter is, like you, I too had a beautiful mother. Who did get up to pranks while my father was away at his wars. Who knows, who I really am. I may indeed be the true Earl of Ronald Ronald, and not an impostor. In this world taught to bow to privilege, my betrothed wants us to assume such a title. I mean it could be merely a matter of a few well placed fivers, and a little tampering flourish of the pen in the various source books of nobility. My dear lady is to give me her answer soon as to our wedding day, accompanied by her accountants' final approval to the financing of my string of betting shops. Riches galore shall not I assure you change me as they clearly have not changed you. And I pray that I shall make my betrothed happy. Of course I want for you to be my best man. And I wonder dear boy, could you possibly see your way clear to tiding me over through what is merely a tiny patch of enforced prudentiality."

Befallen
This present
Self respecting
Man of honour

377

27

One left Rashers contentedly reading his chuckling way through the volumes of *Punch* in the library. Crooks before departing for the funeral, administering a bottle of champagne found hidden in a turf basket, while the new boy butler bowed and pulled his forelock, miraculously succeeding in lighting Rashers' cigar.

In a pair of boots and sou'wester, Sexton drove me in the victoria to Pete's and Willie's cottages. Great grey clouds rolling in from the west. One coffin following the other, borne on the men's shoulders on the long trek. The rain beginning to fall. The wind rising. The grieving household collected under the ancient tall yew tree in the cemetery. The last inches of the deep grave still being dug. The wet now slashing down in sheets across our faces. The vine and holly leaves rustling on the walls of the church ruin. Over the ancient names and dates, the gravestones dripping dark grey. Luke and Thomas under their battered brown hats, throwing shovels aside and jumping up out of the hole.

"Jesus, Mary and Joseph anoint us in our hour of need."

The need being boats instead of burial boxes. For as you might know, the digging men would hit a spring. Water pouring up as hard now from the bottom of the grave as it was pouring down from out of the sky above. Both coffins as they were lowered, bobbing up. Floating one on top of the other. Feet pushing and pressing them back down. Like trying to put a cork in a dyke holding back an ocean. Shovels hurrying into the clay, heaving it on. Sexton advising me by my elbow, as we lowered a boulder and pushed a lumpful of sodden soil thumping on the elm box.

"Ah Master Darcy, not only did old Pete and Willie die dancing, they be drowned as well."

The muddy grave at last heaped high with sods. The funeral over. Gate squeaking shut. Watch the mourners disperse. They go, their dark backs, black on the green meadow. Fading away in the lashing gale and rain. As I go a bachelor to circle back out through the woods. Along by the lake. To smell the pine. The moist rot under the ancient old oaks. The haunted bridge. No lady in her veils there now. My mother's jewels. Saved from my father's squandering. Lets me stay here. To live. And maybe even die. Near the mosses and ferns. To listen again to Sexton. In his potting shed.

"Ah Master Darcy, let me tell you, the winter long weight of the dark clouds would break a man. To keep you there in the big house behind your shutters. Incarcerated so that you wouldn't know the sun had come out. And if you did, you'd be blinded by it and scurry back into the darkness."

Now I turn off this path. From where the overgrown rhododendrons make so much dark under their leaves. Climb over the fallen beech. Carved into the bark. It says. Kill Kildare. Step upon the turf mould, and push through the briars. Towards this boathouse. I alone. Just another inmate of another great house. Whose roof beams may crack over the front hall. While the pasha and lord of the manor cowers within. Trembling in the delirium traumas. No doctor, parson or loving hand to come near me. Left to my own devices. A whisky bottle on the table for breakfast. To help fade into the oblivion. Drowning both sorrows and fortune. And I come here. The old row boat sunk deeper in the water. A rat scurries. Climb these stairs. Up to this room. Push open the door. The dusty floor. Blown with leaves. Rain spattering the window. The cobwebs and her wicker chair. Where she sat. In all her sins. Hear her voice. Your child torn out of your arms. Such sorrow never grows cold nor old. Only makes great long years for every tear to dry.

Darcy Dancer walking to the window. Wiping away the dust on

the glass pane. Swans flying in to land on the lake. Floating down white from the skies through the billowing sheets of rain. That will leak from the dining room ceiling tonight. Into my soup. Call Crooks to place a suitable piece of Meissen to catch the drops. Put a sauceboat upside down on Rashers' head to keep his hair dry. And that sound. Is cheering. Chirps of song. Defiant birds sheltering in under the boathouse eaves. Their anthem sung that spring will come. Bring sap alive in the whitethorn and briar. A horn. Blows. The hunt. Cheer on hounds, pounding after sly boots fox. They must be beyond up over the big meadow hill. The likes of Baptista and the Colonel. While I'm here with you. Dearest friend. Tread with me please, over the loamy dark ground. Upon which my cheek, which never touched yours, will rot in death. Nothing trivial did you ever say. And from anything your voice could ever speak, I would never run. Not out of this room. Not away. I would but wait. And will. For you to find me here near this thick bough of this fallen ancient beech. Alone in a lonely heart. Hush. The dark. On the shores of the lake. A star speaks. Go glad at death, sad at life. Through any years. While the sky is smoky grey with rain. And green and yellow with rainbows. And purple.

Like the ribbon
You wore
In your hair

380